THE LADY OF THE MARK

· ALEX HANSON ·

First hardcover edition April 2022

Cover Design: Damonza.com

Maps by: Chaim Holtjer

Editor: Tasha Taylor

ISBN 979-8-9853751-1-4

Published by Alex Hanson

This book is dedicated to my advisor, mentor, and friend,
Dr. Jeffery Bartone.
Thank you for believing in me when no one else did.

Author's Note

This series follows a guild of sword-wielding warriors. The good guys aren't perfect, and the villains don't hold back. If you don't like reading about trained killers who suck at talking about their feelings and the ones who love them anyway, these books aren't for you. No character is guaranteed to make it out alive. This book contains mature scenes that may be considered offensive or disturbing to some readers. See below for a full content list for this story, but be warned: there may be spoilers.

This book contains sensitive content including but not limited to: murder, torture, sexual assault, implied non-con, character death, unexpected pregnancy, and medical procedures (no abortions).

Playlist

Wild Things — Alessia Cara
River of Tears — Alessia Cara
Stone — Alessia Cara ft. Sebastian Kole
River — Bishop Briggs
Honor For All — Jon Licht & Daniel Licht
The Drunken Whaler — Artist Unknown
There Goes My Heart — The Mavericks
What A Crying Shame — The Mavericks
I Should Have Been True — The Mavericks
O What A Thrill — The Mavericks
Blown Away — Carrie Underwood
Sit Still, Look Pretty — Daya
Closer — The Chainsmokers ft. Halsey
Walkin' After Midnight — Patsy Cline
Let Me Love You — DJ Snake ft. Justin Bieber
Cold Water — Major Lazer ft. Justin Bieber & MØ
Knockin' Boots — Candyman
Need You Now — Lady Antebellum

Polco Street

Rovik's Estate

Trista

THe

Jespa

RIVER

Prologue

TEN MEN STOOD amidst rubble that once was a bridge. Their red robes whipped in the wind and their boots soaked up river water as they gazed over the still-smoking ruins. One man knelt in the Jespa, clutching a fallen comrade who'd been battered and broken in the blast moments ago.

"I'm sorry, brother," he said. He looked toward the crumbled rock and twisted steel of the bridge. If he'd run a little faster, killed his enemies a heartbeat quicker... He closed his eyes, said a prayer, and let the body go. The river gathered it up and carried it away, and he watched until the red robes were swept out of sight. Only then did he stand.

"This war is lost," he said. "Polco Bridge is destroyed, the fences on the Western bank are complete, and the sovereign is nestled in his mansion far from our reach." He shook his head. "Our losses are too many, and our victories too few." He waded back toward the shore and looked at his men, at the defeat heavy on their faces. "That doesn't mean we stop fighting. Now that the city's been divided, our blades are needed more than ever. The West may wall us off like animals, but I won't lay down my sword, not while the East starves and dies of sickness."

He hoisted himself up onto the remains of a stone pillar and gazed down at his comrades. "We formed this brotherhood on a vow to keep Trista united. Lady Fate wasn't with us this time, so I'll make a new vow." He drew his sword and raised it high in the air. "I vow to watch over Trista's Eastern streets, be a champion for those our sovereign has forsaken, and await my chance to reunite our great city! Who will join me?"

His men cast weary glances at one another, but slowly, one by one, they drew their weapons.

"I won't bend to the will of a tyrant! I won't abandon our people! Not while I still have blood to give! What say you?"

The men raised their weapons and roared as one.

❧

Ten men in red robes received The Mark: two interwoven letter Ms branded on their left cheek, a vow of brotherhood they could never erase.

"We are The Men of the Mark," they chanted in unison, and their eyes burned with new conviction. "And we still have blood to give!"

Chapter 1

2nd and 30 of Autumn, Jesparia's 7th and 20 year of Rovik[1]
A century after Trista's demarcation

SHAILA STOOD ON the Western bank of the Jespa river, searching the water for a sign of the maiden she was to meet here. She took down her hood and breathed deep the sweet scent of renistrila[2] blossoms on the breeze. Clear, moonlit nights like this always reminded her of the night she herself swam the Jespa, the night she dove in from the Eastern shore and emerged dripping and exhausted on this very spot. It was supposed to be the start of her new life...

"Shaila, my dear!"

As if summoned from her memories—or perhaps her nightmares—the very man who plucked her from the river seven years ago stepped from the shadows.

"I came to see if the river would spit a beauty tonight," he said. "Instead, I find the most beautiful gift the Jespa ever gave me standing right where I first met her!"

---

1 A detailed breakdown of the date system can be found on page 369.

2 Renistrila AKA "reni": A bright flower that grows in water. A full description can be found on page 377.

"What are you doing here, Krig?" Shaila asked. "This is *my* night to collect."

"Yes, I know. Rumor has it you've been very generous with your *collections*. You've handed over some remarkably handsome girls to several establishments throughout the city. A few of my biggest rivals in fact," he added with a pout. "How about throwing me a morsel instead?"

"For *you*, Krig? Never."

"My dear, you wound me," Krig said, touching a hand over his heart with a wicked grin. "I'd hoped our history might—"

"Our history?" Shaila huffed and turned her back on him. "I'd let these girls drown before giving them to you."

His boots crunched on the stones as he came closer.

"I hear you're now the mistress of our very own Archdynast Rovik. You're welcome."

"Why should I thank *you*, of all people?"

"You stepped from the river as a terrified and naïve girl, Shaila, and I made you a woman. I set free the vixen who would one day bed a sovereign. I'm proud of you, my river reni." He was close now, too close, and he plucked a lock of her long, honey hair off her shoulder, twirling it in his fingers. "Why not show me what tricks you use to entertain Rovik, for old times' sake?"

Shaila stiffened, ready to strike—

"Help!" came a cry on the wind.

Shaila dashed to the edge of the water. The head of a young girl bobbed with the swells halfway across the river. A heartbeat later, it disappeared and didn't resurface.

Shaila yanked open her robes and kicked off her boots. She ran down the bank, following the flow of the river several yards before diving in headfirst. With skill and grace, she cut through the water downstream from where the girl went under, guided by nothing but moonlight and instinct. She was relieved when a pair of flailing arms collided with her own. Shaila wrapped an arm around the young girl's waist and swam toward the surface, praying for the strength to escape the Jespa's grasp with every stroke. When their heads broke the water, the girl began to sob.

"I have you," Shaila yelled, then she swallowed a mouthful of river water that nearly made her choke. "Kick your legs!"

They inched toward the shore as the river swept them further downstream. The old Polco pier was coming up fast, and beyond that, the currents grew fierce. If they were carried past the pier, their chances dwindled with every passing stone. The last wooden beam of the pier would pass by just out of her reach, so Shaila made a choice: she tore the weeping girl's arms from around her and, with a mighty shove, pushed the maiden directly into the path of the upcoming beam.

"Grab it!" Shaila screamed over the roar of the water, and the youth came to her senses in time to wrap her arms around the post. Shaila's nails barely brushed the wood as the river carried her onwards. "Jump the beams!"

Shaila passed the pier, and the Jespa raged as it picked up speed. A current from underneath yanked her down hard, and she spun under the water, losing all sense of Earth and sky. Her arms and legs kicked, her heart prayed, and by some miracle, cool air rushed into her lungs as her face broke the surface. She caught a glimpse of the shore and put the last of her strength into reaching it before the river could suck her under again. Her arms and legs burned when her feet finally touched the rocky riverbed.

Shaila gasped and spit water as she crawled up onto the pebbled embankment. With a shaking hand, she snatched a fistful of the stones and clutched them to her lips.

"Thank you," she whispered. "Remlar[3], protector of seas and lord of rivers, I thank you with all my heart and soul—"

A scream pierced the night.

Shaila peered upriver where Krig held the maiden by the arms and was wrestling her up the embankment.

"Let me go!" the girl cried as she struggled for freedom.

Shaila staggered to her feet and ran, tripping twice in her exhaustion. Krig nearly had the girl up to the cobbled street when Shaila wrapped an arm around his neck from behind. Krig lost his footing in the stones and

---

3 Remlar: The god of water. A full description can be found on page 371.

slid down the embankment. Shaila twisted, throwing him off balance, and they both fell, tumbling clear to the water's edge. Shaila got to her feet first, and she seized Krig's hand, bent his arm around her own, and yanked until his elbow threatened to pop.

"Stop! Stop!" Krig hollered.

Shaila kept the pressure on his arm as she leaned toward his ear. "If I ever see you near the river after dark again, the Jespa and I will see to it no one ever finds your worthless corpse."

"Our sovereign will hear about this!"

"You think my lover's loyalties would lie with you, a slave-trading piece of filth, over the woman who shares his bed and body? You're done forcing yourself on helpless girls." She let him go. "Get out of here, Krig. I hope I never see your repulsive face again."

He gathered himself from the rocks, spit at Shaila's feet, then stalked away, muttering to himself. When he was gone, Shaila sighed and sat in the stones, closing her eyes as she caught her breath at last. Her threat was an empty one, but she prayed Krig couldn't tell the difference. If he indeed sent word to Rovik...

"Thank you!" the maiden said as she took to her knees at Shaila's side. "I owe you my life."

Shaila glared at the youth. "Who in Vedia[4] taught you to swim?"

"N—no one," the girl replied, wide-eyed at Shaila's anger. "This was my first time."

Shaila swore as she climbed to her feet. "You should pray your thanks to the gods for showing you more care than the fools who threw you to the Jespa tonight."

"This was *my* choice!" the girl insisted as she rose and brushed the stones from her sodden pants. "My father, he's old now, and my brothers... my brothers are starving... I'm a burden to them." The girl began to weep again.

Shaila sighed. "All right, there's no need for that." She put an arm around the youth's shoulders. "Remlar took pity on us both. You're safe now."

---

4 Vedia: The underworld. A full description can be found on page 372.

"Who was that man?"

"A leech who owns the biggest whorehouse in Trista."

"It seems I owe you twice then."

Shaila studied the girl for the first time. Her black hair fell in tight ringlet curls to her shoulders. Her face was fair with a dusting of freckles across her cheeks and nose. She was young. Too young. Her looks were handsome enough by the East's standards, sure, but most upperclassmen in the West would give her no more than a passing glance.

"What's your name, child?" Shaila asked as she started back up the shoreline toward her robes and boots.

"Detarii, ma'am."

"How old are you?"

"Sixteen."

"Did anyone tell you what would be expected of you here? Where you'd be employed?"

Detarii shook her head. "They said someone would meet me on the Western bank and put me where I'm needed."

"*Where you're needed*," Shaila said with a humorless laugh. "They don't even tell you girls the truth anymore, do they?"

"What truth?"

Shaila found her boots and sat to pull them on. "Why do you think only the prettiest maidens get to swim the river, girl? You can't be this naïve."

"Because the West only wants the handsome ones."

Shaila cocked a brow.

Detarii's shoulders sagged. "A cathouse? Is that truly all there is for me here?"

"That's the fate of most who swim the Jespa, but there's another option." Shaila turned away from the hopeful look on the maiden's face as she pulled on her robes. "I can offer you a position in Archdynast Rovik's house. The pay is paltry—you'd earn more at the whorehouse—but you'd live and serve in our sovereign's mansion as a maid or a cook instead."

"I'd like that very much," Detarii said. "I can cook and clean anything. I helped look after my father and brothers when my mother died. Thank you ever so much..."

"Shaila."

"Thank you, Shaila."

Detarii looped her arm around her savior's, and Shaila nodded, swallowing back a wave of guilt as strong as the Jespa's currents as she ushered the girl away up the embankment.

"Welcome to your new life."

⁂

Across the river, in a second-story window of a long-abandoned warehouse, a man robed and masked in red watched the scene on the far bank through his spyglass. His eyes followed Shaila's every move until she was swallowed by the darkness of the Western streets, then he too slipped away, silently, like a ghost in the night.

⁂

When Shaila and Detarii stepped into the mansion, the younger woman stared up in awe at the grand ceiling, the winding central staircase, and the stained-glass windows. The door to the servants' hall burst open, and Alonso, Rovik's head of staff, marched across the foyer in clipped, even strides with his hands clasped behind his back, his chin held high, and his coattails whipping.

"Shaila," he barked as if to an errant child. "Who is this? And why are you dripping horrible river water all over the clean tile?"

"This is Detarii, our new member of staff."

Alonso gave the girl a scrutinizing look, then he leaned near Shaila's ear. "What do you expect me to do with this?" he asked. "Rovik told you only to bring back beauties."

"She's the fairest I've seen in weeks."

Detarii beamed at Shaila's praise.

"How old is she?"

"Nineteen," Shaila answered before Detarii could do so first.

Detarii's eyes flicked to Shaila in uncertainty, and Alonso groaned as he rolled his eyes.

"Just take her, Alonso," Shaila said. "She's already here."

Alonso sighed. "You'll be the death of us all, Shaila. I should never have gotten mixed up in your antics." He motioned to Detarii. "Well, come along then, girl. There's much you need to learn."

Detarii gave Shaila one last grateful smile over her shoulder, but before Alonso could usher her away, a call came from the staircase.

"Is this a new addition?"

Marcel, Rovik's head of security and personal bodyguard, descended the stairs, his club swinging back and forth on his belt with every step. His crisp brown uniform was pressed to perfection, and his short black hair was slicked straight back out of his face with so much grease it looked permanently wet. He never smiled.

Alonso stopped and reluctantly turned Detarii for Marcel's inspection.

Marcel seized the girl's chin and turned it one way then the other. He studied her face then her figure with a look of cold indifference. He looked at Shaila with a disapproving scowl before releasing Detarii and dismissing her with a wave. Alonso quickly steered the girl away.

"I know the game you play, woman," Marcel spat.

"I play no games at all," Shaila replied.

"You've brought back nothing but scraps from the river this whole season. How curious it is that the day our sovereign first took you to bed, the Jespa stopped spitting handsome-faced girls. Filling this estate with castaways will not preserve your position in this house."

"No? Perhaps you could teach me *your* tricks then."

Marcel's lip twitched. "I suggest you start doing your job properly from now on." He leaned toward her. "Or would you rather end up in The Cellar? You know how our sovereign likes to deal with those who disappoint him." Shaila's icy stare never faltered under the threat, and Marcel snorted in disappointment. "He wants to see you. Immediately. Go clean yourself up and report to his quarters."

"Whatever Sir desires," Shaila said sweetly. She swept her dripping hair forward over her shoulder and wrung it out in her hands. A stream of icy water splashed onto Marcel's feet, and he jumped back with a hiss as it soaked through the tops of his shoes. Shaila smiled as she sauntered away up the stairs.

Chapter 2

ARCHDYNAST ROVIK HAD taken many mistresses over the years. He grew bored quickly, but he never lacked for options. Many women vied to be his next mistress with the hopes of giving him a child. To bear an heir of a sovereign meant a future bathed in power and wealth, but of the countless women Rovik had bedded, only one ever birthed a babe: a daughter named Amii. That was years ago. There were rumors he was sterile, but because of little Amii, women continued to pursue him anyway.

Not Shaila.

At first, Shaila was quite happy with her new position as a maid at the sovereign's estate. At the age of one and twenty, and for the first time since she'd swum the Jespa, she thought she'd found the better life she came West for. Then she heard the whispers of Rovik's appetite for beautiful women and thought again.

Shaila went straight to her quarters to prepare for her sovereign and found the clothes he'd chosen for her for the evening waiting on her bed: a skirt that ended well above the knee and a top that was little more than a brassiere as it covered her breasts and not much else. The fabric was paper-thin and feather-soft, not a local creation certainly. There was a new pair of shoes as well—black leather with raised heels that made her at least an inch taller and came to a point so small she didn't know how she'd ever walk in them.

'*His idea of a gift,*' she thought with a roll of her eyes.

Once dressed, she sat at her vanity and dried and brushed her hair till it shone. To ward off the smell of the river, she rubbed a few drops of rose oil between her hands and ran them through her locks as well.

Looking at herself in the mirror, in clothes fit for nothing more than Krig's cathouse, Shaila thought about her old life in the East: the filthy streets, the sickness, begging near the bakery for bread while her father looked for work but never found any. She should've stayed there. Damn this city with its ancient grudges. Damn the river that split East from West. And damn the man who kept the walls built tall between them.

Shaila stood and almost lost her balance on the first step in her teetering heels. With a shake of her shoulders, she dismissed her woes and focused. Her shoes clicked loudly on the hardwood as she left her room, and so, to calm her nerves, she counted the taps clear across the house—all eighty-four of them.

Marcel was stationed by the bedroom door when Shaila approached, and he opened it for her.

"Oh, you're welcome, madam," he sneered when she passed him without a word of thanks.

A fire burned on the hearth. Rovik stood staring into the flames, still dressed in his dark blue suit with a glass in his hand and a bottle of Sazeen whiskey sitting, uncorked, on the mantle. His pin-straight brown hair had broken free of its styling and hung down in his face. He was tall and slender with deep blue eyes and a charming smile.

Shaila stopped in uncertainty at the sight of the whiskey.

"Just the woman I wanted to see," Rovik said with a grin. "What are you waiting for? Come here."

The distance between them vanished with eight more ticks of her heels.

His eyes slid down her body, stopping at obvious places to stare. "Do you like your present?" he asked. "That cloth cost a small fortune. Came all the way from Se Trosk A Vol."

"It's beautiful," Shaila lied.

Rovik made a small snort, took a swig from his glass, and smiled as he held it out to her. "Drink?"

She knew she should accept with gratitude, but the look in his eyes told her not to take chances with him tonight. She shook her head.

He shrugged and drained the glass himself. "I'm rather fond of you, Shaila," he said as he poured himself another drink. "You're different."

The whiskey spilled over the side of the glass and ran in amber streaks down the side and over his fingers, dripped, and splattered on the toes of his shoes. He put the bottle back on the mantle and took another deep drink then reached out and ran a moist knuckle across Shaila's cheek.

She closed her eyes and nearly recoiled but stopped herself in time. She smiled instead as if her reaction had been one of pleasure.

He smiled wickedly back at her. "There it is. The disgust. I see it no matter how hard you try to hide it. You're not like the others, the ones who clamor to my bed. You detest me. It's… refreshing."

Shaila's heart gave a little jump, but she wrinkled her brow and tilted her head in what she hoped was a look of honest confusion. "Whatever do you mean?"

"I knew the very first night I took you to my bed there was something about you, something more you tried so hard to hide from me. I saw it in your eyes. I felt it when I touched you, but I was powerless to find it. Then, this very evening, a courier delivered a most amusing note not minutes after you came home from the river. Is there anything you wish to tell me?"

"Nothing, my sovereign," she said, her heart hammering.

"Such an amusing tale it was. When I read it, I laughed and thought this man, this Krig, he must be mistaken. The woman he describes who wrestled him to the ground and twisted his arm, she couldn't be my Shaila, not the woman who utters barely a word in my presence and moves about my house like a ghost. But then I asked myself, could this be the Shaila I've tried so hard to find? What do you have to say for yourself?"

"A man at the river wanted the girl I went to collect. I wanted to bring her here instead. I did what was needed to claim what was rightfully yours."

"She must have been quite the beauty, this girl you fought so hard to claim for me." As if struck by sudden inspiration, he snapped his fingers with a grin. "Let's find out, shall we? Marcel!"

Marcel marched in with Detarii in tow. She looked confused and uncertain but gave Shaila a small smile.

The blood drained from Shaila's face.

Rovik waved Marcel away, and the guard excused himself, leaving Detarii standing awkwardly by the door, blushing a deep crimson.

"Come here," Rovik called, and Detarii came without hesitation. He took the girl by the arm and spun her toward the fireplace to study her in the light of the flames.

"Look at these freckles," he said as he traced a finger down the girl's cheek. "And these curls." He tugged one and watched it spring instantly back into place. "What's your name?"

"Detarii, sir."

"How old are you?"

"Nineteen."

Rovik tilted his head and clucked his tongue. "Now, now, no lies, my dear. I care not a bit about the number, but you must be honest with me if no one else." He took both her hands in his own and dusted a kiss across her knuckles. "Tell me."

Detarii blushed a deeper red. "I... I'm sixteen, my sovereign."

"Good girl," Rovik murmured, and his oozing voice made Shaila's stomach churn. "And did Shaila tell you why she chose to bring you to my home?"

"She told that man before, in the foyer... she told him I'm handsome."

Rovik glanced back at Shaila who refused to look away. "My darling Shaila is to bring me only the fairest girls from the Jespa. She herself came from the river years ago. Did she tell you?"

Detarii shook her head.

"Come here, Shaila dear."

Shaila glided across the room to his side, and Rovik took both girls by the hand, leading them to a full-length mirror mounted on the wall. He placed them side by side and waved at their reflections in the glass.

"Look at her, Detarii," Rovik said in awe. "Look at her deep, brown eyes, that silky skin, the way her hair shines in the dying light of my fire. Is she not beautiful?"

"Yes, sir," Detarii said.

"My dear, can you honestly stand beside such a creature and tell me your looks rival hers in any way?"

A look of heartbroken truth dawned in the girl's eyes as she studied herself in the mirror, her gaze flicking from her face to Shaila's beside her.

"No, sir."

Shaila touched Detarii's arm and glanced at Rovik in the mirror. The calculating look on his face turned her blood to ice.

"No, they certainly don't." Rovik yanked the girl away, calling again to his faithful guard as he marched her across the room. When Marcel came back, Rovik shoved Detarii at him so hard she tripped over her own feet and fell into his arms. "See this rat drowned in the river where she belongs!"

"No!" cried two voices in unison. One was Detarii's as she fought and sobbed in Marcel's grasp. The other came from Shaila, and, as soon as the word escaped her mouth, she knew there was no going back.

Rovik raised a hand to halt Marcel at the door. "Have something to say, my dear?"

"Let her go, Rovik," Shaila demanded, no longer hiding her disgust.

Rovik's eyes lit with eager expectation. "Marcel, send the girl to this Krig, with his sovereign's blessing." Detarii and Marcel left with haste leaving Rovik staring at Shaila with a smile of victory. "The hate I see in your eyes," he growled with anticipation, "I'm eager to see how deeply it burns."

Shaila clapped her hands in slow, mocking applause. "Bravo. What a display that was, truly, my sovereign. You showed such strength, such cunning... by preying on a helpless child."

"Her fate is *your* doing. You think I didn't notice what wretches you've dragged in my door this past season? You've been using my name to hide away the beauties I sent you to fetch. Afraid you'll be replaced, lover? You needn't be. I've finally found a woman with a fire as hot as mine. And now she's got nothing left to hide."

"And nothing left to lose."

Rovik laughed. "By all means, Shaila, show me why I should fear you."

He moved so fast Shaila had no time to react before he backhanded her across the face, and she lost her balance on her heels and fell. She scrambled to get up, but he came down on top of her, pinning her to the floor on her belly. For a moment, the briefest of heartbeats, she was a terrified fourteen-year-old girl again, lying on the bank of the Jespa with river stones scraping her back as a man took all he wanted despite her pleas. She'd promised herself... never again.

"No!" Shaila screamed, and she brought her elbow back, aiming for Rovik's face, but she caught him in the shoulder instead. He cupped the back of her head, like a caress, before he slammed her face into the floor. There was a burst of pain in her nose and a gush of warmth on her lips. The taste of copper in her mouth made her growl. She threw her head back as hard as she could. He released her with a cry of surprise to hold his own streaming nose.

Shaila twisted onto her back, swinging madly for his face, but he caught both her wrists in his hands.

"Come now," he goaded. "You can do better."

Shaila wrestled one of her legs free from under his and yanked it up fast, kneeing him in the groin. All the air escaped him in one low groan, and he fell to the floor, clutching his manhood and gasping. Shaila thrashed to free herself from under his dead weight. With an angry cry, she kicked out as hard as she could, and the heel of her shoe plunged into his thigh.

Rovik screamed, tore the shoe from his leg, and threw it away in a rage. Shaila rolled back to her belly and crawled out from under him, her eyes on the door a few feet away. He seized her by the ankles and slithered up her body like a demon escaping the fiery depths of Vedia.

"Where are you going?" he snarled. "Things are just getting fun!" He wrapped both hands around her throat and squeezed. Shaila's choking gasps made him laugh as she beat her palms on the floor in vain.

Across the floor, lying between her and the door to freedom, was Shaila's bloody shoe. The heel was broken, and the wood inside had split at an angle down to a deadly point. She reached out her hand, and her fingers barely brushed the leather once, twice, but the third time she managed to snatch it up, grip it firmly, and plunge the point into the back of Rovik's hand. He screamed again and let her go.

Shaila rounded on her sovereign and lunged, stabbing her broken heel into the side of his neck three times with a scream of rage for every jab. The wounds were not deep, but Rovik pushed her away with a howl of panicked pain, clutching his bleeding neck. Shaila scrambled to her feet, seized the door, and made her escape at last into the hallway beyond.

Marcel's arm caught her around the middle and yanked her up off her feet.

"Something tells me you've not yet been dismissed," he purred in her ear.

Rovik staggered to his bedroom door. He held his hand over the wounds in his neck as blood seeped from under his fingers. Not enough to kill him, sadly.

Marcel shook Shaila violently by the arm. "You vile little whore!" He drew his club from his belt.

"Let her go," Rovik ordered, and both Marcel and Shaila stared at him in surprise. "But she's no longer allowed to leave the house. You win this time, my golden goddess." Three angry holes wept red down the side of his neck, staining his shirt at the collar, but he smiled as if every drop were a gift. "I look forward to our next *chat*."

Shaila shoved Marcel away. "I'll never come willingly to this room again!"

"Of course not," Rovik said with a soft chuckle. "Where would the fun be in that? Goodnight, Shaila dear."

Shaila turned and hurried off before he changed his mind, blinking back angry tears while still keeping her head held high. Marcel's laughter followed her around the corner, and as soon as she was out of sight, she broke into a run to escape it.

The man in red lowered his spyglass with a small shake of his head. The confrontation he'd just witnessed baffled and amused as much as it worried him. Three nights prior, and on countless other occasions, he'd watched Shaila go willingly to Rovik's bed with a bow and a smile. What changed? Why now?

Drauses chewed his lip behind his mask as he stared out into the dark, wondering if his plans should be postponed. He hated the thought of a year's worth of work going to waste, but better that than it all falling to ruin over a woman who couldn't decide if she were a whore or a... a what? A vigilante? A *madwoman*? Despite his concerns, he had to admit Shaila knew how to handle herself. Using her shoe as a weapon... he smiled to himself.

The squeak of a floorboard set his heart racing, and he slid to the shadows in the back of the room.

A moment later, another man in red robes and a mask crept into the now seemingly-empty room.

"Drauses?" called the newcomer. The door snapped shut, and he jumped and spun, reaching for the sword at his hip. He shook his head with a hiss through gritted teeth when Drauses stepped from the shadows.

"To Vedia with you, Drauses! Are you trying to frighten my heart in two?"

"Serves you right for trying to sneak up on me, Dagon," said Drauses. "Be thankful a fright was all I chose to give you."

"I came to talk."

"It couldn't wait an hour until I came back to headquarters?"

"I'd rather talk in private." Dagon took a seat on the window frame and stretched his long legs. "This task the Liege has given you, it stinks like week-old greeg[5]. You shouldn't go alone tomorrow night."

Drauses leaned against the remains of an old desk, heard the wooden skeleton creak dangerously under his weight, and wisely chose to stand upright again. "The Liege feels I should be the one to retrieve the girl, and I'd have it no other way."

"We all know how much Amii means to you, and I'm not suggesting you set her fate in another's hands—"

"Just what *are* you suggesting? Get on with it."

Dagon scratched his chin, choosing his words carefully. "Let my ward and I go with you, if for nothing more than my peace of mind."

"You would defy our Liege out of worry over me? Do you think me a dulled old fool, friend?"

"Yes, Drauses, I believe you've gone feeble with age," Dagon said

---

5 Greeg: A deep green fish commonly found in the Jespa River.

with a snort. "You know I'd fight any man who dares claim you're not our guild's best Master. But as strong as you are, even you can't handle a whole estate full of our enemies alone."

"This is to be a quick and silent strike. The fewer bodies involved, the less chance it should fail, and if it all goes wrong, the less we lose."

"No offense to our brothers-in-arms, but if we lost *you*..."

Drauses waved away his friend's worry. "All will be well. Have faith in the plans my ward and I have made."

"Yes... your ward. And how long has it been since you last heard from him?"

Drauses narrowed his eyes. "A message came yesterday. How else would I know when Amii will arrive?"

Dagon took a small blade from his pocket and used the tip to pry a stray stone from the bottom of his boot. "Just last week you worried he was slipping in his duties."

"I told you that in confidence," Drauses hissed.

"And I've told not a soul," Dagon barked right back. "Not even my *own* ward, and I keep very little from Aro, as you know. Surely you can understand my concern."

"All will be well," Drauses insisted.

Dagon shook his head again with a sigh, stowed his knife away, and slid down off the sill. "Truth be told, I expected no other response." He took a device from his pocket and held it out to Drauses. It was a small metal box with half a dozen switches and knobs across its face. There was a short antenna at the top with a single gold gear affixed to its base. "Take this."

"Did Julta give you this of his own free will, or did you steal it when our inventor's back was turned?" Drauses asked.

"I asked him for it and for his silence on the matter. Aro and I have its twin. We'll wait for your call in the dark tomorrow night, Drauses. If none comes, we'll assume all has gone wrong and come running. Take it."

"If it pleases you."

"It does," Dagon replied with a firm nod, and he shoved the device into Drauses' hand then clapped him on the shoulder. "Now come. Aro and I will walk back with you."

"Have I gone so feeble to need an escort home as well?" Drauses grumbled.

Dagon laughed. "You bellyache like a toothless old bastard."

"Mind who you call old. You're but a few years my junior, brother. If my foot rests in my grave, you're digging your own as we speak."

The laughter of two old friends carried them out into the dark where they were joined by a third red-robed man, impossibly tall, and the three of them made haste back through the empty streets toward warm food and soft beds.

⚶

Alone once more in her room, Shaila locked the door, knowing it made not a lick of difference anyway. She peeled off her clothes and threw them to the floor then limped into her tiny bathroom where she filled a basin with cool water and scrubbed the blood and ruined makeup from her face.

"Clean yourself up, pull yourself together, and try again tomorrow," she whispered to herself. The old mantra did little to comfort her anymore. What on Earth was she to do? At least it seemed Rovik wasn't going to kill her. No, he'd just abuse her body day after day. This was no life at all. She was confined to the house now, no longer allowed to rescue those girls who made her life as Rovik's whore worth living.

Shaila curled up on her bed and stared out the window at the stars. The tears she'd kept at bay for hours—no, make that weeks—would obey her no longer, and she wept even as she chastised her own self-pity. Tears wouldn't solve this problem.

She wanted to kill him.

Could she kill him? How would she do it? A blade to the throat? A gun to the temple? Exhaustion stole her away as she imagined all the ways she could end the life that plagued her own.

⚶

Rovik sat on the edge of his bed with his head tilted to the side as Marcel tied off the last of the stitches in his neck and cut the thread.

"Do you want me to bandage it as well?" Marcel asked.

"No." Rovik stood and went back to the mantle to pour himself another drink. The fire had burned down to nothing but embers. "Is everything in place for tomorrow?"

"Yes, sir. I passed along the forged letter from Amii's school. Drauses contacted me this morning, and I assured him all was ready for him. Do you still wish me not to alert my men?"

"Tell them nothing. Drauses will grow suspicious if he meets too much or too little resistance within the house. Whoever falls to the Master's blade tomorrow will be a necessary sacrifice for a greater cause."

"Understood, sir."

Rovik groaned and adjusted his pants which still hugged painfully tight in the groin. Perhaps he was too quick to dismiss Shaila. Even through the pain of a needle sewing up his thigh and neck, his desire for her burned unabated, but he'd gone and drowned himself too deeply in whiskey to face such a spirited woman tonight. She'd likely kill him if given the chance, and though the thought only aroused him further, she might well succeed in his current state. As tempting as such a row sounded, he couldn't risk it.

"Would you like me to call one of the other servants to see to your *other* needs?" Marcel asked.

Rovik took a drink to hide his smile. Marcel rarely failed to please, but letting the man know how much he was appreciated was unwise. "Why bother when there's a perfectly capable soul here already who's all too eager to please?"

"Sir?"

"You *are* eager to please me, are you not?"

"Yes, sir."

Rovik's eyes flicked down and back up again with a brisk nod. Marcel hesitated at first but quickly pulled himself together and sank to his knees. When he reached for the buttons of Rovik's pants, the sovereign hauled him up by the shirt and shoved him toward the door.

"Get out."

Marcel bowed his head and took his leave with a little more haste than usual.

Rovik smiled again. It was good to test, on occasion, the loyalty of those who swear their fealty, especially one as close as Marcel, for a man's right hand is always in prime position to plunge a knife in his master's back. Come this time tomorrow, the infamous Master Drauses would learn that lesson firsthand.

Chapter 3

THE NEXT DAY, Shaila wandered from one empty section of the house to another. She ran into Alonso around lunch, and he was uncharacteristically pleasant after a look at her swollen face. No one mentioned she'd be joining the Archdynast in his room again that evening, which was fine with her for she was still deciding how best to kill him. Poison sounded appealing. She pictured herself standing over him, watching as he choked and writhed, but where would she find such a weapon?

As Shaila headed for the kitchen for her supper, the sound of heavy footsteps stopped her short in the third-floor corridor. They came from Rovik's office, and since the sovereign was the last person she wished to see, she ducked into an empty bedroom to avoid him. Through a crack in the door, she watched Marcel slip from the office and make haste down the hall toward the stairwell with a cautious glance over his shoulder.

Marcel was one of the few allowed in the sovereign's office. Why was he sneaking? Once he was gone, Shaila came out of the bedroom and went to the office door. Rovik's sanctum. What weapons might he have stowed away in there? She reached out and touched the knob, gently, as if the metal might wake and scream she was an intruder. Her heart fluttered when it turned in her hand without difficulty.

The room was lit by moonlight pouring in an open window. Shaila had never been invited into the sovereign's office, and only Alonso himself was allowed to clean it, so she made a quick study of the room, searching for anything she could use to take Rovik's life. On the wall opposite the window hung a case containing several firearms and one beautifully crafted sword, each nestled in their own bed of red felt. The door of the case was a lattice of iron bars held shut with a single lock. Shaila stroked the bars and stared at the sword within. Such a beautiful, silent, deadly weapon. She fantasized for a moment how it would feel to plunge it, hilt deep, into Rovik's belly.

Shaila pulled on the door in case she got lucky twice, but it was locked. A desk sat against the wall to her left, and she slid into the chair behind it. The drawers yielded nothing more than parchments, quills, and empty ink wells, but the top left drawer was locked, and she chewed her cheek at the thought of the keys she sought lying inside, just out of her reach.

Shaila went back to the case and yanked up on the door, attempting to ruin the hinges. When that didn't work, she pulled on it with all her might instead to break the lock, but it was too well-made. The hairs on the back of her neck stood up in warning as the curtain jutted in the corner of her eye. She turned her head, and cold, sharp steel brushed her throat.

A hood and mask concealed all but his eyes. They met hers. The stories Shaila had heard as a child seemed like pure fantasy, but the long red robes and mask were unmistakable, and the blade against her throat was certainly real enough. This was a Man of the Mark, a member of a guild Shaila believed a myth until that very moment.

She knew why he was here; there was only one man worth the trouble.

"Kill the bastard, please," she said as she started to shake. If she was to die here, she wished to know Rovik would soon see the same fate.

The Mark's eyes drilled into hers for a long moment, and she thought she saw a look of recognition in them before he withdrew his blade and swept from the room like a phantom or a dream.

Shaila touched her throat then looked at her fingers. The tips were red with blood. How close had she come to death? And why, by the Odas[6], did he spare her? She dashed across the room and into the hall

---

6 The Odas: The gods, collectively.

in time to watch the tail of his robes slip into the stairwell. Shaila raced after him, vowing to help him however she could.

∽

Drauses knew Shaila was following him, but he had neither the time nor the desire to stop and explain himself. He had to find Amii. The dining room where the royal family would be sitting down to dinner any minute now was on the second floor, so he swept down the staircase to the second story.

A guard stepped out of the hallway into the stairwell as Drauses reached the landing. Drauses snatched a small knife from his belt, and the guard's eyes widened just before the blade plunged into his chin. Drauses caught the falling body and laid it silently on the floor then continued into the second-floor corridor. A gasp from behind announced the mistress had spotted his first victim. Despite his attempts to ignore her, he looked back over his shoulder to find her stooped down next to the dead guard, examining the wound in wonder as if she were curious.

Drauses' ward was supposed to raise the alarm as a distraction, but the house was so quiet his footsteps echoed down the hall. His gut churned, Dagon's doubts whispered in the back of his mind, but he marched on. A guard walked out of a nearby door, and Drauses slit his throat, forever muting him. The alarms finally sounded as Drauses picked up speed.

Three guards rounded a corner down the hall and drew their weapons. Drauses bolted down the hall straight for them. Two of them took uncertain steps backward. They were right to be afraid. He threw his knife into the chest of the nearest man as a second pulled up his gun. Drauses dodged left then right then rolled as bullets whistled past him. One shot ripped through his upper arm, but he rushed on and kicked the gun out of the guard's hand. Drauses caught it and fired a single shot right between the eyes of its owner.

As the second guard fell, the third switched on his hot stick: a whip of metal coils that glowed blue with electricity. He brought the coils back then lashed them forward, and the whip wrapped around Drauses' arm like a snake.

Agonizing jolts of electricity shot through Drauses' body. He grit-

24

ted his teeth and willed his hand to wrap around the coils, grip tightly, and yank it out of the guard's grip. He swung the heavy handle around and smacked the guard across the face with it. The guard staggered, and Drauses drew his sword. His blade whistled through the air as it sliced through the guard's chest and throat. A spray of hot blood speckled Drauses' face as he watched his last opponent fall.

Drauses clutched his chest for a breathless moment, willing his heart to slow. He was getting too old for electric shocks. He retrieved his knife, wiping it clean on a dead man's jacket. Despite the three guards, the hall was suspiciously empty.

Drauses walked on past the bodies and turned the corner. The dining room door at the end of this last hallway was ajar. A warning tingle crawled up the back of his neck. Rovik and the girl should be fleeing by now, seeking safer places and more guards, but there was no movement at all. Something was amiss, but he moved on down the hall anyway to see for himself. He pushed the door open slowly with the tip of his sword and peered into the empty dining room.

Not only were Rovik and Amii not here, but there was no evidence a meal had taken place in this room at all; the chairs were all pushed in with not a single dish in sight. Drauses swore as he drew Dagon's device from his pocket. He spun the gold gear as hard as he could, and it climbed the antenna, sending out tiny pops of electricity until the front panel lit up. He adjusted a few knobs and flipped a switch then spoke in a language known only to the guild.

"Dagon, are you there?"

"Yes, brother. Go ahead," came Dagon's reply. His voice crackled and cut out twice, so Drauses adjusted one of the dials before speaking again.

"Something is—"

There was a sharp burst of pain on the back of Drauses' head, and the world went black.

⤫

Shaila stood with her back to the wall around the corner from the dining room. She peeked around in time to watch The Man of the Mark crumble in a heap at Marcel's feet. Two guards came rushing down the hall to join them.

"About time," Marcel barked. "Where have you been? Never mind. Bind his hands and feet."

"Quickly, he's coming to," said one of the guards.

Shaila peered down at the floor and jumped at the sight of a dead guard at her feet who was staring at her with a look of blame as if she were the one who ended his life. A knife was attached to his belt, and she knelt and slid it from its sheath. It was a short blade but heavy and well-made.

Shaila looked around the corner again at the captured Man of the Mark as Marcel and his men set him up on his knees.

"You traitorous filth!" the Mark spat, glaring up at Marcel. "You swore an oath!"

"I serve a new Master now," Marcel said, "and he has far more to offer me than a guild of filthy Easterners ever will."

The Man of the Mark spotted Shaila at the end of the hall, and he stared at her over his mask. She looked from the Mark's face down to the blade in her hands and back again, then she stood and stuck the weapon carefully up the sleeve of her shirt. She took a deep breath and said a silent prayer for courage before running down the hall and into the dining room at a full sprint.

"Marcel!" Shaila cried as she burst into the room, breathing hard as if she'd just run clear from the other end of the house. "The mansion is under attack!"

Marcel rolled his eyes at her. His men chuckled.

"Yes. We already caught the intruder." He motioned to the man in red.

"Where is the other one?" Shaila asked.

"Other one?" Marcel asked in alarm.

Shaila glanced at the Man of the Mark. "I... was in the third-floor hall when... they came from the sovereign's office. There were *two* masked and hooded men."

Marcel rounded on the captured Mark. "Who did you bring with you?" he screamed, but the Master merely glared back with no reply. Marcel swore and ran his hand through his hair, peering about the room in a panic. "You," he snapped at the nearest guard, "come with me." He pointed to the other guard. "You stay here, watch him, and kill him if he moves."

Marcel and his chosen guard rushed past Shaila and back down the hall.

Shaila spotted a hint of black on the dark red carpet. She bent and picked up a small metal box from the floor.

"I think he dropped this," she said, offering it to the remaining guard.

He snatched the device away and turned it curiously in his hand, adjusting the knobs until the box gave a shrill screech that made him yelp and nearly drop it.

Shaila took the knife from her sleeve and stepped up behind the guard, her heart thundering in her chest at what she was about to do. She held her breath as she reared her hand back and plunged the knife in his back.

The guard screamed, and Shaila yanked the knife away, rearing back for another blow, but he rounded on her, pistol raised. The Man of the Mark fell to his back on the floor and kicked his bound feet at the guard who tripped and fell with a bang that rattled the walls. Shaila came down on top of the guard, swiping with her knife over and over, slicing his fingers, arms, and once across his cheek. He shrieked and raised his arms to protect his face. Shaila gripped the knife tightly in both hands and plunged it into his exposed throat.

The guard thrashed and choked as Shaila scrambled away against the wall with both hands clutched over her mouth, watching the blood pool across the carpet toward her shoes. The dying man took hold of the knife and ripped it from his body causing yet more of his blood to gush with each beat of his heart. His gasps slowed then ceased completely as the life drained from his eyes.

The Man of the Mark struggled back to his knees. He said something, but Shaila was frozen, staring at the dead man at her feet.

"Look at me!"

Shaila jumped and looked up into the Mark's eyes.

"You've come this far," he said. "See it through!"

Shaila nodded and snatched her bloody knife from the floor, but when she came near, a wave of nerves shivered through her. This man, this killing machine, was death in human form.

And she was about to release him.

She shook so violently that when she went to cut his bonds, her hand slipped, and she cut him by accident. He flinched but said nothing. She tried again and this time managed to cut the tie without injuring him further.

He took the knife from her and sliced his feet free. He jumped to his feet and snatched his sword from the table. Shaila yelped when he seized her by the front of her shirt and shoved her against the wall.

"Those two men in red you mentioned, where did they go?" he demanded to know.

"I lied to send Marcel away," Shaila said in a rush. "I thought you were the only one in the house. Are there more?"

He released her without answering and searched the dead guard. He found the metal box and wiped it free of blood as he adjusted the knobs. After a click and a whine, the box chirped, and he spoke into it in a language Shaila had never heard before. What confused her more was the clear voice that replied from the box as if it were a living thing. She stepped closer for a better look but, at a glare of warning from the Mark, backed away again. He spoke twice into the box, listened to each reply, then rushed from the room and down the hall, leaving Shaila staring after him in bemusement.

Shaila ran after him back into the stairwell, but he headed up the stairs instead of down. How on Earth did he plan to escape the house through the upper floors? He ran all the way to the fifth floor, and Shaila shadowed him to the last bedroom in the eastern hall. The window was smashed and a long wooden plank placed on the sill to create a bridge into the building next door. Two more Men of the Mark stood in the darkened window across the way.

The Mark moved to step up onto the board and make his escape, and without thinking, Shaila rushed across the room and grabbed his arm to stop him. His hand whipped around, seized hers, and twisted hard to the left, snapping her wrist. She screamed, and the look of surprise on his face said he'd forgotten all about her until that moment.

"Drauses, we must go!" said one of the men in the other building. Shouts echoed in the hall.

"T... take me with you," Shaila said, clutching her broken wrist to her chest.

"Drauses, now!"

"You owe me this much!" she insisted.

His eyes softened above his red mask, and when he held out his hand, she took it.

⟡

Drauses sat on a windowsill with a small mirror propped against the window frame. By reflecting the moon in the glass, he used its light to stitch the bullet wound in his upper arm while Shaila slept on his robes across the room. She'd fallen asleep during the boat ride across the river, and though he knew he should've been long gone by now, he couldn't bring himself to leave her here to wake alone in the dark.

When he was done with his stitching, he took down his hood and removed his mask. His dusty brown hair fell in waves to his shoulders. He inspected himself in the mirror as the breeze coming in the window dried the sweat on his face and neck. There was a cut above his right brow. His nose was freshly bruised over the prominent bump in its bridge, evidence of the many times he'd broken it over the years. Beside one of his jutting cheekbones, his shadow of day-old beard stubble was interrupted by a long scar that ran down his left cheek from under his eye clear to his chin. An inch higher and the wound would have blinded him.

Shaila sighed and shifted on the floor, and Drauses quickly turned toward the window and replaced his hood and mask. When he looked at her, her eyes were open and watching him warily.

"Awake at last," he said.

"So it would seem."

"What's your name?" he asked. Drauses already knew, but there was much more to this woman than what little Marcel had told him in his reports, there had to be. She was the only reason he escaped with his life tonight. Such gumption was rare, especially in the privileged West. That was the only reason he took her away, he told himself, but he could sense the pebble of truth beneath that lie: he was curious and captivated by her, a deadly mix if handled improperly.

"Shaila," she replied, sitting up. "You're Drauses? Is that what your partner called you?"

"Yes."

Shaila tried to push herself up off the floor but yelped when her arm buckled at the wrist.

"Apologies for that," Drauses said. "You startled me. Never touch a Man of the Mark unannounced. I was gentle. Another might have snapped your neck."

"Why are you still here?"

'Why indeed?' he asked himself. He was about to do something either incredibly smart or profoundly foolish. Only time would tell.

"Tonight went horribly wrong," he said. "I was betrayed." He started packing up the tools he'd used to stitch his arm into a small leather case that sat open on his leg. "But another came to my aid when I needed it most." He studied her in the moonlight. "Why did you help me?"

"I thought we had similar goals. I want Rovik dead."

Drauses narrowed his eyes. "Why? Why would you beg me to end your lover's life?"

Shaila curled her lip. "My lover? You think I harbor some feelings for that monster?"

"I know only what I see with my own eyes, and I watched a woman go willingly to her sovereign's bed for weeks then beg an assassin to end his life. Why?"

The look of disgust on her face relaxed into one of wonder instead. "You were watching me?"

"I asked my question first."

Shaila snorted but answered him anyway. "A long, tiring tale of circumstances led me to Rovik's bed. Very few of which were of my choosing."

"Then why not leave?" Drauses challenged. "Surely someone as resourceful as you could've easily slipped away."

She broke eye contact for the first time but kept her chin held high. "In the early days, I stayed because my mother and father gave everything they had for my future. To go back to them with nothing would be shameful. Later, I stayed for the girls."

"What girls?"

"I thought you were watching me," she said cheekily, but when he didn't rise to her taunt, she continued. "I stayed for the maidens who swim the river because someone in the East deems them handsome enough. I met them three times a week on the Western shore on Rovik's orders, but I hid the fairest ones. I kept them from houses of pleasure and from Rovik whenever I could."

"Why? I've watched Rovik for nearly a year. Before you, he only ever treated his lovers with care."

"That's true. But do you know where they went once he was done with them?"

"I don't," Drauses confessed.

"I watched those girls come for a full season, so many I lost track of the names, but I never once watched one go. They'd simply vanish one night and be replaced the next. I asked around for a few to quiet my suspicions and instead had them confirmed. To the best of my knowledge, not one of Rovik's girls was ever seen again."

Shaila climbed to her feet, carefully this time, and sighed. She looked suddenly years older.

"I knew Rovik's bed was a death sentence," she said, "and that I would someday end up in The Cellar like the others. But I couldn't run knowing he'd simply take another in my place. So, I stayed. I laid night after night with a man I loathed to save other young lives from terrible fates, which is far more than anyone did for me when I washed up on the Western shore."

"You were born in the East?" Drauses asked in surprise.

"Obviously." She rolled her eyes at him. The audacity.

Drauses nodded, bemused but content with her answers and intrigued all over again. This woman was a beautiful puzzle he very much wished to solve.

"You asked me to take you away," he said. "I chose to do so. And now, I'll give *you* a choice. I can let you go, set you free of this place to live whatever life you wish. You'll never see me again. Or, you can take

Marcel's place at my side as my ward. I'll train you, discipline you, teach you focus and self-control. If you learn what I can teach you and prove yourself, you'd become a Man... excuse me, a *Lady* of the Mark. You'd join my guild and help keep the peace in the East while leading the rebellion to overthrow Rovik. Perhaps we do have similar goals after all."

She stared at him as if his madness might be catching. "No, thank you."

"No?" He was shocked by her answer as well as his own haughty expectations. "May I ask why?"

"After freeing myself from one man, why would I willingly crawl under the boot of another?"

"Our wards aren't slaves or prisoners. They're willing apprentices, free to leave their Masters' sides if ever they wish. You could call off our arrangement at any time."

"What's in it for you?" Shaila asked, narrowing her eyes. "Surely there must be something you'd want in return."

Drauses set his medicine kit aside and rose from the sill at the implication, casting his towering shadow over her in the moonlight. "The Men of the Mark hold much higher standards than that, I assure you."

"Apologies," she replied, and he was surprised to note the blush that colored her cheeks at his rebuke. "It's been far too long since I could trust another."

He took back his seat on the sill. "What if I told you something personal? A secret of my own that doesn't concern the Marks? Could you trust me then?"

"That depends on the secret."

A smart answer. "You know of Rovik's daughter?"

"Everyone knows of Amii."

"What if I told you she's *not* our sovereign's child?"

Shaila shrugged. "Those whispers surfaced years ago. Amii might've been born of Rovik's mistress, but she's most likely not his blood."

"No, she's not his blood. She's mine."

Shaila raised a brow. "You're sure?"

"As sure as a man can be. Amii's mother was Rose, the only daughter of Rovik's half-brother Dellar, the slaver. When Dellar found out Rose was with child, he sent her West to live with Rovik."

"Why?"

"To keep her away from me." He couldn't look at Shaila knowing his eyes would give away his pain. "He needn't have bothered. Rose died in childbirth two seasons later."

Shaila was silent for a long time, and Drauses looked up, reading the doubt on her face.

"In the name of mutual trust, I'll add to my offer," he said. "I have connections here in the East, as do my Brothers of the Mark, connections who could help those girls you mentioned. You could continue to help them from *this* side of the river. In return, ask your contacts to pass on any information they can on Rovik, his men, Amii and her whereabouts, anything they think may be useful to us. There must be plenty of Westerners who want Rovik replaced as badly as we do."

Shaila nodded thoughtfully. "It may take time to convince them to work via couriers," she muttered.

"Is that a yes?"

Shaila studied him for a moment then held out her good hand. "I'll fight with you."

Drauses chuckled. "If only it were that simple." He removed his hood and mask again.

Shaila tried and failed to hide a smile when she saw his face for the first time.

"To become my ward, you'll have to swear yourself to me and obey my every order," Drauses explained. "Training with a Mark is not an easy endeavor, and I'll expect nothing but your very best efforts. You'll give me blood, and sweat, and tears—"

"Trying to make me change my mind?"

"Merely being honest. I can tell you very few details about the guild before you become a full member, but I promise never to lie." He stood and offered her his medicine kit. "Training can start right now. Brace your wrist."

"I don't know how," Shaila said, but she took the kit anyway.

"I know. I won't touch you; it's against our code. You'll do this yourself with my instructions. It's the best way to learn."

"How long will I train with you?"

"Until I've nothing left to teach you. You won't be a member of the guild until you prove yourself. Even then, you'll remain under my tutelage until I give you leave."

"How do I prove myself?"

"You must fight one of our own. If you win, you'll become a Mark, but if you lose, you'll be cast out. There are no second chances. It takes several seasons to prepare for a proving, and many still lose."

"And you think I can learn to fight well enough to win?"

"Anyone can learn to fight. Learning to listen and obey without question is much harder." He cocked his head to the side. "Can you obey, Shaila?"

She smiled. "I can obey just fine when I put my mind to it."

He almost smiled back. She was a quick learner with a sharp tongue. This was going to be fun.

He nodded. "Then get started."

Chapter 4

3ʳᵈ and 50 of Summer, Jesparia's 9ᵗʰ and 20 year of Rovik

SHAILA STOOD IN the third-story window of an abandoned apartment building, looking out at the darkening alley below, tinted slightly crimson in the dusk light. As she sang quietly to herself, Drauses walked up behind her. He almost interrupted her but couldn't bring himself to. Instead, he stood and listened to her sing of the gods and praise them for their beauty, grace, and mercy. He closed his eyes when she finished the tune with a note that gave him chills.

"You should rest," he said. "Tomorrow is far too important for you to exhaust yourself."

"Did you sleep the night before your proving?" Shaila asked.

"No," he admitted with a sly smile.

"Fret not, Master Drauses, I'll bring you no shame tomorrow."

"My shame is the least of my worries."

"Surely you're not worried for *me*. What happened to 'your fate is your own concern now'?"

He fought not to laugh at her ridiculous imitation of his voice, so he sighed instead. "Masters give wards the tools to succeed, and it's up to you how you use them. But, in the end, we always care, and so we worry."

"So insightful. You should write poetry."

He snorted. "I've never been good with rhymes."

She laughed.

It was always like this between them. They were Master and ward always, but there was something else, something Drauses had never experienced before with his previous protégés: friendship. Though other Masters, Dagon included, often formed lifelong bonds with their wards, Drauses saw his charges as students and treated them as such. It was his job to teach the next generation of Marks, but the father-and-son-like relationship many of his comrades found with their wards wasn't something Drauses wanted. In fact, he worked hard *not* to let those sorts of attachments form for he felt they were nothing but distractions from a greater goal.

But with Shaila, it was different.

Despite his best efforts, he couldn't keep the usual distance between them, and the closer he let her get, the more he enjoyed her company.

"You don't have to lie to me, you know," she said, interrupting his thoughts. "Not anymore."

"What do you mean?"

"I understand what Marcel took from you two years ago." She looked over her shoulder at him, and the setting sun crowned her with a halo of fiery light. "I know why you picked me, and I won't fail you."

"Why did I pick you?" he asked, perplexed.

"Because training a woman is a grander feat than training a man. My success would restore your honor—"

"That's not why," he rushed to say, but then he was lost to explain further. Did she truly believe pride was the only reason he chose her? Was she right? His ego was certainly wounded by Marcel's betrayal, and what better way to nurse it than a challenge when he doubted himself most? How many times over the past two years had he pictured his brothers' shocked faces when his lady ward won her proving?

When she turned back to the window, he resisted the urge to touch her shoulder and assure her their partnership meant more to him than pride. He wasn't so sure himself anymore.

The sun had set, and the streets of Trista were lit by a half-open moon[7]. Shaila stepped up onto the windowsill.

"I should go," she said. "Two sisters will swim tonight if I'm not there to convince them otherwise."

She poised to jump out of the window, to Drauses' horror, and he reached for her in protest. She leapt before he could utter a word. He dashed to the sill to watch her swing from the downpipe on the side of the building and jump to a balcony across the alley. From there, she made her way down to the ground as gracefully as a cat. He shook his head and smiled. Even after two years, she could still surprise him.

The next morning, Drauses led Shaila through a complicated maze of sewer tunnels. She worried they might be lost, but her Master moved confidently, chose his turns with ease, and in no time, he stopped at the bottom of a ladder. Its rungs were the cleanest things Shaila had seen in hours, but they still stained her palms a grimy green when she climbed them. At the top, Drauses slid aside a large circular hatch and climbed out into an old factory. The walls were riddled with peeling paint and the floors covered with a layer of dirt no amount of scrubbing would ever clear away. Shaila looked at Drauses, but he gave nothing away as he led her up a narrow set of stairs toward the second story.

The building transformed before her eyes. Clean paint covered the walls, the wooden floors were immaculate, and the smell of something delicious wafted through the halls. The echoes of voices grew louder as they walked. They stepped out into the wide-open factory floor, and at least fifty men turned to look at the Master and ward, newly arrived. The silence that fell set Shaila's nerves on edge, and she swallowed hard, willing herself not to stare back at the dozens of eyes locked on her from every direction.

Shaila wore her hood and mask as tradition dictated. They hid her sex from the staring men around her, which was how she wanted it. No Mark would know her secret until she was one of them. Though Drauses

---

7 A full description of the moon's phases can be found on page 370.

disapproved, often loudly so, she was confident her Master wouldn't give her away since he was a reserved and private man himself. Everywhere Shaila looked, Masters pointed, wards elbowed each other, whispered together as Drauses swept through the room. He paid them no mind. Shaila followed closely behind, mirroring his cool calm.

Drauses approached an older man at the back wall who stood alone, gazing out at the men around him like a shepherd overseeing his flock. The old man grinned and drew Drauses into a one-armed hug when he walked up.

"Drauses, it's been far too long," the older man said, his voice wheezy with age.

"Apologies, my Liege, I was busy with training."

Shaila bowed her head in respect. So, this was the Liege of the Marks, Gragern, the Elder Master who oversaw headquarters and had final say in all major decisions concerning the guild and their war with Rovik. For as important a person as he was, Shaila had a hard time getting Drauses to tell her much else about him.

Gragern studied Drauses thoughtfully then nodded. "It was likely for the best after the incident with your last ward." He looked at Shaila with a cocked brow. "I see you've brought your *new* ward. Is he here to prove himself today?"

"Yes, sir," Drauses replied, and it was only then Shaila realized he hadn't smiled once.

"A proving!" Gragern cried. "There hasn't been a single one this whole season."

A man with untidy black hair came to Gragern's side. "Did I hear right?" he asked. "Is there to be a proving?"

"Indeed," said Gragern. "Drauses, I presume you remember my ward Miika."

"Of course. Miika, how are you?"

"Just fine, Master Drauses, sir. Has an opponent been chosen for your ward's proving?"

"Not yet."

"I'd be happy to do the honors," Miika said with a grin.

Shaila immediately sized him up. He wasn't as tall as Drauses but was broader in the shoulders. His hair hung down a little past his ears in chaotic waves. What drew her attention most was his eyes: they were a deep, enchanting green. But when he looked at her, his smile was wrong. It felt... false somehow.

"An excellent idea, Miika," Gragern said.

Drauses shifted on his feet.

"Go prepare, Drauses," Gragern said. "Our wards to battle in ten minutes."

Drauses and Shaila made their way across the room where the others were already clearing tables and chairs from the floor to create a ring.

As they stood waiting for the match to begin, Shaila peeked over at her Master. The scar on his cheek bobbed as he clenched his teeth. Was he nervous? His previous ward had shamed him, and that treachery wounded him deeply, she knew, though he refused to talk about it. She would heal some of that pain today, she vowed.

"Are you well?" he asked.

"Yes," she replied in a whisper.

"Miika is one of our strongest fighters. He's rebellious. Watch him closely."

"Why did he volunteer to face me?"

"His reasons matter not. Miika has nothing to lose in this fight, but for you, this battle means everything. Focus, breathe, and show them what a Lady of the Mark is made of."

Shaila smiled under her mask and nodded.

Miika stepped into the circle to a round of cheers. It was time. Shaila made to step in as well, but Drauses touched her arm. She looked back in surprise.

His eyes drilled into hers much like they did the night they first met, but this time, they were heavy with worry. Was that worry for her or for his reputation should she fail him? He opened his mouth to say something then closed it. His scar bobbed again.

"Good luck," he said simply.

Shaila entered the ring wondering what he'd truly wanted to say and why he'd changed his mind.

The Liege raised his arms, and the congregation fell silent. "This is a proving fight," he announced. "The ward who wishes to join the Marks must claim the mask of his opponent. If he loses, a Mark he'll never be. Fighters ready? Begin!"

Shaila fell into her stance how Drauses taught her: all her weight on her right leg, bent at the knee, left leg stuck straight out behind her, balanced on her toes, left arm tucked behind her back, right hand touching the floor with the tips of her fingers. She bowed her head and closed her eyes, tuning out all the noise from the spectators and focusing on her opponent, his breathing, his gait as he circled her. He sucked in a small breath and sidestepped once before he struck.

She struck first.

Shaila spun and kicked the backs of Miika's knees. He stumbled forward with a hiss of rage and came back with his elbow, aiming for her face, but she grabbed his arm and used his own momentum to propel him backward. The crowd roared with laughter when he landed on his backside.

Miika rolled and jumped to his feet. Shaila stood waiting and taunted him forward with the bend of a finger. This time, he ran in to face her head-on, throwing blow after blow. She blocked him easily and landed her own blow to his chest that knocked the wind out of him. He stumbled back, sizing her up anew with a glare, then he reached into his robes and yanked out a short leather club.

Drauses had assured her this would be a hand-to-hand fight only. Why was her opponent allowed a weapon? She took several steps back and looked at Drauses.

Drauses stepped into the ring and came between her and Miika. "This fight is no longer a fair proving," he announced, and he looked at Gragern. "My Liege, your ward needs correcting."

Gragern only shrugged. "I'll allow it."

"A proving has *never* included armed—"

"Your ward has trained for two years, Drauses, twice as long as needed for a proving," Gragern said as he crossed his arms. "Either he's ready for an extra challenge, or he's weak enough to need twice the tutelage to win even a simple match of hand-to-hand. Which is it?"

Drauses' chest heaved, and his hand balled into a fist at his side, but when he looked at Shaila, his eyes were the same worried blue they'd been before the match started.

She nodded once, determined to see the fight through.

"Very well, my Liege," Drauses said, then he stalked from the ring.

Shaila rolled her shoulders and refocused. She stared at Miika's weapon, recognizing it as the same kind Marcel used to carry. The handle was leather, which meant it was flexible, but it was no more than a foot long, so its reach was minimal. The end was likely weighted. Its blows would hurt. A lot.

Miika came in fast again and swung a punch Shaila easily blocked, but then he caught her in the arm with his club. The weapon cracked hard against bone, and she hissed through her teeth and retreated. He swung again, aiming for her face, and she had to block the blow with her arm again. His club struck the same spot as before, which made her double over in pain, and Miika rushed in. Shaila spun on her feet and landed two quick jabs to his side. He staggered back, and Shaila kicked him hard in the stomach, putting him down to one knee.

Shaila moved in, spotting her chance to end the fight fast, but Miika lashed up with his club and smacked her in the chest. Her lungs locked under the blow, and she clutched her chest, fighting to breathe. Miika rose and pivoted and struck her across the face with his club. A burst of bright light and pain ripped through her head, and she crumpled to the floor.

Shaila fought to stay conscious as she searched the faces around her for Drauses. She couldn't find him. Miika no doubt thought he'd won, but she wasn't done with this fight… She would lie here a moment and catch her breath… just another moment…

❧

It took all of Drauses' self-control not to burst into the ring, rip that damnable weapon from Miika's hands, and beat him to death with it.

Miika strolled once around the ring in victory, but there were no cheers. He'd cheated, but the Liege had allowed it, and though Drauses shared in his brothers' disbelief at this injustice, he had bigger concerns at present.

Shaila needed him.

She was motionless on the ground, and Drauses took a step toward the ring to go gather her up before he remembered the match wasn't over yet. Miika had to collect Shaila's mask to claim his victory, and Drauses wished the ward would get on with it already. He'd protest this proving in council with the other Masters, but the outcome wouldn't matter if Miika caved in Shaila's skull. Drauses was poised to rush across the ring when Miika walked over to Shaila's body.

Miika loomed over Shaila with a smile, but when he bent down to take her mask, her body rolled, and her legs sprang up and wrapped around his neck. With a swift and powerful twist, she yanked Miika down headfirst against the floor with a sickening smack.

Miika slumped over, unconscious, as Shaila staggered to her feet. She nearly fell over as she bent and removed Miika's mask, but then she straightened and held it high above her head. Drauses laughed with relief.

The room burst into applause, but then Shaila yanked off her mask, dropped her hood, and shook her hair from her robes, and the entire room fell deathly silent all over again.

Shaila turned in a slow circle, looking to each bewildered face with a smile. Drauses grinned like a fool when she came and presented him with Miika's mask. He took it with a swell of pride glowing warmly in his chest.

They'd done it. Against all odds, he'd trained the first Lady of the Mark, and she'd won her proving fairly, even at a disadvantage. If any man objected to her addition to the guild, Drauses would invite them to try his hand with her in the ring. That should silence any protests. All the Masters and wards stared, but Drauses ignored them as he touched Shaila's shoulder.

"A true Lady of the Mark indeed," he said. His smile faded in alarm when a trickle of blood dripped down the side of her face. A second later, her eyes drifted shut, and Drauses leapt forward to catch her as she fell. He hoisted her up in his arms, clutching her tight.

"Step aside!" he bellowed, and the men cleared a path as he carried her away.

❧

Shaila's head throbbed as she opened her eyes to bright lights and probing fingers.

"Master Drauses?" she called groggily.

"I'm here."

"Does this mean I lost?"

Drauses chuckled from somewhere nearby. "No, you won the fight fair. It doesn't matter if you spew your guts, wet yourself, or pass out afterward, a victory is a victory."

"Men have wet themselves?"

"Once or twice."

Shaila tried to sit up.

"Hold on there," said a voice she didn't recognize, and a small hand held her still by the shoulder. She blinked up into the face of a slender, balding man in glasses. His brown eyes were warm and his smile slight and soft.

"Shaila, this is Dr. Rikar."

"Boon, if you please," the doctor said.

"Boon is the guild's physician in residence. He's been here longer than I have."

Boon clicked his tongue. "Yes, I've been stitching most of the Masters back together since their own provings. And don't ask me which of them is more stubborn; it's a toss." He gave Shaila a wink. "They preach obedience, and yet not one of them can follow a doctor's orders."

Shaila chuckled with a wince.

"Alright, let's see to these wounds. Drauses?"

"Yes, yes, I'm going," Drauses said. "I've some business to attend to anyway. I'll be back soon." He gave Shaila a parting smile then took his leave.

"Why did he have to go?" Shaila asked.

"I take my patients' privacy seriously. Whatever they choose to share with the others is up to them, but I don't allow anyone to stand in on exams."

"So, you won't tell me any scandalous stories about my Master then?"

Boon shook his head. "No one would come to me with what ails them if I was prone to gossip. Now take a deep breath while I check if these ribs are cracked."

§

Drauses went back to the factory floor where the furniture had been replaced and various card games and conversations re-commenced. He made straight for Gragern at the front of the room.

"A word, my Liege?" Drauses requested, and Gragern glided off to the side of the room where they could talk in semi-privacy. "What did you mean by allowing your ward a weapon during a proving?" Drauses barked once they were alone.

"I made my reasons perfectly clear already, Drauses. I wanted to be sure the extra time you took training your ward wasn't wasted. I wasn't disappointed. A woman. Ha! You never fail to surprise, brother. This struck quite a blow to my own ward's pride, I'm sure."

Drauses shook his head in disbelief at the Elder's daring. "Is there any news on Amii, sir?"

Gragern's smile faded, and his gaze wandered away across the room. "I'm afraid not." He looked back at Drauses, his eyes full of accusation. "Since the man who kept us informed turned traitor, we can do nothing but watch from a distance and wait for some lucky chance to try again. So far, Rovik has kept the girl far out of our reach."

"And the list of names I gave you? Have they been of any use?"

"I decided not to use any of the Western contacts," Gragern said dismissively.

"Whyever not? They all came highly recommended."

"By whom? Your new ward?" Gragern studied Drauses' face, concluded he was right, then snorted. "Forgive me for doubting the word of someone I've never met. These are delicate issues. We wouldn't want our brothers to think I'd fallen afool."

"Where do you need me, my Liege?" Drauses asked, struggling to remain respectful. "Now that my ward is a Mark proper, we can join this fight—"

"It's taken care of. Don't concern yourself."

"That's my child!"

"A child you cared none about until she was our best chance to overthrow Rovik."

Drauses winced. "You know that's not true, sir."

"Your last attempt to aid our efforts pushed us back several years."

"How were we to know Marcel—"

"*You* should have known!" Gragern thundered, and several Masters nearby glanced over curiously at the Liege's outburst. "He was *your* ward, *your* responsibility. If he couldn't be trusted, it was *your* job to realize he was corrupt."

Drauses refused to look away like a chastised youth. "I live with that fact every single day. I stand ready to help mend the damage I've caused."

"The damage was mended long ago. We had to move our entire headquarters, terminate all active assignments Marcel was privy to, and question any brothers who were close to him. But you weren't around for any of that."

"I was training a new ward, someone who can fill the hole Marcel left in our ranks and then some."

"Yes, well, if I need you or your ward, I'll inform you. Just make sure you chose one we can trust this time." He let his backhanded insult hang in the air between them for a moment before he continued. "How is she?"

"Boon is caring for her."

"She's cunning."

"Shaila is dedicated and focused. She'll make a fine Sister of the Mark."

"Do you know why there's never been a lady in our guild before?" Gragern asked, but he continued without waiting for Drauses to answer. "Compassion has no place in the life of a Mark. More often than not, compassion gets us killed. The weaknesses of the softer sex are no secret, even to men like us, Drauses. Be careful. Someday, your ward will have to act on her own and thrive without your guidance or your praise." And with that, Gragern walked away.

Drauses stared after the Liege, lost in a flurry of thought.

"Master Drauses," a familiar voice called.

Drauses smiled as he turned. "Aro," he greeted. "Good to see you."

They shook hands. "Where's your Master? He no doubt would've said hello by now if he was in residence."

Aro was a full head taller than Drauses and had to duck his towering frame through doorways. He was as thin as a pole and kept his dark brown hair cut short, so unlike the other Men of the Mark with their long and often shaggy manes. His hazel eyes were soft and welcoming, as was the smile he rarely went without.

"Master Dagon is on a personal holiday with Master Ithail," Aro said.

Drauses smiled in happy surprise. "Good for him. He's been alone far too long."

"My thoughts exactly. He'll be upset when I tell him he missed your ward's proving." Aro stepped close and lowered his voice. "I feel it's my duty to tell you that Master Dagon has been waiting, quite impatiently, might I add, for your return to headquarters. There's something he's been wanting to discuss with you. I believe it concerns—"

"I know what it concerns, Aro," Drauses said. "You can tell your Master I'm not interested in discussing our Liege's retirement with him again."

"I'd rather you tell him that yourself," Aro said with a chuckle. "Besides, I think there's more to it than that. Even the wards are starting to whisper."

"They can whisper all they like. I've no interest in leading them. They'll have to choose another."

"Nevertheless, Master Dagon would be cross with me if I didn't ask you to stick around until his return so he can speak with you. He's due back in three days."

"I'll tell him I got the message. Take care, Aro."

The two men shook hands again before Drauses headed for the guild's workshop.

Julta, the guild's inventor and handyman, was newer to the guild than one would expect. The respect he received from the men could rival Boon's since he alone kept them all equipped with shiny new toys. He could create any weapon imaginable with bits of recycling and was constantly improving his own designs. Drauses knocked on the door of Julta's workshop before he entered.

Julta was stooped over a counter, fiddling with a wire that popped with electricity. As usual, he worked with no gloves nor any other form of protection. Drauses kept his distance and watched as Julta's hand slipped, and the wire shocked his palm. Julta yelped and danced in place for a moment to rid his skin of the sting, but then he launched right back into his task without delay.

Drauses cleared his throat loudly.

"Master Drauses!" Julta greeted cheerfully once he tore himself from his work.

"Hello, Julta," Drauses replied with a smile. He'd always liked the inventor's energy and eccentric, brilliant mind.

"Master Drauses, Master Drauses, come!" Julta called, motioning Drauses forward with a flourish. "Hand over that old blade of yours and let me give it a good look-see, hmm? A quick sharpening perhaps?"

"You know I prefer to maintain my own equipment."

Julta sighed. "I'm glad the others aren't like you. I'd go mad if I could never tinker."

"There's something else you can do for me instead."

"What might that be?"

"I need a weapon. Is there anything new to your stocks? Some brilliant design?"

"Looking to replace your blade? Finally ready to upgrade?" Julta's excitement had him bouncing on his feet.

"It's not for me."

"Then it must be for your new ward!" Julta exclaimed as he leaned on his hands over the counter. "Our very first Lady of the Mark! Oh yes, I know all about the cunning lady ward already. I watched her proving from a distance. She's small and fast, stealthy too, if I had to guess. She needs something quick, something quiet, something deadly and beautiful, like her. Wait, *wait*! I have just the thing!"

Julta darted from one side of his workshop to the other, searching this way and that, his long black hair flailing around his face as he swiveled and whipped until he found what he was searching for: a black case held shut by a long leather strap. Julta placed the case on the counter and swept his hair out of his face before unbuckling the strap and flinging the lid open. Inside sat a small silver crossbow.

"This," Julta said with a sweep of his hand over the weapon, "is perfect." He lifted the crossbow from the box and flipped it over to reveal two small leather straps on its underside. "It's bound to the arm above the wrist, see? And you push in the sides…" Julta squeezed the sides of the crossbow, and it folded up on itself into a mere silver rectangle. He strapped it to his own arm for demonstration. "It hides up the sleeve until you press this button." Julta pressed, and the crossbow sprang forward and fell into his hand, ready to shoot in less than a second. "It's quiet, deadly, and beautiful, no?"

"That it is, Julta, but does it come with bolts?" Drauses peered into the empty case.

Julta's shoulders slumped. "It does, but it's so new, I've not yet had the chance to do much with them. These won't do at all." He pulled a small bundle of bolts out from under the counter. They looked no different than any Drauses had seen before. "This weapon deserves better. Fire, poison, gas, *explosive*! Yes!" Julta slapped the counter in excitement, and Drauses jumped then laughed. "You give me time! Give me time, and I'll make better ones, but for now, take these." He handed the bundle over with a look of disgust.

"This is very nice, Julta. Well done, yet again."

"It's nothing, Master Drauses. I love to create! But I wish you'd let me sharpen your blade." He looked hungrily at the sword at Drauses' hip.

"If I gave you my blade to sharpen, boy, it would come back with a dozen new functions."

Julta giggled. "You know me well, sir! Yes!"

"Julta, do you think you could get me something else? Something you can't craft?"

Julta drew closer, his eyes dancing with wicked expectation. "A challenge? Name it! I love this game." He clapped his hands together.

"I need tickets to an event on the West side."

"What sort of event?"

"The opera," Drauses said with a wince.

"The lady loves music, does she?" The inventor clicked his tongue. "Don't look at me like that. Your secret is safe with me. I can find such a trifle, easy enough."

"Make sure it's a masked event."

"Of course, of course. Do you need formal wear as well?"

"You can do that?"

"It'll take a few days."

"That's fine."

"Then come back and see me soon, Master Drauses." Julta bowed so deeply his nose almost touched the counter.

Drauses nestled the crossbow back in its case and left the workshop with a burning desire to give it to Shaila as soon as possible. His ward had made him proud, and he wanted to reward her.

Chapter 5

DRAUSES CAME DOWN the hallway in time to catch Miika as he was about to enter the clinic. The ward wisely turned on his heels and made haste in the opposite direction at the sight of the Master. Drauses hurried after him, calling, and Miika stopped, turning to eye Drauses warily as he came near. Drauses merely offered his hand.

"No hard feelings about your loss today?" he asked.

Miika regarded Drauses' hand, his eyes flicking from it to the Master's face and back again. Tentatively, he reached out and took it. Drauses smiled then tightened his grip painfully around Miika's hand. He yanked the ward close, reached into Miika's robes, plucked the club from the ward's belt, and struck him across the face with it. Miika's nose broke with a loud crunch and a gush of blood. Drauses grabbed him by the throat and pinned him against the wall.

"Since your own Master won't discipline you, allow me to do the honors," Drauses sneered. He squeezed his fingers tighter around Miika's throat until the ward was gasping. "The next time you consider pulling a weapon during a proving, think twice." Drauses let Miika go and hit him once more, across the mouth. The ward fell to his hands and knees. He coughed on a mouthful of blood then spit one of his teeth out on the floor.

"If you come within arm's length of my ward in future," Drauses continued, "I'll give her leave to kill you. Be assured, if she does not, I'll happily do it for her." He dropped the club on the floor by Miika's feet. "Stay away from the clinic until Shaila and I leave."

Drauses stalked away.

❦

Gragern looked up from behind his desk as Miika stumbled into their shared quarters. The look of surprise on the ward's face said he hadn't expected his Master to be there.

Gragern stood up. "What happened to you?"

"Master Drauses felt compelled to avenge his ward," Miika mumbled through bloodied lips and a broken nose.

"You should've known going after her with a weapon would bring you this fate. Drauses is not the kind of man to let an injustice slide. It's less than you deserve. Care to explain yourself?"

"You asked me to beat her by any means necessary. You let the proving continue despite my club. I thought—"

"It's not the weapon that angers me. It's the fact that, despite said weapon, you still lost. You had the upper hand, and she bested you! Losing to a woman. Are you a whelpling? And you wish to have leave of me and become a Master? Ridiculous!"

"That woman moves like—"

"She's trained by Drauses, considered the best Master of his time! I thought you understood that challenge. Woman or not, any ward under his tutelage would be an expert fighter, which clearly you are not. And now, thanks to you, a woman has been accepted into our fold. A *woman*! Odas help us."

"I'm sorry, Master Gragern." Miika lowered his eyes as he was expected to do, but Gragern saw the defiance in them, even if it was pointed at the floor.

"Yes, sorry," the Liege said as he came around his desk. He walked calmly over and punched Miika hard in the stomach leaving him doubled over and gasping yet again. "A sorry excuse for a Man of the Mark. Get out of my sight while I decide how best to deal with this and with you."

Miika bowed, dripping blood on the floor before staggering from the

51

room. Gragern scowled at the small red dots on the wood at his feet then smudged them with his boot.

Things were put into motion, most of which Gragern hadn't forced himself, but he'd use them to his advantage, regardless. This new ward, the Lady of the Mark, she would be the key to everything, Gragern knew. He could feel it. He'd simply sit and wait for his moment to tip the fates in his favor.

⋖⋗

"A fractured ulna, bruised ribs, and possibly a slight concussion," Shaila recited while Boon fitted her arm with a brace.

"The fracture is mild, but I want it stable while it heals," Boon said. "Wear this brace until I give you leave to stop. Understood?"

Shaila glanced at Drauses who fixed her with a narrowed eye. "Understood?" the Master repeated sternly.

"Yes," Shaila grumbled.

Drauses crossed his arms.

"Stop looking at me like that."

"How am I looking at you?"

"Like I'm a wounded bird. I'm fine."

"It seems our new Lady Mark is as stubborn as her comrades," Boon said with a smirk. He peered sideways at Drauses. "I wonder where she learned that."

"What've you got clutched under your arm?" Shaila asked.

Drauses held out a thin case wrapped in a belt. "For you."

Shaila unwrapped the belt, opened the lid, and lifted the crossbow out with wide eyes.

"It's meant to be worn on the arm," Drauses explained. "Concealed in the sleeve until needed."

Shaila studied the leather straps and set the crossbow on her arm. She struggled through the brace to tighten the straps until Drauses took pity and fastened them for her. Once it was secure, she fitted one of the bolts into place and fired it into the wall. Boon strolled over, yanked the bolt free, and handed it back to her with a disapproving click of his tongue.

"Perhaps take your new toy out of my clinic," he said, trying to sound stern but failing.

Drauses showed her how to collapse the crossbow, and she smoothed her sleeve down over it, hiding it completely.

"Do you like it?" Drauses asked.

"I do," Shaila replied, and she smiled when he visibly relaxed. "Thank you."

"Thank Julta. He's the mastermind behind all our gadgets. If you wanted your weapon to transform into a full suit of armor, I daresay he'd manage it somehow."

"Julta? What a curious name."

"For a very curious man," Boon said with a laugh.

"Come," Drauses bid. He offered to help her to her feet, but with a roll of her eyes, she stood on her own, ignoring his hand and his help as she made for the door. Drauses shared one exasperated look with Boon who could only smile back. "Many thanks to you, Boon, as always."

The physician bowed his head. "Masiila[8] be with you both."

&

Over the next few days, Shaila spent most of her time introducing herself to her new brothers-in-arms. At first, only a few seemed willing to share more than a casual greeting with her, but after a few awkward hellos, she found it easy to urge most into cheerful and often lengthy conversation. She often wondered if they genuinely liked her or if they were merely being polite to a pretty face. Several asked to train with her as soon as her arm had mended, but she didn't know how Drauses would feel about that and had yet to ask him. Even with her brace, her Master insisted *their* daily training continue as it always had.

"Your enemies won't slow for an injury," he declared the morning after her proving. "Neither will I."

Their training sessions drew an audience now, and at first, Shaila was

---

8 Masiila: The goddess of healing and the underworld. A full description can be found on page 372.

conscious of the eyes watching her through the long glass windows of the training room.

"Block them out," Drauses ordered. "Always know what's around you, who presents as a friend and who a foe, but unless they take a swing, they don't concern you."

After a time, training felt like it did before, when there was no one and nothing in the world but this: Master and ward, attack and defend, step and counter, swing, block, watch Drauses as he shifts his weight, adjust, watch for the twitch of his eye before a feint, spin, jab. His smile. Always his smile when she did it right.

She wished he'd smile more often.

❧

Three days after Shaila's proving, Drauses went back to the workshop to pick up the items he'd asked Julta to find for him. He set a crate of odds and ends on the counter as payment, and Julta dove into it, pawing through the rubbish like a starving man searching for a feast. The inventor plucked some bit of scrap from the box with a sound of pleasant discovery, though Drauses couldn't tell what made that piece special from the rest.

"This is quite the collection," Julta said.

"There are two more crates like this one. I'll bring them round at first chance." Julta stared up at the Master in stunned disbelief. Drauses shrugged. "I was gone awhile."

Drauses gathered his parcels from the counter, and Julta remembered himself in time to bow low in respectful parting. "I'm here to serve, Master Drauses," he said, then he looked up with such conviction it gave the Master pause. "I… don't know that I should speak about such things… but I want you to know, I think you'd make an excellent Liege."

Drauses felt the blood drain from his face.

Julta thought he'd misspoken. "Forgive me," he muttered. "My opinion has no bearing on the matter. I shouldn't—"

"It's alright, Julta," Drauses said, finding his tongue. "I'm grateful for the faith you have in me, but I've no desire to be the next Liege."

"Desire is a thing of our own choosing, Master Drauses, but leadership is often chosen for us, as it should be."

Drauses weighed the wisdom in those words for a long, silent moment then nodded once and took his leave.

Shaila was talking with another ward across the room when Drauses found her on the factory floor. She laughed at something the youth said and touched his elbow. Drauses recognized the ward. His name was Xeda, and he was the youngest man to join the guild in two generations. He would soon be twenty years old but was a mere sixteen when he won his proving, an impressive feat that brought great pride and respect to his Master, Ithail. By Drauses' calculations, Xeda had to be the closest to Shaila in age. The thought irritated him, and he snorted to himself when Shaila laughed again. Xeda joined in her mirth, staring at her in awe as if she were the moon and stars.

'She's my *moon and stars*,' Drauses thought, then he cringed both in shock and shame at such possessiveness. What in Vedia had gotten into him?

Drauses watched Shaila gaze about the room, searching for something or someone in the crowd. When her eyes landed on Drauses, she smiled. Drauses felt a sliver of satisfaction when Xeda realized the lady ward's attention had wandered. Xeda glanced at Drauses and made his excuses at the look on the Master's face. He walked away as Drauses came to Shaila's side.

Shaila cocked an accusing brow at her Master.

"What?" he asked, feigning innocence.

"Would it kill you to smile? I'll never make friends if you glare at them all like that whenever they speak to me."

"Surely you can do better than Xeda for company." Even as he said it, Drauses knew he was being unfair. Xeda was a good man, an accomplished ward, and had never given Drauses reason to speak badly of him before. "Apologies. It's not my place to choose your companions."

"Xeda seems like a nice enough young man. Emphasis on *young*, but that's hardly his fault." She motioned to his burden of boxes. "What's all this?"

"The reason we need to leave now. Come on."

◈

Shaila dropped down into the sewer first and helped Drauses down with his load.

"I've heard some interesting rumors these past few days," she said as he climbed down the ladder.

"We've better things to do than gossip."

"Even when it's about *you*?" she teased.

Drauses chuckled. "What tales are my brothers telling this time? If it's that one about the game of naked spindle…"

"There's talk you'll soon become the guild's next leader."

Drauses' smile vanished. "I've no desire to become Liege."

Shaila stopped in the muck. "I think you'd be a great leader. Why don't you want to head the guild?"

Drauses rounded on her. "How old do you think I am? Our Liege is by all accounts retired. He never leaves headquarters, doesn't go on assignments, doesn't train except with his ward. He sits, watches, and dictates. I'd go mad in such a state of rest."

"Oh, how I know that," she replied with a bark of laughter. "You can barely sit still for any length of time. But don't you think the guild would grow stronger from your leadership?"

"What do I have to offer that Master Gragern does not?"

"You don't think he's too old?"

Drauses made a face but otherwise brushed her question away. "You should be careful who hears you say such things. Master Gragern won't take kindly to slander." They walked in silence for a while before climbing another ladder to street level.

For the past two years, Shaila and Drauses lived in an apartment building an hour east of headquarters. Most of the building was empty when they first moved in, so they both chose their own apartments in the same hall. The separate living space gave Shaila privacy even with Drauses living next door. The few other tenants in the building enjoyed having a Mark for a neighbor. Drauses' presence offered safety, something in short supply on this side of the river. The number of occupants in the building had doubled since they'd moved in.

"Have you given any thought to our living arrangements?" Shaila asked as they let themselves in the front door of their building.

"What about them?"

"Will we stay here or move to headquarters?"

"Masters and their wards move into headquarters after the proving, but the wards all share quarters. That won't work for you, so accommodations will have to be made."

"I'd prefer to stay here. I like my privacy."

"Privacy? With me just on the other side of the wall? You should be amongst your peers, making friendships, bonds of brother and sisterhood with those who may one day defend your back, not secluding yourself away across town."

"Perhaps I prefer *your* company."

Drauses stopped a few stairs short of the third-floor landing. He turned and towered over Shaila who stood several steps below him.

"You can't clutch the tail of my robes forever," he said

"I'm not some whelp." Did he truly think of her that way?

Drauses' scowl softened, and he shook his head. "I know you're not, Shaila." He sighed. "I know being the only woman in the guild is a challenge all its own. You likely feel like an outsider, but these are good men, some of the best I've had the privilege to know. They can teach you a lot, more than I can alone. I don't just want you to succeed; I want you to thrive. Do you understand?"

"I think so."

It looked like Drauses had more to say but changed his mind and continued up to the landing in silence instead. They went into Shaila's apartment and tossed the boxes on her kitchen counter.

"We're going across the river this evening," Drauses announced.

Shaila's stomach jittered. "What business do we have in the West?"

"No business tonight, only pleasure."

"What are you up to?"

Drauses smiled but didn't answer. He opened the larger of the two boxes and lifted out a long red dress.

"Oh, that'll look stunning on you," Shaila teased.

Drauses rolled his eyes, set the dress back in the box, and gathered the rest back into his arms. "Meet me in thirty minutes," he said as he headed for the door.

"You're truly not going to tell me where we're going?" she called after him.

"Twenty-nine minutes!"

Shaila held the dress up by the shoulders with a sigh of delight. It was long and silky, simple but elegant. She dashed to her bedroom to prepare, eager to see what surprises Drauses had in store.

❧

Drauses was already standing in the hall when Shaila stepped from her quarters half an hour later. He glanced at her, then quickly looked again. She'd twisted her hair up in an elegant knot, secured with a couple of thin wooden sticks. Her shoulders and back were bare as the dress's straps clung to her upper arms instead, giving the impression the garment may slip down her frame at any moment. The cloth hugged tight to each of her curves clear to the floor. It was split up one side to the knee, revealing a long, slender leg every time she took a step.

The moon, the stars, the sun—this woman was all of it and more. He should worship at her feet, but instead, he opened his mouth to say something witty then promptly closed it again lest he make a fool of himself. Her steps clicked when she walked. There'd been no shoes with the gown; where in Vedia had she gotten heels, the sly fox?

She walked up with a look of expectation, and he watched with satisfaction as her eyes raked him up and down.

The outfit Julta chose for Drauses was a simple set of black pants, a white shirt, and a black tie, a classic, but the long black jacket was custom altered for a Mark who needed to conceal a sword in a crowd. Julta had done well. Drauses had tried his best to look presentable. He'd even washed and shaved his face.

"Do I pass inspection?" he asked. He was rewarded with a faint blush across Shaila's pale cheeks.

"Do I?"

"I'd make one adjustment. May I?" She nodded, and Drauses plucked the sticks from her hair. Her locks tumbled across her shoulders and down her back. "Leave it down. Please."

Shaila smiled, her blush growing deeper. He offered her his arm, and she took it.

"What've you got there?" she asked, pointing to one last parcel under Drauses' other arm.

"I'll show you later."

Drauses hated formal affairs, but Shaila had done so well, brought him such honor during her proving; she'd earned this. Masters often rewarded their wards, sometimes extravagantly so. Shaila loved music, so this would be a special treat for her, something he hoped would banish her suspicions that he'd taken her as his ward for nothing more than pride.

Her accusation still stung, but he knew better than to tell her the truth, the reason training with her these past two years had been such a joy for him, the reason he couldn't tear himself away the night he set her down, sleeping and helpless, in that filthy place after rescuing her from Rovik's estate. She'd enchanted him with her beauty and her bravery, then again with her endless dedication in training. She had potential, that was true, but this was about far more than her skill as a fighter.

He was falling for her. But it wasn't meant to be.

The guild's codes were clear: Masters were not to lie with their wards. This secret must remain with him and him alone lest the truth of it jeopardize her place in the guild. For her future, he would seal away his heart and his desires. For Shaila, he would live a lie. Starting tomorrow. Tonight was theirs.

⁕

On the river in the center of town, where once the largest bridge in Trista connected the East and West, an old man ferried people across the water for a fee, unless you were with the Marks, then you crossed free of charge. The ferryman's name was Alek, and he was Master Gragern's younger brother. Though his sibling ruled a notorious guild of warriors, Alek had always been content with his simple life on the river. He wore a brown flat cap pulled down low, a long brown wool coat, and matching slacks. He clutched a corn cob pipe between his lips but was never seen smoking it.

"Drauses!" Alek exclaimed. "My, you're dressed to dance the night away. And with a pretty lady on your arm as well. Good evening, Shaila dear."

"Alek," Shaila greeted. "It's a pleasure as always."

Drauses introduced her to Alek a few days after she became his ward. Since that day, the girls she failed to persuade to stay in the East sailed across the river in the safety of Alek's little boat. Shaila tried to pay the ferryman every time, but he'd shake his head.

"No, ma'am," he'd say. "You can't put a price on a young maiden's life."

Shaila owed Alek more than she could ever repay.

Alek helped Drauses and Shaila aboard, then they swept across the water toward the Western shore. They moored next to a large gate that blocked one of the smaller side alleys. Drauses and Alek agreed on a time and place to meet again later, then the boat pulled away back across the river. Drauses took a small tool out of the inside pocket of his jacket. In under a minute, he picked a lock, unraveled a chain, and held the gate open for Shaila.

"After you," he said.

"Will you teach me that?"

"All things in time."

Drauses replaced the chain and clicked the lock back into place, then he took the final box from under his arm and held it out to her.

She was nervous to look at first, but she smiled when she lifted the lid. Inside were two masks. One was a black felt jester. The other was far more delicate, a red cat made from soft feathers and silk. Drauses handed her the red cat mask, and when he put on the black one, Shaila laughed.

"No doubt Julta's making a joke," she said. "The ever-serious Master Drauses forced to laugh all evening long." She laughed again, harder still.

"Yes, yes. Very amusing."

They linked arms as they set off down the alley.

The West bustled with life as always. Carriages sped up and down the streets, and shoppers rushed from one store to another, anxious to complete their shopping before closing. When Drauses and Shaila turned the corner onto the main cobbled street, the theater came into view. Small groups of people, mostly couples, crossed streets and sauntered down sidewalks dressed in their best.

Shaila gripped Drauses' arm a little tighter when they fell into step with the crowd moving toward the brightly lit theater.

"A show!" she exclaimed. "Is this a jest?"

Drauses showed her their tickets.

She laughed with delight. "I could kiss you!" She expected him to huff or softly rebuke her as he always did when she said such things, but he was silent. In fact, she could've sworn she saw his lip twitch as if he were suppressing a grin. Their eyes met, and she thought she saw a look of longing in his. But then it was gone, and they continued walking in silence with the crowd.

Chapter 6

AS DRAUSES AND Shaila walked up the sidewalk toward the theater, a group of men bustled by with their ladies. Shaila hid her braced arm behind her back until they'd passed and only relaxed when she and Drauses walked alone again.

"Stop fretting," Drauses said. "I doubt a single soul notices that bandage. Their eyes are far too occupied with that stunning dress."

"Was that a compliment?" Shaila asked in feigned shock.

"An attempt at one, I suppose."

"You mean to say the Men of the Mark don't give lessons in charm?"

Drauses laughed. "I daresay not."

"I've been meaning to ask after the guild's name. '*The Men*' is fairly straightforward, but what is '*the Mark*'?"

Drauses tore his eyes from the slip of soft skin that peeked out of her dress at the knee as she walked. "The founding Masters of our craft, those who first formed the guild, branded themselves on their left cheeks to signify their lifelong commitment to our cause. They wore masks when they needed to conceal it, but in time, the masks themselves became as notorious as the Mark. Eventually, we kept the masks and ceased with the brand." Drauses chuckled to himself. "I ended up with my own mark on that very cheek anyway."

They approached the front doors of the theater and fell silent as strangers pushed in close. Shaila sidestepped nearer to Drauses who slid his arm protectively around her as they shuffled forward with the crowd. At the door, they produced their tickets, and, once inside, an usher rushed up to examine the slips more closely and guide them to their seats. He led them past the entrance to the main floor and up a set of stairs, marching them down a corridor toward the more private seats and showing them into the last box in the hall.

"How on Earth did Julta get such good seats?" Drauses mused as they sat. The usher dropped a curtain behind them.

"Perhaps you shouldn't ask," Shaila said. "It would be akin to asking a magician to reveal his tricks."

"Think it'd bring me bad luck?" he asked with a smirk.

"I think every man is entitled to his share of secrets. You needn't know every answer, Master Drauses, lest you take all the mystery out of life."

Usually, such rebukes irritated him, but when they came from her, he found he seldom minded. Her points were often just, which made them hard to deny.

Drauses scanned the other boxes, especially the one set center stage, the best seats in the house, forever reserved for the sovereign. The box was empty, to Drauses' relief. He could enjoy the evening with Shaila without Rovik's shadow looming over him. The lights dimmed, and the curtains rose as the show began.

The woman singing on stage had a beautiful voice, and though Drauses understood none of the language she sang, he found the music moving nonetheless. These sorts of events were not in his taste, but he was enjoying himself this time, likely due to the company he kept.

Shaila slid to the edge of her seat and at one point closed her eyes to better absorb the music. Drauses smiled, congratulating himself on a perfect surprise as he looked past Shaila and up at Rovik's box. His smile faded.

Rovik had gone to his box sometime after the start of the show, but Drauses didn't care about that at the moment. All he cared about was the small figure seated to the sovereign's right. He could barely make out her dark curls in the lights from the stage, but when she leaned forward, her face came into full view, and it reminded him so much of Rose that he gasped.

Amii.

⁂

Shaila heard Drauses' sharp intake of breath, and she looked over at her Master to find him staring off across the theater. She followed his gaze to the best box where Rovik sat, engrossed in the show. To his right sat little Amii, and Shaila's heart shot up into her throat.

Drauses' daughter was in this very building tonight.

The lights came back up, signaling the end of the first half, and Drauses jumped from his chair and moved into the corridor. Shaila followed him. Instead of heading back down toward the lobby where guests most often went during intermission, he headed for a door at the end of the corridor marked 'staff only.' He shoved it open and let himself into a staircase where he took the steps up three at a time.

"Where are we going?" Shaila asked as she struggled to keep up in her heels.

"As high as we can get." The door at the top of the stairs opened to the night sky, and Drauses stepped out onto the roof. "Prop that door open," he ordered as he fished for something in an inside jacket pocket. "It'll likely lock behind us otherwise."

Shaila yanked off one of her shoes and let the door close against it. She hobbled across the rooftop in her one remaining heel, her dress and hair whipping in the wind as Drauses fiddled with a small black box she barely recognized.

"Is that the trinket you carried the night we met?"

"Not the very one, but one of its brothers. Julta invented these so the Marks could communicate from a distance, but we might be too far to get a signal here." Drauses spun the gold gear and adjusted the dials, swearing under his breath when the box gave a hideous squeal. He smacked it against his palm several times, and it made a single, cheerful chirp.

"Thank the gods," Drauses murmured. He spoke into the gadget, calling to someone in the same language he used that night in Rovik's house. It was several minutes and many dial tweaks before there was an answer. Julta's distorted voice rose from Drauses' palm. Drauses barked orders into his hand, then all fell silent.

"What's happening?" Shaila asked.

"Julta's fetching the Liege."

"What language are you speaking?"

"It's the Marks' own creation. Few know it anymore as it's a dying tradition. We only use it in the West where our enemies may be listening."

Master Gragern's voice drifted up from the device, and Drauses launched into a quick discussion that grew more heated with each exchange. Drauses spoke faster, and his voice rose until he was shouting at the Liege before he switched the gadget off with a long string of obscenities.

"What did he say?" Shaila asked.

"He refuses to give me any direction at all!" Drauses fumed. "He's left this entirely up to me! It's as if he's forgotten how important the girl is to us—"

"Us? I thought you wanted to rescue Amii because she's your child. Why else is she important?"

Drauses closed his eyes and tapped the box against his forehead a few times. When he looked at her, his eyes were conflicted. "I suppose it's time I told you. That night two years ago when I snuck into Rovik's mansion, I was there to take Amii away, but not because she's mine, not entirely anyway. Amii is the key to everything, Shaila. Rovik has named her his heir. That means the West will accept her as their sovereign. If she grows up under Rovik's heel, she'll be taught to rule this country as it is now: fractured and ruined. But if she were with us, she could unite East and West. She's the only one who can."

"You want to use her?" Shaila asked in disbelief.

Drauses shook his head. "I can't see it that way," he said, but he avoided her eyes. "Rovik put her on this path by naming her next to rule. He gave her this fate, a fate she never would've had if…" His eyes found hers again, and she saw the pain in them. "Amii will rule one day whether she wants to or not. This isn't the life I want for her, but it's the one fate has handed, and I'll see it plays out right."

Shaila nodded. "I'm with you. Just tell me what to do."

Drauses started to pace. "Do you think we can handle this on our own?"

"I'm unarmed."

"I have my sword."

"You do?"

Drauses showed her his sword sheathed in a folded slip of leather sewn inside his jacket. "I don't have anything for you."

"You with a sword is enough. Rovik tried to sneak in after the start of the show. If he wanted to be inconspicuous, Marcel is likely the only one with him and Amii tonight. Surely the two of us can handle that much."

Drauses stared off in thought, then nodded his head. "Alright. We'll wait and watch from a distance. If the chance comes, we'll act; if not, we'll go back to the guild and form a better plan with the others."

"I'll follow your lead," Shaila said.

Drauses scooped up Shaila's shoe. When she took it from him, she also took his hand, and the sudden uncertainty in his eyes made her heart flutter.

"We can do this," she said with conviction. "We'll bring your daughter home with us."

Drauses looked down at her hand. "She doesn't know me," he said. "My own child wouldn't pause at the sound of my name."

"All the more reason we should try. Let's give Amii a father worth loving."

Drauses nodded with fresh resolve and held the door open for her. They took their seats as the lights dimmed again.

Shaila watched the stage as if nothing at all were amiss, but she could see Drauses in the corner of her eye as he stared across the theater at Rovik's box. She couldn't bear the tension anymore, so she nudged Drauses' foot with her own. He jumped and looked down to where her hand hovered, palm up and open, above his knee. He picked his hand up from his lap, one finger at a time, and laid his palm on hers. She slid her fingers between his and set their joined hands on his thigh. Drauses' thumb stroked the back of her hand, and she shivered.

"Look at me," he said, his voice deep and rumbling.

"I can't," Shaila said breathlessly. Her heart hammered in her ears, all but blocking out the music.

"Why not?"

Shaila watched the stage where the singer was down on her knees, pouring her heart out in her song, begging her man to love her as deeply as she loved him.

"I know our code. I know what it could cost us to give in to temptation—"

"Shaila."

She turned, drawn by the sound of his voice saying her name, and the look in his eyes was every bit as intense as she'd feared it would be. He raised his hand toward her face, hesitated and stopped, then breathed deep and took her by the chin.

"It wasn't pride," he said.

"Yes, it was," she whispered. "But it's more than that now, isn't it?"

"Yes, it is."

Drauses lifted her mask as the music swelled, and he touched her cheek. Shaila sighed when he lifted his own mask then held her breath as he leaned closer.

This couldn't happen, it was against their code, but she didn't want him to stop, and she was sure he wasn't about to... until his eyes slid past her, and he froze.

Shaila turned and looked up at Rovik's box where Amii was on her feet. The girl spoke to Rovik for a moment then disappeared behind the curtain with Marcel on her heels.

Drauses and Shaila jumped from their seats in unison and were halfway down the corridor before they realized they were still holding hands. Shaila let go and pulled her mask back down. Drauses peered sideways at her then pulled his own mask down as well. What just happened between them warranted a serious discussion, but it would have to wait.

Right now, it was time to focus.

They could hear Amii's voice as they started down the stairs toward the lobby.

"You're not coming into the restroom with me!" she said.

"You've got no parts I haven't seen before, child," Marcel sneered.

Amii protested yet again with a stomp of her foot, and Marcel relented. "Fine!" he barked in annoyance. "I'll wait here, but you better be quick!"

"Oh, thaaank you soooo much," Amii snapped before she turned with a huff and stalked into the lady's room.

Drauses and Shaila descended the last few steps of the grand staircase, pretending for the moment they were an ordinary couple slipping away before the horde. When they started across the lobby, Marcel eyed them with increasing suspicion. The men's restroom was on the other side of the lobby, but Drauses walked at Shaila's side like a dutiful lover escorting his date to the lady's room. Marcel allowed them to get barely more than an arm's length away before his suspicions prompted him to act. He tried to raise his pistol, but it was too late. Drauses blocked the weapon, and Marcel's eyes widened as the Master yanked off his mask.

"You!" Marcel sneered.

Drauses knocked the gun from Marcel's hand, and the pistol slid away across the carpet. Drauses reached into his coat, but Marcel rushed in before Drauses could draw his sword. The two men locked into a fierce battle of hand-to-hand, throwing punches and kicks and dodging each other's moves perfectly, like twins.

Shaila watched the fight from a distance, ready to intervene if needed, but her goal was Amii above all else. Drauses was counting on her.

Marcel lost his footing, and Drauses landed three solid blows before the door to the lady's room opened and Amii walked out. Drauses looked over at his daughter and let his guard down for the second Marcel needed to recover himself and land a blow of his own.

Amii took in the spectacle and opened her mouth to scream, but Shaila snuck up behind her and clamped her hand over the girl's mouth. She hauled Amii back toward the stairs to bide her time since Marcel and Drauses blocked their way to the door. Amii bit down hard on Shaila's hand, but Shaila couldn't let go and let her scream the roof down. Shaila hissed through her teeth and breathed through the pain. The girl gave up when the taste of blood in her mouth made her gag.

"Relax!" Shaila said. "We're here to rescue you."

Amii tried to speak, so Shaila relaxed her grip enough to hear.

"*Rescue* me?" Amii said, muffled behind Shaila's bleeding palm.

"You're here to *kidnap* me!" She kicked Shaila in the shin and tried to twist away, but Shaila only held on tighter.

Drauses was gaining the upper hand, and he caught Marcel across the jaw with a blow that sent the man staggering. Drauses spun and kicked Marcel's legs out from under him. Marcel landed hard on his back, and Drauses moved in to finish the job.

"Stop!" came a shout from above.

Shaila backed up under the stairs, dragging Amii with her as Rovik walked slowly down the steps, gun drawn. He was so focused on having Drauses right where he wanted him, he never took a second to consider the Master might not be alone. As he descended, Shaila moved closer to the steps, waiting for the right moment.

"I should've killed you years ago," Rovik said.

"Yes, you should have," Drauses agreed. "I'm sure you realized even then that I'd come to take back what your brother stole from me."

"You tried once before and failed."

"I'll never stop coming, Rovik. Not until I have her."

"She was never yours!" Rovik hollered.

Amii squealed under Shaila's hand as they crouched near the foot of the stairs.

"Amii is *mine*!" Rovik continued. "*My* child! *My* heir!"

"Simply saying so doesn't make it true, no matter how deeply you wish it were so."

Rovik's foot touched the lobby floor, and Shaila held her breath, ready for him to take that final step to his doom.

"Once you're dead, there won't be a soul left to contradict it," Rovik replied, and he cocked his gun.

Rovik took the last step down, and, in one motion, Shaila shoved Amii out of the way and leapt for the gun as the sovereign pulled the trigger. Shaila shoved the gun up as the weapon went off, shattering a stained-glass window high up the wall. Drauses rounded on Marcel who was scrambling across the carpet for his pistol.

Shaila twisted the pistol from Rovik's grip, but before she could take aim, Amii ran full force into her chest, right into her bruised ribs. The hit knocked the wind out of her, and she struggled to keep her composure as Amii rained tiny blows on her and Rovik made a lunge for the gun.

Shaila didn't want to hurt Amii, but fending off her and Rovik at the same time was too much, so she shoved the girl in the chest, and Amii fell on her backside on the floor. Shaila spun and smacked Rovik in the face with the gun, and he stumbled backward, tripped on the stairs, and landed flat on his back. Shaila aimed at his heart. She yanked off her mask and smiled when recognition dawned in his eyes.

"Shaila," Rovik said in wonder.

She started squeezing the trigger.

"No!" Amii flung herself across Rovik's chest.

Rovik tried to push her off. "Get back!" he ordered, but she wouldn't listen.

Amii began to cry. "Please. Please don't!"

"Shaila," Drauses called.

Shaila looked back at her Master who had Marcel down on his back on the floor with the tip of his sword on the man's neck. He motioned toward the doors as applause erupted in the distance. The show was over. She snatched Amii by the arm and dragged her away, holding the gun on Rovik as she walked backward to Drauses' side.

"Now!" Drauses cried, and he and Shaila turned and fled out the front doors, dragging Amii along with them.

Shaila kicked off her shoes and ran down the sidewalk, clutching the sobbing twelve-year-old under her arm as she went. She followed Drauses into the alley they'd arrived through, and they sprinted together to the gate at the end. Drauses pulled out his pick and attacked the lock as fast as he could in the dark. Alarms began to wail in every direction.

Drauses yanked the chain away and shoved the gate open, ushering Shaila and Amii through ahead of him. Once they were all on the other side, he secured the gate to buy them more time, but just as the lock clicked into place, a shot rang out, and Drauses jerked backward, clutching his chest with a cry of pain. He went down on one knee.

"Drauses!" Shaila screamed as she rushed to his side, but he was already back up on his feet.

"Go!" he screamed, pointing up the river. She did as he ordered, checking over her shoulder regularly to be sure he was still with them. When Alek's boat came into view, Drauses stumbled and fell on the pebbled bank. Shaila fell back, tossed Rovik's gun into the Jespa, and wrapped her free arm around her Master.

"Just go," Drauses said again, weaker this time.

Shaila struggled to get him up on his feet. "Not without you!"

Alek came running up the riverbank and took the Master's other side. They dragged Drauses the last few yards to the boat where he collapsed on the floor. Shaila shoved Amii in a seat, then took to her knees at Drauses' side.

A large patch of blood was growing across the front of his white shirt, and there was a sickening wheeze every time he drew breath.

"What do I do?" she asked.

He took her hand and placed it over the hole in his chest. "Press."

She pressed down on the spot and panicked anew at the feel of his blood gushing under her hand. She shook violently.

"Shaila," Drauses said, his voice suddenly stern. "Look at me." She did so as a helpless tear slid down her cheek. "Take care... of her."

"You're not leaving us tonight!" cried Shaila.

"Promise me."

Shaila sobbed as the wind whipped her tears into her hair. "I promise," she replied in a broken voice. "But that's not my permission to die, you hear?"

Drauses gazed up at the stars without replying.

"I hope he does die," Amii spat.

Shaila rounded on the girl with anger as hot as the blood on her hands. "You've no idea who he is! He's your—"

"No!" Drauses yelled, then he coughed and winced. "Not now. Not yet."

Shaila shook her head at the ignorant girl and turned her attention back to her Master who'd gone deathly pale.

Alek pulled the boat up to the Eastern shoreline, and the ferryman helped hoist Drauses from the boat. They carried the Master between them through the darkened streets with Amii tugged along by the elbow. Headquarters was only a few blocks away, but Drauses leaned harder on them with every step, and Shaila prayed for more time. By some miracle, they made it to the building, and Shaila smashed her fist repeatedly against the front door. No one ever used this entrance for sake of secrecy, but she prayed someone would hear the racket and come anyway.

"Boon!" Shaila screamed as she began kicking the door as well. It sprang open, and three Masters stood glaring in the doorway, but at the sight of blood and their brother's pale face, they rushed forward and took Drauses into their arms.

Among the ones who hauled him away, Drauses spotted a familiar face. "Dagon…"

"What've you gotten yourself into this time, brother?" the man Drauses called Dagon replied.

Drauses slumped against Dagon's shoulder and fell unconscious before he could reply.

Master Gragern came rushing up, and when his eyes landed on Amii, he smiled with pure joy.

"Shaila, come here," Gragern ordered, and she hesitated as she watched the others carry Drauses away down the hall. "Now," the Liege barked, and she did as he ordered with Amii in tow. "Thank you for your help, Alek. You can go now."

The ferryman quickly took his leave. Outsiders weren't allowed in headquarters, even one as trusted as Alek.

"I see your mission was a success," said Gragern.

"Barely, sir," Shaila said. "Master Drauses may yet pay too high a price for this victory."

"Drauses understands the girl's importance." Gragern held his hand out to Amii. "Come with me now, child. I'll explain everything."

Shaila tightened her grip on Amii's elbow. "Master Drauses asked me to look out for her in his stead."

"I'm the Liege here, and my orders rise above all others!" He bid Amii away again with a bend of a finger, but even after all that had happened between them, she was hesitant to leave Shaila's side. "Come, child. I don't bite."

With small, tentative steps, Amii did as the Liege bid, and Shaila had no choice but to let her go.

"Would you at least save certain *details* for when Master Drauses can speak to Amii himself?" Shaila requested.

Gragern eyed her coolly. "I'm not sure Drauses will ever get that chance, but I'll bite my tongue for now."

"Thank you, sir."

"Please," Amii begged on the verge of tears, "tell me what you want from me."

"All will be revealed in time, girl," Gragern said.

"I beg my leave for now," Shaila said in a rush.

"Go then," Gragern barked. "I want an update soon."

Shaila bowed and sprinted away through the factory. Drauses was already laid out on one of Boon's tables when she arrived at the clinic. The doctor dashed about, moving equipment, throwing certain tools, and gathering others in a frenzy.

"Julta!" he screamed. "Get in here now! Everyone else, out!"

The rest of the men scurried out, but Shaila and Dagon came closer instead.

"Can I help?" Shaila asked.

"Tell us what you need, Boon," Dagon said.

"I need you to go and let me work!" Boon hollered.

Dagon relented and headed for the door, but Shaila didn't move. Julta smacked into her as he ran into the room. He rushed to Drauses' side and ripped open the blood-soaked shirt. He examined the wound then put his ear down close to Drauses' chest.

"I hear air," he said.

Boon swore and rushed over to examine the wound himself. He looked back at where Shaila still stood, frozen halfway across the room. "I said get out!"

Shaila slowly backed away. She shut the door on Drauses' pale, lifeless face and immediately began to hyperventilate.

"He'll be alright," Dagon said, and Shaila jumped, having forgotten he was there. "He's too stubborn to die. Every time he comes close and we think this is the end for him, he comes out stronger on the other side. This'll be no different."

"How many times has he come so close to death?" Shaila asked.

Dagon smiled. "At least half a dozen. I'll tell you all about them sometime when Drauses is back on his feet and able to argue with me over every detail."

Shaila shivered, and Dagon stripped off his robes and set them around her shoulders. She pulled the warm robes closed over her blood-soaked dress with a nod of thanks.

Dagon was shorter than Drauses by about half a head but bulkier all around. His wavy black hair was gathered in a long ponytail high on the back of his head. His eyes were an equal mix of green and blue set in a square face.

"Your ward said you were away," Shaila said.

"I was, yes. I got back little more than an hour ago, and my, did the men have tales to tell me. I hear your proving left quite an impression."

Shaila tried to smile but failed.

"You should go rest. It'll be a while before that door opens again."

"I'll wait here." She leaned against the wall across from the clinic door. "The Liege wants an update soon."

"Will you send word to me as well?"

Shaila nodded.

Dagon bowed and walked away leaving her staring at the door of the clinic and fretting after her Master's life on the other side.

Chapter 7

ROVIK STOOD IN his grand foyer with a bat in his hands and Marcel on the floor in front of him.

"What in Vedia happened tonight?" the Archdynast screamed as he smashed the bat down on Marcel's left hand. The resulting scream irritated him more, so he struck the bodyguard in the mouth next.

"I f… failed you," Marcel sputtered through the blood. "I'm sorry."

Rovik smashed him in the shoulder with the bat. "You assured me you could handle a single evening show! The wedding is but a week away, but now my girl is gone!" The bat came down on an arm, and the bone snapped under the blow. "She's out there, the Odas only know where, with *him*!"

Another smash to the mouth left Marcel sprawled flat on his back. "I can fix this," he whimpered.

"You'll fix nothing. You won't even be *breathing* soon." Rovik raised the bat above his head, ready to cave in Marcel's skull.

"Wait!" Marcel cried, shielding his face behind his broken arm. "There's a Man of the Mark who's loyal to me!"

"You've corrupted another Mark?" Rovik asked. He lowered the bat but narrowed his eyes. "How?"

"We're… old friends. He can help us get the girl back, but you'll need me. He won't work with anyone else!"

"Why have you never mentioned this before?"

"I've never needed to."

Rovik stared down at the bleeding lump of flesh on the floor, and though his eyes remained doubtful, the bat clattered to the tile. Rovik came closer and pressed his boot down on Marcel's throat, slowly increasing the pressure. Marcel's fingers dug into the leather as his face started turning colors.

"Get my daughter back or you're a dead man," Rovik snarled, then he removed his foot and scowled as Marcel gasped and coughed. "Someone get him a doctor." He turned and headed for the stairs. "And send word to my niece," he called as he climbed. "I want her here by this time tomorrow."

∽

Shaila was sticky all over with dried blood and her eyes were drooping by the time the clinic door opened again. She jumped to her feet and rushed forward.

"Is he..."

"He lives," Boon said, but she saw the unspoken words in his eyes.

"Tell me," she pleaded.

"I've done all I can for him, Shaila, but he lost so much blood." Boon sighed. "I'm not certain he'll wake."

Shaila swallowed the lump in her throat. "Can I see him?"

Boon stepped aside and waved her in.

Drauses had been moved to a cot near the far wall. His chest was wrapped in thick bandages, and his face was as pale as before. Shaila sat on the cot next to his and reached for his hand, watching his face for signs of life as she took it. There were none. She traced his knuckles with her thumb, remembering their moment in the theater. She bent and kissed the back of his hand.

"You can't leave me now," she whispered. "Not with my heart tied up in such knots. You've come this far, Drauses. Come back and finish it. Come back to me."

She shifted her foot and knocked something out from under the cot. It was Drauses' black coat with his mask sticking out of the pocket. She plucked the mask out and twirled it in her fingers. By some miracle, it was whole and free of blood. She studied the laughing jester for a long time, fighting tears.

If Drauses never woke, would they give her a new Master? The thought made her chest ache. If she lost him, could she even stay with the guild through that pain? Shaila winced at what Drauses would say if he knew how cowardly her thoughts had become. Of course she'd stay with the guild; it's what he'd want. Plus, there was Amii. Shaila made Drauses a promise. She had to look after Amii now in his stead.

She needed to get on with it. Right now.

Shaila leaned near Drauses' ear. "I'll be back soon," she promised.

She left the clinic, still carrying Drauses' mask, and went straight to Master Gragern's quarters. Though she rapped loudly on his door, there wasn't a sound from the chambers within. He must've retired for the evening. Perhaps she should do the same and come back first thing in the morning. She wondered vaguely where the Elder was keeping Amii.

"He's not in there," said a voice right behind her.

Shaila spun with arms raised ready to defend herself, but it was only Miika. He crossed his arms with a smirk.

"You startled me," she accused, but he made no attempt to apologize. "I assume you know where I can find him, then?"

"In his office."

"At this hour?"

"The Liege rarely sleeps."

Miika looked tired himself, but it was hard to tell under his two blackened eyes. One was from her proving, she knew, but the other came a day or so later along with the deep purple patch across his jaw and the hole in the top left side of his mouth where at least one tooth was missing. Despite the bruises she still wore from his weapon, Shaila felt rather sorry for him, though from where the impulse came, she didn't know exactly.

Shaila pointed down the hall. "It's that way, yes?"

"Third door on the left," he said with a jerk of his head.

Shaila bowed her head in thanks, but when she made to step around him, Miika refused to budge. His wide shoulders ate up the narrow passage, and she was forced to touch his arm as she scooted past him. She looked back over her shoulder to catch him staring after her with a mischievous grin on his face.

"Did no one ever tell you it's rude to stare," she called, but he kept right on looking, nonetheless. She stopped and turned around, her curiosity getting the better of her. "Was it worth it?"

"Come again?" he asked as he tore his eyes from the ruined dress showing through the gap in Dagon's robes.

"Your face. Whatever you were fighting for, was it worth it?"

Miika narrowed his eyes, snorted, and walked off down the hall.

Shaila headed in the opposite direction. She was bid to enter without delay when she knocked on Gragern's office door. As Miika said, the Liege was awake and fully dressed even at such a late hour.

"Shaila," he greeted coolly.

"I have news."

"You look as if you'll soon fall over, and you're filthy. I can't say I approve of your attire either."

"Sorry, sir," Shaila replied, too tired to stick up for herself.

"What's your news?"

"Boon stopped the bleeding. We're merely waiting for Master Drauses to wake now."

"And Boon says he'll certainly do so?" The Elder asked with the hint of a knowing smile.

Shaila hesitated. "He's hopeful."

Gragern chuckled. "You can't fool me, woman. To try is folly. Your Master's fate is likely a grim one. I doubt he'll ever wake, and so I'll do what I should've done the moment you brought me the girl. Miika!"

Miika arrived in seconds. Where in Vedia did he come from? He reminded Shaila more of a servant than a ward as he stood still as a statue and stared at his shoes, waiting for his orders.

"Bring the girl," Gragern barked.

Miika disappeared again and came back quickly with a weary-eyed Amii in tow.

"Amii," Gragern began. "It's time you learned the truth of who you are, where you're from. What do you know about your mother?"

"Her name was Rose," Amii replied as she rubbed the sleep from her eyes. "She worked for my father and died when I was born."

"You're mistaken, little one. Your mother didn't work for your father because Rovik is not your blood."

Amii looked from Gragern to Miika to Shaila. Shaila saw no surprise on the girl's face at this news; Amii already knew.

"Do you... Who is my real father?" Amii asked, her chin held high.

"Your father's name is Drauses," Gragern answered.

Amii's eyes flicked to Shaila's, and her face grew pale.

Shaila's eyes burned with effort not to cry.

"Did he die?" Amii asked in a small voice.

Shaila could only shake her head.

"Our doctor is doing the best he can to see that doesn't happen," Gragern reassured her. "You've been lied to all your life, child. You deserve the truth, and that's what you'll find here. Ask anything you like, and I promise you honest answers. Thank you, Shaila. You may go."

"Sir, what's to be done with the girl until Master Drauses wakes?" Shaila asked.

"I'll watch over her."

"Master Drauses asked me to look after her in his stead. I wish to fulfill that promise."

"You're in no condition to take on a child," Gragern barked. "Look at yourself!"

Shaila glanced down at her ruined dress and tugged Dagon's robes tighter around herself. "I just need a bath," she mumbled.

Gragern smiled. "We'll let Amii decide, shall we? Who would you like to be your guardian until your father mends, girl?"

Amii and Shaila both cringed at the word 'father.' Shaila knew there was no way Amii would choose her, not after everything that had happened that evening. Amii studied her, but Shaila looked away, wishing the youth would get on with it so she could go back to the clinic and sleep on one of the cots near her Master.

"I want to go with her," Amii announced.

Shaila's eyes popped up in surprise.

Gragern scowled. "Very well. Shaila, you're under house arrest until further notice. The room at the end of the northern hall is empty with several clean beds. It's been assigned as '*ladies' quarters*,'" he said in disgust. "There's a washroom across the hall. Amii is under your care. If any harm comes to her, you'll answer for it. Dismissed."

Shaila held her hand out to Amii who took it without hesitation, and the two girls hurried away like prisoners fleeing their warden.

⸙

Shaila sat on one of the beds in the newly dubbed ladies' quarters and rubbed her face with an exhausted sigh. She needed a bath, sleep, to hear her Master's voice… She was still clutching his mask, and the sight of it twisted her stomach in knots, yet she couldn't stop looking, remembering.

Amii came and regarded the mask herself. "That was his?"

"Yes."

"Will you tell me about him?"

"Are you sure?" Shaila asked, a tad too bitterly. "Will you believe the words if they come from me?"

"I chose you, didn't I?" Amii snapped, and she crossed her arms.

Shaila ran her finger down the jester's cheek. "Your father saved my life two years ago, and now he trains me as his ward. He's strong, brave, and honest."

"But he kills people!"

"Never the innocent. Marks only kill those who deserve it."

"Marks? The Men of the Mark? That's who you are?" Amii dropped her arms and sat on the bed across from Shaila's. "I thought those were just stories."

"So did I, once upon a time."

"Do *you* think he'll… die?" There was genuine concern on the girl's face for the first time.

"I don't know," Shaila replied. She could bear this conversation no longer in her current state. She stood up and set the mask on her bed. "Will you be alright here while I clean up?"

Amii nodded.

"Don't wander off or Master Gragern may decide I'm not fit to take care of you after all."

"I'll stay here, I promise."

Having a genius inventor in residence had its advantages. With a few turns of a dial in the bathroom, Shaila had hot running water thanks to Julta's brilliance. It was a revolutionary concept: water was heated then piped throughout the entire building for easy cooking and bathing. The Marks' headquarters was the only place in the city with such a commodity, but once the city was whole again, they'd change that, among so many other things.

Shaila tried to focus on the task at hand—scrub hair, wash face, rinse—but her composure was cracking, slipping away as fast as the bloody water gurgling down the drain at her feet. Her throat constricted until she couldn't breathe, and she sank to her knees. The tears came, and she was powerless to stop them this time. She owed her entire existence to this man, her mentor, her best friend; the only friend she'd ever had in her life.

"I beg you not to take him yet," Shaila prayed to the Odas between sobs. "If I've ever in my life done anything to please you, then I beg you: let him stay, let him wake, let him come back to me."

Of course, there was no reply, no booming voice from Odavail[9] to answer her, but she felt stronger now, strong enough to stand up, rinse off, and wrap up in a towel. Once she'd composed herself, she crossed the hall back to the bedroom. Amii was asleep on her cot, so Shaila took off her towel and used it to scrub her hair dry. When she looked up, Amii was awake and watching her through puffy, bloodshot eyes. Shaila had never been shy of her nudity, so she went on drying her hair, then she knelt and searched the chest at the foot of her bed for clean clothes.

"What happened to you?" Amii asked, pointing at the bruise on Shaila's chest.

Shaila touched the mark with the tips of her fingers. "I got these the day I joined the guild."

"I thought you said you've been here for years."

"I trained with your father for two years, but I became a Lady of the Mark only four days ago."

---

9 Odavail: The realm of the gods where pure souls go after death.

"So, this is all still new for you?"

"Very much so."

"Maybe we can learn together."

Shaila tried to smile as she tied up her robes. "Maybe."

Amii sat up on the bed. "I'm sorry for what I said before. I was angry."

"I know, little one. I'm trying to forgive and forget."

"I hope I get the chance to tell him too."

"As do I."

"Your name is Shaila?"

"Yes."

"How did you meet my father?"

Shaila stretched out on her bed with a sigh. She was tired but not likely to sleep tonight anyway, so she searched for how best to start her tale. "Well, it started with an open window…"

For the next three days, Amii followed Shaila everywhere like a shadow. The girl asked so many questions, and Shaila did her best to answer every one. Having been away at a school in Ilython since she was five years old, Amii knew very little about her own country. She'd never seen the East before the day Shaila dragged her here, and one look at the headquarters' lower floor was enough to show her how low this side of the city had fallen over the past century. Shaila couldn't understand why Rovik allowed the girl's ignorance to continue for so long if he truly meant her to rule in his stead. To set Amii on the right track at last, Shaila explained that most of Rovik's wrongs could be righted by a fair and just sovereign, which was what they hoped she would become free of Rovik's influence.

Shaila told Amii of the laborers at the Sazeen brewery who all walked out one day and refused to work a moment longer without fair pay. Since those who owned the brewery and decided such things were already rich and living in luxury in the West, they refused. This began a long rebellion during which the East refused to work and the West refused to care, choosing instead to invest their coin in the one commodity they had to sell on their side of the river. Brothels multiplied and grew with help from a few who found and sent West any and all Eastern beauty, creating the system that landed Shaila in Rovik's clutches. Riots broke out as Eastern-ers stormed the Western shore, demanding the wealthy help those who couldn't help themselves. The sovereign at the time, Paryth, refused to lose the support and coin of his Western brethren, and so he ordered the walls built on the Western shoreline.

The brewery laborers who started it all saw the situation quickly deteriorating and decided to band together to stop Paryth. They took up arms and launched strikes at the newly constructed sections of wall as well as Paryth's forces that worked to keep the Easterners sequestered until the wall was complete. Though these men fought bravely, many of them giving their lives in the process, they were too outnumbered. The day Paryth ordered Polco Bridge destroyed was the day those men vowed to continue watching over the Eastern districts and fighting to reunite Trista someday. And thus, The Men of the Mark were formed.

Amii hung on every word Shaila spoke, and often Shaila had to remind the girl that these weren't stories from a fairytale but the history of her people, people to whom she could one day bring justice.

"Won't the West put up a fight if I order the walls torn down?" Amii asked.

"Not if they think there's coin to be made in the process," Shaila explained. "You see, even though the brothels have kept the West well-fed since the East was banished, Western fortunes have suffered since the walls were built. Trista used to have a thriving whiskey and lumber trade, both of which quickly went dry during the rebellions. With the promise of jobs and fair pay, the East could once again open the mills and brewery. There would be coin aplenty to be made by all."

Shaila saw the weight of responsibility in Amii's eyes, and she put a hand on the girl's shoulder. "Fret not, little one," Shaila said with a smile. "We'll be beside you every step of the way. So will your father," she added with a heavy heart.

The morning after Drauses' injury, Shaila asked Dagon to deliver a personal message to Alek for her, three messages in fact: one for the ferryman himself and two he was to take across the river for her. She did her best to keep up with her duties to the river-swimming damsels from afar, but Alek never sent any correspondence back to tell her how things were going without her.

Shaila found it nearly impossible to sleep at night. She would sneak into the clinic in the dark and sit on the cot next to her Master's. Twice, she dozed off there, soothed to sleep by the warmth of his hand in hers.

꙳

On the fourth day, before tucking Amii into bed, Shaila came to sit with Drauses first. She ached to hear his voice, even one of his gruff rebukes. With his hand clutched in her lap, she launched into speech, and the words kept coming. She needed to talk to him; her heart would wait no longer.

"Amii knows you're her father," she said. "It wasn't my decision to tell her, so please don't be cross with me. She asks me regularly to tell her about you, but I fear my words do you no justice. You'll likely tell her you're a mere stubborn, foolish old man who fights like a whelp."

Shaila traced his fingers with her own in her lap then flipped his hand over to draw circles in his palm. "Please wake up," she begged, the tears starting to well in her eyes. She swallowed hard and blew out a large breath. She couldn't break down again. Her finger went on drawing that small circle in his palm over and over.

His fingers twitched.

Shaila leaned closer and stared expectantly at her Master's face, but his eyes didn't open. She drew the circle again and got another twitch.

"Drauses?" she called. When she got no response, she leaned closer still. "Wake up, Drauses. I need you." She squeezed his hand and was shocked when his fingers tightened around hers.

Slowly, his eyes cracked open, and he groaned.

"Drauses?"

"Where... am I?"

"Boon's clinic. You've been here four days."

His eyes popped open, and he raised his head. "Amii?"

Shaila laid a calming hand on his shoulder. "She's alright. I've watched over her like I promised."

Drauses sighed in relief and closed his eyes. Shaila was afraid he was slipping away again and softly called his name.

"I'm still here," he answered wearily.

"I should fetch Boon."

"No need," Boon said as he rounded a corner by the clinic's back door. Had he been standing on the other side of the wall? Shaila paled at the thought of how much the physician might've heard. He walked to the foot of Drauses' cot and glanced at their joined hands. Shaila let Drauses go then stood to leave.

"Where are you going?" Drauses asked.

"To fetch Amii."

"Wait. I want to talk to you first."

Miika stood with his back to the wall outside the clinic and listened for a full twenty minutes as Boon fretted over Drauses. Once the doctor was satisfied Drauses was in no immediate danger, he excused himself to fetch water for the Master. When he stepped into the hall, Boon flashed Miika a look of condemnation.

"You know I don't like you using my clinic for your spying," Boon chastised in a whisper.

"And *you* know I have no choice in the matter, doc," Miika replied, crossing his arms as he sidestepped closer to the open doorway.

Boon sighed and patted Miika on the shoulder. "I know, son." Miika looked away under Boon's stare until the physician walked on, leaving the ward to his duties with a shake of his head.

Miika leaned his head back against the wall and closed his eyes as he listened to the hushed conversation in the next room.

"Tell me what I've missed," Drauses requested.

"Well firstly, Amii knows the truth."

"Why?"

"Master Gragern took the decision from my hands. I asked him to wait but..."

Miika snorted to himself. The Elder was good at making quick enemies.

"You look tired," Drauses remarked.

"I haven't slept well since you fell."

"Why's that?"

Miika rolled his eyes. If a woman admitted to losing sleep over your well-being, you didn't question it lest she decide you're not worth her worries after all.

Shaila sighed before replying. "There are no words to describe how it felt to watch you lie here lifelessly day after day nor ones to tell you how happy I am to see you wake."

Miika peeked around the wall to catch Shaila's warm smile and to watch Drauses refuse to return it.

"You shouldn't have spent so much energy worrying over me," Drauses chastised.

Shaila blinked in hurt surprise and lost her smile. "Where would you rather I place my energy?"

"You should've focused on training. Have you done *any* while I've been here?"

Shaila blinked several more times and sat back on her cot. "No."

"Any ward in the guild would battle Gindar[10] himself for a chance to train with you, likely most of the Masters as well. But you spent those days *sulking?*"

Shaila studied her hands in shame.

"Fool…" Miika muttered.

"I'll fetch Amii," Shaila said suddenly, and she got to her feet.

"Shaila," Drauses called, but his ward shook her head and refused to look back as she headed for the door. "Shaila!"

Miika hurried away down the hall and out of sight.

Though bound by his duty to report everything he'd just witnessed to his Master, Miika couldn't shake the image of Shaila's face, turned down and burning red with shame and regret. She'd been expecting something far different from her Master's lips, that much was certain. Were they intimate? Such a breach of their codes would be quite the scandal, one

---

10 Gindar: The god of death, war, and domestication. A full description can be found on page 374.

that would help Miika regain lost favor with his own Master, but why did the thought of telling Gragern this news make him feel so… so…

⁂

Drauses stared at the door of the clinic for a long time after Shaila left. He felt like he'd kicked a small child or helpless animal. Either would've brought him more joy than the look on Shaila's face as she fled. She'd been so clearly relieved to see him wake, and he repaid her by lashing out at her heart. But it had to be done.

What happened between them at the theater was a moment of weakness mixed with adrenaline at the thought of what they were about to do. He'd let his heart run away with him after he'd sworn to keep it buried deep within. She was holding his hand, losing sleep, worrying herself sick…

More often than not, compassion gets us killed.

"It's for the best," Drauses muttered miserably to himself.

The clinic door opened again, and Amii peered in.

"Hello?" she called shyly.

"Hello there," said Drauses.

She stayed in the doorway, either unwilling to draw closer or unsure if she should.

"Come," he beckoned.

Amii shuffled in, staring at his heavily bandaged chest as she came halfway across the room.

Drauses waved a hand dismissively. "This is nothing."

"I watched them drag you here. It's something."

Drauses nodded. "You're right. It's something. I'm sorry you had to see it."

Amii's eyes slid away to the floor. "I'm sorry too… for what I said before."

Drauses barely remembered her words in the boat. "It's alright."

Amii eyed him warily.

"I know this is a shock—"

"Not really."

"No?"

"I've known for some time that I'm not Rovik's child. He calls me such, but…" She shook her head.

"How did you find out?"

"Gossip mostly. And a feeling I've had for a long time. He treats me like an heir, not a daughter. If he's not my father, someone else must be. Here you are."

"Here I am. For all I'm worth."

Amii cocked her head to the side. "Shaila speaks highly of you."

Drauses' stomach twisted. "I'm sure she does, as is her duty. Wards are not to speak badly of their Masters."

"Shaila's been very honest with me," Amii said with confidence. "I think if you were a bad man, she'd tell me so."

Drauses smiled. "We'll get to know each other so you can make that judgment for yourself, alright?"

Amii nodded.

"Where's Shaila?"

"She went to bed, but she won't stay there." Amii came a bit closer, a mischievous smile on her face. "She kept disappearing after I went to sleep, so last night, I *pretended* to sleep until she left, and I followed her." The girl grinned, proud of her cunning. "She came here and didn't come out until breakfast… You look pale. Did I say something wrong?"

"He needs rest," Boon said as he walked in with a fresh, dripping pitcher of water. "Run along, little one."

Drauses held out his hand, and Amii slowly crossed the last few steps to his bedside to take it.

"Good night, Amii," he said, wrapping his fingers around hers with a gentle squeeze.

Amii stared at his hand for a long moment. "Can I come back tomorrow?" she asked softly.

"Please do."

All through his fitful night of sleep, Drauses woke countless times and checked the room for any signs of Shaila in the dark. She never came.

Chapter 8

1st and 80 of Summer, Jesparia's 9th and 20 year of Rovik

DRAUSES SAT IN a chair taking dozens of deep breaths while Boon poked and prodded around the small scar on his chest.

"Everything sounds good."

"Am I free to work?" Drauses asked eagerly. Though he'd been doing light workouts to help keep in shape, Drauses was burning to get back to regular training.

"Yes, Drauses," Boon replied with a smirk. "Cautiously, of course."

Drauses had spent the last few weeks at headquarters under Boon's watchful eye. He'd reconnected with his brothers, particularly Dagon, and had gotten to know his daughter as his body healed. He could almost call himself happy if it weren't for the storm brewing between him and his ward.

Shaila had kept an unusual distance since their quarrel. She tended to Amii, and the two of them were near inseparable, but she avoided her Master, vacating rooms as soon as he entered and spinning on her heels when she saw him coming her way. He didn't blame her, but the more distance she put between them, the more Drauses wondered if he'd made a mistake. He didn't know how to fix things without giving away how deeply he felt for her, so he left well enough alone, hoping in time she'd forgive him on her own. What a fool he was.

As soon as he left the clinic, Drauses went searching for Shaila. It was time for them to work out their contretemps, one way or another. He found her in the training room, and he watched through the wall of windows as Xeda taught her a new move. Drauses recognized the fighting style. It was more modern than he preferred himself but still based on traditional technique, Ithail's specialty. Drauses watched the sparring for ten minutes or so before changing into training clothes himself. When he came back, Xeda stepped out into the hall covered in sweat with a freshly bloodied brow. He nodded to Drauses as he passed.

Shaila was placing a training knife back in its proper place in a cupboard by the wall when Drauses walked in. She glared at him.

"What are you doing here?" she asked.

"Boon gave me leave to train. I thought I'd see what new things you've learned. Unless you're too tired." His tone rang with a challenge, and he almost smiled when she immediately rose to it.

"I'm fine. Let's go a round if you want."

Drauses took two sticks from an old whiskey barrel by the wall. He threw one to Shaila who caught it and spun it several times to measure its weight and resistance. A small audience had gathered at the windows to watch the Lady of the Mark spar with her Master, the men's favorite spectacle. Drauses twirled his own stick in his hands, flashing a grin, trying to lighten the mood. Shaila didn't return his smile.

Drauses came in fast with a strike she blocked effortlessly, but he immediately followed with a kick to the back of her leg that knocked her down to one knee.

"Watch your footwork," Drauses barked as she got back up. He came in again with the same move, which Shaila blocked with the correct footing this time, but she dropped her arm, exposing her face. He brought an elbow in fast and stopped an inch from her nose to show he could've broken it if he wished.

"Keep that arm up," he ordered. "Again."

He repeated the move until she countered it correctly, then he swung the stick around to smack her in the back. She surprised him with a forward roll, and his blow sailed right over her. She rolled up to her knees and clocked him in the back of the head. She brought her stick down low to sweep his legs out from under him, but he jumped over it.

They faced each other again, moving in a slow circle, until Shaila ran forward, swinging her weapon in quick strikes which he blocked, one after the other. She struck faster and harder, feigned a left blow, which Drauses fell for, then smacked the Master hard in the stomach. He doubled over, and she came in close for another blow, but he reached out and grabbed her right wrist, her dominant hand, blocking her hit... or so he thought. She punched him fast and true on the nose with her left hand.

"Who by Vediida[11]'s graces taught you to throw left-handed?" he asked, pinching his nose to check for a break. So, she wanted to make him pay in blood? Two could play that game. Drauses suddenly grimaced with a hiss of pain and clutched his chest.

"Drauses," Shaila said with such concern it made him feel guilty for what he was about to do. When she drew too close, he swung his weapon up and smacked her in the nose. They were even now.

"Never let your guard down," Drauses chastised.

Shaila glared in indignation as she wiped the blood from her face. Drauses swiped his hand under his own nose and glanced down briefly at the red streak on his palm. Shaila jumped into action, falling into a sideways roll, and she struck him in the shin with one end of her weapon then his chest with the other. Before he recovered his balance, she kicked out at his knees, but he grabbed her foot mid-kick and yanked it up into the air, knocking her off her feet. She landed hard, flat on her back.

He hovered over her. "Had enough yet?"

Shaila growled and jumped back to her feet. Her eyes burned with wrath, her face was flushed, and she was shaking. He'd unleashed a she-beast, the very one he once watched stab Rovik bloody with her own shoe, and now he had to deal with her.

Shaila took several deep, cleansing breaths, but she didn't move. Drauses went on the offensive, and Shaila stood her ground, blocking his hits and biding her time. Having been out of practice for weeks, Drauses

---

11 Vediida: The god of the underworld. A full description can be found on page 372.

felt fatigue hit him hard and sudden, and his form began to falter. He knew the moment Shaila spied her opening. She moved quick as a cat and smacked her Master hard in the backs of his legs. He fell to his knees, and she struck him in the stomach. He doubled over, and she finished him off with yet another blow to his face.

Drauses lay stunned on his back across the mat. When Shaila came close, he made one last attempt to strike back, but she tore the stick from his hand, brought up her knee, and snapped the weapon in two. She threw the pieces away with a cry of fury. With the last of his strength, Drauses rolled to his side and swept his leg across the floor, kicking hers out from under her, and she fell to her back as well.

Though technically a draw, Drauses knew this fight went to her. He got painfully to his feet and reached down to help her up.

"Good match," he said with a smile.

Shaila glared back at him and got to her feet on her own. She stalked from the room, slamming the door in her wake. Drauses looked out the windows at the group gathered at the glass, and wards and Masters alike all scattered like mice.

Shame burned hot in Drauses' gut, shame for his weakness in training, shame that his brothers knew his once devoted ward had spurned him, but most of all, shame that he'd hurt her heart, that she believed him nothing but a self-centered old man who chose her for his own selfish pride.

Drauses stalked from the room and down the hall toward the ladies' quarters.

✑

Shaila fled to her room in a rage. She kicked the chest at the foot of her bed then yelled in pain and fury. The doorknob rattled. She'd locked it out of spite.

"Shaila, open this now," Drauses' voice drifted through the door. She ignored him at first, but he pounded on the wood, refusing to be turned away by a locked knob. She crossed the room with a growl and threw the lock. He shoved the door open and slammed it shut again so hard she jumped.

"Care to explain yourself?" he barked.

"Whatever do you mean?" she asked, feigning innocence.

"I mean that ridiculous display just now! Need I remind you who is ward and who is Master?"

"You needn't. You've exercised your dominance in all things, *Master* Drauses, even so far as to tell me what emotions I'm allowed."

Drauses shook his head. "Don't speak in riddles. Talk straight with me. What's your grievance?"

"My *grievance* is that, for three days, I lived in my own Vedian misery waiting for news that you'd either woken or died!" Angry tears were trying their best to make her a fool, but she swallowed them back. Her voice broke and gave her away, regardless. "No one could tell me if you would ever... if you would come back to us or... and I was afraid. I was afraid for my Master and my *friend*! Watching you wake was one of the happiest moments of my life, until you... How dare you tell me I shouldn't care! Perhaps you wish me not to care about you because *you* don't care about *me*!"

"That's not true," Drauses said in a rush. "I only wish to know that you can go on without me. I don't want my death to affect your future."

"My life became *yours* the day I agreed to be your ward. We're together nearly every minute of every day. If you were gone, it would affect my life whether you wanted it to or not."

"Shaila—"

"I'm not a machine!" she thundered. "I feel emotions, same as you would if it were me who came so close to death, unless that bullet deflated your heart the same as it did your lung."

"Are you asking how I'd feel had our places been reversed?"

"I suppose I am."

"I would've been distraught."

Shaila opened and closed her mouth twice. "Distraught?"

"Yes."

"Then why did you say those awful things to me?" she asked tearfully.

Drauses paced across the room away from her then back again, running his hand through his hair. "It's my job to make sure you can survive without me, to teach you independence so that you can go on in the guild on your own and take care of yourself."

"Yes, when you've given me leave of you. When I'm ready. That's not the same as you *dying* without warning!"

"You and the other wards will go on when the other Masters and I are no more. That's the way of things. I have to know my death won't cripple you."

"Don't talk like that. I won't discuss your death as if it's—"

"Inevitable?" Drauses fumed with a throw of his arms. "I'm a Man of the Mark, Shaila! I'll die someday and likely before my time as countless of my brothers have before me. I've already come close several times."

She turned her back on him with a huff.

Drauses took her by the shoulder, spinning her to face him again. "You see this mark?" he asked, pointing to a long scar on his abdomen under his shirt. "I was nearly gutted by a knife. I almost bled to death that day too."

"Stop," Shaila said through clenched teeth.

"How about this one?" He ran his hand down the scar on his face then down his chest where she knew a second scar ran from shoulder to waist under his shirt, a continuation of the same wound. "A hot stick. It stopped my heart." Shaila's eyes filled with angry tears again. He turned his head and pointed to his neck.

"Or this one," he continued. There was a thin line of a scar across the right side of his neck under his jaw. "A man tried to slit my throat. So you see, I've been *very* fortunate to last this long. I'm not immortal. The sooner you realize I'm none of your concern—"

She slapped him. Hard. The sound of it cut through the room like a whiplash, and Drauses froze, his chest heaving and cheek reddening. He seized her and backed her hard against the wall. She simply stared up at him, wide-eyed and shocked by her own daring.

Tears trickled down her cheeks. In the past two years, through exhaustion, injury, and frustration, she'd never let him see her cry. He reached up in wonder and wiped one away, stroking his thumb down her cheek from eye to jawline, then he leaned close, sighed softly, and kissed her.

Shaila's heart was in her throat, and a shudder rippled up her spine.

She wrapped her arms around him, stroked his back, his hair, his chest, touching him everywhere she could reach after two years of restraint. He smelled of sweat and blood, and… him, only a hundred times stronger than she'd ever experienced before. She broke their kiss to breathe him in.

"Drauses…" she murmured.

He pulled away to her dismay, leaving her flushed and breathless against the wall.

"I'm sorry," he whispered, then he turned and rushed from the room.

Shaila touched her swollen lips. What was he sorry for? Kissing her or nearly dying?

Amii came bounding in seconds later.

"Was that Father just now?" she asked.

"Yes," Shaila replied absentmindedly.

"I called to him, but… Are you alright?"

"Yes." For the first time in weeks, everything was indeed alright. All her anger was gone.

She'd forgiven him.

⤙

That night, Shaila slept the best she had in weeks. She couldn't call her and Drauses' row resolved, exactly, but her heart found peace enough to let her drift into pleasant dreams.

Pleasant dreams can be cruel things when one wakes to a startling reality.

Shaila roused in the dark when the sound of footsteps, no more than the shuffling of slippers across the floor, put her on high alert. A man robed in black stood at her bedside. Before he had a chance to act further, Shaila wrapped her legs around the man's waist and twisted, knocking him to the ground. She rolled out of bed on top of him and wrapped her arms around his neck.

"Who are you?" she demanded to know.

Amii screamed as another black-clad intruder dragged her out of bed. Shaila snapped the neck of the man in her arms and took the knife from his limp fingers. She rushed up behind Amii's attacker and slit his throat from behind. Amii screamed again as the bleeding man collapsed at her

95

feet, but Shaila took her hand and pulled her away, blocking her view of the dead men on the floor around her.

"Calm, Amii dear. I have you."

"Who are they?"

"I don't know. We need to go. Get dressed, quickly!"

Shaila still had the knife clutched in her hand when the door flew open. She moved to strike but canceled her attack at the last second when she recognized the man in the doorway.

"Father!" Amii cried.

Drauses took a knee, and his daughter wrapped her arms around his neck.

"I won't let them take you from me," Drauses vowed as he hugged her tight. "Never again, I promise."

Amii nodded through her sobs, and Drauses hauled the girl up into his arms. Shaila peered out into the hallway and gasped at the black-robed bodies that littered the floor. Drauses had carved quite a path on his way to rescue his daughter.

"Who are they?" Shaila asked.

"I don't know, but they're everywhere," Drauses said.

"Amii, close your eyes," Shaila ordered. She looked at Drauses. "I'll lead. Stay close."

Shaila ran as fast as she dared through the blood pooling on the wood floor. An assassin in black jumped from a door to her right, and she stabbed her knife into his heart before he could ready his weapon.

Miika fought two enemies at once at the end of the hall. One of them smashed him in the mouth with the hilt of his sword sending him staggering backward, and the other moved in to finish him off. Shaila threw her blade which stuck in the back of the second attacker's skull. Miika made quick work of the other.

"Thank you," Miika said between gasping breaths as they joined him.

"Do you know who these men are, Miika?" Shaila asked as she retrieved her knife.

"Master Gragern called them Black Blades."

"Black Blades?" She stooped again to one of the dead men at Miika's feet and tore a sword from dead fingers. The blade was black as coal.

"You've heard of them?" Drauses asked.

"Yes. They're men for hire, loyal to who pays them best." She tossed the sword away in disgust. "There's only one man with that kind of coin."

"Rovik," Drauses sneered.

"They came up through the sewers," Miika said. "How in Vedia did they learn the way?"

"Where's the Liege?"

"He fled through the back staircase in the southern corridor. You should too. Get the girl away from here."

"Thank you, Miika," Shaila said, then she and Drauses took off down the hall.

At the end of the southern corridor sat an old office the Marks used for storage. Its far window opened to a set of steel steps the Men of the Mark had installed in case of a fire. When the trio approached the office, there were voices from within.

"I watched him slip away just minutes ago."

"What kind of Liege leaves his men behind to die?"

"Their leaders have always hidden behind their comrades like whelplings."

Drauses hugged the wall and set Amii on her feet beside him. He peeked quickly into the room then held up two fingers. Shaila moved Amii back yet further and stood at Drauses' side. With a few hand signals, he told her his plan, and Shaila nodded.

Drauses darted in the door first, and Shaila followed right behind. His knife soared and stuck deep into the left assassin's back. A split second later, Shaila's knife also flew, but her target was faster. He knocked her knife away with his arm. She ran in close as he raised a pistol and smacked the gun away. She elbowed him in the face, punched him between the legs, grabbed his head, and yanked his face down hard across her drawn-up knee. He fell unconscious onto his back, and Drauses plunged his sword into his heart.

"Amii," Drauses called, and the girl scurried to his side, avoiding the bodies on the floor as if they might still nab her.

Shaila slid out the window onto the staircase. Once she was sure they were alone, she held her hand out to guide Amii across the sill. The metal landing creaked under the added weight. The girls waited for Drauses to join them, but he leaned on the window frame and looked at Shaila with regretful determination.

"Take her to our place," he said. "You'll be safe there until I can come for you."

"What about you?" Shaila asked in alarm.

"I have to go back. I can't abandon my brothers."

"No, you must come with us!" Amii cried.

"I can't, child. Shaila will protect you, and I'll join you soon. I promise."

Shaila reached for Drauses, and he took her hand.

"Be careful," she said with a squeeze. He nodded then disappeared back into the darkened room. "Come, Amii. He'll be alright."

Shaila tucked the girl under her arm, and they wove their way through the narrow staircase and rushed off down the alley.

Chapter 9

SHAILA AND DRAUSES' building was at least an hour's brisk walk in the daylight. With Amii shuffling along at her side and only moonlight to guide them, it was well over two hours before the building came into view. Shaila didn't have her keys but getting into the building was easy. She knocked on the window of a ground-floor neighbor who happily let them in. Her apartment was another matter entirely.

Shaila ushered Amii into the vacant apartment next to hers and made her lock herself in the bathroom. Next, she opened the living room window and stepped out onto a ledge a mere three inches wide. One painfully slow step at a time, she slid across the wall toward her own apartment window, muttering prayers the entire way. She lost her footing once and almost fell but grabbed a downpipe to steady herself at the last second. Several minutes went by while she stood clutching the pipe, laughing to keep from crying. Her bravery returned, and she continued her slow but steady shuffle along the ledge. She finally made it to her window and nearly wept in relief when it opened without protest. She slid into her apartment and stood in the middle of her kitchen, praying thanks to the gods she managed not to fall to her death.

When she went back to the empty apartment, Amii rushed up. "You're mad! I thought you'd fall for sure!"

"I told you to wait in the bathroom!"

"It stunk in there. That was amazing, Shaila! Mad, but amazing!"

"Perhaps we can keep this to ourselves, yes? Your father won't be so impressed."

Amii laughed.

When the sky began to lighten, there was a knock on Shaila's door. She'd left her crossbow behind, so a kitchen knife was all she had to defend them with. She clutched it behind her back as she peered into the hall through a mere crack in the door.

It was Miika.

Shaila pulled the door open with a sigh of relief.

"Master Drauses gave me these," he said, and he handed over her keys.

"Is he alright?"

"As well as ever. He told the Liege and me where to find you, and others are arriving in intervals. The two of you are to come down to the first floor with the rest of us."

Shaila much preferred to keep her distance from the Liege. The old man set her nerves on edge which was something she didn't need more of at present.

"We'll stay here for now, thank you kindly."

"It wasn't a request."

"Tell your Master that Amii and I will stay right here where Master Drauses expects us to be."

Miika tilted his head. "He won't be pleased."

"I care very little about his pleasure."

He laughed and crossed his arms. "You're a witty thing."

"And?"

"Merely an observation."

Shaila crossed her arms as well. "Do you want to know what I *observe* about you?"

"Oh, I'm simply *brimming* with anticipation."

"I think the dog barks far worse than he bites."

Miika leaned on the doorframe with a wicked glint in his eye. "And I think the kitten should watch herself in the wolf's den."

"Is that a warning or a threat?"

"Where would the fun be if I told you?"

They were nose to nose, both refusing to look away.

"You never answered me," she said.

"I forgot your question. It must not have been very interesting."

"Was it worth it?" she asked.

Miika's hand came up so fast Shaila flinched on instinct. He merely scratched his nose with a cocky grin, winked, then walked away.

⚘

Gragern was busy setting up a makeshift headquarters in a ground floor apartment when Miika returned.

"Where are they?" Gragern asked.

"Not coming."

Gragern grunted, swallowed the harsh rebuke he so wished to deliver, and said instead, "It's for the best. There's a dire matter I need to discuss with you in private anyhow."

"What matter is that?"

"One that could earn you leave of me." Gragern smiled at the hope in his ward's eyes. "Miika, what I'm about to ask of you may seem crass, but you know I always have my reasons, yes?"

"You've yet to steer the guild wrong, my Liege."

"I'm glad you're so loyal to me. There's no one else I could trust with this." It was all too easy to stroke Miika's ego. "I need you to forever silence the Lady of the Mark."

Miika went pale. "You want me to… to kill Shaila? Why?"

"Not that I need to explain myself," Gragern snapped, "but she's a danger to this guild. She was a mess while Drauses laid in the clinic."

"Her Master was dying—"

"And she was a useless carcass of emotions. I warned Drauses his ward would crumble without him, and she did just that the second he fell. She's a weakness we can't afford. You saw evidence of an improper relationship between them as well. Though I can't prove it, I suspect she may also be involved with this attack on our headquarters."

"What makes you suspect that, sir?"

For once, Gragern was happy Miika asked, and he leaned nearer to his ward as if to deliver a juicy secret. "When Drauses first took Shaila as his protégé, he sent me a list of Western contacts he wished me to reach out to. None of the names were ones we'd ever had dealings with before, and I was skeptical as to their trustworthiness, so I never acted on them. The day of Shaila's proving, Drauses revealed the names came from her, and he expressed dissatisfaction on behalf of his ward that none of the contacts were ever utilized."

"What does that have to do with the Black Blades?"

"I believe Shaila learned I never reached out to her contacts and did so herself."

"You think she revealed our headquarters to someone in bed with Rovik by accident?"

"I don't think it was an accident at all."

Miika looked skeptical.

"Do you not find it odd that the Black Blades attacked the very day Shaila's Master was deemed fit for combat? If Shaila and Drauses are having improper relations, she wouldn't want the sword to fall on him while he was injured and unable to defend himself."

Miika considered this a moment. "Why not turn her out, then? You're the Liege. You can banish her."

"If your suspicions about their relationship are correct, Drauses might decide to exile with her, and we can't lose him, not with these new enemies pursuing us. It'd be better to eliminate her entirely, break Drauses and the guild off cleanly from this threat. Don't you agree?"

"I don't know."

Gragern smiled. "I have the best interest of this guild in mind as always, Miika."

"Killing our own is against our code."

"I'm the Liege of this guild. I *am* the code. If I say something must be done against our laws, an exception can be made. Make it look like an accident if you wish. I don't care how you go about it, but I need your oath you'll never speak of the deed to anyone."

"I'd never betray you," Miika said with conviction, though he was still pale.

"I know how much I'm asking of you, Miika. Do this for me and your brothers, and I'll give you leave of me at last. What say you?"

Miika studied his Master's face for a moment then bowed his head. "I'll do your bidding, my Liege."

Gragern clapped Miika on the shoulder. "Good man, Miika. Now, to more urgent matters. See that all empty rooms are prepared for our brothers. They'll be aching for baths and beds when they arrive."

⊸

Shaila watched out the window over the next few hours while Amii dozed on her bed. Occasionally, she'd spot a red-robed figure in the alley below. It was midday when there was another knock on the door. When she peered into the hall this time, her heart gave a happy leap at the sight of Drauses' face. He was covered in blood but none of it looked to be his.

"Where's Amii?" he asked.

"Sleeping," Shaila whispered.

Drauses held out a familiar box wrapped with a leather strap.

"Thank you!" She snatched up the case, retrieved her crossbow from inside, and fastened it to her arm, vowing never to be parted from the weapon again. Once she smoothed her sleeve down over it, she looked up to see Drauses staring into the case.

His jester mask was inside where Shaila tucked it for safekeeping weeks ago. His eyes came up and bore into hers. She swallowed as he started toward her, and her lips parted when he pinned her to the counter between his arms. He leaned close.

"I fought with everything I had through the halls last night," he muttered in a deep, husky voice that set her heart beating frantically, "through enemies I knew would bleed you dry if given the chance. In those moments of pure Vedia, when I didn't know if you were alive or dead, I made a decision."

"What decision?" she asked breathlessly.

"If we lived, I vowed to finish what I started with that kiss."

His face inched closer to hers. Shaila closed her eyes as she breathed in his intoxicating scent again, this time mixed with the smell of blood, the blood of the enemies he slaughtered to get to her last night. She leaned closer with a small sigh, reaching to bury her hand in his hair.

Amii called out from the bedroom.

Shaila jumped as if zapped by a live wire, and Drauses squeezed his eyes shut with a groan.

"Shaila?" Amii called again, louder this time, and Drauses slid aside.

"Here, Amii," Shaila called.

Amii came out of the bedroom still rubbing the sleep from her eyes. "Father!" She ran to him, and he hugged her tight.

"I'm sorry, but I can't stay," Drauses said. "I only came to see you were both ok. I'll be downstairs in Master Gragern's quarters for the time being."

"What will you be doing?" Shaila asked.

"Helping where I can. We need to prepare funerals for the ones who fell and find new headquarters for the rest. Our valuables must be retrieved from the factory. We don't need our enemies seizing them. Boon and Julta are already grumbling about their stocks. I doubt you'll see much of me for a while."

"But you'll be right downstairs?" Amii fretted.

"I'll let you know if I plan to leave the building," he assured her with a smile and a loving touch on her cheek. "I'll send a man to watch over you both."

"We'll be alright," Shaila said. "Go. Come back to us when you can."

❧

Rovik sat behind his desk as a figure in black robes and a mask strolled into his office.

"Take that thing off your face," he barked.

The Blade removed her mask, and he smiled. He never tired of looking at her. She had the same long mahogany curls as her daughter. Her eyes were a stormy grey, and her cheeks were a pale pink, as if she were always on the verge of a blush. Her lips were painted a dark red and they curled back over her teeth as she sneered.

"You promised me this would be a quick and easy deed," she fumed. "I lost half my men! Where was the Mark you claim is on your side? Those who survived said they never saw a single Man of the Mark raise a sword for us."

"Of course not," Rovik barked. "He dare not turn a blade on his own lest he gives up his position as spy."

"You want to know what I think, Uncle?" She leaned on her hands on his desk. "I think Marcel played you for a fool the same way he played Drauses. Once a traitor, always a traitor."

"If I want your opinion, Rose, I'll ask for it."

Rose narrowed her eyes. "I won't send my men to slaughter again."

"The Marks will be expecting that anyway. We've lost our element of surprise. We need a more efficient way for Marcel's inside man to gather intel. I know your brother employs several men of genius. Can any of them help us with this?"

Rose stood up straight once more and considered it for a moment. "There may be one."

"Get him here. Immediately."

She nodded and turned to go.

"Rose?"

She looked back from the doorway.

"Get our girl back, please."

"She's *my* girl, not yours. You were supposed to keep her safe; you promised me. Pray I can fix this, or else my brother will get involved."

"Don't threaten me, girl!"

"At least you're smart enough to acknowledge he's a threat," Rose said with a dangerous smile. "You screwed up, Rovik. Just sit back while the family cleans up your mess. As always."

Drauses spent the next four days in constant motion, helping the wards set up a temporary training room on the ground floor, scouring maps of the city for a new headquarters, sending teams of men back to the factory for supplies, and making funeral arrangements for their fallen brothers. Of the four Marks lost, three were wards and one was a Master. Though none of them were among Drauses' closest friends, he grieved them all the same.

Drauses wanted to find new headquarters right away, but Gragern was content to stay put for the time being. He contradicted Drauses at every turn it seemed, more than was necessary. Drauses wondered if it was the result of trying times or something more, something personal. The constant resistance irritated him more and more each day.

A guard was stationed on the third floor and switched out every six hours to help Shaila watch over Amii. Drauses himself had only been upstairs to change once a day since they arrived. He couldn't find a single moment alone with Shaila, but perhaps that was a good thing for now. There was far too much to do for such distractions. He pushed on doing all he could for the guild as the hours and days bled together.

On the fifth day, Drauses was exhausted to the point he could no longer focus, so he begged his leave of Gragern's quarters and climbed wearily to the third floor to sleep in his own bed for a night. Just one night and he'd be right back to it all in the morning.

Xeda stood guard outside Drauses' apartment.

"Is everything alright up here?" Drauses asked.

"All is well," Xeda replied. The door was open so he could see and hear inside from the hall.

Drauses did a quick sweep of his rooms and found Amii asleep in his bed. So much for his plans to sleep there himself tonight.

"Where's Shaila?" Drauses asked from the kitchen.

"She went next door not long ago," Xeda called.

Drauses knocked on Shaila's apartment door and called her name but got no reply, so he let himself in.

Shaila rushed out from her bedroom wrapped in nothing but a towel.

"Is something wrong?" she asked in alarm.

"Wrong…" His eyes took in every pale, exposed inch of her, from her bare shoulders down to her toes. His stomach jumped when he realized there wasn't anything under the towel. Just her. "No, nothing. I went to check on Amii, and you were gone."

"I went to wash up while Amii slept. I'll go back as soon as I dress."

There were dark circles under her eyes. To the best of his knowledge, she guarded Amii day and night. When had she last slept?

"It's alright," he said. "Amii is important, but so is your well-being. Take all the time you need and get some rest tonight, ok?"

Shaila nodded.

He'd said all there was to say, so he should be leaving... but he wasn't. The sight of her rendered him immobile, rooting his feet to the floor. Her eyes met his expectantly.

'Leave, leave. Leave! Leave now, you fool!' Drauses screamed to himself, but he couldn't tear his eyes away. He closed them. Nothing short of steel determination made him turn around and make toward the door.

"Drauses."

He froze. With one word, his own name spoken with enough feeling to steal the breath from his chest, she tore away his resolve. She wasn't calling to him as her Master, not her brother-in-arms or a friend, but as something more, something deeper. He shouldn't look back. If he did, it would all be over. The door was right in front of him, open and calling to the very last shred of his self-control...

He looked back over his shoulder.

Shaila stood still as stone in the middle of the room with her towel clutched shut in one hand. She loosened her grip, and the cloth slipped through her fingers, fell away, and pooled at her feet. Her skin was milky white in the moonlight, and he knew from experience how soft it was. How had he never noticed her figure before? Full breasts, slender waist, rounded hips... any man would fall at her feet and beg to touch her. He certainly wanted to.

Drauses reached behind him with a shaking hand and pushed the door shut with a snap, blocking his escape and sealing his fate. Shaila walked his way, slowly, as if uncertain what he might do. She raised her hand, brought it an inch from his face, and held it there. He leaned into her touch and closed his eyes at the warmth of her palm on his cheek. Her thumb caressed his lips which parted to let out a shaky breath.

He reached for her, sliding his fingers up her neck into her silky hair. He pulled her closer and kissed a trail across her jaw and up her cheek to her ear. She smelled sweet, like flowers and honey. He buried his nose below her ear to breathe deep of it, and the last of his self-control shattered.

"Touch me," he whispered.

Shaila untied his robes and pushed them off his shoulders. He let them fall. She slid her hands under his shirt, and when her palms touched bare skin, he growled low in his throat. He tore the cloth over his head and threw it away then kicked off his boots as she unclasped his belt. When she slid her thumbs into the waist of his pants, he thought about stopping her. This was the point of no return, he knew, but no sooner did the thought enter his mind than it was swept away again by the look of longing on her face.

She shoved his pants down.

⁂

Drauses' body was now, for the first time, completely bare for Shaila's admiration; and admire she did. Years of training had sculpted every muscle from chin to toes, but there were also scars, many scars, across his shoulders, his chest, his stomach, and down both legs. The one made by the hot stick was by far the worst of them. It must have been so painful. Shaila made to touch it but stopped with her hand poised over his skin, asking permission one last time. He nodded once, and she traced the mark from his shoulder clear to his hip, stroking every peak and valley in between. She leaned forward and kissed his chest as her hands stroked his back.

Drauses closed his eyes with a sigh, and when he opened them again, they'd changed. A fire Shaila had never seen before roared inside those blue pools. It burned away the last of his trepidation. He seized her and kissed her hard. She gasped when his hand slid down her belly and between her legs. She clung to his neck as his teasing fingers made her heart beat a hard, rushing rhythm in her ears, and her legs started to tremble.

"Drauses?" she murmured in uncertainty.

With few exceptions, Shaila always guarded her body and chose the few lovers she knew with great care. Even with those she let in passed her walls, she never trusted them enough to let desire sweep her away. As a result, lovemaking usually left her feeling empty and disappointed. But here with Drauses, her defenses wouldn't last. He'd shatter her walls tonight, and she was afraid.

"Do you want me to stop?" he asked.

Despite her nerves, that was the last thing she wanted. "Odas, no."

Drauses groaned and swept her off her feet into his arms. He carried

108

her to her bedroom and laid on top of her on the bed, pushing her knees apart as he settled between her thighs.

His hand touched her first, slow and soft. He petted her until she squirmed then slid a single finger inside her, finding a rhythm with it as his thumb worked maddening circles around her most sensitive places. He captured her mouth in a deep kiss that she broke a moment later on a moan so carnal it shocked her that such a sound could come from her lips. Drauses growled in response, and his hand disappeared. He leaned back and positioned himself at her entry, but then he froze. There was nothing left to stop him, but he stopped nonetheless and looked deep into her eyes. He waited there, giving her one last chance to say no. She kissed him to hide the tears welling in her eyes and pulled him closer in welcome.

When he entered her, they sighed in unison.

Drauses was in no way a small man, but he was slow and gentle and soon had her gasping with every thrust. Her hand found his hair, and she gripped a tight fist of it and pulled hard. It was his turn to gasp, and he moved faster, harder. He slid his thumb through her folds again, circling her sensitive flesh with each thrust of his hips.

"Tell me how best to please you," Drauses said breathlessly. "I want to hear you cry out my name."

"What you're doing... perfect..." Shaila said between small gasps. "Don't stop!"

"Never."

In the frenzy, their lips met as they raced together toward the brink. Shaila arched off the bed as she came apart in his arms, crying out his name. Drauses pulled her closer and buried his face in her neck as a heat filled her, his heat.

As their hearts slowed, and the trembles ceased, Shaila stroked Drauses' hair, brushing it back out of his face one lock at a time and marveling at the feel of it between her fingers. Though the words she longed to say were poised on the tip of her tongue, she kept quiet, not wanting to ruin the moment should he decide he didn't feel the same way. She could tell him tomorrow, or next week, or never. The words didn't matter, not if he'd stay right here in her bed and in her heart like this forever. What were a few words compared to this?

Chapter 10

THEY DRIFTED IN and out of sleep in each other's arms for the rest of the night. Come morning, Shaila was draped across Drauses, sleeping peacefully on his shoulder with her silky locks fanned across his chest like a blanket of gold. While she slept on, he took a few of the strands in his hand and let them fall softly through his fingers with a contented sigh. The blanket had slipped to expose her to the morning sunlight, and he thought there wasn't a more breathtaking sight in the world... until she roused, looked up, and smiled at him. The moon. The stars. The sun. She was everything. He was only ashamed it took him so long to notice.

Shaila gathered herself up, stood, and stretched with an arch of her back that sent her hair rippling and her breasts heaving. Drauses shot up and looped an arm around her waist, yanked her into his lap, and kissed her. He'd planned for it to be a quick deed, one last taste of her lips before he rose for the day, but it carried away into something much more, and they were soon breathless and aching for each other.

She pulled away and placed a finger against his lips. "If you do that again, we'll lose the entire morning finding out how far one kiss can go."

"I fail to see the problem with that," he said.

Shaila smiled and traced the scar on his cheek with her thumb. "Amii. If she wakes alone, she'll worry."

He sighed in defeat. "You're right."

Shaila eased the sting of her rejection with a tender kiss on his cheek. "What happens now?" she asked softly.

"I don't know," Drauses replied with a small laugh. "Let's not fret over it. No need to give it a name or a purpose yet. Let's just be us, for a while."

Shaila nodded.

He took her chin in his hand, unable to resist stealing one more kiss. When Shaila moaned against his lips, he rolled and laid her back on the bed beside him.

"Drauses—"

Her protests died when he locked his lips to her breast. His hand went between her thighs as his tongue slid across her nipple. Drauses was a patient and attentive lover, and he touched and suckled until she was writhing and ready to fall to pieces for him all over again. With her nails dug deep in his back, Drauses dragged her straight to pleasure's peak and let her fly. She shook in his arms, her face burning a deep crimson she tried to hide behind her hair. He brushed it away.

"Beautiful," he murmured.

Shaila smiled and closed her eyes. She settled on his shoulder again, and Drauses was content to steal a few more selfish minutes with her in the dawn's golden light.

❦

Amii was reading under Aro's watchful eye when Drauses entered his apartment sometime later. Aro volunteered to sit up on the third floor more than anyone. He seemed to enjoy Amii's company which made Drauses more than happy to put him on guard most often. If Aro was fond of Amii, he would protect her far better than the wards who fell asleep out of boredom.

"Father," Amii greeted with a smile. It took Drauses' breath away how much she looked like her mother when she smiled. The thought of Rose made Drauses want to crawl back down the hall and hold Shaila protectively in his arms.

"Where's Shaila?" he asked, constructing his ruse.

"Xeda said she was with you," Aro said with a raised brow.

"I checked in with her last night as always," Drauses replied. "I was needed back downstairs right after."

Aro frowned but offered no protest.

"I think she's still in her room," Amii said as she turned the page in her book. "She looked very tired yesterday."

"I'm here." Shaila swept into the room, securing the last tie on her robes as she walked. "Forgive me, Master Drauses, I overslept."

"It's alright," Drauses said with a wink only she could see. "You likely needed the rest."

Shaila tried a casual smile, failed as it slipped into a smirk, bit her lip instead, and shook her head to hide it all. "Amii, are you hungry? Aro, coffee?"

"I should check in with Master Dagon," Aro said.

"Oh, please stay a bit longer, Aro," Amii begged. "Tell me another of your jokes."

Aro chuckled then nodded, persuaded by nothing more than the youth's hopeful face. "One cup of coffee, Amii, then I must be on my way."

Amii pouted but was soon laughing uncontrollably as Aro treated her to a witty jest.

Shaila busied herself in the kitchen making breakfast, and Drauses found himself staring, watching her with new eyes. She was a goddess, a silky, golden beauty... and she was his lover now. The thought made him grin like a fool. By the time he tore his eyes away, Amii was smiling at him.

"What?" he asked innocently.

"Oh... nothing."

Drauses raised a brow. Keeping this secret was going to be more difficult than he anticipated.

☙

Once the bodies of the fallen were recovered from the factory, Boon acted as mortician while pyres were built using dry wood gathered from a crumbling building down the street. Drauses spent the afternoon overseeing final preparations, and when all was ready, he notified the Liege who ordered the guild to gather in a nearby open lot at dusk.

Since the forming of their guild a hundred years ago, the Men of the Mark had always burned their fallen where the rest of the country buried their dead. The founding Masters revived the tradition of pyres and oil used in ancient times, believing this was the proper way to send warriors to meet the Odas. Trista's East side was all too familiar with what rising columns of black smoke meant, and it never failed that whenever the guild held a funeral, the streets nearby would go quiet and still as if the city itself were in mourning with them.

The pyres were arranged together in a row. Four men carried each fallen Mark between them on stretchers of red cloth. The dead wore their hoods and masks, as was tradition: masked at proving, masked at pyre. The Master of each fallen ward laid any possessions their protégé held dear in his empty hands, and the ward who lost his Master placed a sword in the hands of his departed mentor.

The bottoms of the pyres were soaked in oil so the fires would burn hot and fast. Master Gragern took up a torch of cloth and oil and snapped his fingers. Julta darted forward with a tiny silver box of his own design and lit the end with a flick of flint and steel. The Liege walked along the row, dragging the torch across the wood until all four slabs were engulfed in flames then tossed it atop the blaze.

"Today we lay to rest four fallen brothers," he said. "We live by the sword and die by the sword, thus is our fate and our duties as Men of the Mark. For these four souls, the fight is over. May they rest in peace."

Drauses glared at the Liege after such a dismal speech. This was not how they sent the souls of the fallen to Odavail, and the Elder knew it. Drauses bowed his head and started a prayer aloud, the proper one, and the men around him were quick to join in.

"We fight beside our brothers with honor and pride. Today a few have fallen, and we weep in pain of loss. We pray these souls pass safely through the gates of Odavail. May they guide us forward while we fight in their stead. While we still have blood to give."

Many of the men started back toward the apartments, Gragern included, who cast a caustic look at Drauses as he went. Amii came to her father, and he placed his hands on her shoulders as they stood together to watch the flames.

Drauses stared at the bodies of his fallen brothers with a burdened heart. This pain in his chest was bad enough for men with whom he barely spoke. He knew it'd be much worse, crippling even, for Shaila the day he was set atop his own pyre. After the night they shared together, nothing could be the same. He cared too deeply for her, and though she hadn't voiced it, he suspected she felt the same for him. It saddened him to know she'd carry on without him one day. Given their age difference, the odds that he would meet his end first were staggering. He'd have to learn to carry the guilt that brought.

Drauses watched Shaila walk around the fire to stand beside Miika. She smiled sadly at her fellow ward, and when Miika smirked back, her gaze lingered long enough to send Drauses' temper crackling like the nearby flames. Why be friendly with a man who nearly beat her to death at her own proving? Did she... could she *like* him? Of all the men with which he might find competition for Shaila's heart, Miika was the last he'd expected.

Drauses leaned down to whisper in Amii's ear, never taking his eyes off Shaila at Miika's side. Amii gave an obedient nod then marched over to take Shaila by the hand. She spoke in Shaila's ear, then the girls turned away from the fire to go back inside on Drauses' orders. Miika watched them go then looked over at Drauses through the flames, his eyes cold and calculating. Shaila and Amii were not yet out of sight when Miika turned on his heel and followed them. A prickle of warning slithered up the back of Drauses' neck, but before he could go after them, a hand landed on his shoulder. It was Dagon.

"We need to talk, brother," he said with a cautious glance around.

Both wards and child were gone, and Dagon was already steering Drauses away in the opposite direction. Dagon led them into the darkest corner of the lot.

"What is it?" Drauses asked with a huff, irritated at the interruption and because he could already guess what this was about.

"I've received some distressing news."

"Oh?" Drauses' heart skipped a beat. Did Dagon know about him and Shaila? If anyone were to notice something was amiss with Drauses, it would be his oldest friend, and Dagon was the sort of friend to confront Drauses first before reporting his suspicions to the Liege.

Dagon peered back toward the fire to check they weren't followed. "I heard from our brothers at the southern gate." Drauses relaxed when he realized this wasn't about his relationship with Shaila, but he tensed all over again when Dagon continued, "They spotted a wagon on its way from Se Trosk A Vol. It was covered, armored, and guarded."

"Weapons?"

"Most likely."

"It must be a substantial delivery to warrant so much protection. We must alert the Liege immediately."

"I already did, brother. Our Elder chose to take no action."

Drauses frowned. "None at all?"

"I got the message in plenty of time to put a group together and intercept the wagon before it came within a day's travel of our southern wall, but the Liege forbade me."

Drauses considered it a moment but couldn't come up with a satisfactory explanation for Master Gragern's decision. "Who did you request to take with you?"

"Aside from Aro, just you and Shaila."

Drauses was puzzled. He knew the Liege had his doubts about Shaila, but he couldn't picture the Elder letting a chance like this slip by, regardless of who took on the assignment. The whole purpose of having scouts in the south was to catch deliveries like this. Allowing Rovik to receive such a shipment was unwise.

"Where is the wagon now," Drauses asked, already forming a plan.

"It entered the southern gate this morning. I waited for the Liege to announce he had some grander plan for the shipment, but he never said a word or sent a single man. Our Western lookouts report it made it to Rovik's door, unhindered, hours ago."

Drauses huffed. "Then why tell me this now?"

"You've been gone for a while, Drauses. You haven't had the chance to witness what the rest of us have seen these past two years. Ever since Marcel's betrayal, the Liege has behaved oddly. This is just the most recent example. I am anxious about our brotherhood's current path, and I'm not the only one."

Drauses groaned.

"You'll stand and listen to what I have to say," Dagon barked. "You've dodged me long enough."

Drauses rolled his eyes but motioned for his friend to continue.

"We used to be a powerful and fearsome force in this city," said Dagon. "Our enemies could barely keep the dividing walls built, our forefathers were so busy tearing them down at every chance. But now? Look at us: burning four fallen brothers at once. When was the last time that happened?"

Drauses remembered quite clearly the last time they'd suffered such losses. "The 5th Year of Rovik. Six Marks were crossing the river from the West when their boat was lit on fire by Rovik's men. Three of them drowned. One died later from the burns."

"And who were the two survivors?" Dagon asked, crossing his arms.

"Master Gragern and your Master, Raiga."

"Raiga was never the same after that incident. Gragern fared better, or so we thought. His ghosts may be catching up to him at last. It's as if he's lost his spine. This attack has everyone concerned for the guild's safety. They don't know who to trust. How did our enemies find our new headquarters? How did they get past our night watchmen?"

"I've asked myself the same questions countless times."

Dagon ran his hands through his hair. "I fear our ranks are fracturing. Gragern's unwillingness to act has sown doubts and fear throughout the men. We were always outnumbered, but we held our own by remaining one step ahead of our enemy. We keep falling further behind." Dagon finally regarded Drauses, locking his old friend in a stern stare. "The men would follow you into Vedian fire, Drauses. Tonight, after Gragern's awful speech, you spoke The Warrior's Prayer. You knew what the men needed and acted accordingly. You were ready to jump to action about the wagon as well, I could see it in your eyes. You're more of a leader than you'll admit to yourself."

"I'm a fighter," Drauses said, and he hated the pleading tone that crept into his voice as he tried to make Dagon understand. "I don't belong back at headquarters plotting and organizing. I belong on the battlefield with a sword in my hand."

"Soon, there may be no more battles to fight. We may splinter apart until too few of us are left to matter in this war."

"You truly believe that?"

"I do. Our Elder failed us today, perhaps more than once. How many more failures can we endure before we have no more blood to give?"

"I'm not the one to lead us to victory," Drauses said quietly.

Dagon sighed and moved to head back toward the fire, but when he drew up next to Drauses, he stopped, rested his hand on Drauses' shoulder, and said, "But perhaps you are the only one who can save us from ruin." Then he walked away, leaving Drauses to stew alone in the dark.

⁓

Miika glanced back once to see if Drauses would follow him. When he saw Dagon lead Drauses away to the opposite side of the lot, Miika raised his hood and donned his mask. The two girls walked along ahead of him, and he sped up his pace, eating up the distance between them with quick and silent steps. He fingered the handle of the knife in his pocket, gripping it tightly. He came up behind Shaila as the knife slipped free of his robes—

His heart seized in his chest, and he couldn't breathe as pure panic stopped him in his tracks. He watched from the shadows as Shaila walked on and out of danger.

Miika put his head in his hands and leaned back against a nearby wall. This deed was the key to earning his freedom from his Master once and for all, so why couldn't he do it? With Shaila's death, he'd no longer be the clueless ward who could never please his Liege. He was bound by code not to speak against Gragern, but now more than ever he wished he could tell the other Masters what their Liege had asked of him. They'd likely see him as a sniveling tattle who buckled under pressure. Being ward to the Elder Master must mean his assignments were more stressful, shrouded even more in secrecy, right?

Miika wasn't so sure this time. He wasn't sure about anything anymore.

◄§

After tucking Amii in for the night, Shaila went to wash up in her quarters and came back to find Drauses' bedroom door closed. She stood in front of it in wonder. Drauses spent day and night downstairs in Gragern's apartment where he could be called upon at all hours if needed. If he was resting here, she should leave him be. After the day's depressing events, she wasn't sure he'd want company. In the end, she couldn't help herself, and she snuck into his room.

Drauses was already fast asleep. She'd slip into bed with him, with no expectations. That sounded better than sleeping alone, at least. She crept across the room and reached for the blanket of his bed just as her foot pressed against a squeaky floorboard.

Drauses leapt at her, drawing his knife from under his pillow. Shaila ducked under his blade. When he recognized her through his sleepy haze, he swore through his teeth and put the weapon away.

"What were you thinking?" he asked. "I could've killed you!"

"Not with that sloppy swing," she teased.

Drauses narrowed his eyes, but his nostrils flared as he fought not to smile. He leapt again, snatching her by the elbow and tugging her down into his lap.

"Tell me, Lady of the Mark," he murmured near her ear, his voice low and husky, "what's worth risking your life in the dark?"

"I thought you weren't good with rhymes, Master Drauses."

He chuckled as he nuzzled her ear. "You've come this far. See it through."

Shaila straddled him as their mouths met, and her fingers wove into his hair as her tongue thrust in his mouth. He crushed his mouth back to hers and met her tongue with the same passion. Lovemaking in a kiss, that was what it was. Her heart began to race.

He stripped off her shirt and gave her breasts the same treatment he did that morning. Shaila arched her back, giving him access to every inch of her chest. His hand dove down the front of her pants, and he soon had her moaning in longing. He lifted her back on her feet long enough to rip her pants to her ankles, then he pulled her to the bed, laying her beside him across the sheets.

"Take off your clothes," she said. "I want to touch you."

They tossed off his clothes together until he was naked beside her. She smiled and brought her hand up, stopping an inch away from his face as she always did.

"May I?" she asked.

"You may," he murmured as he leaned into her touch. "In fact, never ask again. Touch me whenever, wherever you like. Only you."

"Can I make a confession?"

"I'm no holy man but, by all means, confess away."

"If I have my way, I'll never be parted from you, Drauses. If that means I must be nothing but your ward by day to then warm your bed at night, I'll gladly do so for the rest of my days. Unless... I know this goes against our codes. I'd understand if you'd rather we—"

Drauses wrapped an arm around her and hauled her closer until their chests touched and their faces were mere inches apart.

"Never," he declared in his deep, gravelly voice. "I'd rather cleave off my own appendages than have you leave my side."

"Speaking of appendages..." She wrapped her fingers around his hard length, and he moaned as she touched him. He only let her do so for a few strokes before he grabbed her by the waist and rolled, dragging her up on top of him. She sank slowly down onto him.

"Hmm," she said with a mischievous smile. "I like this." She arched her back, taking him deeper in her body. "I have such control from up here."

"Oh, I can control plenty from down here." He bucked his hips up hard, and she gasped as his body plunged into hers. She rode him up and down with subtle, teasing thrusts of her hips, and kept that torturous pace until he could take no more. He bucked his hips again over and over. Shaila moaned and closed her eyes.

"Look at me," he said, and her eyes fluttered open again. The look he wore for her, such passion and desire, was enough to send her over the edge, and she struggled not to shout.

Drauses rolled on top of her and thrust so hard she cried out into his neck. He pulled her nearer, bent her legs at the knees, and nestled deep between her thighs until her body took all of him. He moved fast, bringing her slowly back up toward another orgasm, and she struggled to reach it again so soon.

"I can't," she whispered breathlessly.

"Yes, you can. And you will."

And she did.

Her pleasure broke again, and her nails raked across his back as she lost all sense of time and space. Drauses was quick to follow, his fingers clenching the bedding so hard she was amazed the cloth didn't rip to pieces in his grip.

He buried his nose in her hair. "Shaila..."

Where was she? Who was she? She didn't care. All she cared about was this man, this assassin in the dark who'd swept into her life through an open window. Drauses scooped her into his arms and tucked her to his side, and she soon fell asleep to the soft thump, thump, thump of his heart under her ear.

≪

Morning light was creeping across the room. No... It wasn't creeping at all; the sun had already risen to full height and lit the room in gold. There was a startled gasp as Drauses blinked the sleep from his eyes. Shaila was still sleeping on his arm, curled against his chest, so where did the sound come from? He peered about the room, slowly remembering where he was, recalling every pleasurable detail of—his door was open.

Amii stood in the doorway with her hand on the knob and her mouth hanging open. Drauses' heart skipped a beat, and he sat up sharply. Shaila stirred with an unhappy groan and looked up at Drauses' pale face. Her eyes followed his to the doorway.

"Amii!" Shaila cried with a gasp as she scrambled to cover herself in the twisted bedding.

Amii stared with wide eyes for a moment, but then her face split into a ridiculous grin, and she laughed as she pulled the door shut. Shaila looked at Drauses. Drauses gazed right back at her, lost for words. He broke the silence with a full belly laugh that consumed him as he flopped back on the bed again. His laughter was infectious, and Shaila snickered with him even as she hid her burning cheeks behind her hands in dismay.

"Oh gods," she muttered into her palms. "What do we tell her?"

"The truth?" Drauses offered, but Shaila looked at him with more questions in her eyes than answers. "I'll take care of it."

⁓

Drauses found Amii reading at the kitchen counter alone once he'd dressed.

"Can I speak to you a moment?" he asked, quietly, so the guard in the hall wouldn't overhear.

"I know what I saw," she said. "Don't tell me I'm imagining things."

"You're no fool; I'd never treat you as such. But, Amii, I have to ask that you keep this between us. You mustn't tell anyone what you saw just now."

"Not even Aro?" she asked with a frown.

"Not even Aro."

"Why? Are you ashamed?"

"Shaila is the last person in this world I'd be ashamed of. Besides you, of course."

Amii grinned. "Good."

"The truth is," he said as he leaned closer, "Shaila and I... we're not supposed to... be doing... what we do," he poorly explained, and he shook his head with a grimace.

Amii was not about to take pity on him. "Why not?"

"It is against our codes as Master and ward."

"Then, why do you do it?"

Why indeed? This tryst was of the heart, not just desire. He couldn't stay away from Shaila now no matter how hard he tried. But how to explain this to a twelve-year-old? He groaned and rubbed his face in his hands.

"It was beyond our control. These things are like that sometimes. This is a trying time, as I'm sure you can understand. It's an issue better left for a later day. Do I have your word you'll not talk about this with anyone?"

"I promise, Father. I don't want to cause you trouble. I like Shaila."

Drauses smiled. "As do I."

"Clearly," Amii said with a giggle.

"Are you two scheming?" Shaila asked as she entered the room. "Did you speak to her?" she whispered to Drauses.

He nodded. "All is well."

Amii giggled again.

Chapter 11

DRAUSES GREW RESTLESS as the days ticked by and they lingered far too long at the apartments. The building wasn't secure and lacked proper space as many of the wards and Masters were forced to bunk together. Gragern stonewalled any attempt to find new headquarters until finally, after days of heated discussion, Drauses convinced the Liege to let him and a small team investigate a few potential locations around the city. This meant leaving Shaila and Amii for days at a time, which worried him but couldn't be helped.

The Marks had been at the apartments for nearly a fortnight when Drauses set his sights on an abandoned lumber mill at the south side of the city. Built a few years before Jesparia's fall, the mill was further away than any of the other places Drauses had suggested but was also less likely to be ruined by time and decay. It'd take the better part of a day to get there on foot, but the longer Drauses considered it, the more he felt sure it would be worth the trip, so he and his team set out.

The mill was large and riddled with scrap they could make use of. It was nestled in an elbow of the river, stretching right up to the Eastern bank and giving them an easy route through the city right to their doorstep. There was a tall wall built shortly after the mill was founded to cut down on the noise from the sawblades during early morning hours. It ran the length of the mill's northern property line but could easily be expanded to secure the whole property. Since the mill sat on the very southern limits of the city, there was plenty of space for expansion as well.

The guild could thrive and grow here in a way it never had before, though it meant their headquarters would no longer be hidden. Perhaps that was a good thing. Perhaps they'd fought from the shadows for too long and it was time they stepped into the light. Drauses even gave the place a name, be it simple and unofficial: The Yard.

Drauses was relieved when the Liege raised no objections to refurbishing The Yard to suit their needs. It was decided that a large team of men would move there at once and begin fortifying a perimeter and making repairs. Unfortunately, the Liege was adamant Drauses oversee this work himself. Since it was no place yet for a child to live, Amii would have to remain behind, and since Shaila was her acting guardian, she'd have to stay as well. Dagon insisted on going south with Drauses, and they decided together that Aro would stay behind as a permanent guard over Amii along with Shaila while they were away. Aro happily agreed.

With a heavy heart, Drauses gathered his belongings and prepared to leave the girls for the foreseeable future. Shaila stood at a distance and watched with worried eyes as he moved about the apartment packing his things. She was as unhappy with the arrangement as he was, but there was nothing to be done.

Amii threw a fit.

"But I don't want to stay behind!" she fumed. "I can help too. I'll work. Let me come with you, and Shaila and Aro too. Please?"

"We all make sacrifices for the good of the guild, little one," Drauses explained on one knee, holding her hands as he begged her forgiveness for circumstances beyond his control. "That's our way. It's not safe for you there, and the men need me. Please try to understand."

After a final storm of angry tears, and at the news Aro would be moving into their apartment full time, Amii eventually let go of her grudges.

The morning of his departure, Drauses whisked Shaila away to an empty room where he kissed her long and hard.

"Be safe and come back to me," she ordered him woefully.

9ᵗʰ of Autumn, Jesparia's 9ᵗʰ and 20 year of Rovik

Drauses had been gone a week when Shaila got word Julta wished to see her. She was curious what the inventor could want, so she let Aro know she was stepping out for a moment.

Julta was bent over a counter holding a piping hot piece of metal when she walked into his workshop. He set the metal to a piece of wood clamped to the counter, and a small flame burst up at the contact. The flame caught Julta's sleeve on fire, and he swore as he dropped the metal into a nearby bucket before swatting wildly at the flames. He caught sight of Shaila in the doorway who stood snorting behind her hand at the spectacle.

"Yes, yes, yes!" he cried as he tore off his jacket, which still smoked a bit at the sleeve. "Come!" He waved her in as he reached under the counter. "I told Master Drauses I'd improve them, and so I have! He's been away too long, so I decided I'd give them to you myself."

"Give me what, Julta?"

"Your bolts, of course! The others are efficient, but I strive for the spectacular!"

Julta produced a leather belt with a long satchel attached to one side. He flipped back the cover to reveal three small compartments full of bolts. Each compartment's bolts had a different color fletching: red, green, and blue. Julta plucked out a blue bolt and held it up for Shaila's inspection.

"Electric," Julta said in awe. "The tip is designed to grip, not pierce the skin." Shaila looked closer to inspect the head: a flat tip surrounded by a series of curved barbs. She watched as Julta placed a pencil to the tip, and the barbs sprang forward like claws to latch onto the wood. Julta promptly let the pencil go as a second later, a burst of electricity surged through it with a flash and a crackle.

"Strong enough to stun, cause immobility, possibly unconsciousness," Julta stated proudly. "Only good for one use though." He tossed the used bolt over his shoulder, and it clattered on the floor. He pulled a green one from the quiver instead.

"Poison."

"Poison!" Shaila cried, and she stepped back from the counter. "Julta, are you mad? I could kill *myself* with such a thing strapped to my hip!"

Julta huffed with indignation. "They're safe until fired, Shaila, of course. The poison is enclosed until the bolt strikes a surface, then it delivers a fast-acting formula of my own design... well, Boon helped, but it was my idea! You'd have to shoot someone with *two* green bolts, possibly three, to kill. One only brings sickness: vomiting, violent shakes, and weakness."

He placed the bolt back in its compartment with the others and drew a red bolt this time.

"Explosive," he said as he held the bolt out to Shaila.

She hesitated before taking it between two tentative fingers.

"Use these with caution. They'll cause lots of destruction. And of course, the resulting blaze will be quite a sight. Use them sparingly. I lack the supplies to make very many."

Shaila nodded and handed the bolt back to him. He returned it to the quiver and closed the flap.

"Hand over your crossbow," he ordered, and he held out his hand expectantly.

"Why?"

"Improvements will be made. I'll be swift and have it returned to you in a day or two."

"What changes will you make?" she asked as she unstrapped her crossbow from her arm.

Julta bit his lip, but Shaila refused to give him the weapon until he answered, holding it out of the inventor's reach with a raised, expectant brow.

"Faster release mechanism, more powerful draw for longer shots, a sight for improved accuracy, and adjustments to accommodate the new bolts," Julta said moodily.

Shaila laid her crossbow in his hand. "Was that so hard? Trust works both ways."

Julta smiled anew as he fingered her crossbow, and she suspected he had more plans for the weapon than the ones he mentioned.

"I wish Master Drauses trusted me as you do," Julta said, his smile fading.

Shaila tilted her head with a frown. "Of course he trusts you, Julta. He wouldn't have given me your crossbow as a gift if he didn't."

"But he won't accept any of my weapons! He chooses to keep his blade and nothing more."

"That speaks more to his particular tastes than to your abilities as an inventor. You've not yet found the right design to tempt him is all."

"I've tried many ideas, but not one has been good enough."

"Keep trying. I'm sure you'll succeed someday. Just don't offer him a hot stick. The Odas know he has plenty of reasons to despise them."

Julta's eyes widened. "Master Drauses despises hot sticks," he muttered. "Of course."

Shaila watched his eyes glaze over as he drifted off into the inner workings of his mind. He darted to a nearby table, pulled out a paper and pencil, and began scribbling frantically, muttering under his breath.

"Julta?" Shaila called. He didn't respond. "Julta!"

He looked up at her, blinked in confusion to find her still there, then waved his hand toward the door. "A day or two and your crossbow will be finished. I've much to do." He went back to dashing about his shop and talking to himself.

Shaila shrugged and took her leave. Julta was brilliant, to be certain, but many considered him insane. She wondered if those two things often went hand in hand as she started up the stairs.

"Shaila!" Miika rushed to catch up to her on the steps. "I'd like to spar with someone who can give me a challenge for once. Care to train with me?"

"That could be fun," she said. "Let me run up and change. I'll meet you in ten."

When Shaila returned to Drauses' apartment, Aro was seated at the kitchen counter folding pieces of paper into little animals as Amii watched with amusement. They had a whole zoo strewn across the countertop. Amii had a paper of her own and sat folding it as Aro instructed her to. A moment later, she held a miniature bird in her palm whose wings flapped with a pull of its tail.

"That's very good, Amii," Aro praised. "Much better than my first try, for sure."

Shaila liked having Aro around. Where the other guards sat silent and bored to tears, Aro played games, told jokes, cooked for them on occasion, and told amazing tales of brave heroes that kept Amii captivated for hours at a time. He was kind and cheerful and took his job as Amii's guardian as seriously as Shaila did.

"How're things in here?" Shaila asked.

"All is well," Aro said.

"Shaila," Amii called. "What do you call a one-legged pirate?"

"I dare not venture a guess."

"A swashhobbler!"

Shaila shook her head in dismay but laughed at the silly quip anyway.

"Care to learn to fold a few creations?" Aro asked. He held a small paper dog out to her on his palm, and she took it with another chuckle.

"No, thank you," she said as she set the little animal on the counter with the rest of their menagerie. "Miika asked to train with me. I came up to change and let you know where I'll be."

Aro's smile faded. "Miika? Has he ever requested to train with you before?"

"No, but he was recovering from an injury for a time. It could've delayed the invitation."

Aro didn't look convinced. "Would you like us to come to the training room with you?"

"That's not necessary, Aro. I won't be long."

Aro nodded. "Be careful. Miika can be a dirty fighter when it suits him, as you know."

"It's about time someone knocked him on his backside, then," Shaila said with a grin.

Aro laughed. "You already did that once."

Shaila changed quickly and bid the two farewell, heading for the temporary training room they'd set up on the first floor. She passed Xeda on her way as he bustled about collecting everyone's dirty laundry.

"Weren't you on laundry duty last week, Xeda?" she asked.

"I volunteered to take it again," Xeda explained. "There's enough going on without us all squabbling over chores."

Shaila smiled. "Wise man."

Miika was kneeling next to a large trunk when Shaila walked into the training room. He took two practice knives from the trunk, kicked the lid shut, and walked over to give one knife to Shaila who accepted with a smile.

"It's about time I get a rematch," Miika said.

"No club this time," Shaila said sternly.

Miika smiled wickedly. "No club, but that's all the promise I'll make."

They bowed to each other then waited, each wondering who would strike first. Shaila wasn't at all surprised when Miika lost his patience and rushed in. She blocked his quick strikes effortlessly before rolling in close and tapping him in the stomach with her knife.

"You lean too far forward when you strike," she said. "It leaves you open to sudden, close attacks. The more upright you stay, the more your opponent will underestimate your reach."

Miika nodded and fell back into his stance. This time, Shaila attacked first, coming in low and quick at first then shifting up higher, searching for a weakness in Miika's form. His defensive moves were much better than his offensive ones—as if the ward spent more time defending himself in training than throwing blows of his own. After a time, she noticed a flaw in his footwork and exploited it to kick him in the shin and followed up with a blow to the face that would have broken his nose if she'd allowed it.

"You are a curiosity," Miika said as he waited for her next move.

"How so?"

"Your Master shows a devotion to you I've never seen before. What is it about you that makes him so... loyal?"

Miika followed with a fast strike she barely had time to block. Was he merely trying to distract her with riddles, or did he suspect something? He smacked her on the shoulder with his knife and smiled in victory.

"Wards show loyalty to their Masters, not the other way around," Shaila replied. She moved to the side to strike left then spun to the right instead and stomped on Miika's foot then clocked him in the ear with her hand. He fell back, hissing.

"I believed that as well," he said. "Until your Master showed me how displeased he was after your proving."

"What do you mean?"

Miika pointed to the gap in his teeth.

"Master Drauses did that?" she asked in disbelief.

"He did." Miika lunged in close, aiming his blade at her stomach, but she blocked it and spun her arm around his to strike close to his chest. He grabbed her wrist to stop her blow, but she struck with her left hand instead. He surprised her by blocking that blow as well.

Miika smiled. "I know Aro's left-handed tricks," he said. He looped his leg around the back of her knee, and with a jerk of his hip and a shove of his arm, he pushed her off balance, and she landed hard on her back on the floor.

She laid stunned on her back for a moment, then she laughed. "You must teach me that!" She jumped back to her feet. "Do it again."

Miika brought Shaila here to try again to end her life. Since the night of the funeral fires, he'd had several opportunities, but he always fell back at the last second, unable to fulfill his Master's orders. He kept trying anyway; he had to. There was a knife in the pocket of his pants, a real one, sharp and ready to cut her down if he got the chance... but he was enjoying himself, enjoying her company. She treated him as an equal, not something to be feared as so many did, not as a whelp like his Master often called him, but her peer, her brother-in-arms.

The Odas save him, he liked her.

He showed her the move in slow motion, and she mirrored him until she executed it flawlessly. Then he showed her how to block the move if anyone ever used it on her in future. She was a fast learner and even offered her own suggestions that made the move more reliable and harder to block. When they were done, she grew suddenly serious.

"Is Master Gragern not loyal to you, Miika?" she asked.

Miika frowned and glanced around the empty training room. Words uttered in private traveled back to his Liege far too often.

"What do you mean?" he asked cautiously.

Shaila came closer, dangerously close. "If Master Gragern isn't fulfilling his duties to you, something should be done."

Miika reached in his pocket to finger the knife he could draw if she came one step closer. "What duties? A ward doesn't make demands of his Master. A ward obeys and accepts that which he cannot change."

Shaila took that last step toward him and touched his shoulder. Now was his time to strike; it was the perfect moment.

"You're wrong, friend," she said, looking him deep in the eyes. "If Master Gragern isn't loyal to you, you should place your own loyalties somewhere else. Never let anyone use you, Miika. It'll poison you from within. Trust me, I know."

Miika didn't draw his knife.

Shaila backed away and beckoned him to attack her again. He considered refusing, for he was no longer in the mood for company having failed yet again to do his Master's bidding, but then she smiled at him. There was no judgment in her eyes, only expectation and patience. So he did as she bid and attacked anew. They went on training together for over an hour, and she had him laughing by the end with tales of her many failures in her early days of training. They were both soaked with sweat and breathless when she held up her hand in defeat.

"You asked for a challenge," she said between gasps, "but I fear I don't yet have your stamina." With her hands on her legs, she bent over double in exhaustion. In truth, Miika harbored a throbbing stitch in his side, but his own stubbornness made him wait her out to see how far she could go. He was impressed but would never tell her so.

"You did alright," he said with a casual shrug.

She gave him back her practice knife. "Thank you for the sparring. I needed the distraction."

Miika bowed his head, and Shaila made to take her leave but stopped at the door when he called her name.

"Perhaps you could do with more distraction tomorrow," he said.

"Same time? You can show me that move you used to best me during your proving."

Shaila smiled and nodded. "Tomorrow then."

Miika polished the practice knives with a rag before returning them to their trunk, smiling like a fool all the while. Training with the Lady of the Mark was the most enjoyable thing he'd done in nearly a full season. He'd all but forgotten the assignment his Master had given him.

Miika had just closed the lid to the trunk when he heard footsteps behind him. He thought Shaila had returned, but his mood instantly soured when he looked to see his Master instead. The Elder shut the door to the training room behind him when he came in. Miika's shoulders sank.

"Did you enjoy your sparring?" Gragern asked with narrowed eyes.

"I'm merely getting to know her fighting style so I—"

"I care not to hear your excuses, whelp."

"I'm sorry, Master Gragern."

Gragern merely stared at Miika, his lip twitching as he chewed it. The silence stretched on until Miika found it nearly unbearable.

"Get out a pair of practice swords," Gragern snapped.

Miika nodded solemnly then did as his Master bid.

Chapter 12

SHAILA WAS QUIET that evening. She was sitting at the kitchen counter, absentmindedly fiddling with one of Amii's paper animals, when Aro came to her.

"Is something amiss?" he asked. "You look troubled."

"Apologies," she said, and she managed a half-hearted smile. "I know I'm sour company tonight."

"Is it to do with Amii?"

"No."

"Are you worried for Master Drauses?"

"No… well, yes always, but no more so than before. Don't fret, Aro, it's nothing of concern."

"Can I help?"

Shaila chewed her cheek for a moment, then regarded him anew with fresh purpose. "Do you know if the guild's codes say anything regarding Masters mistreating their wards?"

"How do you mean 'mistreat'?" Aro asked.

"I can't give specifics. I don't know them myself."

"Well, usually if a ward has a grievance against his Master, he takes it to the Liege who decides what action should be taken, if any."

Shaila's shoulders slumped in defeat. "I was afraid you'd say that."

"You don't want to involve Master Gragern?"

"Is there a way?" she asked hopefully.

"I don't believe so," Aro replied. "What's this about? Has Master Drauses—"

"Gods no! I'm not the one with a grievance."

"Who then?"

Shaila shook her head. "I can't tell you."

"Don't you trust me?" He looked a bit hurt.

"Of course I trust you, Aro. I'd never leave you alone with Amii otherwise. But I want this person to trust *me*, and so I need to be the kind of person they can trust. This isn't my secret to tell."

Aro nodded in understanding. "I'll help however I can. You need only ask."

Shaila sighed. "With our Masters away, it's likely best if we stay clear of it altogether."

Aro grinned as he leaned against the counter next to her. "Why do I get the feeling you've no intention of staying clear of it at all?"

Shaila laughed. "Perhaps you've spent too much time with me as of late."

Amii came to beg Aro to build a house of cards with her. He put up no fight and went to her bidding with a smile, leaving Shaila to fret alone.

⟡

The next day, Shaila went down to the training room as she and Miika planned, but he never showed. She lingered for thirty minutes with no sign of him before she crossed the hall and knocked on the Liege's door. No one answered. She gave up and was halfway up the stairs to the second floor when the front door opened in the foyer below and Miika strolled in. She smiled in welcome until she got a better look at his face. He was bruised again, worse this time, with his hand set in a crude splint and his arm hugged close to his chest as he walked, nursing bruised or broken ribs, she guessed. At the sight of her, he turned on his heels and marched right back outside.

Shaila followed him. "Miika?" she called.

He stopped and slowly turned to face her. One eye was blackened, the other swollen under a split brow. One cheek was deep purple next to a split in his upper lip.

"Gods, Miika, what happened to you?"

"It's none of your concern," he snapped.

"Master Gragern did this, didn't he?"

Miika stomped over, took her by the elbow, and marched her down a nearby alley. "Shut your mouth!" he fumed. "Do you want to make matters worse for me?"

"I can help you if you just—"

"We're not friends! You'd do well to stay away from me."

Shaila reached to touch his shoulder, and Miika flinched away. His reaction said more than his words, and Shaila understood. Someone had abused him and his trust time and time again.

"I consider you *my* friend, Miika," Shaila declared. "I'm asking my *friend* to talk to me straight. If your Master is abusive, something should be done."

"Let me worry about my own Master. He says I'll have leave of him soon anyway. I've one assignment left, and I'll finally be a Master."

"Can I help?"

Miika laughed humorlessly, then winced and clutched his side. He turned his back on Shaila and stood staring down the alley. She debated leaving him alone but decided that wasn't what he needed right now. Instead, she laid her hand softly on his shoulder. He didn't flinch this time, merely looked down at her hand for a moment before staring back off into empty space.

"Whatever's happening in your life," she said, "if you ever wish for help, you only have to ask. I'll do all I can for you."

"I appreciate the sentiment, *friend*, but this is my burden. My choice."

"I know you'll make the right one. Whatever your Master has asked of you, it can't be as hard as living this way another day. If your reward is freedom, then do it and do it fast. Then you'll be a Master. Maybe you'll train the next Lady of the Mark," she added with a smile.

"Odavail forbid! One of you is enough." Miika sighed, then coughed and winced again.

"Come along," Shaila said sternly, and she took Miika by the arm.

"Where are we going?" he asked, refusing to budge.

"Do you trust me?"

The look on Miika's face was a mix of indecision, calculation, and perhaps even a little fear. He studied her for a long moment, his eyes flicking back and forth between hers until he finally answered. "Yes," he said in a voice so quiet Shaila barely heard him.

She tugged his arm again. "Then come along and let me tend to you."

"Yes, ma'am," he said with a smirk.

They walked back inside and up the stairs to her apartment. She ushered him in then shut and locked the door behind her.

"Take off your shirt," she ordered.

"Shouldn't we have dinner first? You've not even kissed me yet."

"Enough with your smart mouth. Just do it."

He untied his robes and laid them on the counter then groaned as he lifted his arms above his head to pull off his shirt. His shoulders were wide and thick, but his waist and hips were narrow. He was every bit as tone and fit as Drauses though he lacked most of the scars. A hideous bruise stretched across his lower ribs.

Shaila pushed him into a chair and knelt on the floor at his side. A burn scar above his left breast caught her eye. It was two identical, capital Ms, each constructed with four crudely drawn, interlacing swords.

"What's this?" she asked.

"A wasted hope from a foolish youth."

Shaila brought her hands up to his chest and almost touched him before she remembered he wasn't Drauses and she shouldn't take liberties without his permission. She paused, waiting for an invitation.

"Oh, to Vedia with you," he spat. "Do it already."

Shaila rolled her eyes as she started probing his ribs with her fingers. She was quick and as careful as she could be as she slid her thumb up each of his ribs. "I think these are just bruised. Possibly a crack or two."

"Oh, joy for me."

Shaila went into her bedroom and came back with her medicine kit. She took Miika's hand and unwrapped the haphazard splint, clicking her tongue in disapproval at the sight of his two swollen, purple fingers.

"This one isn't set properly," she said. "It needs to be adjusted."

"Do it."

"Are you sure you wouldn't rather see Boon for this?"

"Either *you* do it, since you feel like playing caregiver, or I'll leave it to heal as it wishes."

"Fine," she said with a shrug. "Are you ready?"

Miika picked his shirt up out of his lap and stuffed the sleeve in his mouth. He nodded.

Shaila held firm to his hand, and with one hard tug, she popped the crooked finger back into place. Miika screamed into the fabric of his shirt with a stomp of his foot then yanked the cloth from his mouth and threw it across the room. Shaila fastened a better splint around his fingers and wrapped them securely this time.

"Thanks, doc," Miika said a bit breathlessly. He got to his feet and gathered his clothes, avoiding her eyes.

"Will you be alright?" she asked.

"I've made it this far."

Miika struggled to lift his arms enough to put his shirt back on, so Shaila helped him. When he was clothed, his face was but inches from hers, and she looked into his eyes, studying the green pools with a slight tilt of her head. The color enchanted her: a swirl of blues and greens with an occasional speck of brown. They flicked back and forth between her own.

He pulled away. "I meant what I said. You should stay away from me."

"Well, since you obviously disregard your own well-being, it falls to me to see to it for you," Shaila declared. "That's how friendship works, you know."

"So... we're friends?"

"Are we?"

"I suppose," he conceded. "Master Drauses will kill me regardless, so it makes little difference what title we give it." He went to the door, unlocked it, and peered up and down the hall, then, all at once, he looked back at Shaila, spun on his heels, and came back to her. With no warning and before she could utter a single protest, he yanked her close and kissed her hard on the lips.

First came paralyzing shock, then her heart began to hammer in her chest. The thought of Drauses turned her stomach to ice, and she made to take a step back, but Miika released her before she could make her feet obey. He held her at arms' length, and for a moment, he looked… panicked, desperate. It scared her.

"Stay away from me," he ordered. "Please." And then he left, leaving Shaila stunned and shaking with a hand over her mouth.

"Shaila?" Aro called from the hall.

"Here," she said, but her voice cracked, so she tried again. "I'm here, Aro."

Aro came around the corner and peered in through the door Miika left open as he fled. Aro looked back over his shoulder toward the stairs then again at Shaila's pale face.

"What happened?" he asked.

"I was… helping Miika set a broken finger."

"He looked rough," Aro said with a nod. "Is that *all* he wanted?"

Shaila raised a brow. "Come again?"

"It's just that you've been spending a lot of time with him."

"Is that a problem?"

"Not at all," Aro rushed to say. "I thought… well, I thought you and Master Drauses…"

Shaila's stomach turned to ice yet again. "What are you saying?"

Aro shifted on his feet, avoiding her eyes. "I thought the two of you were involved."

Shaila crossed her arms as she struggled not to show the truth on her face. "Why on Earth would you think that? Masters and wards aren't allowed to be intimate."

"You think every Master and ward follows all the rules?" Aro asked with a slight smile. "Our codes are strict, Shaila, and no one's perfect. We give ourselves to our Masters, eat, sleep, and breathe their guidance and praise. In return, they devote themselves to us just as fully. We can't help but love them, each in our own way. I daresay plenty of Masters and wards have gone to bed together over the years as a result."

Shaila shook her head. "Drauses isn't like that. He—"

"*Master* Drauses," Aro said with a grin. Shaila's shoulders slumped, and Aro read the worry on her face. "You can trust me," he insisted.

Shaila sighed and leaned against her kitchen counter. "Are we that obvious?" she asked miserably.

Aro shook his head. "I'm around more than most, so I see the little things. Fret not. Your secret is safe with me."

"Why?" Shaila asked with a curious tilt of her head. "We're breaking the laws of the guild. Why would you turn a blind eye to such a thing?" She studied him. "Are you and Master Dagon..."

"No. I do love him, but more like a father."

Shaila smiled, her anxiety melting away. Aro was a true friend.

Aro cleared his throat. "So, is Miika the ward? The one you asked about last night?"

"Aro, please. I can't."

"I understand. But if it *is* Miika, I beg you to tread lightly. He has a reputation, and his Master—Oh, gods." Aro's eyes widened as he realized the full gravity of the situation. "The Liege..."

"I'll be careful. I promise."

Aro nodded and peered back out into the hall. "I must get back to Amii. Will you join us?"

"In a bit." Shaila shoved away from the counter with a look of determination. "I was promised some training, and I aim to collect."

"I doubt Miika is in any shape for sparring."

"Our enemies won't slow for injury. Neither should we."

19ᵗʰ of Autumn, Jesparia's 9ᵗʰ and 20 year of Rovik

Miika dug out the bottle of Sazeen from his meager store of personal effects. The bottles were highly sought and mostly extinct, but he'd found one, by Lady Fate's good grace, and had hidden it away years ago. He hunted down a deck of cards then headed upstairs. Drauses had been gone for weeks, so there was nothing stopping Miika from spending an evening with the Lady of the Mark.

When Shaila dragged him to her quarters and insisted on tending to him, she'd shown him the first shred of care he'd known since he was a child. Over the next week or so, she came around every day and insisted they train together despite his injuries. He thought the kiss would ward her off for good considering the feelings he suspected she had for her

Master, but it didn't. If anything, it had made her all the more determined to get closer to him—a dangerous notion for them both. She wanted him to call her a friend, but he'd never had one before. Was it trust that grew a friendship? He didn't know how to trust. He wasn't even sure *she* could trust *him*. How can you call someone a friend while secretly planning to kill them?

Miika laughed humorlessly to himself as he climbed the stairs. What a mess he was in. All he knew for certain was he'd left all his weapons in his quarters tonight. Perhaps that showed a sense of trust, for all it was worth. He knocked on Drauses' door, trying not to imagine what the Master would do if he found Miika anywhere near his quarters. Aro answered, blade in hand. Miika smiled as he pushed the door open, ignoring Aro's questions. Shaila stood by the kitchen counter with a look of stunned surprise at the sight of him.

"Good evening," Miika greeted.

"Miika," Shaila said with a nod.

"I brought cards and whiskey." Miika lifted both for her viewing. "I thought I could whip you at a game of Suits as well as I did in training this morning."

"You didn't beat me in training. We were evenly matched, sir, and I can hold my own at cards as well."

Miika shrugged. "Then you've nothing to fear."

Amii bounded into the room. She spotted the cards in Miika's hand. "Ooo, games?" she asked with excitement. "Can I join you?"

"Of course," Miika said.

Once Amii was promised games, any and all arguments were squashed, as she would have it no other way. They dragged Drauses' square dining table to the center of the living room and set a chair at each side.

"Aro, join us?" Shaila asked.

"I'm supposed to keep guard."

"What could happen with the three of us in the same room?" Miika asked. "Surely six eyes are enough for you to relax a little."

After a moment's consideration, Aro sank into a chair, and Amii grinned like a fool as she took the seat to his right.

"Can we play Jests?" Amii asked.

Miika sat across from her. "That's a child's game."

"One game for the girl," Aro said. "Unless you're afraid she'll best you."

Shaila sat across from Aro, took the cards from Miika, and dealt for a game of Jests. Having been outvoted, Miika conceded with a shrug, and damned if the twelve-year-old didn't indeed beat them all at the game, giving Miika a wide smirk as she played her last card.

"Again?" she asked.

"We're moving on to Suits, Amii," said Shaila. "Do you know the rules?"

"Some. But I've only played it once before."

Miika dealt, and the game began with Shaila checking Amii's cards to give suggestions until she caught on to the rules. Aro bested them in the first round, but Miika won the next two. Shaila sat quietly observing her cards then stomped them all for the next three rounds and won the first game. As she dealt the next set of hands, Miika cracked open the bottle of Sazeen. Aro eyed it longingly as the seal popped. Miika put his nose above the bottle and breathed deep of its sweet scent. He got up from the table and searched Drauses' kitchen cupboards for glasses.

"Aro, are you indulging?" Miika asked.

Aro glanced at the open Sazeen on the table then at Miika who stood waiting with his hand on a glass. After a pause, Aro nodded, and Miika came back with three glasses.

"Who says *I'll* be drinking the stuff?" Shaila asked.

"I say," Miika said, and he poured three full glasses of whiskey and set them around the table.

Amii eyed Aro's glass with curiosity. She reached for it, but Aro slapped her hand away.

"Just a taste?" the girl pleaded.

"No," Aro said firmly.

Miika slid his glass across the table, and Amii grinned as she picked it up. Miika jumped with a yelp of pain when something struck his shin hard enough to make his toes tingle. He eyed Shaila with a raised brow then laughed.

"By the Odas above, woman, you're brutal," he said, rubbing his abused leg. "She's in no danger from a single sip."

Amii raised the glass to her nose and sniffed. She took the smallest of drinks, made a face, and coughed as the whiskey burned down her throat.

"That's vile," she croaked, shoving the glass back at Miika.

"Curiosity kills," Aro replied, and he took a large gulp from his glass as Amii watched with a horrified curl of her lip.

The game continued with Shaila winning the first round before Amii surprised them by taking two in a row. She came close to winning until Miika came up in points in the last few rounds and stole the victory. As they set up for a third game, Miika poured his third glass of whiskey, and he was starting to feel its effects. Aro matched him drink for drink and pushed his glass over for more as well. Shaila had only just emptied her first glass. Miika refilled it despite her protests.

Soon the cards lay strewn across the table, forgotten, as conversation won out and the glasses drained faster. Aro told the tale of how he met Master Dagon which involved four near-naked, slightly intoxicated young men who were bored beyond good sense, a wager, a footrace, a swim in the cold winter Jespa waters, and a wrestling match with a live pig coated in cooking oil. The whole scene was unknowingly watched from a distance by Dagon who approached the winner of the wager, their very own Aro, and offered to make him a ward—provided he promptly dress himself.

Chapter 13

ARO FELL ASLEEP in his chair, his head lulling to one side as he snored. Shaila shooed Amii off to bed as well when the girl started to yawn. Miika sat fiddling with a card, flipping it over and over in his fingers until, suddenly, he flung his arms out and gathered them all into a pile. He re-stacked the deck, shuffled it, and fanned the cards out in front of Shaila.

"Pick one," he said.

Shaila was happy to see Miika enjoying himself. He seemed so relaxed and carefree, not at all like the man she'd met weeks ago. Now and then, during their hours spent training, she caught glimpses of this person through cracks in an otherwise perfect shell of indifference and self-preservation. It seemed he'd left his armor behind tonight, and she wondered why he didn't let others see this side of himself more often.

She smiled and humored him, drawing a card at random.

"Don't tell me what it is. Stick it back in the deck."

She slid it back into the middle of the stack, and Miika cut and shuffled the cards several times. He smiled wickedly and held the deck out to her, face down on his palm.

"Put your hand over the cards but don't touch them. Close your eyes. Think about your card. Picture it. Do you see it?"

"I see my foot in your backside if you don't get on with it."

"Draw the top card," he instructed. "Is it the one you chose at the start?"

"Nope," she replied with a grin.

"No? Hmm, pity." He took the next card off the pile. "How about this one?"

Shaila chuckled. "Perhaps you should practice this trick some more before attempting to impress with it in future."

"You may be right. But first, check your pocket."

"My *pocket*?" she asked, and she laughed again.

"Just check your damned pocket, woman," Miika said with an exasperated sigh.

Shaila did as he asked, and her eyes widened. She sat in stunned awe as she plucked her drawn card from her robes.

"Is *that* your card?" Miika asked with a smile, then he laughed at the look on her face. He leaned over and snatched the card from her fingers. "Let us see which card Fate dealt the lady, shall we?" He flipped it over and laughed even harder. "The queen of hearts. How fitting!"

Shaila grew sullen. To hide it, she took his injured hand in both of hers. Without asking, she unwrapped his broken fingers with care and gently pinched each one to feel the bones. Satisfied everything was healing correctly, she replaced the splint and wrapped it anew, but when she let him go, Miika grabbed her hand before she could pull it away. He traced the lines on her palm with his two good fingers.

"You're very beautiful," he said.

Shaila snorted. "I know." She pulled her hand away, sullen once more.

Miika frowned. "You accept the compliment without argument; one might think you were conceited if it weren't for the disgusted look on your face."

"Is there a question in there somewhere?"

"Why does being beautiful upset you?"

"That's quite a personal question."

"Come now, *friend*. You want me to talk straight with you. Shouldn't you offer me the same?"

Shaila played with her glass, swirling the amber liquid inside around and around. It reminded her of Rovik, so she set it back down on the table without taking a drink. "I'd be happy with half as much beauty and would gladly give the rest to another woman eager to have it."

"So, you wish to be beautiful, just not *as* beautiful? What twisted notion is that?"

"A woman too beautiful is often judged by her beauty over other qualities," she explained, though she knew he wouldn't understand. "She can never know for sure if her friends prefer her good company, her wit, her skills, or if they just like staring at a handsome face."

"Can't they all be mixed in equal portions?"

Shaila shrugged and drained the last of her drink. "I don't know," she said with a sigh. "I've often wondered if Master Drauses would still have offered to take me as his ward if I'd been of average looks or less. Perhaps he would've left me to rot in Rovik's bed if I'd been homely."

Miika choked on his drink. "You laid with Rovik?" he asked between coughing sprees.

Shaila narrowed her eyes. "Not willingly."

Silence fell between them during which their eyes would meet for the briefest of heartbeats then dart away. After a moment, Shaila cleared her throat.

"Alright," she said with new determination. "I answered your questions. Will you answer some of mine?"

"I suppose that'd be the fair thing to do since we're *friends* now," Miika grumbled.

Shaila started with something simple, yet still personal. "Do you have any family?"

"I have a father somewhere, but he may be dead for all I know."

"You've never tried to find him?"

"I've no desire to know him. He abandoned mother and me when I was a babe. All he left me were his eyes, or so my mother used to say."

"They are quite striking eyes," she said with a kind smile.

Miika merely shrugged at the compliment.

"Do you know his name?"

"Vernan."

"And your mother?"

"Her name was Minista, and she died years ago."

"Anyone else?"

"A hot-blooded aunt, my mother's older sister. She never liked me much though. After my mother died, I struck out on my own as soon as I was able. I don't know what became of her either."

Shaila could tell that subject was a sore one, so she moved on. Her next topic was no less invasive, however. "How long has Master Gragern been beating you, Miika?"

Miika looked over at Aro who was still snoring away, dead asleep. Miika drained his drink then took Aro's still half-filled glass before he answered.

"There was never a time when he didn't," Miika admitted. "Things have been this way for me since I became his ward, since the very beginning."

"How long ago was that?"

Miika hesitated. "Ten years," he said, staring down at his glass.

Shaila's mouth fell open. "Ten years?"

"Must you say it like that?"

"I mean no offense, Miika. I just... To endure this way for *ten years*..." She shook her head, lost for words.

"It fit the pattern of my life. It was no shock at all to me when it happened the first time. I thought at first this was the way of every ward and Master. It was a time before I realized that wasn't true, that I was the only one punished this way. Nevertheless, I accepted it as the hand Lady Fate dealt me. I've had worse."

Shaila leaned forward and took his hand in hers. "You deserve better. Please, let's speak to Master Drauses about this."

"Master Drauses doesn't care for me. Especially since your proving."

"Damn you men!" Shaila spat. Aro snorted once at her sudden outburst. "When will you all put that behind you? Isn't it obvious I've forgiven you? Truthfully, I harbored no grudge from the start so there was nothing to forgive. I'm sick of hearing about it."

"I doubt your Master will ever be that forgiving."

Shaila sighed in exasperation. "Even so, he won't turn his back on this. He's not the kind to let injustices continue under his nose, and this is an injustice of the highest degree. You know it is."

Miika regarded her warily, then he drained Aro's glass and let out a long breath of defeat.

"Alright," he conceded. "Let's talk to him then, if you truly think it'll make a difference."

"What have you got to lose at this point?"

Miika winced but didn't reply.

She gave him a reassuring smile, and his eyes roamed her face for a silent moment, landing at last on her mouth where they lingered. Her smile slipped a little, and he shook himself, breaking his stare.

"I should go," he said suddenly. He got up from his chair and staggered, grabbing the kitchen counter to keep from falling over. Shaila leapt up and wrapped an arm around his waist.

"You're not walking downstairs like this," she said. "Sleep here tonight."

Miika laughed. "Sleeping in the notorious Master Drauses' quarters? Ha! What a privilege. I'm better suited downstairs with the other commoners." He pushed away and made a step or two toward the door but stumbled again. Shaila came and took his arm, draping it over her shoulders.

"Come along, commoner. To bed with you."

Miika let her march him to the bedroom. At the very least, she could give him one night of rest, free of his Master. She cringed at what Drauses would say to Miika sleeping in his bed, but what he didn't know wouldn't hurt him. She yanked Miika's robes off, then his shirt, and pushed him down to sit on the bed. The sight of the odd burn on his chest dug up her curiosity.

"Miika, tell me about this symbol on your chest. Did you do this yourself?"

"A persistent, stubborn thing aren't you?" he barked. He collapsed on his back across the bed with a deep sigh. "It's a symbol I found amongst Gragern's notes years ago, shortly after I became his ward. Our Masters of old burned it on their cheeks when they joined the guild."

"This is The Mark?"

"I altered it a bit. The original was just letters. I drew mine in swords with a nail I heated over a flame until it glowed. I had to do it in a mirror, so it's... it wasn't meant to be seen by others."

"Then why do it at all?"

Miika stared up at Shaila with the most feeling she'd ever seen in his deep green eyes, no doubt unleashed by the copious amounts of whiskey in his blood.

"For me," he confessed. "To remind myself I wasn't alone anymore. I was a naïve youth and hadn't been shown the extent of Gragern's malice." Miika snorted in humorless laughter then scowled. "I thought I'd found friends."

Shaila sat beside him. "You have friends now. You're not alone. No longer and never again."

Miika reached for her hair in a daze. He touched the locks softly, staring at the strands in wonder as they ran through his fingers as if he'd never seen anything like it before.

"You'll be the death of me," he murmured, then his arm dropped to his side, and his eyes closed. Seconds later, he began to snore.

Shaila continued to stare at The Mark on Miika's chest for a long time with a sinking sadness in her gut for the youth who was once so full of hope to burn it there. She reached out to touch it but changed her mind. She left him sprawled across the bed and went to sleep in Amii's room for the night.

Drauses entered the apartment building as the sun began to rise. He, Dagon, and two other Masters had traveled through the night to be back at the building by dawn. The work at The Yard had gone far more smoothly than anticipated, so much so that they decided it was time to bring in Julta so he could begin working on the things only he could install, like running water. Drauses insisted on coming back as well, claiming he wished to personally oversee Julta's transfer to The Yard. In truth, he ached for Shaila in the worst way. He could bear it no longer and cared not a bit what the Liege would say about his return. He hurried up the stairs to the third floor, determined to make up for lost time with her that very morning before the others woke.

Drauses let himself into his apartment and froze in his tracks. His table was in the middle of the room strewn with cards, glasses, and an empty whiskey bottle. Aro sat in a chair at the table, slumped to the side and snoring. Where were Amii and Shaila? He stomped across the room and shook Aro roughly by the shoulder. The ward slowly stirred and blinked up.

"Master Drauses?" he muttered.

"What happened here?" Drauses fumed.

Aro winced at the Master's raised voice. "Miika brought cards and Sazeen last—"

"Miika?" Drauses thundered. Aro's eyes widened as he realized he'd made a grave mistake. Drauses flew down the hall and into Amii's room only to find her asleep in bed and perfectly safe. As he marched further down the hall, he could hear shuffling in the bathroom, but his bedroom door came first. He peered inside, expecting to find it empty. His blood turned to ice at what he found instead.

Clothing littered the floor, and Miika lay sprawled across Drauses' bed wearing nothing but pants, the covers and sheets a rumpled mess beneath him. It was obvious what had happened here while Drauses was away. Shaila must be in the bathroom, cleaning away a night spent in Miika's arms. Drauses stormed into the room. His heavy footsteps woke Miika who quickly realized the danger he was in and scrambled to get to his feet. Drauses was faster.

Drauses grabbed Miika by the back of the neck and flung him face-first into the nearest wall. Miika broke his fall with an already injured hand, and the fingers hit hard, making him cry out in pain. He spun to face the Master and blocked the first couple of blows, but Drauses soon broke his defenses. He punched Miika square in the nose. Drauses set his arm over the ward's throat, cutting off his air. As Miika gasped for breath, Drauses took his splinted hand and slammed it against the wall, breaking the bones anew. Miika choked with fresh pain under Drauses' arm, his feet skidding across the floor and his nails scraping at Drauses' sleeve.

"I told you I'd kill you," Drauses sneered, and he pressed harder.

Suddenly, there was an arm around Drauses' own throat. A blow to the back of his knees buckled his legs, and a powerful yank threw him backward. He tumbled hard across the floor then looked up in time to watch as Shaila helped Miika up from the floor, pinching the ward's nose in her sleeve to stem the bleeding and fussing over him as a lover would. Drauses' chest tightened in heartbreak. So she'd chosen Miika after all. He got to his feet, and Shaila rounded on him.

"What in Vedia is the matter with you?" she screamed.

"I was going to ask you the same! You couldn't take your lover to your own quarters? You had to carry on this way behind my back and *in my bed*?"

"I slept in Amii's room last night, you ignorant ass!"

Miika moved for the door, but Shaila grabbed him by the elbow.

"Where do you think *you're* going?" she asked.

"I'm leaving," Miika sneered. "This was a bad idea."

Shaila hauled him back toward the bed.

"Sit and stay!" she commanded with a finger in his face.

He wiped the blood from his nose with his good hand and sat.

Next, Shaila took a handful of Drauses' robes and yanked him out the door then shoved him ahead of her down the hall. Aro stood in the living room looking sheepish.

"Wait outside," Shaila barked, and he rushed to do as she asked. As soon as the door closed behind him, she turned again on her Master. "And you... Do you have *any* idea what you've done?"

"I found Miika half-dressed in the bed we share," Drauses defended in a heated whisper. "What was I supposed to think?"

"You're supposed to have more faith in me than that," she shot back. Her face was flushed, and her balled fists said he was not yet safe from a blow or two. "He came to play cards last night. He stayed because he was staggering with whiskey, and I refused to let him die falling down the stairs. I finally convinced him to seek your help, and you've likely ruined it all!"

Drauses cocked his head, his anger slipping away to confusion and curiosity. "Seek my help? With what?"

Shaila crossed her arms with a huff.

"Tell me, please."

"Miika's in trouble, and he's refused to tell a soul about it or let anyone help him. Just as I convince him he can trust *you*, you barge in and try to kill him on sight!"

Drauses ran his hands through his hair. "I'm sorry if I've—"

"Sorry? *If?* You better be a great deal more than sorry, Drauses. I'm so furious with you, I could just—" He reached for her hand, but she yanked it out of reach and backed away. "Don't touch me! Not until you put this right!"

"Alright, alright." Drauses pulled up a chair at the table, pushing aside cards and empty glasses as he sat. "Sit down. Start at the beginning."

Shaila sat, but it took her several minutes to calm down enough to tell the tale. "Miika has been suffering for years, right under the guild's nose."

"Suffering how? Is he ill?"

She shook her head. "Drauses, Gragern's been beating Miika for years, abusing him disgracefully whenever the ward displeases him in the slightest. I've seen the wounds myself: cuts, bruises, and broken bones."

Drauses' first instinct was complete disbelief. Miika was sneaky, mischievous, and a known liar when it suited him, but the look on Shaila's face said she believed every word. She was smart enough not to fall for an ill-conceived ruse.

"And Miika admitted these injuries came from his Master?" Drauses asked carefully.

"At first his loyalty held his tongue. But I pressed him and got the truth. I already had my suspicions—"

"And she was a right pain in the backside," Miika interjected from across the room. He'd gotten his nose to stop bleeding and was fully dressed. "She nagged me ruthlessly until I gave it up and told her everything."

"You would've suffered in silence, the Odas only know for how long, if I hadn't intervened," Shaila said.

She rose, walked to the bedroom, and returned with Drauses' medicine kit. She motioned Miika into the chair beside her, and when he sat, he stuck his hand out to her without being asked. She took off the ruined pieces of splint and growled at the sight of his newly battered fingers. She threw Drauses a furious glare.

Drauses stood and went to the kitchen. He reached to the top shelf of a corner cupboard and fished out a bottle of whiskey hidden behind some dishes. He set it on the table in front of Miika.

"Thanks," Miika said. He took several large swigs straight from the bottle before nodding for Shaila to continue.

Shaila popped the first finger into place, and Miika pounded the tabletop with a fist but managed not to scream. More whiskey poured down his throat before he nodded again. When the second finger cracked, Miika jumped from his seat and kicked the chair across the floor, howling in pain and rage. Shaila retrieved the chair, set it in place, and shoved Miika back into it. She used Drauses' kit to make a new splint then bandaged Miika's fingers as he chugged spirits and belched.

"Pardon," he muttered.

"You realize the gravity of these charges, yes?" Drauses asked.

"I do."

"Why haven't you sought help before?"

"If I'd come to you with this grievance years ago without Shaila to vouch for me, would you have believed me?" When Drauses didn't answer, Miika nodded. "I thought not. Besides, we're not supposed to speak against our Masters. Was I supposed to run to you like a whelp?"

"This is a serious infraction, Miika," Drauses said with a finger to the tabletop. "Wards have rules, but so do Masters. We're not allowed to hurt for cruelty's sake. If this is true—"

"*If?*" Shaila raged.

Miika stopped her rant before it started with a raised hand. "There's more. Over the years, Master Gragern has entrusted me with many assignments of… a delicate nature. I won't speak on most of them, they don't concern you, but I'll tell you those that do. The first was Shaila's proving. I drew a weapon because my Master made it clear I was to win the fight by any means necessary. He wished Master Drauses' ward thrown from the guild, and he left it to me to accomplish such, our codes be damned."

Drauses was struck by a pang of fresh guilt. He'd attacked Miika after the proving. The thought that Gragern had forced his ward to do such a thing was hard to believe, but it explained why the Elder allowed the fight to continue.

"Most recently…" Miika hesitated and hung his head. "He promised to make me a Master at last… if I…"

"What did Gragern want, Miika?" Drauses asked, his gut already sinking in dread.

Miika stared at Shaila with pain in his eyes. "Your life."

Shaila gasped and looked at Drauses who towered over Miika. He leaned on one hand across the table to get in the ward's face.

"Don't you dare entertain that notion for a single second," Drauses spat.

"I hated it from the start," Miika rushed to explain. "But I told myself the Liege must have his reasons. He's asked me to do questionable things before which ended in the right. But this… After the proving, I suspected his reasons were no longer noble."

Shaila rose from the table and walked a short distance away.

"Shaila, I swear, I couldn't do it." Miika tried to get up to go to her, but Drauses put a hand on his shoulder and shoved him back into his chair. "That's why I confided in you. I wish you no harm."

"Are there others coming after me?" Shaila asked.

"He's always left his foul whims to me, but there's no knowing for sure if he made other plans."

Shaila nodded, her face set with determination. "I have to leave."

"No!" Drauses and Miika exclaimed in unison.

"Temporarily," Shaila continued. "Until we know for sure how deep this order goes. I'm a danger to Amii with a target on my back."

"You're not going anywhere," Drauses declared.

"I could go with her," Miika offered. "I could take both girls away and keep them safe until you—"

"No," Drauses barked. He shook his head and rubbed the bridge of his nose. "What a mess."

"I'm sorry," Miika said. He took another long drink of whiskey.

"Why does the Liege want Shaila dead?" Drauses asked.

"He told me he believed Shaila was feeding information back to Rovik," Miika said. "He blamed her for the Black Blades' attack on the factory."

"That's ridiculous," Shaila said. "What reasons did he give to suspect me?"

"Something about Western contacts he chose not to utilize. He tried to convince me you were sending messages to spies in Rovik's corner, but I think the real reason he wants you dead is Drauses." Miika looked up at the Master in question. "He fears you. There's been talk for years about you taking his place someday. When Shaila won her proving and became the first Lady of the Mark, that talk grew louder. Master Gragern doesn't want to stand down as Liege yet. He told me to defeat Shaila during her proving to shame you. When that didn't work, he sent me to kill her instead. I think he means to break you."

If Shaila *was* killed, it most certainly would break him, Drauses knew. It would shatter his heart and his will to go on. The Liege knew where to hit to make him hurt.

"Why not come after me directly?" Drauses asked.

Miika snorted. "You think I could take you in a fight?"

Drauses didn't reply.

"Me neither. The Elder may once have been our best fighter, but he's old now. He knows a match with you would be his end. I think he hopes you'll get yourself killed and save him the trouble. He's buying himself time until then."

Drauses studied Miika thoughtfully. This news was grave and based on nothing more than Miika's word. Could he trust him?

"I need to speak to Dagon," Drauses announced. He crossed to the door and yanked it open. "Get in here." Aro walked in looking uneasy, likely thinking he was in some sort of trouble. "Stay here and watch him. If he tries anything stupid, kill him."

Drauses walked down to the second floor and knocked on Dagon's door. There wasn't an immediate answer, so he kept rapping louder until it flew open. It was Ithail who stood in the doorway wearing nothing but an old, battered pair of training pants. His shoulder-length, light brown hair was usually pulled back with a tie, but now it hung freely about his face. It made him look years younger.

"I need to see Dagon," Drauses said.

"He's washing up." Ithail pushed the door open wide. "Come in. I'll tell him you're here."

Drauses sat at Dagon's kitchen table while Ithail disappeared down the hall. There was a murmured conversation then Ithail reemerged, fully dressed, with his hair secured yet again. He busied himself making coffee.

"He'll be along—"

"I'm here," Dagon said as he swept into the room, pulling a shirt over his damp chest as he walked. "What's happened?"

"We have a problem," Drauses announced. "I need your advice."

"I should excuse myself," Ithail said. "This sounds private."

"Thank you, Ithail," Drauses replied.

Dagon went to give his lover a parting kiss while Drauses found an interesting spot on the wall to study.

"I'll come 'round before I head south again," Dagon murmured. Once Ithail took his leave, he took a seat and gave Drauses his full attention. "Alright. What's so dire it couldn't wait until our meeting this afternoon?"

⁓

"That is just the happenings of the past few *weeks*, Dagon!" Drauses exclaimed. The two Masters sat over steaming cups of coffee while Drauses unraveled the whole tale. "The Odas only know what other things he's made Miika do these past ten years. The ward refuses to speak of them, likely out of shame."

"Odas above," Dagon muttered. "Miika. All those injuries over the years. We assumed he was getting himself into trouble, picking fights where he shouldn't."

Drauses shared in his closest friend's guilt. "I went after him for Shaila's proving. I served what I thought was fair justice, beat him with his own club. Turns out he pulled the weapon under Gragern's orders."

"We were all shocked when the Elder let that proving continue." Dagon took a drink from his cup then swore under his breath. "I reported Miika to the Elder for stealing from Boon's clinic after hours. Boon made light of it and tried to convince me to let the infraction slide, but I told the Liege anyway. The next day, Miika showed up with a broken arm Boon had to operate on to fix properly. I didn't connect the two until now."

"Perhaps Miika was stealing supplies to patch himself up when needed. Shaila's taken to fixing him lately. He must avoid Boon whenever possible."

Dagon nodded. "Miika has protected his Master for a long time. If these accusations are true, Gragern doesn't deserve such loyalty. Can you imagine if Miika had been taken in by one of us? How far he could have gone. What a waste."

Drauses stared down into his cup. "It's not too late. We'll see things put right for him."

"Why come clean now? Could this be another ruse? Some elaborate trap set by Gragern? By Miika himself?"

"It's a possibility, but I don't think so."

"What made him come to *you*? I think you'd be the last person he'd consider an ally."

"It was Shaila," Drauses replied with a small smile. "She realized something was amiss. Miika confided in her, and she convinced him to speak to me."

"And you came to *me*?" Dagon jested. "How do you know *I'm* not poisoned by our Liege's influences?"

"You, Dagon, become corrupted?" Drauses laughed. "We've been closest friends for years. Of course I came to you. Who else?"

"This is the worst timing for this." Dagon moaned. "The Masters aren't together to discuss this in council. We can't make a decision without a vote."

"I agree."

Dagon tapped a finger against the side of his cup as he thought. "We need to step up our work at The Yard and move the guild as soon as possible. Once we're all together, we can take care of this."

"Gragern can't know we plan to vote him out."

Dagon grunted in agreement. "Nor that we know about Miika lest he brings vengeance down on the ward."

"You know what this means?" Drauses asked.

"We can't both go back," Dagon said with a nod.

Drauses cleared his throat and made to argue why he should be the one to stay.

"You should stay, Drauses, of course," Dagon said before Drauses could utter a word. "Your ward is the one in the sights here. There's your daughter's safety to consider as well. It's only fitting you should stay and watch out for them both."

Drauses was relieved. He'd go crazy with worry if he left now.

"I'll take more hands back with me than we planned," Dagon continued. "It's going to leave you thin back here, but the more men we move south, the faster repairs will get done."

"What of Aro? Will he accompany you?"

"Perhaps I should leave him here with you again. He enjoys watching out for Amii."

"I've been meaning to ask you about that. Why does he like spending time with someone so young?"

Dagon scratched the stubble on his chin and leaned back in his chair. "Aro's childhood was... troubled. He doesn't like to discuss it, but I've gotten the full story over the years. Spending time with Amii likely reminds him of happier times. You can rest assured he takes his duties as Amii's guard most seriously. I'll tell him all we know, and he can act as diligent eyes for you while I'm away."

"Unless Miika supplies cards and drink," Drauses muttered.

"Come again?"

"The three wards indulged in whiskey and Suits last night. I walked in this morning to find Aro drooling on himself in my living room and Miika half-naked in my bed."

Dagon roared with laughter and slapped the table. "Do you remember the time Master Raiga walked in on the four of us playing naked Spindle?"

Drauses laughed. "He threatened to rid me of my manhood if he ever saw it rubbing on his furniture again."

The two Masters recounted the tale, wiping tears of laughter from their eyes.

"Oh, Drauses, whatever happened to times like those?" Dagon asked with a sigh. "We used to stop and enjoy friendships from time to time. Just look at Miika. How did we miss a brother's suffering for so long?"

"Shaila's the only one who's gotten close enough to Miika to see the situation for what it is."

"Perhaps she cares for him," Dagon remarked. Drauses ignored the sudden pang in his gut as his friend continued. "I think we've spent too long in darkness and dread. Once we get the new headquarters up and running and sort out this Gragern mess, we should have a carouse like old times. Let the men loosen up a bit and enjoy each other's company. They deserve it."

"Speaking of enjoying others' company," Drauses said cheekily, "I wasn't expecting to find Ithail half-dressed in your quarters at such an hour."

Dagon smiled down at his coffee. "Liar," he said with a snort.

Drauses laughed. "Aro mentioned it a while back. How long have you…"

"Not long, not even a full season yet, but… I don't know. Something tells me this could be long-term." Dagon shrugged. "Perhaps that's merely wishful thinking. Ithail may not want to tether himself to one so many years his senior."

Drauses recalled his and Shaila's extensive age difference and shook his head. "I wouldn't worry about such things if I were you. Be happy, Dagon. You deserve it."

Dagon shrugged again and took a sip of coffee to hide the bashful look on his face.

Drauses gracefully changed the subject. "What should we do with Miika for the time being?" he asked. "Should we convince the Liege to send him to The Yard with you and the others? That would place him out of danger and give you extra working hands."

Dagon grunted. "Too suspicious. We never include Miika in important tasks."

"I'll watch over him as well then," Drauses declared. "I'll distance him from the Elder as much as possible and make excuses where I can." He stood from his chair. "Be quick with your work, Dagon. So many rely on it now."

"I will, brother. Watch your back, front, and both sides while I'm away."

Chapter 14

DRAUSES ORDERED MIIKA and Aro to pack their things and move together into Shaila's apartment for the time being. Miika went to his quarters and gathered his robes, his shoes, training clothes, favorite knife, and one small cigar box of personal possessions from his closet, all the while surprised by how free he already felt. He'd never let anyone touch him again, he vowed. Well, except for Shaila. She could touch him whenever she liked.

Miika was gathering the last few pieces of his medicine kit when a noise from behind made him whip around, blade drawn. Gragern stood in the doorway, arms crossed and smiling.

"Where are you off to?" the Liege asked sweetly.

"Anywhere but here."

"Lower that blade boy."

"No thank you."

"Need I remind you that disobeying me is not in your best interest."

"Living here isn't in my best interest either. I'm going to stay in an empty apartment and have my own space."

Gragern took a threatening step forward. "You'll get your own quarters when you've earned them."

"After these past ten years, I've earned much more than that."

Careful not to turn his back to the Elder, Miika gathered his things and waited for the old man to move. Gragern inched aside and let him pass. Miika struck out fast for the door. The sound of soaring steel gave him a heartbeat's warning before a knife buried into the back of his thigh.

Miika clutched the wall and yanked the blade from his leg with a cry of rage. He rounded on Gragern as the old man barreled toward him. Gragern made to strike, but Miika lunged with the knife and sliced the Master's forearm. Gragern backed away as blood soaked through his sleeve.

"I won't lie down and take this anymore," Miika snarled with his weapon pointed in the Liege's face. "If you come at me again, you better be ready to bleed." Miika gathered his things from the floor and limped backward toward the front door, his weapon drawn the whole way.

Gragern pulled back his sleeve and examined the wound in his forearm. He swiped a finger across it, marveling at the sight of his own blood dripping down his hand.

"I don't mind bleeding," he said, and the crazed look in his eyes made Miika turn and flee.

Using the wall as a crutch, Miika limped one slow, painful step at a time back up to the third floor. He could feel the blood dripping down the back of his leg. He stumbled into his new apartment and tossed his stuff on the counter, rummaging through it for his medicine kit.

He found his bottle of alcohol and dabbed it on a rag then stripped off his pants. With a shaking hand, he pressed the rag to his thigh, smashing his teeth together in an effort not to scream and break things. The damnable thing would not stop bleeding. He grabbed a new rag from a drawer in the kitchen and soaked that one red too, but it kept flowing. He was about to swallow his pride and limp down to see Boon when a voice from behind made him jump clear out of his skin.

"It needs stitched," Aro said.

"Yes, and I can't see to do it myself," Miika grumbled. "Care to do the honors?"

"Are you sure you wouldn't rather have Shaila do it?"

"You think I want her stitching under my bare ass with the mood she's in today? Likely she'd stab me with the needle out of spite. You do it."

Aro rifled through Miika's kit until he found what he needed. He threaded and sterilized a needle, then knelt and started stitching, fast and efficient.

"Master Dagon told me about your situation," Aro said. "But I already knew."

Miika jumped and growled at a biting stitch. "How?"

"Shaila questioned me about errant Masters, then I saw you bolting from her quarters all bruised and bandaged, and I made assumptions. Turns out they were true. I want to say I'm sorry."

"For what?" Miika asked with an indifferent shrug. "You're not part of the problem."

"You used to ask me to train with you from time to time when I first joined the guild," Aro said with a look of guilt. "I always gave you excuses. I'd heard you were a dirty fighter and thought you'd try to snap my neck. Eventually, you stopped asking, and I was relieved. I feel badly about that now."

Miika glared down at Aro. "Listen here: I didn't do this so you all would feel sorry for me. I could've gone on doing Gragern's bidding as long as needed if his orders were just. When they ceased being so, I stopped doing his bidding, simple as that. You keep what you know to yourself, even after Gragern is dealt with. I want to be a Master, but I'll earn it on my own and not have the title handed to me out of pity."

"I'll keep your secret, brother, but as I'm one of the few who know the truth, if you ever need help, I stand ready to assist. As a friend."

"There's that blasted word again," Miika said in exasperation. "*Friend*. Like I'm supposed to know what in Vedia to do with friends. If I'd known confiding in others would promote *feelings*, I might've thought twice."

Aro cracked a smile as he broke the thread. "Welcome to the softer side of humanity."

Miika growled and snatched the needle back. He gathered his things and stalked off to the bedroom, slamming the door on Aro's laughing face, but once he was alone, he shook his head with a small laugh of his own. 'Brother?' 'Friend?' How could two simple words carry such weight? Even Drauses was on his side now, by some miracle of the gods. He owed it all to Shaila. The Lady of the Mark was every bit as powerful as Gragern feared, and now she was Miika's ally. His friend. She'd given him hope, the strength to stand up for himself, and the chance to break free of Gragern at long last.

And he loved her for it.

⇜

There was a knock on Rovik's door.

"Come in," he called. He sat at his desk nursing a glass of Sazeen. Rose stood at Rovik's side. Marcel glowered at her as he walked in, but when he spoke, it was to his sovereign.

"I have news," Marcel announced.

"It's about time," Rovik barked. "Spit it out."

"A rift has formed within the guild. Their Liege's corruption has been brought to light, and the Masters are moving more men south, scrambling to hasten their work there. Their building will be as empty as we can hope for in a day's time. We should strike while their numbers are few."

"No," said Rose.

"I wasn't speaking to—"

"Enough," Rovik ordered, swirling his whiskey. "We need a smarter approach to this. As soon as they finish their work at the old lumber yard, they'll move Amii with the rest, yes?"

"That's their plan," Marcel said. "But, sir, if we allow the girl to reach The Yard, I fear we'll never get her back. They're securing the place like a fortress."

"I've no intention of letting her reach it," Rovik mused. "We should wait and strike as they move south. They'll be in the open, likely dispersed. With our inside knowledge, we'll know the moment they go on the move and can convene on Amii in force. The Black Blades will aid in this, yes?" he asked with a glance at Rose, who nodded.

"We'll have the element of surprise," she said. "My men can handle it."

Marcel nodded. "Very well. I'll notify my informant."

"Who is this man you've corrupted?" Rose asked.

"The fewer who know, the less chance he's discovered," Marcel replied.

"I don't think so. Either tell me who your informant is, or I'll tell my engineer to pull the plug on your communications."

Marcel looked at Rovik. "Sir?"

Rovik grinned. "It's only fair, boy. Why should she stick her neck out for a man who won't do the same?"

Marcel chewed his lip, shook his head, then swore. "He's my brother."

Rovik raised a brow. "A *blood* brother? Really?"

"Yes, sir."

"And you don't think Drauses would expect your sibling to betray them?" Rose asked in disbelief. She turned to her uncle. "We can't trust anything this man has reported! Every bit of intel is probably fed by Drauses himself."

"Drauses doesn't know," Marcel explained. "My brother feared my shadow would affect his chances of joining the guild, so we told no one."

"Likely story," Rose sneered. "What's his name?"

"Go to Vedia!"

Rose opened her mouth to retort, but Rovik held up his hand.

"Let him keep the name. For now." He locked Marcel with an even stare. "You're not yet back in my good graces, but this is a start. Get out."

As the door closed behind Marcel, Rose sat on the corner of Rovik's desk.

"Don't tell me you still want to marry Amii off to that dog," she said in disgust.

Rovik sighed. "I don't know. Let's see if he can fix his mistake, then I'll decide." He stood from his chair and took hold of Rose's hips, pulling her into him. "Come to my bed tonight, for old times' sake."

"No," she said sternly. "I indulged you years ago, but I told you: never again."

Rovik huffed and picked up his drink. "Then you get out too."

Chapter 15

MIIKA AND ARO were settled in Shaila's old apartment, and Shaila's belongings were now scattered about Drauses' quarters. Drauses watched cautiously as Shaila bustled around, stowing her things. He'd hoped placing Miika out of Gragern's reach would help lighten her mood, but she still wouldn't speak to him unless he addressed her first. As the day dragged on, Drauses was more and more desperate to get her alone. He'd let her have at him in the training room and draw all the blood she liked if she'd forgive him after. Amii helped distract him for a time with a game of cards. She told him all about the fun she'd had the evening prior.

"Miika let me try a sip of his whiskey," she confessed.

"Did he now?" Drauses asked.

"I almost spit it back in the glass. Such awful stuff." She wrinkled her nose at the memory.

"I'm glad he gave you a taste if it put you off the drink forever."

They both fell silent as Shaila came into the room. She stared moodily around, searching for something, then snatched up a handful of toiletries from the counter. She caught them staring, and their eyes snapped back to their cards. She stalked from the room and locked herself in the bathroom.

"What did you do?" Amii asked, wide-eyed.

"What do you mean?"

"Don't play innocent. She should be happy to see you, but I've never seen her this angry."

"I have. Once."

"Well, you better fix it for both our sakes."

"I will as soon as I can."

"Do you need me to leave?" she asked as she set down her cards.

"Where would you go?"

"Next door." She took her father's cards and gathered the rest from the table as well. "I'll ask Aro to play Jests."

"Very well. I'll walk you to the door. Have Aro return you before day's end. Don't wander anywhere alone, sweetheart. Not even down the hall."

She rolled her eyes, so much like Shaila that it made him smile. "I won't. Stop fretting."

Drauses watched from his doorway as Amii bounded down the hall. She knocked at the boys' door and, when Aro answered, let herself in. The ward peered out at Drauses with a cocked brow.

"She was bored," Drauses said with a shrug. "Asked to come sit with you instead."

"Tell him we'll babysit, but he owes us drinks," Miika called from inside.

"I don't need a babysitter," came Amii's heated reply.

Aro laughed. "We'll entertain for a while."

"Don't let her out of your sight," Drauses warned.

"I never do."

❦

Shaila stood in the bathroom yanking her brush through her hair more forcefully than she meant to. The bristles caught a snag, and she hissed as it yanked painfully at her scalp. She tossed it in the wash basin with a growl and stared at herself in the mirror. Her face was flushed with anger, and a perpetual scowl etched an unsightly wrinkle in her brow. Drauses pinning Miika to the wall, the ward bleeding anew and gasping for air, the Master spitting deathly threats… Oh, how furious she was at the whole spectacle! Miika had suffered enough, and Drauses' temper, unbridled jealousy, and ignorant abhorrence for the ward set Shaila grinding her teeth, a habit she thought she'd kicked as a child.

She threw on her robes and stalked from the room. She peered into the living room, but Drauses and Amii were gone. Perhaps they went to find more cheerful company. Some time alone may be for the best right now, she decided, so she went to the bedroom to finish stowing her things. When she walked into the room, she found Drauses sitting on the bed with his hands clasped together on his knees, waiting for her.

"Where's Amii?" Shaila asked.

"Next door. She wanted to give us privacy."

Shaila crossed her arms. "And just what do we need privacy for?"

"For this." Drauses stood but didn't come closer. "When I walked in this room this morning…" he closed his eyes. "I was consumed by jealousy and acted without thought. I'm sorry."

"I'm not the only one owed an apology," Shaila said sternly.

Drauses winced. "No, you're not."

"You've secured Miika to safety and taken the first steps needed to free him from Gragern, and for that I am thankful. But that's not enough, Drauses."

"I understand. I'll make things right with Miika. I promise." Drauses looked briefly down at his boots then back up at her. "If you'd rather have time away from me, I can go. I can return to The Yard tomorrow and have Dagon stay behind to protect you instead."

Shaila was torn. She wanted to be angry with him—he deserved it—but under no circumstances did she want him to leave again. He waited for her answer; she had none. He turned to go. Shaila leapt forward to stop him, but he spun and caught her first, yanking her into his arms.

He smelled so good, so familiar. The weeks without him seemed much longer. He took her chin in hand and tilted it up until she looked into his eyes. He kissed her, hard, as if she were the drink to save a dying soul, and a shiver ran through her. There was no way she was letting him leave. Both her hands swept up into his hair, and she pulled it, hard, fueled by her anger.

He backed her against the nearest wall and pinned her there. His fingers loosened every tie on her robes, and he shoved them open to find her naked underneath. He growled low in his throat as he put his lips to a spot below her ear that made her moan. He pushed her legs open with his feet as one hand delved down to touch her where she already stirred for him. His fingers teased and thrusted. She started to tremble. Her breath caught in her chest, and she cried out into his robes as she came apart at his touch.

Drauses yanked off his robes and shirt. Shaila tugged down his pants. He shoved her robes off her shoulders to the floor and sank to his knees in front of her. He trailed his fingers down one of her legs and seized her ankle, tugging it up over his shoulder.

He put his mouth to her between her legs, and Shaila moaned and leaned her head back against the wall. There was nothing to hold on to, so she threaded her hands in his hair again, twirling it around her fingers as her breathing sped once more. His mouth caressed her, teased her, wound her into a tight, tense spring until, with a wicked flick of his tongue, she spiraled out of control all over again.

She was held up on her feet by his arms alone as her legs went wobbly. He stood and shifted her captured leg from his shoulder to the bend of his elbow then slowly slid inside her. She sighed and whispered his name like a prayer.

"Yes, my lady?" he replied.

"You've nothing left to prove," she said. "I'm no longer angry."

He chuckled then thrust deep to hear her cry of surprise. "By the time I'm done with you, you won't remember your own name."

Their lips met as he fell into a slow, steady rhythm. She wanted more. She reached out and slapped him hard on the backside to spur him on. The move ripped away his self-control, and he rammed into her body. She threw her arms around his neck and clung to him as he brought them both to the brink. They cried out a garbled mix of exclamations as they burst over the edge together and fell…

&

When Drauses came to his senses again, he was lying on his back on the floor. Shaila was still wrapped around him: her arms around his neck, her face buried in the side of his throat, and her legs tangled with his. He pushed her hair back to find her flushed and breathless but was startled to find tears trickling down her cheeks as well. He sat up, dragging her into his arms.

"What is it?" he asked with concern.

"Nothing," she said tearfully.

"But you're crying." His thumb brushed a drop from her cheek.

"Drauses, I... I love you."

It felt as if the air was sucked from his lungs. His heart pumped harder now than when he'd taken her against the wall a moment ago. She was looking at him uncertainly, awaiting his reply. He kissed her tenderly.

"I love you too," he murmured against her lips.

"You do?"

"I do. This morning, with Miika..." he closed his eyes in pain and hugged her close. "I thought I'd lost you to another."

"There's no one else for me, Drauses. No one but you."

'*What more is there to life?*' he thought. This breathtaking woman loved him, and he loved her. He stared at her, seeing her in a new light: Pera's light[12]. She was so beautiful. He ran his hand over her body from forehead to heel to ensure she wasn't an illusion. What benevolent acts had he committed to deserve this fallen angel?

"Does this mean I'm forgiven?" he asked.

She laughed through her tears and curled up against him. "Yes, dearest, you're forgiven. But promise me next time you won't rush to violence."

"Apologies again, my lady." Shaila yawned, and Drauses laughed. "Am I boring you?"

"I'm just tired. It's been a trying day."

The sun was setting. Amii would be back soon, so Drauses stood and set Shaila on her feet. As he gathered his clothes from the floor, she reached out and slapped him on the backside again. He dropped his things and made a lunge for her, but she snatched up her robes and rushed from the room, laughing as she ran to safety in the bathroom.

⌇

12 Pera: The goddess of love and fertility. A full description can be found on page 375.

In the dead of night, as the rest of the building slept, Aro rose from his chair where he'd been feigning sleep for the past hour. With silent steps, so as not to wake Miika in the other room, he crossed the apartment, unlocked the door, and snuck out into the deserted hall. He took to the stairs, avoiding the steps he knew to creak and groan as he went, checking regularly over his shoulder for followers. The front door of the building opened on ancient hinges, and he stepped out into the chilly night air. He slid a piece of wood into the door to prop it open then darted away in the dark.

9th and 40 of Autumn, Jesparia's 9th and 20 year of Rovik

A ward arrived from The Yard about four weeks after Dagon left with Julta. They'd almost completed all the construction and repairs, and the new headquarters was ready for the entire guild to move there permanently. On one hand, Drauses was impatient to resolve the situation with Gragern. They were lucky they'd had no incidents since they secured Miika away from the Liege, and Drauses didn't wish to push his luck any further. On the other hand, he was enjoying his time with Shaila and Amii and even Aro and Miika. Though Drauses was the one making final decisions as Master, the group discussed issues together as a team.

Ever in the back of his mind, Drauses could feel an uneasy trepidation creeping up on him. As time passed, he felt more and more certain something was wrong. When word came it was time to move, the feeling threatened to engulf him entirely. He ignored it as he told the others it was time to take their leave.

Shaila moved about Drauses' apartment, pulling things from drawers and cupboards and closets. Everything the man owned, which was far more than she expected, was strewn across tabletops and beds, ready to be sorted, folded, and packed. Shaila tried to make haste since Drauses wished to leave at dawn, but she was finding it hard to keep motivated. The past two weeks had left her so tired she'd spent more time sleeping than much else. She blamed the training they did all hours of the day and her passionate lovemaking with Drauses every night.

Miika came bursting into the apartment with a disheveled Amii thrown over his shoulder who pummeled the wards back as he walked.

"Put me down now, Miika!" Amii hollered in fury.

"As you wish, my lady." He tossed her up off his shoulder and made to drop her but threw his arms out and caught her before she hit the floor. Amii screamed then laughed as Miika set her on her feet. She smacked him twice more before fleeing down the hall to her room.

"What was that about?" Shaila asked.

"I told her to move her backside or I'd throw her over my shoulder. She didn't believe I'd do it, so I had to prove her wrong."

"Of course you did. Where's Aro?"

"Moving the last of our things into the hall. We're done next door. It looks like you still have a long way to go, though."

Shaila yawned widely behind her hand.

"Are you alright?" Miika asked. "You look weary."

"I'm fine."

"Need some help? Why are *you* taking care of all Master Drauses' rubbish?"

"He's helping Boon pack the clinic. From what he says of our physician's extensive stocks, I got the easier job. But an extra set of hands would be appreciated. Thank you."

The two of them sorted through Drauses' kitchen and living room, deciding what needed to go now, what could wait, and what could be left behind indefinitely. With the important pieces packed into the bottom of Drauses' knapsack, Shaila flipped the top of the bag closed and stood staring down at the kitchen counter, exhausted.

"Go lie down for a bit," Miika urged. "We must all be at our best tomorrow."

"There's still too much to do."

"You can take an hour, surely. I'll wake you after a while."

Shaila chewed her lip. "Will you watch over Amii?"

"No. I think I'll lock her up on the roof for pigeon fodder."

Shaila smiled. Miika had changed so much in the past few weeks. "I'm happy for you."

"Happy I'm going to turn the girl into bird food?" he asked obtusely.

"You know what I mean."

His shoulders slumped a bit. "We're not out of this yet."

"Don't do that. Don't ruin this for yourself. We won't let anything happen. You're free now, Miika. Enjoy it."

Miika gave her a sheepish smile, and when she returned it, he leaned toward her, his face inching ever closer to hers. Shaila's lungs seized in her chest, but she made no move to stop him. Why couldn't she stop him? She was frozen as he softly touched a palm to her cheek, and then, at the last second, she found her will and turned away.

"Hmm, not the reaction I was hoping for," Miika murmured.

"I'm sorry. I... I can't..."

"Why not?" he insisted, and he stepped closer, still caressing her cheek while she refused to look him in the eye. He sighed. "There's already someone else."

It wasn't a question, but she nodded anyway.

"It's Master Drauses."

Her eyes snapped to his in alarm. "Miika—"

"I already had my suspicions." He dropped his hand from her face. "It's alright. He's the better man. Your secret is safe with me."

To her surprise, the thought of being found out didn't concern her as much as the look of disappointment and pain in his eyes. "It's no fault of yours my heart's already taken. In another time, another place..."

Miika smiled. "I know."

She laid her hand over his on the counter. "I only wish you happiness. You deserve so much of it."

"I *am* happy. Don't look at me like that. It's true. This is the best life I've known in years. I'm surrounded by people who care about me. *Friends.*" He snorted at the word. "I'm no longer Gragern's slave and still a Man of the Mark. Truly, I didn't believe such a day would ever come. I know who to thank for that." He took her fingers in his hand and squeezed them. "Thank you."

"Trying to sweet-talk your way to a kiss now?" She asked with a grin.

Miika chuckled. "Care to hear a secret? A longing I've known since I was a child?"

"Tell me."

He leaned in and whispered, "I've long wished for a sister."

"Oh, stop it," Shaila said with a click of her tongue.

"It's true, I swear. Not a brother, young or old, but a sister. A *little* sister. I used to imagine sweeping in to save her from thugs and scaring monsters from under her bed. Perhaps I wanted to be someone's hero," he mused with a shake of his head. "But if you and I are never anything but friends, then I'll count you as the sister I always wished for."

Aro walked into the room, and they slid apart.

"Everything's in the hall, ready for morning," Aro announced. He glanced around at all the things still littering the room. "Umm…"

"Shaila's not feeling well," Miika said. "We'll take a break and entertain the whelp while she rests for a bit."

"I'm not a whelp!" Amii hollered from down the hall.

Both men laughed, and Shaila gave them a weak smile before heading off for some much-needed rest.

Chapter 16

ROSE APPROACHED ROVIK'S office as Marcel was leaving it. She made to walk by him, but he blocked her path.

"A word?" he asked.

"I can't imagine you'd have anything of interest to discuss with me."

"It's about Amii."

Rose tried her best to ignore the little kick to the gut her child's name always brought. She'd long ago given up any right to care for the girl, but somewhere inside her dwelled a small sliver of maternal instincts, a lingering touch of the goddess Heniira[13] no doubt. It only ever reminded her how much she'd failed as a mother. Perhaps that was the point.

"You know if we manage to retrieve the girl, Drauses will never give us a moment's rest until he has her back," Marcel said.

Rose rolled her eyes. "We've kept Drauses at bay for years. We can do so again."

"Or we could finally kill him."

"You just want back in Rovik's favor."

"Do my motives matter? Drauses has been a thorn in our sides for years. We should deal with him once and for all."

Rose laughed. "Many have tried, boy."

"None who know him as well as I."

---

13 Heniira: The moon goddess. A full description can be found on page 370.

She snorted but couldn't deny he had a point. "Go on."

"Drauses gets too absorbed in his emotions. It's clear he can't think straight when it comes to *that woman*," he said with disgust. "We could exploit this weakness."

"How so?"

"Drauses has a history of betrayal by those closest to him. I doubt it would take much to convince him Shaila's done the same. It would fluster him, break him. Surely the two of us can handle one grief-stricken Master."

"She'll refute any accusations we make. He'll never listen to us over her."

"What if she's not there to defend herself?"

Rose crossed her arms. Perhaps this little worm could be of some use after all. "Alright. I'm listening."

⊰

Drauses came home to find Aro, Miika, and Amii playing cards while piles of his possessions remained still strewn about the half-empty apartment. As soon as he entered, Miika rose from his chair and beckoned him for a private word in the kitchen.

"I'm worried about Shaila, sir," Miika said quietly.

"Has something happened?" Drauses asked.

"She looked about to drop of fatigue some hours ago, so I told her to rest. I've tried rousing her several times since, but she seems unable to get out of bed."

"Is she sick?"

"I don't know. Perhaps Boon ought to have a look."

"I'll check on her. Thank you."

Drauses found Shaila sleeping soundly in his room. So soundly, in fact, that she was snoring, something he'd never heard her do before. It made him chuckle as he crossed to the bed. He shook her, called her name, and got barely more than a grumble for his efforts. He kissed her, hard and long until she roused with a small gasp. She sat up in a panic.

"How late is it?" she cried.

"Well past dinner time."

Shaila swore and rushed to get out of bed. "I'll strike Miika dead. He said he'd wake me!"

"He said he tried. He's worried you're sick."

"I'm fine. I was tired, and I let the day slip away. I'll wash up and get the rest of our things prepared for morning."

When she made for the door, he grabbed her by the elbow and pulled her close. He touched her face, brushed her hair off her cheeks to check them for flush, peered into her eyes...

"I'm fine, really."

"Prove it."

She smiled and locked her lips to his. He deepened the kiss until she pushed herself away.

"Satisfied?" she asked.

"Always with you, my lady."

"Stop worrying. All is well."

Shaila disappeared into the bathroom while Drauses sent the men away to rest since they'd all be rising early the next morning. Once they were gone, he sat at the table where Amii was building a towering castle of cards.

"Is Shaila alright?" Amii asked. She dropped a card into place to start another floor.

"Just tired. We've been training hard."

"Do you love her, Father?" Amii asked.

Drauses smiled. "I do."

"It must be very easy to love someone so beautiful."

"Beauty has no say in love."

Amii looked at him doubtfully.

"It's true," he insisted. "In fact, beauty can hinder love."

"Who says?"

Drauses closed his eyes in thoughtful silence for a moment, recalling words he hadn't heard nor spoken in many years. Once he remembered them all, he began to recite:

> *"Swift men be to love her*
> *that lady of greatest beauty,*

but few is the count of men
who learn to blind their eyes
and look anew on her
with sight of soul and heart
to let that which lives within
make her fairest yet
to please the senses total five.
How hard I weep for brothers
who know not their losses
of heart, of soul, of sense
who need only close their eyes
to know love's truest sight. "

When he opened his eyes again, Amii was staring at him, mouth agape.

"What was that?" she asked.

"A piece of an old poem written long ago to teach others how to find true love."

"You read poetry?"

"That's the only poem I know."

"What's it called?" she asked as she placed two more cards on her castle.

"*Rubric for My Beloved.*"

"What does it mean?"

"It means to love a beautiful woman, you have to ignore her beauty. Only when you see her other qualities can you see how beautiful she truly is."

Amii tilted her head curiously. "Do the same rules apply to handsome men?"

"I don't know."

"You do know you're handsome, don't you?"

He fought not to smile. "I've never given it thought," he lied.

"I know Shaila loves you, too, the same way as in that poem."

"How can you tell?"

Amii shook her head so hard her hair nearly smacked into her castle. "I shouldn't tell you. You may get angry."

"Oh well, now you'll most certainly tell me even if I have to tickle it from you."

Amii giggled. She placed two more cards on her tower before leaning close and dropping her voice to a whisper. "I know she loves you because she told Miika so."

"Oh?"

"Do. Not. Get. Angry," the girl ordered through her teeth. "You must promise me."

"I promise."

Amii nodded and leaned closer still. "I heard Miika and Shaila talking in the kitchen earlier. I think he tried to kiss her, but she told him no because she already loves you."

So Miika tried his hand. Drauses had wondered when the ward would make his move, and he'd finally done so. And Shaila refused him. A bubble of satisfaction warmed Drauses from within. He smiled and picked up a card to help Amii finish her tower.

"You're not mad?" Amii asked.

"Well, of course not. I did promise, after all."

The bathroom door opened, and Drauses put a finger to his lips. Amii giggled again then placed the last card at the very top of her tower a second before the whole thing shook and fell, scattering cards every which way.

Shaila came in, attacking her damp hair with a towel. She paused halfway across the room to pick up a stray card from the floor. She studied it thoughtfully, almost sadly, before turning away.

"Can the two of you help me finish the work that needs done? Amii, you still have half your things to pack." She set the queen of hearts back on the table then gave Drauses a rather hinting smile. "You, sir, a hand please?" She started toward the bedroom.

The look she gave him over her shoulder set his heart racing, and he rose to follow, eager to do her bidding.

⟡

Shaila was sleeping soundly on his arm, but Drauses was awake and running over every step of their plans again and again. Something was amiss, some detail unchecked, but he couldn't find it. The feeling he'd forgotten something vital crawled under his skin, refusing to let him rest as he ought. He decided to take one last look in his knapsack, and as he slid his arm out from under Shaila, she stirred and sat up.

"What is it?" she asked in alarm.

"Nothing. Go back to sleep."

"If it's nothing, why does it keep you awake?"

"I don't know."

She reached for his arm. "Are you worried? You needn't be."

"So much could go wrong tomorrow," he said. "I need to check I've done all I can."

"Hmm, like get enough rest? Seems you're failing at that." She pushed him back flat on the bed and curled up again on his chest. "Amii will be traveling safely with us, and the rest of the men can handle themselves. Tomorrow night, we'll sleep at our new and improved headquarters which is said to be the safest place in Trista."

Drauses sighed. "I know."

"There's something else," she whispered in a silky voice that stole his breath away.

"Tell me."

"I love you."

"Well, that's something, my lady. It goes a long way to soothing my nerves."

"Show me what else I can do to help, Drauses."

Though he got very little sleep, Drauses had to admit that by morning, the Lady of the Mark had all but erased his worries.

Drauses was up before the sun. He made rounds to every door to ensure every last man was roused and ready to leave by dawn. Each ward and Master was given a bundle of Boon's vast stock until every bandage was accounted for. The men were broken into six groups, and Xeda passed out Julta's communication devices so that each team had one for emergencies. Drauses kept a close eye on Gragern who stood waiting with the men he'd chosen to travel with. He smiled when he spotted Miika.

"Boy!" the Liege called, and with so many eyes around them, Miika was forced to acknowledge him.

"Yes, my Liege?"

"I've changed my mind. You'll travel with me today."

Miika looked at Shaila who looked at Drauses.

"Do you suspect trouble today, my Liege?" Drauses asked.

"I should ask you the same question," Gragern replied. "You want Amii to move through the city unseen, yes? Adding to your team only detracts from that goal. My ward will go with me to help you be as inconspicuous as possible."

Aro stepped forward to stand at Miika's side. "In that case, I'll come with you, too, my Liege," he said with conviction.

"No!" Amii cried. "Aro!"

Shaila shushed her.

"That's a fine idea, Aro," Drauses replied with an approving nod, and he looked at Gragern, waiting with the rest to see if the old man would object.

Having talked himself into a corner, the Liege could do nothing but force a smile as Aro joined his group as well.

Drauses released the first two groups under cover of darkness. Next, he sent Miika and Aro's party away with Gragern in tow as the sun began to rise. By the time the last two groups were deployed, the sun was shining brightly.

"Are you ready?" Drauses asked the girls once they were alone.

"You let Aro go with that monster!" Amii raged.

"Aro volunteered to keep Miika safe," Shaila said.

"But what if he gets hurt?"

"Did I ever tell you about the time Dagon saved my life?" Drauses asked.

Amii blinked several times and shook her head. "No. What does that—"

"He fought off half a dozen men while I laid unconscious on the floor at his feet," Drauses continued. "I would trust Dagon with my life, and Aro has been Dagon's ward for years now. I trust Aro as fully as I do his Master. He is strong and clever and has Miika to watch his back."

Amii still looked doubtful.

"Aro taught me how to best your father in training," Shaila said, though she knew it was a far stretch of the truth. "He never saw it coming."

"It's true," Drauses chimed.

Amii peered from one to the other with a suspicious wrinkle in her brow.

"The sooner we head south, the sooner you'll be reunited," Shaila said with a soft brush of her hand on Amii's hair.

Amii nodded with fresh determination and shouldered her pack higher onto her back.

Drauses gave Shaila a wink as they ushered Amii along between them down the street.

∽

Miika walked at the back of the group with Aro at his side. Gragern walked a few yards in front of them. Every so often, one of them would search around in a full circle for any hint of danger. A sudden bang from down an alley made them jump in unison, and Miika shook his head at his own anxiousness as a cat darted out from behind some boxes.

"Any idea what he's planning?" Aro whispered.

"None," Miika replied.

"When he makes his move, I say we—"

"*I* say you duck your head and find some cover. You should've stayed away."

Without warning, Aro elbowed Miika hard enough in the ribs to seize his lungs.

"What was that for?" Miika choked, rubbing his side.

"You irritate me."

Miika smirked. "Do I?"

"You claim to be grateful for your newfound friendships, and yet you still keep us all at a distance. You can't have it both ways."

"I never asked for this! If not for Shaila's prying, I'd have—"

Aro shook his head and laughed. "You may think you've fooled the lady with that lie, but none of us, especially Shaila, are gulled a bit. You never could've killed her, Miika. You love her."

Miika scoffed but couldn't think of a retort.

"Furthermore," Aro continued, "your plight went unnoticed by the guild all those years because you refused to confide in us. Your isolation, by the Liege's manipulation or otherwise, made us turn a blind eye to you. Perhaps that's what you wanted, but this brotherhood relies on trust. It's the very bones and blood of the guild. Without it, we weaken from within. Why do you think so many of the Masters wish to see Gragern replaced? They feel the rifts where once there were friendships and fraternity. Our Liege has let us fall apart, one small crack at a time."

"Wise words from a ward," Miika commented.

"They're Master Dagon's. He credits much of his own success in the guild to his close friendship with Master Drauses."

"He has good reason to feel that way."

Aro raised a brow. "What do you mean?"

Miika hesitated, unsure how much he should divulge. Being new to such discussions, he didn't know the boundaries between friendship and confidentiality.

"Let's just say Master Dagon might've walked a much different path in the guild if not for a certain friend who kept his spirits up and his morals aligned during trying times in his early years as a Mark."

Aro narrowed his eyes and fell silent as they continued their steady march south. Miika looked around again for anything out of place in time to catch a glimpse of a dark figure in a window of an abandoned storefront. He no sooner blinked, and the figure was gone. He grabbed Aro's arm.

"What is it?"

Miika looked back from where they came and watched a Black Blade stroll out of an alley several blocks up the street.

"Ambush!" Miika screamed, and a heartbeat later, bullets began to fly.

⋘

The first half of the day went by smoothly for Drauses, Shaila, and Amii. They stopped to eat in what was once a park full of kept grass and apple trees. The trees, left unattended, had seeded and spread throughout the entire square but still produced deliciously plump apples. Amii picked a few from low-hanging branches. They ate in an old gazebo in the center of the park. The wooden-skeleton frame was home to a tangled web of wild roses that wove in and out of the beams and boards. Petals of red and white blanketed the gazebo floor, and their sweet scent blew around the trio in the breeze. As they gathered their things to leave, Amii stumbled across the remains of an old fountain buried deep in the overgrowth. The basin still held water, by some miracle, and in the edge of the pool grew a single blue renistrila blossom, an odd sight this far from the river. Drauses snipped it off with his blade and slid it in his daughter's hair.

"Beautiful," he told her, and she beamed at him.

When they left the park to continue south, just as they cleared the thicket of apple trees, Drauses took Julta's device from his pocket to check for any communications from the others as he'd done periodically all morning. He spun the golden gear, and as soon as the device powered on, Miika's anxious voice rose up from the box.

"Can anyone hear me?"

"We hear you," Drauses replied. "What's wrong?"

"Thank the Odas! We were ambushed in the old shopping district. We're surrounded!"

Shaila jerked Drauses' hand close and spoke into the device herself. "Is everyone alright?"

"A stray bullet struck Aro, but the wound looks minor."

"Aro!" Amii cried in a panic.

"Has anyone else answered your call?" Drauses asked.

"No, sir," Miika said, and there was a crack of gunfire in the background as he spoke. "I've been calling for a while with no response."

"Why is no one else listening?" Shaila asked.

"I don't know," Drauses replied, then he spoke into the box again. "We're not far from you. Keep in cover. Help is coming." Drauses put the box back in his pocket and looked at Shaila. "I'll go. You and Amii continue down this road until you hit Acadia Street. Take a right and follow it to the river. The Jespa will lead you straight to The Yard."

"No," Shaila replied. "You stay with Amii. She's safer with you. I have my crossbow and can make short work of many from a distance."

Drauses shook his head. "No. I—"

"There's no time for debate, Drauses. Gragern may well use the distraction to his advantage. Take Amii, continue south, and I'll meet you there." Before Drauses could argue further, Shaila turned and dashed away down the street.

"Shaila!" he screamed after her, but she soon turned a corner and was out of sight.

Drauses cursed and ran his hand through his hair.

"Will she be alright?" Amii fretted.

"Yes... yes, of course she will, little one," Drauses reassured her, but the girl looked far from convinced. "And Aro too. Don't fret."

Amii nodded, staring off down the street with worry. Her flower teetered above her ear, and Drauses tucked it back into place.

"Come along," he said. "We should keep moving."

She took his hand as they continued on, each lost in their own anxious silence.

⤷

Shaila knew the route, and it should have taken only fifteen minutes to reach her comrades, but when she turned down an alley to cross into the shopping market, footsteps from behind made her whip around. A Black Blade rushed up wielding a hot stick. Shaila drew her sword as he reeled his weapon back over his head. With a roll to the side, she evaded his blow by inches. Behind him, two more Black Blades came around the corner. She rolled in close as the whip lashed out again, and it struck her shoulder as she smacked him in the face with the hilt of her sword. The whip brushed her for but a second or two, but it was enough to send a wave of rippling pain through her entire body.

Shaila kneed her attacker between the legs then drew her sword across his throat, but his comrades were immediately upon her. She blocked a blade from the first and kicked the second in the stomach. Shaila fell to the ground in feigned shock from a single blow to the face, but as she fell, she drew her crossbow. She rolled to her back and fired, hitting the nearest Black Blade square in the eye. She jumped back to her feet and rounded on the last assassin who drew a gun. She threw her sword at him, which he had ample time to dodge, but not enough to then dodge *her* as she dashed in, jumped, and wrapped her leg around the back of his neck. She yanked him face-first to the ground, then wrapped her arms around his neck and twisted. He convulsed as his neck snapped.

Shaila climbed back to her feet, recovered her sword and bolt, and hurried down the alley before more of her enemies could descend.

Chapter 17

DRAUSES AND AMII continued down the route he and Shaila discussed in case she was forced to turn back. Drauses waited twenty-five minutes before calling Miika to check for Shaila's safe arrival. To his dismay, Miika reported they hadn't seen her. Something was wrong.

Drauses could see the river but kept his distance from the wide-open spaces of the waterfront and instead passed through various buildings and down alleys, following the Jespa from afar. They were but a few short hours from The Yard, but Drauses felt a rising sense of dread. He looked back over his shoulder every couple of minutes, fretting over the silence with his heart thumping in his ears.

Not an hour after Shaila's disappearance, he saw a body, black like a shadow, slip into the street behind them, and, like a man possessed, every nerve, every muscle came alive as Drauses shifted from protective father to murderous Master of the Mark. With a growl, he drew his sword and took Amii by the elbow, nearly yanking the girl off her feet as he rushed them off between two buildings to the next block over where he broke into a run down the sidewalk.

"What is it?" Amii yelled as she struggled to stay on her feet at her father's side. A gunshot rang out, and she screamed as the bullet ricocheted off the roadway at her feet, dusting her shoes with bits of stone. Drauses yanked her to his chest, swearing loudly.

Drauses backed them against the front door of the nearest building, a long-ago abandoned tavern. The door swung in on rusty hinges, and they ran inside and through the bar. The kitchen was a skeleton of rotten appliances that stank of mildew and rust. It lacked windows, leaving them to find their way in the dark. Drauses led Amii through the maze of counters to a door in the back of the room that opened to the daylight of a back alley. Drauses searched left and right but saw no danger. He stepped out first to be sure it was safe before allowing Amii to follow, but as he took the girl's hand, a shatter of glass to his left startled him as a Black Blade burst through a window of the building next door and rolled out into the alley.

Drauses shoved Amii back inside to safety as he rounded on the Blade. He'd struggled very little with these Western fighters in the past. Their style was sloppy, their footwork was wrong, and they left themselves open to blows far too often: all evidence they lacked proper training. It was much to Drauses' surprise when this particular Black Blade locked swords with him in a stance nearly identical to his own. He was small in frame, agile and lithe like... like Shaila. Of course.

This Black Blade was a woman.

She met his strikes blow for blow, and they each searched the other's form for weaknesses, finding none. The fight may well have lasted an eternity, so evenly were they matched, were it not for footsteps that told Drauses they weren't alone. He pivoted and found the new arrival was none other than his previous ward.

"Where's the Lady of the Mark, Drauses?" Marcel asked smugly.

Drauses' eyes flicked from the Blade to Marcel as he considered his chances against them both. He didn't like his odds but knew he had to overcome them for Amii's sake.

Marcel came in for a swipe with his sword. Drauses blocked it, but the Black Blade swung a heartbeat later. He ducked and rolled and struck out at the back of Marcel's legs. Marcel jumped over the blow as the Black Blade kicked Drauses in the chest. Drauses fell to his back on the sidewalk. Marcel came in quickly, but the Master managed to block his sword from cleaving his skull. Drauses kicked Marcel's ankle so hard it gave an awful crack, and Marcel screamed and staggered away. Drauses jumped back to his feet as the Black Blade rounded on him again.

Her strikes were fast and accurate. She swung a kick Drauses jumped back to avoid, then he spun on his heel in an upswing, but she expected that and blocked it with her own blade before knocking him in the ribs. He gasped for breath and backed away, watching Marcel in the corner of his eye, expecting him to rejoin the fight, but he only stood there watching. What was he waiting for?

The Black Blade swept back her hood and pulled off her mask, and a sickening wave of shock and betrayal ripped through Drauses as he recognized the face staring back at him. Her dark hair and grey eyes matched Amii's. She hadn't aged a day.

"Rose?" Drauses muttered in awe.

She smiled and swung at him with her blade. Drauses blocked her blows as he reeled inside. Not only was Amii's mother alive, but she was a Blade! How could this be? She continued to strike at him, and he blocked each one. Only now, he didn't strike back.

Marcel leaned against the side of the tavern wall and laughed. "Why do you refuse to fight the lady, Drauses?"

Drauses ignored him and kept his eyes on Rose.

"Our beautiful Shaila has made good use of your weakness for a handsome face," Rose declared, and her voice was exactly as Drauses remembered it: soft and deadly, like daggered silk. "She's been quite the well of information."

Drauses' eyes widened. Had they captured Shaila? That must be why she never reached Miika! Rose attacked Drauses again, faster, harder, while Drauses tried to concentrate over the growing panic in his chest. When she found no opening in his form, she fell back again.

"It's no wonder our sovereign trusted her with such a delicate assignment," Marcel chimed. "I must say, I was against it at first, but Shaila has surpassed my highest expectations."

Drauses froze and looked at Marcel in disbelief at what he suggested: they hadn't captured Shaila... She was one of theirs? Not possible. Drauses came back with his blade and struck at Rose with renewed vigor, but he missed a step. Before he could recover, she sliced her blade across his forearm. He hissed in pain and fell back again.

"I planned to kill you the night I lured you to the mansion," Marcel continued. "But then Shaila asked, 'Why kill one Mark when we could topple the entire guild from within?' She spoke of a better, grander plan, and oh my, has she executed it flawlessly! A beautiful damsel saves an assassin's life then pleads for his help. He takes her as his ward, and she infiltrates his entire brotherhood, enchants them all; such blind and foolish men they are."

Rose lowered her blade and cocked her head. "Everything began to fall apart the moment Shaila became the Lady of the Mark, didn't it?" she asked. "What havoc she's wreaked amongst your kind."

Drauses was breathing too fast, making himself lightheaded as his heart hammered in his chest. It wasn't possible, no, not possible at all. Shaila wasn't a spy. Everything they'd said was common enough knowledge. It proved nothing.

Rose stepped forward with a smile. "How skillfully Shaila convinced you to ignore your instincts in the dark last night, Drauses. There was a snake lying close, waiting to strike. It laid coiled in your arms."

"You lie!" Drauses shouted. How could they know such private things... unless? No! He hadn't been betrayed. Not again.

Rose clicked her tongue. "Temper, Drauses. It was always your downfall. Did you never wonder why a woman would work so hard to bed a sovereign only to beg a stranger to end his life?"

Drauses had wondered that very thing himself the night he took Shaila away; in fact, he'd asked her the same question. She'd had answers, of course, answers Drauses had accepted without question like a fool. Raw, overwhelming heartbreak and dread spread like fire through his chest as he considered this horrible possibility.

Rose locked blades with Drauses again, shoving into his stance, then she spun and struck him in the stomach. Drauses couldn't focus. Shaila's whispers in the dark the night before played over and over in his head, an echo of her sweet, soothing voice, full of hope and love, but they didn't calm him this time. They crushed him, heart and soul. *'There's something else... I love you... Show me what else I can do to help, Drauses...'* He missed another block and took a blow to the face that sent him staggering. Rose stalked closer.

"You'll die here now," Marcel sneered. "A grief-stricken Shaila will return to your beloved brothers, her cover intact. She'll darken her blade with so much blood, starting with the ward whose heart she's already ensnared. Maybe she'll warm Miika's bed as well before she ends him. It makes no difference to us."

Drauses had no words. He was struck silent and immobile by the pain of utter betrayal... again. They knew too much. They knew everything. Shaila was sent to be his downfall, and she would be.

'Show me what else I can do to help, Drauses...'

"You were right about one thing," Rose said, her grey eyes staring intensely into his blue. *"Rubric for My Beloved* applies perfectly to our beautiful Shaila. It's just too bad the poem doesn't teach how to spot a wicked heart in a lady finest fair."

Rose kicked out at Drauses again, striking him in the chest, once, twice, three times, in a spinning whirl. Then she shifted to her opposite leg and kicked his blade out of his hand. It flew through the air and clattered to the ground behind her.

'There's something else...'

Rose spun in close and punched him twice in the kidney then once in the face before kicking out one of his legs to bring him to a knee.

'I love you...'

Shaila had betrayed him, used him. She didn't love him at all.

Rose drew a shorter, oddly shaped blade from her robes, reared back, and plunged it into Drauses' middle. He cried out in pain of both body and heart.

Marcel limped into the tavern. Rose withdrew her blade and placed the bloody tip against Drauses' neck, daring him with her eyes to make a further move against her. He waited for her to slit his throat and get it over with. She didn't. Instead, she reached into Drauses' robes, plucked Julta's box from his pocket, and stomped it to pieces under her boot.

"Father!" Amii cried as Marcel hauled her out into the alley. Drauses watched as she tried to fight the guard off, swinging madly for his face, but Marcel merely laughed and swatted her arms away as if they were nothing more than buzzing insects.

Rose backed away, gathering Drauses' sword from the ground as she went. Together, she and Marcel turned and fled down the street. Amii's blossom tumbled from her hair as they dragged her away between them, kicking and sobbing her father's name.

"I'm sorry," he whispered as they turned a corner out of sight.

∽

"Master Drauses," Miika called into Julta's gadget. "Master Drauses!"

"This is your fourth try," Aro muttered. "He's not going to answer."

They were sitting in an old store front that, in the days of old during the building's prime, once sold jewelry of the highest quality. The display cases all stood empty now, the glass long smashed to shards and the counters full of holes from the Black Blades' bullets. A stray shot had clipped Aro nearly as soon as the bullets started flying, but the rest of the Marks were crouched behind displays and walls, unharmed. The bodies of the few Black Blades who'd attempted a head-on rush into the store now littered the floor around them, staining the wood red.

Gragern was secured away in a back room. The other Masters ushered him there and insisted he stay put for his own safety. Their actions ensured Miika's continued safety as well, but he didn't care. His only concern, for the moment, was Aro.

His fellow ward looked paler and paler by the minute, and Miika was at a loss as to why Aro was losing so much blood. The bullet had passed straight through nothing but meat. No bone was broken, no organ pierced, and yet blood kept pouring down Aro's arm in a steady river. His entire right sleeve was now a dark shade of crimson. They'd abandoned their heavy packs when they ran for cover. Miika's medicine kit and his bundle of Boon's supplies had all he needed to tend Aro's wound, but it sat useless in his knapsack in the street outside.

"I wish I had a gun," Miika grumbled.

"We don't fight with firearms," Aro replied. "They're cowards' weapons."

"We're the ones cowering behind cover."

"Each Blade who's stepped foot in here has bloodied our swords. They can do nothing but run out of bullets then stroll in to their deaths."

"I doubt you have that much time."

Aro leaned his head back against the display case they were seated behind. "So do I."

Miika glanced around his cover, and his eyes fell on the body of a Black Blade lying halfway across the room. Under the dead man's left arm glinted the handle of the very pistol that shot Aro. Miika estimated it would take him about three seconds to reach the gun. He was preparing to make a dive for the weapon when several gunshots rang out and bullets went whizzing past his head. Aro grabbed a handful of Miika's robes and yanked him back behind the display to safety.

"Stay put, you fool!" Aro fumed, then he grimaced and closed his eyes, gripping his shoulder.

"You'll die if we just sit here!"

All of a sudden, the Blades outside were shouting. No, screaming. Somewhere nearby there was an explosion, the force of which shook the jewelry store and sent bits of dust and dirt raining down on the men trapped inside. Gunshots began again, but none of the bullets flew into the store this time. Miika and Aro looked over the top of the case as another explosion shook the building. A moment later, a Black Blade landed dead on the sidewalk, his face turned into the jewelry store, eyes staring blindly at the Men of the Mark. There was a bolt stuck dead center in his forehead.

"Let's go, brothers," Miika called as he scrambled out from behind the case. He snatched the pistol from under the Black Blade as he rushed toward the door. "Our sister has arrived."

Several of the other Marks grabbed guns of their own off their fallen enemies as they followed Miika out of the store. Miika hit the sidewalk and froze in shock at the carnage around him. Two of the buildings across the street were ablaze with Black Blades pouring from the windows and doors like morbid living smoke, beating their robes and rolling in agony in the street to douse the flames. Miika ran ahead and raised his pistol. He'd used guns before and considered himself a decent enough marksman. He shot, and the nearest Blade fell dead. The other Marks were not as skilled with firearms, and, though many fired, only a few Black Blades fell to their bullets. Several more fell speared by bolts, however, and Miika searched up and down the street but couldn't spot the Lady of the Mark who fired them.

The last of their enemies decided this was not their fight after all and scattered up the street and down alleys. When the last black hood vanished from sight, Miika heard a whistle from above. He looked up to see Shaila on the roof of the jewelry store with a triumphant grin on her face. He waved, and with a quick slide down a ladder he hadn't noticed until now, she joined him on the sidewalk. Miika stowed the borrowed pistol in his robes and made to shake her hand. She yanked him into a tight hug instead.

"Are you alright?" she asked.

Miika squeezed her tight in his arms. "I am, but Aro needs aid." It was then Miika realized Aro never followed them into the street. "Follow me." He retrieved his knapsack, shaking off bits of broken glass and debris as he led Shaila back into the jewelry store and pointed toward the case he and Aro had used as a shield. Aro was still seated behind it, leaning against the wood, white as a ghost. Sitting beside him on the filthy floor was Gragern. Shaila froze. Miika drew his gun again.

"Hello there," Gragern greeted sweetly.

"Get away from him," Miika sneered, taking a menacing step toward his Master. Shaila put an arm out to stop him.

"I'm done here anyway," The Elder Master said with a grin, and he got to his feet and headed out of the store to join the others.

Shaila and Miika stared after him in bemusement then knelt at Aro's side.

"What did he say?" Miika asked.

"He made threats," Aro said. "He has information he could use to bring me grief."

"What information?" Shaila asked as she pressed her hand over Aro's wound.

Aro hissed in pain. "About my family," he said through gritted teeth.

"What did he want in return for leaving your loved ones alone?" Miika asked. Aro glanced up at him sadly, and Miika guessed the truth. "My death."

"I'll do no such thing, Miika. Trading one life for another is against our code."

Miika rubbed his hands down his face in dismay. "This is my fault."

"None of this is your doing," said Shaila.

"You don't understand. Where do you think Gragern learned all he needed to threaten Aro this way? I gave the Elder this information, at least most of it."

"What do you mean?" Aro asked.

Miika refused to look at him out of shame. "You admitted you avoided me when you first became a Mark. It was smart of you to do so. Gragern had me learn all I could about each new ward. He wanted to know everything about every Man of the Mark. It took me nearly three seasons, but I eventually found out about your family. I gave him names and... much more."

Aro stared at Miika for a long moment then nodded once. "It's alright, Miika. I don't blame you for this."

"That's fine," Miika said sourly. "I can blame myself enough for both of us."

⤚⥽

Shaila helped Aro strip off his blood-soaked robes and shirt. She gasped at how saturated they were.

"Gods, Aro," she whispered. Miika handed her gauze which she pressed firmly to the seeping wound. When she pulled the gauze away a moment later, it was already soaked with blood.

"How long ago did this happen?" she asked.

"Over an hour ago," Miika replied.

Shaila regarded Aro who wouldn't meet her eyes. "Miika, will you please see to it that the rest of the men are uninjured and ready to move as soon as possible?" she asked. Miika nodded miserably and took his leave. "Care to tell me what's going on here?" Shaila asked once she and Aro were alone.

"Is a man not entitled to bleed when a bullet goes straight through him?"

"Aro, your body has made no attempt to stop this bleeding. There's no sign of clotting. Talk straight with me. Please."

She dug around in Miika's kit for more gauze and bandages. She didn't ask him again but rather left it up to him to confide in her or not. She packed the hole in his shoulder, both front and back, then began wrapping it as tightly as she could.

Aro sighed in defeat. "I take medicine that thins my blood near to water," he admitted. "It prevents clotting."

Shaila gaped at him. "Why would you do such a foolish thing? You could bleed to death!"

"It's necessary for... it's to care for a condition I have."

"Does Boon know about this?"

"He's the one who gave me the pills."

"So this condition is monitored by Boon?"

"Yes. I see him regularly."

"Is it serious?"

Aro hesitated to answer which was answer enough.

"It's very dangerous for you to be a Mark, isn't it?" she asked. "Much more so than the others." She laid his right arm across his chest and wrapped the bandage clear around his back and shoulder to pin the appendage in place in a makeshift sling. Aro grabbed her wrist, halting her efforts to care for him. She looked into his anxious eyes.

"Shaila, I beg you, tell no one of this," he pleaded. "I'm a Man of the Mark. I'd be nothing without this guild. This is the life I choose to live until Lady Fate takes it from me. Please don't force her hand. Don't tell Master Drauses."

She regarded him thoughtfully and tried to pull her arm away. Reluctantly, and with a look of imploring terror, he released her.

"You say you see Boon regularly?" Shaila asked.

Aro nodded. "I'm well looked after, I assure you."

"Who else knows about this?"

"Just you."

"Not even Master Dagon?"

"No."

Shaila finished securing his arm to his chest. Once she'd anchored the last of the bandage, she took his hand in hers.

"It's not my place to speak of your private affairs," she said. "I won't hinder your future as a Mark if you assure me you'll look out for your health to the best of your ability and Boon's."

"I have so far and plan to continue doing so."

"Then your secret is safe with me."

Aro sighed with relief and squeezed Shaila's hand. "Thank you."

"Thank *you* for trusting me. I know it's not an easy thing to do in such trying times. I'm honored." Shaila made to stand, but he refused to release her hand, and she knelt anew at his side. "What is it?"

"I was there that night years ago," he said, staring at her fingers. "The night Master Drauses took you from Rovik's estate. I was one of the other masked men who traveled with you across the river."

Shaila gave him a small smile. "I already knew that."

"You did?"

"You're as tall as a house. I knew it was you the day we first met."

He shook his head with a small chuckle, then turned surly again. "I thought Master Drauses was a fool that night," he admitted. "I didn't tell a soul for two years that his new ward was a woman, for I feared you'd bring him nothing but shame. I'm so sorry, Shaila, for lacking such faith in you. I've never been so wrong."

Shaila shook her head and stood, helping him to his feet at her side. "You men and your foolish guilts," she said, then she sighed and hugged him, catching him by surprise. He'd not yet come to his senses enough to hug her back before she pulled away. "You knew nothing about me, Aro. You had a right to your opinions and your doubts. What matters is the faith you have in me now. I consider you one of my closest friends."

Aro smiled and nodded, his face burning red in a rare blush. "Yes, I... I consider you the same," he replied.

"And I'll protect your secret as if it were my own. Now stop troubling yourself over opinions made before we were ever introduced, and let's focus on getting to our new home in one piece, shall we?"

Shaila checked one last time that his wound was behaving as it ought. Though a small amount of blood had soaked through the bandage, the bleeding had slowed considerably. He should be alright until they could get him to Boon. She shooed him out into the street where Miika had gathered the rest of the men. All packs were accounted for and returned to their various owners, save for Aro's which Miika had slung over his free shoulder.

"Miika, do you have your box to call Master Drauses?" Shaila asked.

"Yes, but I fear you won't reach him," Miika replied. He handed over his device. "When you took longer than expected to get here, I tried many times to contact him and got no response."

"Did no one else respond either?"

"No one."

"That's not good," Aro said.

"No, it's not," Shaila agreed. She fiddled with Julta's device but got no better results herself. She was suddenly very anxious to be on their way. They spurred the men to motion, and the group continued south once again.

⚜

Drauses knew what it felt like to die, and he waited for the familiar, crippling cold to come. Rose and Marcel were long gone, Amii's screams had faded in the distance. He was alone, sitting propped against a wall, holding his bleeding middle.

The breeze kicked up and swept Amii's blossom down the alley. It bumped into Drauses' boot, and he plucked it up between bloodied fingers. He'd failed her again. He'd done nothing but fail her since her birth. Drauses gave life to a beautiful, smart, and headstrong child, then he left her in the hands of the most sordid sorts for years. Just when he thought he could right that wrong, he placed his trust in the wrong person and lost her all over again. The entire brotherhood could fall to Shaila's deceptions. If only he could warn them. But Rose smashed Julta's box.

Drauses pulled back his hand from the wound in his middle and saw the blood soaking into his clothes, but there wasn't as much of it as he expected. In fact, he felt very little pain. He got slowly to his feet. He was shaking, though not from illness or injury, but indignation and delayed adrenaline. He took a few tentative steps and though his middle burned, it was bearable. Perhaps by some miracle, he could still make it back to The Yard. He headed off, slow but steady, down the alley.

That Vedian woman would do no more damage if he could help it.

Chapter 18

MIIKA, ARO, AND Shaila arrived at The Yard around sunset. Shaila was stunned at the high stone wall erected around the place. There was a metal gate that opened on creaking hinges as they drew closer. The buildings inside all had new additions and recent maintenance. There were several brand-new structures as well; the most prominent of which was a one-story building standing at the back near the river with a bright red cross painted on the front. Boon was already organizing boxes of supplies and carrying them inside, happy as a lark. To the left of Boon's new clinic sat a small shack with an open workstation out front next to a large iron furnace: Julta's new workshop. Shaila was staring around in awe at all the work the men had done when Master Dagon stepped out from one of the side buildings.

"Aro," he called as he crossed The Yard toward them. "Are you alright?"

"We had a run-in with the Black Blades on our way," Miika explained.

"I'll be fine," Aro assured his Master.

"Shaila," Dagon said in surprise. "You're supposed to be with Drauses and Amii."

"Haven't they already arrived?" she asked, her panic rising. "They should've been here hours ago."

"Why did you leave them?" Dagon asked.

"That was our fault," Miika said. "We were ambushed and called for help. Shaila doubled back to save our backsides."

"Why were *you* the one to answer the call?" Dagon asked Shaila. "I thought the plan was for you, Drauses, and Amii to slip through the city silently and undetected."

"Shaila and Drauses were the only ones to answer our distress call," Aro explained. "Did anyone else run into trouble?"

"No. Everyone is here except for Drauses and Amii. No one reported a single mishap nor your call for help."

"Perhaps Julta's boxes failed," Shaila said.

"Don't let Julta hear you say that," said Dagon. "He gets testy when his genius is questioned."

Gragern shuffled past and headed off across The Yard, calling greetings and shaking hands like a celebrity as he went.

"We shouldn't take our eyes off him," Miika muttered.

"He made threats at Aro during the commotion," Shaila explained. "He's evil and desperate: never a good mix."

"I'll call in favors with a few other Masters and have him secured in his rooms for the time being," Dagon said. There were shouts from the gate as it opened again. "This must be Drauses at last."

"Thank the Odas," Shaila muttered as she headed for the gate.

Miika, Aro, Dagon, and a handful of others followed, and they watched in horror as Drauses stumbled in the gate. He was unarmed, his face was battered, and he was holding his bloody middle. Amii was nowhere to be seen.

"What happened?" Shaila asked as she rushed for the man she loved. "Where's Amii?"

Drauses glared at her. "Surprised to see me?" The ice in his voice froze Shaila in her tracks still several yards away from him. "No doubt you thought me dead. That was your plan, wasn't it? But your comrades failed to end my life, so here I stand." Even as he said it, he swayed on his feet, but when Shaila darted forward to catch him, he shoved her away in disgust.

"What in Vedia are you saying?" she asked. "Where's Amii?"

"Rose took her!" Drauses shouted.

"Rose? Amii's mother?" Dagon asked.

"You said Rose was dead," Shaila said in confusion.

"I don't want to hear any more of your lies, you evil witch," Drauses hissed with a bloody finger pointed in her face.

Shaila shrank at his words. Miika growled at her side, and she touched his arm to calm him lest he did something foolish. Drauses turned on him next.

"Are you part of this as well?" Drauses demanded to know. "She has you so bent to her will, it wouldn't surprise me."

"I'm part of no deception," Miika replied heatedly. "And I don't believe for a second that Shaila is either."

"Then you're a fool."

"What is it you believe I've done?" Shaila asked, reaching a hand toward her Master, pleading to his good sense. "Tell me straight."

"Our brothers at the factory were cut down, Amii's been taken, and I nearly lost my life all because of you. I won't allow you to do any more damage with your treachery!"

"I would never betray you this way. I—"

"I should've killed you the night we met," Drauses said, his voice barely more than a growl and his eyes full of such hatred that Shaila took a step back, wounded and afraid.

Almost every man around her now owed Shaila their lives. At Drauses' words, they bristled, all except Miika who drew his sword in a rage. Shaila held him back.

"Stow that blade, boy, lest you find yourself skewered at the end of it," Drauses ordered.

Dagon jumped to action. He yanked Miika's arm back and twisted until the ward hissed in pain. Miika tried to jerk away, keeping a firm hold on his weapon, but Dagon swept his feet out from under him, and the ward landed hard in the dirt. Dagon pinned him there beneath his boot, but Miika still refused to give up his sword.

"Miika, let it go," Shaila beseeched. "Please. Let me handle this."

At her urging, Miika loosened his grip and allowed Dagon to swipe the weapon away. The Master hauled him to his feet and marched him by the elbow across The Yard. Aro took point at Shaila's side instead with a look on his face barely friendlier than Miika's.

"Aro, take *her* weapons as well," Drauses ordered. Aro didn't move, neither did any of the others around her. Shaila unbuckled her crossbow, her quiver, and her sword. She handed it all to Aro.

"Keep them safe for me," she told him softly.

"Shaila, you're no longer a Mark," Drauses announced. He turned to Aro. "Get her out of my sight. If you're so concerned with the lady's safety, you can guard her door. No one comes or goes unless I give the orders."

"Yes, sir," Aro snapped. He put a gentle hand on Shaila's back and led her away until Drauses could no longer overhear him, then he said, "Master Drauses is clearly mistaken. Dagon will put this right."

As if on cue, Dagon rejoined them, walking on Shaila's other side as if she were a prisoner needing an escort.

"Where's Miika?" Shaila asked.

"I sent him to cool off," Dagon said. "Nothing more. All will be well. Have faith."

"Drauses has lost his mind!" Aro fumed.

"If so, he'll put everything to right once he finds it again. He's upset right now. Give it time."

◅

Dagon and Aro marched Shaila into the western most building and up to a third-floor office. Once his Master left the room, Aro closed the door on Shaila's pain-filled face. He would stand guard and watch over her until sense returned to her Master, he vowed.

Dagon eyed him up and down. "You're filthy," he commented. "I can stand watch while you clean yourself up and see Boon."

"No thank you, sir," Aro replied. "I'll stay right here."

Dagon looked surprised, but he nodded. "It's important to show loyalty to our Masters, but when we feel so passionately that one is in the wrong, it's just as important to stick to our beliefs lest we let a corrupt brother wreak havoc on us as Gragern has done. I'm proud of how you handled your anger with Drauses just now."

"Thank you, sir."

"See to it Boon gets a look at that shoulder before infection sets in," Dagon ordered, and he turned away.

"Master Dagon?" Aro called. "Why is it you rarely mention your own Master, sir?" he asked, spurred by Miika's curious comments earlier that day.

Dagon's face was set in stone, an unreadable and unmoving expression, as he stared at his ward. "This guild, this life, it... requires more than physical strength, Aro, and sometimes, though a man may rise victorious in battle, his mind loses the war. Such men may be a welcome force in battle, but they make poor brothers otherwise. When a man knows nothing but pain inside, in the privacy of his own mind, there comes a point where he needs to let it out lest it eat him alive. Unfortunately, the ones closest to him often become the targets of such outbursts."

"Did Master Raiga beat you too?" Aro asked in horror.

Dagon shook his head, his eyes giving away some deep internal pain Aro had never seen there before. "Sometimes I wished he would," he said softly. "Then at least the wounds would heal." Dagon came back to his ward, and he put a hand on Aro's shoulder. "Miika's Master battered his body, a serious mistreatment for any ward, to be certain, but there are other ways for Masters to abuse their protégés. Words can hurt as badly as a blow. Never sharpen your tongue to heal your pain, Aro, lest you one day bleed your own ward dry. Do you understand?"

"I think so, sir."

Dagon smiled. "Good." He gave Aro a brisk nod but continued staring at him, deep in thought for a long moment, then he nodded again as if he'd come to some conclusion Aro wasn't privy to before taking his leave without a word of explanation.

Drauses lifted his shirt so Boon could inspect the wound in his middle. It was still bleeding, but only just, and caused him very little pain. Boon narrowed his eyes and probed around the slit with his fingers.

"What're you looking for?" Drauses asked. "Stitch the blasted thing shut."

Boon stepped away and grabbed a long, thin metal tool from a nearby counter. "Don't move," he ordered before sliding the instrument into the wound.

Drauses certainly felt pain now, and he struggled to remain still as

Boon rooted around in his abdomen. After a moment, the physician stood up straight and shook his head.

"Drauses, are you sure it was a *blade?*"

"Yes, Boon," Drauses grumbled. "Unless that word has some new meaning."

"But this is barely more than a scratch..." Boon mused.

"I'll consider myself lucky."

"Lucky...yes."

Bandaged and medicated, Drauses stalked off across The Yard toward his new quarters. He'd spent the last few hours with nothing but his thoughts but was no closer to figuring out what, if anything, he could trust about Shaila. This whole mess with Miika and Gragern for example: what should be done about that? Was the Liege truly corrupt, or had he simply caught on to Shaila's betrayal from the start? Was this all an elaborate ruse? Was Miika in on it?

Perhaps she just wanted Gragern out of the way. She'd mentioned before that she thought Drauses should lead instead. If he'd stepped up as Liege with Shaila as his ward, it would have given her endless opportunity to damage the guild. But if that was her goal, why send Marcel and Rose after him? Nothing made any sense, and Drauses was spent, emotionally as well as physically. He decided to sleep on it and consider it all with a fresh mind in the morning.

⤙

Aro was standing guard at Shaila's door when Miika came strolling up, alone and determined.

"How did you slip away?" Aro asked.

"The men, including your own Master, feel Drauses has lost all good sense," Miika said. "They let me go but kept my blade." He nodded toward the office door. "Is she alone in there?"

"She is."

"Good. I'll relieve you."

Aro laughed. "Do you think me a fool?"

"No, brother," Miika replied with conviction. "I'm giving you the choice to walk away now and leave me to take the fall for what's about to happen."

"What *is* about to happen?"

"The lady is leaving. I'm going with her."

Aro scoffed. "And I'm supposed to stay free of blame if I leave *you* here on guard? Master Drauses will have my head."

"You take your chances, but we're leaving regardless. You could always come with us, or you could try to stop us, I suppose. Pray choose quickly, friend."

It seemed Aro's mind was already made up for he handed over Shaila's weapons without much delay. "Good luck," he said simply, and the two men shook hands before he turned and walked away.

Miika didn't blame his fellow ward for choosing to stay. Aro had ties to the guild Miika never had, and, in truth, Miika himself wouldn't be leaving either if he didn't care so deeply for Shaila. He waited until Aro was well out of sight before he opened the door and walked in.

Shaila sat at a desk near the wall with her head in her hands. At the sound of the door, she looked up, but her face fell when she saw who entered. Clearly, he wasn't the man she'd wanted to see. It was a blow to Miika's heart, but he shoved it aside.

"What're you doing here?" she asked.

He held out her weapons. "I'm told friends are supposed to look out for each other's well-being." He placed her things on the table in front of her. "Consider this my best attempt to repay all you've done for me."

Shaila left the weapons untouched on the table. "Miika, I can't let you do this. Drauses will—"

"To Vedia with Drauses," Miika barked. "If your Master refuses to see sense, then it falls to us to learn the truth. There's no point sitting here, unarmed in miserable innocence, while he broods. Since you're no longer his ward, he has no say in it anyway." He nodded to her weapons, and she picked them up with a sigh. "So what do we know? Any idea who's to blame for all of this?"

"None," she replied. "Drauses and I moved alone with Amii and picked our path as we went. There was no planned route our enemies could know ahead of time. They waited until I left Drauses' side then attacked when he was most vulnerable. How did they know?"

"Could they have heard our message when we called you for help? They would've known you were splitting up."

"Perhaps, but that wouldn't have told them Drauses' position."

"Then you must've been followed."

"No. We kept careful watch."

"That just leaves you and Drauses, Shaila! There must be something else."

"What do you think I've been sitting here pondering? The weather? I'm at a loss, same as you."

Miika growled in frustration. "Did you and Drauses decide what route he and Amii would take in your absence?"

Shaila blinked several times in sudden realization. "Yes. Right before I left him, Drauses mentioned which streets were best to take to reach the river and that the Jespa would lead us home from there."

"And not a word was spoken about your route until then?"

"Not one. Drauses chose it as we went, and I never asked after it as we traveled."

Miika began to pace. "If you're certain you weren't followed, then the moment Drauses spoke his plans aloud must have been overheard by our enemies. But how?" He stopped to stare at her thoughtfully.

"What is it?" she asked.

"Stand up, give me your robes."

She raised a brow but stood and did as he asked without question. He took the cloth in both hands and shook it. He ran his hands along her hood, turned it inside out, examined every button, then dove his hand into the pockets. He felt something odd in the left outer pocket, so he turned it out. There was something stitched into the fabric.

"Give me one of your bolts," he said, and when she handed it over, he used its sharpened edge to split the seam of her pocket. From between two layers of cloth, he pulled out an odd copper disk.

"What by Vediida is that?" Shaila asked, stepping closer to examine it.

Miika held it between his thumb and finger up to the dying light through the window. It was flat and round like a coin but quite thick. He could barely make out a seam along the edge where two halves came together, so he placed the disk on the floor and pressed it under his boot heel until the casing cracked in protest. When he picked it back up, it fell apart in his palm to reveal a jumble of wires and one tiny red blinking light inside.

"It's electrical and quite complex," Miika commented, tilting the device back and forth in the light for a better view. "Perhaps Julta could— wait, do you see that?" As he spoke, the light inside stopped blinking and lit solid red, and when he went silent again, it went back to blinking steadily. "Is it *listening* to us?" he asked in horror, and the red light lit solid once again at his words.

They shared a look of bemusement before Shaila snatched the device from his hand and crushed it under her own boot until the light went out entirely. She plunged her hand into Miika's pocket to find another copper disk sewn into that one as well. It met the same fate as its brother.

"Do you realize what this means?" she asked.

"We've a rat among us," Miika announced in disgust.

"Someone must be told. Every word the guild utters is being heard by our enemies!"

"They'll never believe it from either of us right now."

"Oh gods," Shaila moaned. "Amii. This is all my fault."

"How?"

"I was supposed to protect her. The Odas only know how long our enemies have been listening. How could I have missed something like this?"

"Did you see that thing?" Miika waved to the bits of wires and casing littering the floor. "I've never seen anything like it in my life. How could any of us have prepared for something like that?"

Shaila shook her head. "Regardless of blame, Amii must be brought back. I won't sit here waiting for others to fix this. Who can we trust?"

"We can trust each other," Miika announced with a nod. "Let the two of us bring the girl back together."

"Miika, I can't let you risk so much. If you leave here with me, you'll ruin your future as a Mark. I'm no longer in the guild; Drauses has dismissed me. I've little left to lose, but you… I haven't fought this hard to save you from Gragern to see you throw it all away on my behalf. And besides, you're unarmed."

"Drauses is a fool," he declared in disgust. "If we bring Amii back, it'll clear both our names. We'll both still be in the guild; I'd bet my life on it. As for me being unarmed…" Miika pulled from his robes the pistol he snatched off the dead Black Blade in the jewelry store. He'd filled his pockets with ammo from the fallen Blades in the street as well. "I believe I can take care of myself just fine."

Shaila stood in thought for a long time, staring at Miika while she chewed the inside of her cheek. "Alright. Give me a moment to pen a note, just in case…"

Miika nodded in understanding and re-pocketed his pistol. Shaila searched the desk and found an old book. A few of its inner pages hadn't yet crumbled to dust. She ripped one free of the binding and sat to write her note. When she was done, she folded it in half and left it on the table.

"Is there no one you wish to leave a message for?" she asked.

"No. I've no one left here."

Shaila nodded and pulled her robes back on. She motioned Miika ahead of her toward the door, and he turned his back to her to take his leave. When his fingers gripped the door handle, something hard and heavy smacked him in the side of the head, and he crumpled, unconscious before he even hit the floor.

Drauses woke with a splitting headache. He reached groggily for Shaila before he remembered everything from the previous day. Guilt and regret twisted his stomach until he thought he might be sick. The look of hurt and betrayal in her eyes had appeared real enough. Perhaps he was mistaken. But then his thoughts started around the same miserable, inescapable loop as before: Who else but Shaila had known where he and Amii would be? How did his enemies know so much if Shaila hadn't betrayed him? How was it that their accusations made so much sense even as he fought so hard to deny them? Perhaps they made *too much* sense, were just a bit *too* perfect. Or was that his own hopeful foolishness?

There was also Boon's suspicions about the wound in his middle. It still pained him very little and had barely bled through the bandage as he slept. The blade Rose stabbed him with wasn't the one she'd use to fight him. She'd taken it from her robes instead of using her sword. Why would she do that? Her intentions seemed clear enough, and yet he knew from past experience that if Rose had wanted him dead, she'd have left nothing to chance. She would've slit his throat, bled him dry on the alley stone, but instead, he'd managed not only to survive but to make his way clear back to headquarters. He met not a single Black Blade as he'd wandered, bleeding and broken-hearted, toward home. Did Rose not only spare his life but ensure he could find his way without hindrance? Where Shaila's guilt was all but unquestionable, Rose's behavior raised nothing *but* questions.

He should speak to Shaila. Even if he couldn't trust a single word she said, she was the only one who knew the truth, and he'd wring it from her one way or another. If she was innocent... Oh gods, his actions were inexcusable and horrid. *'I should've killed you the night we met.'* Did he truly say such a horrible thing? Unable to stomach his guilt a moment longer, he leapt from the bed. He had to see her. Now.

As he drew near the office Shaila was supposed to be held captive in, Drauses discovered a group of men gathered around the open door. He ordered them to make way and marched in to find Miika leaning against a desk with blood trailing down the side of his face. Boon was already at the ward's side, peering into his eyes.

"Are you nauseous?" the doctor asked.

"I'm fine, Boon," Miika grumbled, taking the rag the physician offered him and dabbing at the blood on his cheek.

"Where is she?" Drauses thundered.

Miika glared at him. "She smashed me with a chair and took off."

The fact that Shaila left Miika behind to take the full brunt of her Master's wrath alone confirmed what Drauses didn't want to accept. Only the guilty run.

Drauses was suddenly, immeasurably furious. He picked up the nearby chair, which was already missing a leg, and smashed it against the wall, over and over, until it fell apart in his hands. He flung the pieces across the room with a scream of rage, and one shattered the window. Miika was still glaring at him, but the rest of his brothers all stared in silent shock. Even Boon stood frozen in awe with a cocked brow and a calculating look as if questioning Drauses' sanity.

Drauses turned away with a huff and stalked from the room, and the others gave him a wide berth as he passed.

✑

Shaila entered the old apartment building and climbed up to the third floor an hour or so before dawn. She had no keys, but her old quarters sat unlocked as they no longer contained anything of worth. She pushed the door open wide, trying her best to ignore the flood of happy memories, and went straight to the bedroom, the place she first made love with Drauses... No, she couldn't think of such things. Not now. Perhaps after she fixed things, they could start again... No, no false hopes, just Amii. Amii was all that mattered now. From under her bed, she pulled out an old burlap bag covered in two years' worth of dust. It contained her uniform from the night Drauses took her from the mansion. She'd left it behind for the move south, never thinking for a second she'd need it again.

She went to the bathroom and changed into the uniform to wear under her robes until she crossed the river. The mansion guards wouldn't expect her to be dressed as one of their own. The outfit didn't conceal her quiver, to her dismay, but the shirt's sleeves were long enough to cover her crossbow and the few bolts she could tuck under its straps. She'd have to leave her sword as well. Going in so unarmed made her nervous, but it couldn't be helped. As she stared at herself in the mirror, dressed as she was that night two years ago when Drauses changed her life forever, his words played over and over on an endless loop that broke her heart anew. *'I should've killed you the night we met.'* She turned away from her own pathetic, tear-streaked face.

Her stomach twisted violently, and a second later, she was bent over the toilet, sick as a dog. The floor was ice cold when she slid down to sit with her back to the wall. She stared ahead, her eyes unseeing as she counted days, weeks in her head. This couldn't be. She buried her face in her hands and wept, realizing at last why she'd been so tired, so sick to her stomach. With a shaking hand, she touched her belly.

Drauses hated her now. This news would no doubt sicken him. What she was about to do could end in her death, but she'd do it anyway; there was no other choice. If she was successful, she could return Amii to her father then disappear to live her life away from the guild. And if she failed... Well, none of it would matter anyway. Her secret would go with her to the grave, and Drauses could go on hating her, free of guilt.

"Clean yourself up and pull yourself together," Shaila told herself the way she used to. She gathered herself from the floor.

It was time to focus.

⁓

At the river, Shaila found Alek sleeping in his boat as always. She wondered if the man had a home or if he lived in his little boat year-round. He roused with a jolt at the call of his name.

"Ah, yes, what can I do for you?" he asked, blinking the sleep from his eyes. He studied her face then smiled as he woke enough to recognize her. "Shaila, my dear! I've not seen you in, what, near a full season? I've kept my promise, though. I sail those ladies across the river every night like you asked me. But tell me, is Drauses well? I've heard no news since your one and only note to me."

"He's well," she replied, trying to smile. "I'm grateful for your loyalty, Alek. You no doubt saved many young lives these past weeks. I've a new favor to ask of you, friend. Would you mind taking *me* across the river tonight?"

"For you, Shaila, I mind not a bit. But why is Drauses not with you?"

"He has other matters far more pressing, and my errand can't wait."

"Well, climb aboard then, my lady."

Alek sailed her across the water to the very place on the Western shore where she brought Krig to his knees. It felt like a lifetime ago. She climbed out onto the bank as the sun peeked over the horizon.

"Where and when should I retrieve you?" Alek asked.

"Polco Pier. Wait as long as is safe for you, but if no one arrives by nightfall, it matters not if you stay."

"Why wouldn't you arrive, Shaila? What's going on?"

"Look for the girl you helped us bring East the night Drauses was shot," Shaila continued, ignoring his questions. "I may be with her, or I may not, but if she shows up alone, don't wait for me. Take her to the Eastern shore immediately, no matter what."

He narrowed his eyes. "Drauses doesn't know you're here, does he?"

"No," she admitted.

Alek looked like he wanted to ask more questions, but let them go to ask instead, "Is there somewhere safe I can deliver the child if she travels alone? The factory?"

"The guild is no longer there." Shaila cocked her head. "Has your brother sent you no word?"

"My brother never tells me anything. It's not my place to know brotherhood business."

Shaila saw no harm in telling Alek the truth. He was as trusted as Boon or Julta amongst the Marks, and Drauses never had a foul word to say about him in two years.

"Take the girl to the old lumber yard," Shaila said. "That's where the guild calls home now. You can easily reach it with your boat. Please get Amii safely to Drauses. Deliver her to his arms only, promise me."

"I'll see it done, you have my word, but see to it you come back with the girl yourself," Alek ordered.

"I'll try my best." She gave Alek a smile of farewell. "Goodbye for now, or forever, Alek." She heard his boat pull away as she climbed up the riverbank and started walking that old, familiar path toward Rovik's estate with a heavy heart.

Chapter 19

SHAILA STOOD ON the sidewalk across the street from the front gate of Rovik's estate, staring at the towering house as she formed a plan, a one-in-a-million-even-if-everything-went-perfectly plan, but a plan, nonetheless. Off in the left alley, she knew there was a smaller, more concealed entrance the servants used to take out the trash, but she still didn't know how to pick locks, so that was a dead end. Instead, she walked left a block away from the house, far out of sight of the guards' shack by the front gate, then crossed the street. She stripped off her robes, tossed them behind a bin, then marched off down the sidewalk toward the front gate. From this direction, it would look like she was coming from the side entrance. As she approached, two of Rovik's men spotted her through the window of the guard house and stepped out, guns drawn.

"Apologies, gentlemen," Shaila called sweetly, her hands raised. "I locked myself out when taking the trash."

She was close enough now for them to see her in the early morning light, and they both smiled when they got a good look. *'Yes, come closer to this pretty face,'* Shaila thought. They both lowered their weapons and took a couple of steps her way. Shaila unleashed a full, dazzling smile, and one man holstered his gun completely. She came closer and could see in the open door of the building behind them now. It was empty. These two unfortunate souls were alone. She was nearly within arm's reach before the still-armed guard raised a brow.

"Isn't that one of the old uniforms?" he asked.

Shaila rolled her eyes dramatically. "Yes," she said with feigned agitation. "I've bugged and bugged Alonso for a new one, but he keeps forgetting me." She pouted to complete the ruse. She was surprised when the guard aimed his gun at her anew.

"Alonso was executed for treason two seasons ago," he sneered.

Shaila hid a wince at the news and smiled instead. "I suppose that's why he's forgotten me," she quipped before grabbing his gun and kicking him between the legs. He never fired a shot, Odas be praised. The other guard reached for his weapon again, but Shaila brought the butt of her stolen gun up and smacked him in the temple, making him stagger. She yanked a bolt from her sleeve and stabbed him in the neck with it.

The guard she left clutching his manhood straightened up again. She kicked him in the chest then grabbed his wrist and jerked his arm to the side, bending it backward as hard as she could. She heard his elbow pop in protest. He opened his mouth to scream, but she punched him in the throat, crushing his windpipe. He went down gasping to his knees, and Shaila drew his own knife from his belt and plunged it into his heart.

Shaila dragged the bodies back into the guard house, concealing them near the wall under the window, out of sight. She retrieved her bolt and checked the pistol to see that it was loaded before tucking it in the back of her pants under her shirt. She kept the knife as well, sliding it in the top of her boot. She stepped over the dead guards, yanked open the window, and hopped out onto the estate's front lawn.

Her uniform wasn't going to get her as far as she'd hoped, and it was smeared with blood now anyway, so she darted through the side yard toward the laundry room. It was at the back of the house and should be empty. Most of the staff would be preparing for breakfast at this hour. When she reached the side door to the servant's wing, however, she found it locked. This door was never locked before. Shaila peered around to check she was still alone, then glanced up at the rows of balconies on the second floor above her. The balcony doors were also rarely locked; she'd try one of those next. Using the door frame and the downspout for support, she climbed the wall to the floor of the balcony over her head. It took all her upper body strength, but she managed to haul her backside up and over the rail, her toes scraping the brick wall every inch of the way.

Shaila was relieved to find the first balcony door unlocked. These rooms were guard's quarters, but most of the men were up and off to their duties by this time of day. The bedroom she let herself into stank of booze and cigarettes. As she crossed the room, someone coughed in the adjoining bathroom, and Shaila swore as the door sprang open a second later. A half-naked guard came staggering out, still drunk. He stumbled several steps before realizing he wasn't alone. By the time his glazed eyes landed on Shaila, she'd already drawn her crossbow, and a heartbeat before the man cried out, his forehead was speared by a bolt. Shaila rushed forward and caught the body as it fell, laying it silently on the floor. She stepped over it, leaving the bolt embedded in his skull, and let herself out.

Several maids bustled in and out of rooms at the other end of the hall. Shaila knew it'd be an hour or more before they reached the room with the dead guard, and by then she hoped to be long gone. She ran into the stairwell and waited for shouts to erupt. All was quiet. Smeared with blood as she was, she'd have to find Amii without being spotted by staff. That was going to be next to impossible, but at least she was armed. If all else failed, she'd silence anyone unfortunate enough to cross her path.

Shaila flew down the stairs to the basement: a jumbled maze of junk and tools with a large stone sink at the back for washing bedpans. She picked her way across the room to a back corner where the basin drained through a large grate in the floor into the sewers. The smell was awful, but Shaila breathed through her mouth and plucked the grate up out of the floor to peer down into the darkness of the tunnel below. This hole was much smaller than she remembered it.

Shaila knelt and stared down into the dark. She wouldn't fit, she knew, but Amii might. It was the girl's only hope. No one would be able to follow her through, which meant she'd be safe as soon as her feet touched the sodden tunnel floor, even if that meant Shaila couldn't go with her. She'd known this was likely a one-way trip, but she'd never imagined she'd make the choice voluntarily. She touched her belly.

"I'm sorry, little one," Shaila whispered. "It's not fair to you, I know. We're not supposed to trade lives, but mine for hers is more than fair. I'm

only sorry yours is forfeit as well. I've never pictured myself as a mother."
She sighed and shook her head. "Forgive me."

Shaila replaced the grate and rose, wiping her eyes as she returned to
the stairwell where she climbed all the way to the fifth floor, the emptiest
level of the house since most of the rooms were vacant. In the east hall,
she chose a room halfway down on the right-hand side and crossed to
the window within. She yanked it open and slid out to sit on the sill. She
closed her eyes and muttered a prayer for the mad stunt she was about to
attempt then slowly maneuvered out and clung to the sill, lowering herself inch by inch while her feet scraped the side of the building, searching
for the window frame of the fourth floor with her toes.

"I'm so tired of dangling from buildings," she muttered with a grunt
as her foot finally connected with the frame below.

෴

Amii sat at the table picking at her breakfast with her fork. Her father
was dead. She'd cried so many tears for him throughout the night that
her eyes now burned with every blink. The only thing that made her
feel the slightest bit better was the news that Rovik's men had failed to
kidnap Shaila. Marcel and the woman who helped him grab Amii were
very upset to learn the Lady of the Mark had gotten away. The fact that
Shaila, Aro, and Miika were safe helped ease the ache in Amii's heart,
but only just.

Rovik sat across the table from her, stuffing his face, overjoyed at the
news his long-time nemesis was finally dead.

"I know what you're thinking," he said.

"I doubt that very much," Amii replied acidly.

"You're angry, grieving for that man, that killer."

Amii slammed her hand on the tabletop. "His name was Drauses,
and he was my father!"

"He was a murderer," Rovik replied calmly. "He killed many people
over the years, and I'm sure he fathered many children as well. He only
took an interest in *you* because you're destined to rule in my place. He
wanted you for your power, nothing more."

"Nothing you say will ever poison me against him," Amii sneered on the verge of fresh tears.

"Perhaps. But there's someone I think you should meet who might make you see reason. She's busy right now with a delicate security issue, but, afterward, I'll send her around to your room so she can introduce herself properly. Tomorrow morning, she'll stand at your side at your wedding."

Amii had known for quite some time about Rovik's plans to wed her to Marcel. She was to be sovereign, but Marcel was to rule. Amii despised Marcel even before she knew how crooked he was. Rovik didn't know it yet, but Amii decided long ago she wouldn't trade promise and prayer with that monster. If they dragged her to the altar, she'd refuse to say a single word. She'd never take that man as her husband. Never. She thought of Aro, who would no doubt kill Marcel in her name if he knew, and a stray tear trickled down her cheek.

"May I be excused?" she asked. Watching Rovik stuff himself was making her sick.

"I suppose," the sovereign replied, spitting bits of food as he spoke.

As Amii got up from the table, two guards came to flank her. They moved with her everywhere throughout the house and had stood at her door the night before as she'd slept. Rovik tried to issue her a good day, but Amii ignored him as she followed the guards out of the room and down the hall.

✦

As Amii and two guards passed the window at the end of the hall, none of them noticed two hands snake under the glass and push it silently open. Shaila slid into the hallway as quiet as a ghost.

She stalked down the hallway behind the two guards as fast as she dared, pulling her borrowed knife from her boot. Whether it was a soft sound or simply intuition, something made Amii look back over her shoulder at that moment. Her eyes landed on Shaila, and she made the tiniest gasp. Both guards began to turn just as Shaila finally reached them, and she plunged her knife into the nearest guard's back. He crumpled as his partner drew his gun. Shaila ducked and rolled as he fired two shots.

He missed both, and she shot with her crossbow, hitting him in the groin. He screamed as she drew her own gun and shot him in the forehead.

Amii scurried away down the hall and watched the carnage with her hands clamped over her mouth. But once the men were dead, she had eyes only for her rescuer.

"Shaila!" Amii cried and flung herself into the woman's arms. Shaila hugged her close until alarms began to wail throughout the house. She took Amii's hand and dragged her down the hall toward the stairs. The door burst open in front of them, and Shaila shot both men who came through. More men came running up the hall behind the girls. One opened fire, and Amii screamed. Shaila pulled the girl into the safety of her chest as bullets flew past them. One grazed Shaila's upper arm, far too close to Amii's head. Shaila gave Amii a small shove, and they broke into a run together toward the stairwell.

"Hold your fire, you fools!" Rovik yelled as he joined the guards in the hall. One guard ignored the sovereign and fired two more shots as Shaila and Amii jumped over the bodies of the dead and disappeared into the stairwell.

They took the stairs two at a time, always on the verge of losing their footing. They made it to the basement with footsteps hot on their tails. Shaila slammed the basement door shut, but there was no way to lock it. She all but dragged Amii across the room to the grate and yanked it open.

"Go!" she screamed, and Amii didn't hesitate to lower herself through the stinking hole.

The girl barely fit and had to all but screw herself through the last few inches until she dangled by the arms. She let go and landed with a thud and a groan in the dark below. Shaila peered down as Amii got to her feet.

"Come on, Shaila!" Amii called up.

"I can't, child."

"What do you mean?" Amii cried. "You have to come with me!"

"Go to Polco Pier," Shaila ordered. "Look for the ferryman, Alek."

Amii started to sob. "Please, don't leave me!"

The basement door crashed open.

"Run, Amii!" Shaila screamed. "Don't look back!" She watched Amii whirl and disappear in the dark. Shaila got to her feet and rounded on Marcel as he drew his blade.

One final stand. While she still had blood to give.

More guards rushed into the basement behind Marcel. Shaila had her crossbow in one hand and the pistol in the other. She fired an arrow past Marcel's head, striking a guard in the throat. Marcel struck the gun from her hand with his sword. It clattered to the floor and fired, and the bullet hit a brick on the wall nearby, ricocheting across the room and sending Marcel's men ducking for cover.

Shaila reloaded her crossbow and took aim at Marcel, but a gunshot rang out again, and this time, the bullet buried deep in her thigh. Shaila screamed and almost lowered her crossbow, but she forced herself to focus and take aim anew. A Blade stood behind Marcel, his face masked, a coal-black sword in one hand, a pistol in the other. Shaila changed targets and aimed at the Blade instead. She fired, but the lithe assassin jerked to the side, and the bolt sailed over his shoulder to bury into a nearby crate.

Marcel dove and tackled Shaila's legs, knocking her to the floor. Shaila used her crossbow as a club and knocked Marcel across the side of his head over and over. The crossbow broke apart in her hands under the strain.

Marcel rolled away in a daze, and Shaila tried to detangle her legs from under his dead weight. The Black Blade rushed in. Shaila made a dive for her dropped pistol, but the Blade came down on top of her, crushing the air from her lungs. Shaila rolled and plunged her last bolt into the Black Blade's side.

The resulting cry of pain was feminine.

Shaila and the lady assassin rolled across the floor, locked in a battle of fists and rage-filled screams, throwing punches and clawing at each other for freedom. Shaila grabbed her bolt and gave it a vicious twist in her enemy's side. The Black Blade surprised her by yanking the bolt from her body and turning it on Shaila herself who raised an arm to protect her face only to have her bolt shoved straight through her left hand. Shaila returned the favor by slapping the Blade with the same hand, gouging at the woman's face with the tip of the bloodied bolt, ripping her mask and tearing at her cheek.

Marcel came to and sat up. He crawled to where the two women wrestled on the floor and struck Shaila in the face with the hilt of his sword until her world went black.

✍

Amii heard the gunshots as she ran through the sewer tunnels. She didn't know what scared her more—that they may kill Shaila or what they'd do to her if she lived.

The sewers were lit only by the light of the grates above her head, small ones that broke the sides of the streets every few hundred feet or so for water drainage, so Amii kept a hand on the wall of the revolting tunnel to keep moving forward and track the turns that came abruptly in the dark. When she could run no more, she wandered aimlessly, choosing her turns at random and praying she was headed closer to the river, but, after a while, she suspected she must be going the wrong way. Should the tunnels not have dumped her out to the water by now? Oh gods… she was lost.

Up ahead, Amii spotted daylight again, a far bigger beam than the meager street drains. She ran for it, desperate to be free of the dark and the stink. She was dismayed, however, to see the grate through which the sunlight poured was far above her head and the ladder that used to hang from it had long ago detached. It laid in the muck at her feet. Amii stood below the hole and stared up at the sky through the bars. The sun shone brightly, and she could hear carriages moving about nearby. It looked midday.

"Hello!" she screamed, and her voice echoed back a dozen times through the tunnels. "Anyone? Please, I need help! Help me! Hello!"

No one replied.

Amii lingered below the grate, crying and staring up at the daylight and shadows of carriages and passersby, so close but impossible to reach. Shaila had sacrificed herself for Amii's freedom. She would be upset to see Amii sitting motionless in dread. Alek was waiting for her at the pier. Maybe Shaila would be there too if, by some miracle, she managed to get away. At that thought, Amii turned away from her beacon of sunlight, wiped her face, and continued on.

❧

Shaila woke to pain. Nothing but pain. Her thigh throbbed, her head ached, her shoulders and wrists burned. She blinked her eyes open and immediately wished she'd stayed unconscious. Her hands were bound together above her head and a chain stuck under the binding hung her from the ceiling by her wrists. Her feet were limp against the floor below, and she struggled to stand to bring her aching arms and wrists some relief. She'd been stripped of all her clothes, and she shivered with cold and humiliation, but she knew much worse was coming. Why else would they have kept her alive?

Shaila was in a small stone room she'd never seen before, but she knew exactly where she was: Rovik's Cellar. It was a place as notorious as it was evil, a little piece of Vedia brought to Earth. It was lit dimly by a fire somewhere behind her that she couldn't see, and along the walls hung all manner of tools, knives, and weapons. There were two men nearby, each dressed in brown from head to toe and wearing thick leather gloves and aprons. They looked up when she staggered to her feet. Her arms were still above her head, but she could breathe easier now, and she worked her fingers to restore their circulation.

"Good morning, sunshine," the taller of the two men greeted. His voice was raspy from far too many cigarettes. The other man smiled, missing half his teeth, and his eyes raked up and down Shaila's naked flesh making her skin crawl. He slithered closer and ran his hands down her stomach, across her hip, then down her injured thigh.

"I wouldn't, Straith," the taller man called in warning. "Boss said don't touch."

Straith smiled his toothless grin, ignoring his comrade as he trailed his fingers up Shaila's inner thigh. He took a step closer.

Shaila struck like lightning, wrapping her thighs around the man's neck and squeezing with all her strength. The bindings at her wrists cut in again, but she gritted her teeth through the pain and held on tightly. The tall man laughed as Straith began to turn blue. As his eyes rolled to the back of his head, a yell cut across the room, echoing off the stone.

"Enough!" Rovik descended the last few steps into The Cellar, strolled over to Shaila, and pressed his thumb into the bullet wound in her thigh. She screamed and released her captive. Straith crawled away, gasping and gagging as his partner continued to laugh. "Secure her legs, Hadra."

The laughing man walked over and pulled something down off the wall. He knelt at her feet and snapped two large metal cuffs around her ankles, still chuckling under his breath. The cuffs were connected to a short chain which he secured to a metal loop in the floor.

Rovik crossed his arms and glared down at the wound he'd just abused. "Who shot her?" he demanded to know.

"It was me, Uncle. Apologies," said a soft voice from the stairs. The lady Blade came down the steps to Rovik's side. "I was unaware you gave a cease-fire."

Uncle? Shaila put the pieces together as the Blade lowered her hood and removed her mask. Her features were so close to Amii's it was startling.

"Rose," Shaila said in awe.

Rose smiled. "Shaila."

"Such an assembly we have here," Rovik mused with a conniving smile. "So many people connected in so many ways. The world seems such a small place after all."

"Yes, very amusing," Rose muttered dryly.

"So you've traded your freedom for Amii's," Rovik said, staring at Shaila. "Tell me, how long do you think that'll last? You're locked up here, your Master is dead..."

Shaila closed her eyes in a feigned look of pain. They didn't know Drauses yet lived. That gave her hope.

"There aren't many who can protect her now," Rovik continued. "The ward she clings to, Aro, and the one so devoted to you, Miika, they're not much of a threat without their two best fighters. I expect to have my daughter back very soon. But for now, I have *you*, my golden goddess."

Rovik stroked her cheek.

Shaila spit in his face.

He laughed. "Oh, how I've missed you, dear Shaila. No lover since has brought me the satisfaction you did. You'll warm my bed yet again very soon."

"I wouldn't be so sure," Shaila said through chattering teeth.

"I don't expect you'll come willingly. That'd be too easy. For now, you need to be punished. A day or two in this hole should realign your loyalties. You'll still hate me, oh yes, but you'll think twice before running away again." He turned to Hadra and Straith. "You don't have free rein," he barked. "Cause pain only. No mortal wounds, no severing of any parts, and leave her important pieces..." he trailed a finger again down her face then fondled one of her breasts, "...free of scars." Rovik turned to leave, but then he rounded on Straith at the last second and punched the man between the legs. Hadra cackled again. "Keep your manhood in your pants. She's mine. If she dies, you'll wish you'd died with her."

Rose continued to stare at Shaila after Rovik walked away. Shaila glared back at her.

"I wish I'd known it was you behind the mask," Shaila said. "I'd have taken greater efforts to kill you."

Rose pouted. "Oh dear, and I thought we could be friends."

"You turned your back on Drauses and Amii."

Rose snorted with a roll of her eyes. "I did no such thing. You think your beloved Master was so perfect, so noble and loyal. *He* turned his back on *me* while his child still grew in my belly. What man abandons his own blood?"

"If you'd gone to him after, you'd have learned he loved you both enough to stay away, to give you a chance at something better than he could ever give you."

A twitch of her brow broke Rose's glare, betraying her true feelings before Rovik called her from the stairs, and she marched away like the loyal dog she was.

Hadra clapped his hands together happily, and Straith picked up one of Shaila's bolts from a nearby table, rolling it in his hands with a sick, toothless grin.

"These look like fun," he said.

❧

As she climbed the stone steps on her uncle's heels, Rose wondered what things Drauses must've said about her and if Shaila's words held any truth.

"What plans have you made to retrieve my daughter?" Rovik asked as they started across the lawn toward the house.

"I've an idea but have yet to voice it to your precious guard," Rose replied.

"Tell me."

"Gragern."

Rovik nodded with interest. "Go on."

"He made a move to corrupt Aro. The Elder spoke of information we could use to control the ward ourselves. We plan to have Amii walk out of their stronghold and right into our arms. If Aro can be persuaded to bring her to us, the girl won't hesitate to follow him."

"Hmm, but what will we do with the Man of the Mark once we have Amii?"

"Converting him to our cause will go a long way to smoothing things with our girl. It's likely, with Aro at her side, Amii will finally fall in line. All efforts should be made to bend him to our will. Perhaps you could task Hadra and Straith to persuade him. He can be Amii's pet, to keep her compliant."

Rovik hummed to himself, then nodded. "I like it. Keep me informed."

A sharp scream rose from The Cellar, and they both stopped to glance back at the metal doors that broke the grass back across the lawn. It seemed Straith and Hadra had begun.

Rovik smiled, but Rose frowned. "You should rein in your men," she warned. "If they break her mind, she'll be of no use to you."

"Are you worried for her?" Rovik asked in amusement. "Feeling a sisterhood with your old lover's latest whore?"

"I know her spirit is what you admire most. If they break it, she'll be nothing but a shell."

At a new, shrill shriek, Rovik chuckled. "There's no breaking that spirit, I can assure you." He turned and walked away, leaving his niece staring back at the door for a long moment before she followed yet again.

❧

Hours ticked by, but Amii had no way of counting them. They may well have been days as the time she spent in darkness bled together. It felt like an eternity. She stopped several times in a fit of tears, consumed in panic and grief. Would she die down here in the dark and the filth? From the near corners and deeply shadowed places of the tunnels came the scurrying and squeaking of rats. The longer Amii stood idle, the louder and closer they got. That drove her to keep moving above anything else.

At long last, she rounded a corner and spotted another beam of light ahead. She dashed forward and sobbed with relief at the sight of the ladder still intact below the grate. She grabbed hastily to a rung, but it was slippery, and her foot slid right off when she tried to climb. She made herself slow down and pick her footing with care.

The grate at the top was heavy and wouldn't budge as Amii pushed. She wouldn't go back down, not with daylight and fresh air so close, so she wrapped an arm around the top rung of the ladder and climbed higher, ducking her head until her back rested against the grate. Using her legs as leverage, she pushed with all her might until the grate lifted, and she slid it an inch or so to the side. She rested for a moment then tried again. Inch by inch, she slid the grate away. Her back stung where the metal dug in and her legs burned from exertion, but she eventually made a hole large enough to squeeze through. After a quick peek to be sure the way was safe, she hoisted herself out into an alley.

Amii scrambled back against the nearest building and sat with her legs drawn to her chest, sobbing into her knees. Never again would she venture into those forsaken tunnels. They were things of nightmares. She searched for any sign of where she was, but this alley was all back doors and garbage bins, so she pushed herself up and staggered on aching legs to the nearest street. The store fronts here looked vaguely familiar, and she wracked her memory as she turned left and wandered up the sidewalk.

People shopping on the street stopped to stare at her filthy clothes as she passed. Amii picked up the pace lest someone recognize her through the dirt and grime. When she came to the end of the street, she knew with sudden certainty where she was. She turned right and broke into a run, rushing the three blocks up to Polco Street. Another right turn and half a dozen blocks later, Amii could see the river in the distance. Polco Street was too busy to try to get through the fence at the end—she would draw far too much attention—so she darted down a few side alleys until she stood alone, staring at the water. The only thing stopping her now was a towering wall of metal links.

Amii was exhausted, but she had one last hurdle to jump. That was exactly what she planned to do: jump it. A garbage bin overflowing with stinking trash sat nearby. Amii tossed off the top layer of rubbish and threw the lid over the top of the can. She pulled it one foot at a time down the alley to the fence. She climbed on top, praying the lid would bear her weight.

She laced her fingers and wedged the toes of her shoes through the wires. With a hop, she flung her right leg over, but she underestimated how hard it would be to hold herself from falling over. She searched desperately with her toes for a foothold on the other side, but her grip was failing fast. She leaned further over, lost her footing, and tumbled headfirst over the fence into the dirt. She landed on her hands, and her right arm took too much of the force. There was a loud pop, and Amii screamed in pain. She lay clutching her arm to her chest and sobbing until she remembered she was on the right side of the fence now. The river gurgled a few feet away, and she staggered to its bank for a much-needed drink and washed her face.

The sun was sinking low as she made her way down the bank to the end of Polco Street. She saw the ferryman moored at the pier and broke into a run. Alek caught sight of her and hopped from his boat to rush to her side.

"By the gods! What happened?" He reached for her cradled arm, but Amii jerked away from him. She had no more trust for strangers. "It's all right, child. Amii is it? Where's Shaila?"

"She's not here?" Amii asked with dread. The last of her hopes for Shaila's safety were dashed. She closed her eyes in grief and pain and burst into a new batch of tears.

Alek waved toward his boat. "Come. Let's take you back to your father."

"My father is... is dead."

Alek shook his head. "That's not so, little one. Shaila made me promise to deliver you to him at the lumber yard."

"Really?" Amii asked, her tears slowing. "Shaila said that?"

"Just hours ago," Alek replied with a nod.

With new hope, Amii climbed aboard, and Alek shoved away from the pier.

"Hold on tight, now," the ferryman warned, and the boat lurched forward.

Chapter 20

THERE WAS A soft knock on Gragern's door. No one had come to see him since Dagon and the others locked him in his quarters, so the noise startled him. There was a click as the door was unlocked, and an unknown Mark shoved through the door, his head and face concealed by hood and mask. Gragern backed up several steps and tensed to draw his blade. The man surprised him, however, by holding out a small slip of paper. Puzzled, the Elder Master took it and read it twice. He smiled.

"Yes, this'll do," he declared. "But I won't make a move until I know who I'm working with."

The Mark hesitated a moment, but then he dropped his hood and pulled off his mask.

Gragern smiled wider then began to laugh. "You were the last I suspected."

❧

Shaila had been gone a day. Drauses sat in his quarters sipping a glass of whiskey. He hated drinking alone. He took a large swig of the amber liquid and willed it to burn him alive from the inside out. Could he be any more of a fool? He seriously doubted it.

First, there was Rose. Drauses had cared for her deeply, even more so when he learned she was with child. He was to be a father. Nothing else in his life came close to that feeling of pure terror and joy. Then, Rose's father learned about the babe, that his precious girl had been lying with a Man of the Mark. To say he was furious did Dellar no justice. When Rose was whisked away to the West, Drauses thought perhaps she and the child would be better off. He was young and foolish, but also knew they'd have a better life with Rovik than he could ever give them here in the East. When he heard Rose died during childbirth, Drauses was crushed with guilt and regret. Now he learned it was all a ruse and Rose still lived. He couldn't decide which hurt worse: her loss or her betrayal.

Next came Marcel. Drauses had once thought the ward so full of potential. Marcel excelled at everything he put his mind to, and what he'd put his mind to was deception. He'd played his Master for a fool and turned traitor. Drauses ignored the signs and even the concerns of his closest friend, so convinced he was of Marcel's loyalty. To be struck down by his own ward was a blow to his pride. He was more than lucky to escape the mansion that night with his life. He thought the gods had intervened and sent him not only a guardian but a prodigious replacement for the ward he'd lost.

Enter Shaila: a breathtaking beauty in the perfect place at the right time. A true damsel in distress. How could any man resist? Her performance that night was spectacular. How dedicated she was for two whole years, so loyal, so focused... Oh so slowly, she'd stolen his heart, one small piece at a time, until she was sharing his bed and had him confessing his love for her. Drauses squeezed his eyes shut at the memory of her falling to tears in his arms.

'Drauses, I... I love you.' Her words haunted him. Drauses leapt from his chair and flung his drink at the wall. It smashed in a shower of glass and whiskey. A second later, there was a knock at his door.

"What?" he shouted.

Miika strolled in.

Drauses rolled his eyes. "Perfect. Please, do come in," Drauses beckoned sarcastically. "What could you possibly want from me?"

Miika didn't utter a word, merely held out a paper to Drauses who snatched it testily. When he realized who the letter was from, he clung to every word.

Drauses,

Once you receive this message, I'll be long gone. Miika and I found listening devices in the pockets of our robes. We know not who hid them there, but it's clear there's a traitor amongst our brothers. I doubt you'll believe me, but I beg you to be cautious. I'm going after Amii. By the time you read this, your daughter will either be with you once more or I'll have failed. Either way, I'll fight to my last breath to see Amii returned to you. While I still have blood to give.

Though you may have doubts, I want you to know I care deeply for you both, and every word of feeling I spoke was pure truth. I know I've no right, but I beg you for one favor: please see Miika's situation with Gragern is resolved. He deserves happiness, as do you and Amii, and I wish it for you all for the rest of your days. Goodbye.

Shaila

"Why didn't you give me this yesterday?" Drauses raged.

"Because she asked me not to," Miika replied. He stared at the paper.

Drauses flipped the letter over and found another note scribbled amongst the typing of the old document.

Miika,

Please forgive me, friend, for leaving you behind, but I can't let you sabotage your future with the guild for me. I beg you not to come after me. Stay and help discover who's trying to ruin the Marks from within. You're the only one I can trust to do so should I fail.

Please keep this note in your possession for one day, or until Amii is safely delivered to The Yard, whichever comes first, then deliver it to Drauses.

*Find happiness, dear Miika, as much of it as you can, and know
that I'll forever consider you my closest and most treasured friend.*

With love,

Your Queen of Hearts

Drauses stared at Miika, lost for words. Miika held out his hand and
deposited several pieces of broken casings and wires into the Master's
palm. Drauses studied them for a moment before searching his own
robes. He wrapped his fingers around a hard, flat object sewn into one
of his outer pockets. He tore the fabric open and pulled out a small
copper disk.

"You understand now, don't you?" Miika said, his fists clenched in
barely controlled anger. "The moment I was discovered in that office and
confessed she was gone, they heard it all. They knew she was coming. She
truly did march off to her doom, alone, for you. All because you believed
the words of our enemy over the woman who loves you. You don't deserve
her, you ignorant fool."

Drauses pushed past Miika and rushed outside. The dark of dusk was
beginning to fall as he stormed across The Yard and into Julta's workshop.
He called for the inventor who appeared a second later from a back room.
Drauses held his finger to his lips, then he dropped all the broken bits and
the still-intact gadget on the counter. Julta didn't hesitate to dive in and
inspect every shard and wire. He pulled out a knife and used the blade
to gently separate the casing on the functioning device. Drauses leaned
close to study the little round pod full of wires and one red light blinking
steadily on and off. Julta dug around its insides for a long time.

"Well?" Drauses barked, and the light turned solid red. Julta stared
at it in awe until it went back to blinking, then, with a flick of his blade,
he cut a single wire, and the light died.

"It's a listening device," Julta said in awe. "A good one. Better than
I could make." His voice dropped to a mere whisper. "He was always so
good at this."

"What was that?" Drauses asked.

"I've seen something like this before," the inventor admitted. "It was much bigger, and very complex, with dozens of wires and knobs. Of course, that was many years ago. He's made impressive improvements since—"

"Who?" the Master snapped.

"My brother, Roth. He was good with trinkets like these."

"I didn't know you had a brother, Julta."

"I recognize his work... but..." Julta stared at the broken pieces on his counter, his eyes drifting off into old memories, completely forgetting about the Master in front of him.

"Go on," Drauses urged.

"I believed my brother dead, sir," Julta said.

"Seems that's happening a lot lately." Drauses nodded down to the bits of copper and wire. "How far could someone hear with one of these?"

"My brother is good at what he does, but he can't work miracles. This device is small. You'd need a powerful receiver to hear it from any distance. There must be one hidden somewhere on the grounds. It gathers overheard conversations from these little disks and sends them... somewhere else." He shrugged.

"So, you're telling me this could only be the work of one of our own?"

"Unless you think it more likely someone snuck in, planted the gadgets in all our pockets, set up a receiver, and managed to sneak back out again undetected."

Drauses shook his head. This discovery didn't prove Shaila's innocence. She could've known about the listening devices from the start. Telling him about them now seemed a bit too convenient. But if she wanted to get back in his good graces, then why did she run?

"Is there anything else I should know if your brother is indeed working with our enemies?" Drauses asked.

"My brother specialized in things of stealth, things to... observe, to gather information, to spy. He liked making weapons designed to fail or to trick: guns that fired backward at the shooter, hot sticks that electrocuted their wielders—"

"What about a blade that wouldn't wound too deeply when thrusted into a body?"

"More like swords that slide back through their hilts and stab their wielders instead, but a weapon like you just described certainly wouldn't be hard for him to create."

"Drauses!" someone hollered outside.

Drauses pushed away from the counter and stepped out of the workshop to see what the fuss was about.

Alek marched across The Yard, waving away the many concerned Masters and wards gathering around him. A disheveled, tear-stained Amii was tucked under his arm.

Drauses' heart soared, and he broke into a run. He fell to his knees and yanked the girl into his arms. He hugged her tightly, relieved beyond words to have her back in one piece. When he pulled away again to voice as much, Amii slapped him across the face. She struck left-handed, a weak blow that caused him little pain, but it stunned him to silence, nonetheless.

"How could you let her go alone?" Amii spat, her eyes full of hot anger and tears.

"She went without my knowledge," Drauses replied. He was being vague, and Amii knew it.

"You knew she was gone, yet here you stand!" the girl raged. "Why didn't you go after her?"

"I... I'm sorry," was all Drauses could reply.

"We can't leave her!"

Drauses held his daughter by the shoulders, beseechingly, begging her forgiveness with his eyes. "I'll make this right, but first I need you to breathe and start at the beginning. Tell me everything. Please."

Amii recounted the whole tale: from Shaila slipping in the second-floor window to Amii's fall from atop the fence. She held her swollen, purple arm up for Drauses' inspection. He pulled the girl into another careful hug, thankful beyond words that she'd made it against such odds. Behind her, Alek turned to head back to his boat.

"Wait, please, Alek," Drauses called. "Your services may yet be needed here."

"What will we do about Shaila?" Amii asked. "I know she lives. Rovik said not to kill her."

Drauses' blood ran cold. If Rovik wanted Shaila alive, he had plans for her, and none of them could be good. "I'll get her back."

"Promise?"

"Yes, child. I promise."

"Amii!" Aro had spotted the girl from across The Yard, and he waved as he approached.

Amii whipped around at the sound of his voice. "Aro!" she cried, and she abandoned her father and ran instead to the ward who took a knee to draw her into a one-armed hug. Back in the company of her most trusted guard, Amii burst into tears all over again.

"What happened, love?" Aro asked.

"Shaila came for me, and Rovik's men kept shooting at us even when he told them to stop. Shaila shoved me into the sewers and told me to meet Alek, but I didn't know which way to go. I kept walking and walking. It was so dark and there were rats everywhere, Aro, I could hear them. I was lost and so scared I was going to… that I'd…" She was sobbing now, and Aro held her close and let her cry into his robes.

"Shh, now," he said. He kissed her softly on the top of the head. "You're safe with us again. I promise I won't leave your side, all right?"

Amii nodded and stood up a little straighter. "Your arm," she muttered when she noticed the sling around Aro's injured limb.

"I'm alright." He touched her arm. "But what happened to yours?"

"I fell."

"Come, you should see Boon."

Drauses walked over, and Aro eyed him warily. The Master turned out Aro's front pocket and ripped another listening device from the fabric before letting the ward lead Amii away toward the clinic. He watched them go, and his heart ached a little when his daughter didn't look back.

"Master Drauses!" Julta called as he rushed across The Yard. Drauses dropped the disk on the ground and crushed it under his boot.

"What is it, Julta? I've no time to waste right now."

"I understand," Julta said. "But I have something I think might help." He took a long sword out from under his arm. "Shaila inspired it, sir."

"Shaila?" Drauses said, his interest piqued. He tentatively took the sword by the hilt and pulled it free of its sheath. The blade was half again as long as Drauses' old sword and much thicker and heavier than he was used to, but the hilt fit his hand perfectly when he flexed his fingers around it.

"Shaila mentioned your disdain for hot sticks," Julta chimed as he bounced on his feet, barely able to contain his excitement. "I present you with the very first hot *blade*. Press the button by your thumb."

Drauses pressed as instructed, and the blade began to glow faintly and hum with a slight crackle.

"I modified it to be quiet, stealthy. No whip for a Man of the Mark, no. A blade! A blade that electrocutes! Press the button under your middle finger."

Drauses did so, and small bolts began to dance across the blade, doing back flips like tiny blue acrobats. It crackled menacingly now, and the hilt grew warm in his hand. Drauses pressed the same button again, and the blade went back to humming. Drauses gaped in wonder.

"In its lower setting, it causes pain and limited loss of motor functions if applied to the skin," Julta explained. "The higher setting will knock an attacker unconscious."

"Julta, how did you accomplish such a thing?" Drauses asked, studying the buttons on the hilt.

"Wait! Wait! There's more!" Julta took a hot stick from the back of his pants that Drauses hadn't noticed before and backed away several steps. He uncoiled the whip in the dirt and switched it on. Drauses eyed the weapon with loathing. "In its higher setting..." Julta waved expectantly, and Drauses pressed the button again to bring the blade to life with sparking electricity. "...If it comes in contact with a hot stick..." Julta pulled the whip back and struck at Drauses who blocked the blow with the sword. The whip snaked around the blade before there was a loud pop and a hiss. Julta shrieked and dropped the hot stick to hold his hand in agony. Drauses switched off his sword and came to the inventor's aid. He inspected Julta's palm which was burned bright red and already blistering.

"You fool, Julta! Why did you do that?"

"It's nothing," Julta insisted. He picked up the discarded hot stick and held it out for Drauses' inspection. "I wanted you to see how your blade can burn out the electrical components in a hot stick." The handle of the whip was a ruined, smoking mess. Julta flipped the weapon's switch several times, but the whip remained a lifeless coil in the dirt. "This sword is a hot stick's worst enemy!" Julta bounced up and down on the balls of his feet again, waiting impatiently for the Master's reply.

Drauses stared down at the sword in his hands, and his face split into a wide grin.

Julta's eyes widened. "You like it?"

"This is perfect, Julta," Drauses admitted.

"Yes! Yes! I've done it!" Julta cried with a pump of his arms and a jump of joy. "I've tempted the impossibly-particular Master Drauses into taking a new weapon!" he screamed. All the watching Masters and wards laughed at the eccentric little man's utter joy. "Shaila told me I could do it if I found the right design, and I did it! I did it at last!"

Drauses strapped the weapon around his waist. "You'll be highly rewarded for this, Julta, I assure you."

"No reward required, sir. I'm victorious in this battle with you and can die a happy man."

Drauses shook Julta's hand. In the corner of his eye, he caught sight of Miika sulking by the door of the bunkhouse, and he walked over to the ward who eyed him back with disgust.

"I'm going after her," said Drauses.

"So I assumed," Miika replied sourly. "I want to come with you."

"I know, Miika, and you have every right to ask that of me," Drauses admitted, "but I fear I'd be leaving us far too thin here if you did. You, Aro, and Dagon are the only ones left who know about Gragern's poisonous influences. And now we have a brother among us trying to sabotage. We need to know if the two are connected and which Master or ward is reporting to our enemies. I ask that you stay instead and uncover this traitor. You're good at gathering information, yes?"

"It was one of the many things Gragern relied on me for."

"Then put that past experience to good use. Between the three of you, I'm confident you'll uncover our hidden rat."

Miika chewed his cheek.

"Please, Miika," Drauses beseeched. "I'll bring her back, I promise, but I must know I'll be bringing her back to safety, not to yet another trap laid by our enemies. And Amii. I need ones I can trust to watch over her while I'm away. Will you do this for me? For the guild?"

"Do you trust me?" Miika asked as he crossed his arms.

"Shaila trusts you. That's good enough for me."

Drauses offered Miika his hand, and Miika regarded him for a long, tense moment before taking it. They shook as brothers and comrades, but perhaps not quite yet friends.

"Make them pay for whatever pain they've brought her," Miika sneered.

Drauses nodded. "I'll burn the whole place to the ground if I have to. Shaila will return with me, and our enemies will pay for every drop of blood spilt, I promise you."

⌁

Miika stood with Dagon and Aro in front of the clinic and watched as Drauses climbed aboard Alek's boat and sped away up the river in the dark.

"Here, Miika," Dagon said as he handed Miika his previously confiscated blade. "So, we've a traitor of a brother among us who plants listening devices and reports to our enemies? I can barely believe it."

Miika nodded. "That's how they knew when best to strike Drauses and how they gathered all the information they needed to poison him against Shaila. We can't speak freely around any of our brothers for fear their pockets may be listening."

"I wonder if this same brother is responsible for Julta's failed communication boxes," Aro mused. "I asked around. No one but Shaila and Drauses heard our call. It's as if their box was the only one functioning properly as we traveled."

"I suspect so," said Miika. "Unless we've more than one traitor in our ranks."

"Are there any leads to trail this rat?" Aro asked.

"None," Miika replied. "Master Dagon, I thought you could question and investigate amongst the Masters, and Aro the same throughout the wards. If you have suspicions, bring them to me, and I'll dig deeper to find the truth of the fellow's loyalties. I'm good at that."

"This is the work of a ward," Dagon said with a nod.

"How are you certain?" Aro asked.

"Just a feeling. I'll scrutinize the Masters anyway, but I believe once all is brought to light, we'll find this corruption in a ward both young and ambitious." Dagon sighed. "Either way, there's nothing to be done tonight. Let's tackle this head-on in the morning."

"What?" Miika asked incredulously. "Master Drauses wishes this matter seen to right away. We should start—"

"Miika, it's been a long day. Most have retired to bed already."

"The longer we delay, the more our enemies—"

"They'll hear little more than snores before first light. That's soon enough to start our investigation." Dagon regarded his ward, changing the subject and cutting off Miika's rebuttal as he asked, "Is Amii well?"

"Boon is splinting her arm. She'll be fine."

"She's a brave little thing."

"She wandered lost in the sewers for nearly a whole day," Aro said in awe.

"You'll find separate rooms for ladies on the second floor. The two of you should stay near the girl until Drauses returns. I'm sure Amii won't object. Gather her as soon as Boon is finished and get some rest."

"Yes, sir," Miika and Aro replied in unison.

The three men bid each other good night with promises to meet again at first light.

⁂

Alek agreed to remain moored at the Western shore until dawn. Drauses knew he would either be back by then or not at all. As Alek nestled down into the bottom of his boat for a nap, Drauses approached the fence at the end of Polco Street. His pick made short work of the lock on the gate, and he left it open as he headed up the street.

The estate was a fortress surrounded by thick walls of stone topped with metal spikes every few inches, each covered in razor sharp barbs that stuck up at all angles. To any stranger, it would seem impenetrable, but to a Man of the Mark, it was child's play. He found a side door in an alley full of trash bins. The lock was large and impressive but still took a simple key. Any lock with a tumbler was no match for Drauses, and he let himself into the grounds with little difficulty. Slow and quiet was his aim. With any luck, he'd reach Shaila without setting off a single alarm, but once he had her, he'd set fire to the house if that was what it took to escape.

Drauses wondered where they were holding his ward. There were several outbuildings: sheds, an office, a carriage house, and a barn with separate stables. Drauses had no desire to search each one from rafters to foundation. He'd grab the first guard he could and start interrogating.

A line of shrubbery hid the Master as he stalked down the wall toward the back of the house. A group of three men stood talking and smoking at the corner of a nearby shed. Drauses drew close enough to listen.

"Straith and Hadra must be taking naps. I've heard nary a murmur in over an hour."

"I, for one, am glad to have a break from the noise. The constant screaming is... unnerving."

"Aww, are you feeling badly for the whore? Perhaps you can convince Rovik to let you take her place."

Drauses' stomach twisted.

"Give me a cigarette."

"To Vedia with you. You owe me close to a pack already."

"Well, give me one more and make it a full pack then, you stingy bastard."

They stood puffing away and jeering each other until one man elbowed another and nodded toward the house.

"Here comes the boss." They ground their cigarettes under their feet as Marcel marched across the lawn.

"What are you all doing standing about?" Marcel fumed.

"Just having a quick smoke."

"Why are so many of us out here anyway? Aren't the worst of those masked bastards dead already?"

"By all means, do my job for me," Marcel sneered. He moved closer, and the guard backed away several steps.

"No need to be that way, boss. I was only asking."

"Drauses lives," Marcel announced. "What say you now about your numbers?"

"Rovik said he's dead."

"Rose and I haven't yet informed him. Rest assured if we had, things would be far less pleasant back here. You're welcome. Drauses may not yet know we have the woman alive, but it's only a matter of time. Do you wish to take a blade in the back because you let your guard down? Get back to work and watch your asses!"

The men disbursed as Marcel marched off toward the barn. One of the guards walked along the long wall by the bushes, stepping steadily toward Drauses' hiding place while the others headed across the grass into the southern spans of the lawn. Drauses let his prey walk closer until he was on the other side of Drauses' bush, then he leapt from behind the greenery and snagged the man by the neck. With an arm wrapped around the guard's throat, Drauses increased the pressure until the man started turning colors. He leaned close to the guard's ear.

"Where are they holding the Lady of the Mark?" Drauses asked. He relaxed his grip enough for the guard to answer. Instead of information, he received a string of insults and was told to go to Vedia. Drauses shrugged and snapped the man's neck.

"After you," Drauses muttered. He hid the guard's body behind the shrubs and moved on.

Chapter 21

ARO MOVED LIKE a shadow across the darkened yard to the eastern wall. It was hours since Drauses had left and everyone else was long ago dead asleep. The ward's eyes raked the wall up and down as he searched for a way to the other side. He couldn't climb it, not with his shoulder in this condition. The gate was guarded night and day by at least two Marks, but at the opposite side of the grounds, a long wire fence—constructed when the lumber yard was running in its prime—stood to ward off intruders from the water. It was much shorter than the wall. Aro thought perhaps he could handle a simple chain link fence.

Toward the left side of The Yard, where the fence met the new wall, there was a ninety-degree corner. Aro took his arm out of his sling and placed his feet against the solid wall, lacing his fingers through the wires of the fence. With a jump, he used his legs as leverage and climbed the fence as quickly as he could, his shoulder burning the whole way. He vaulted over the top and landed on his feet on the other side in water up to his ankles. Climbing back over upon his return would be harder, but he'd manage. He put his arm back in the sling and sloshed down the riverbank.

Aro walked next to the Jespa until he was far enough from The Yard not to be spotted by the sentries, then he passed between a couple of buildings to the street. He put several more blocks between him and headquarters before he stopped and pulled an odd silver tube from his pocket. He put the end of the tube to his lips and blew into it. To any person near, not a sound was made, but the tune wasn't meant for human ears. Aro stood on the sidewalk alone for several long moments, waiting. He was met with nothing but silence, so he tried again.

From the far distance came a single deep bark. Aro smiled and signaled one more time. The answering bark was much closer now, and a moment later a giant black shepherd came bounding around a corner into the street, ears flapping and long curly mane whipping in the wind. The canine pounded down the sidewalk to Aro who took a knee to greet the animal affectionately.

"You clever girl," he crooned. "I knew you'd find me just fine." He produced a morsel from his pocket to the animal's delight. At her neck, Aro unscrewed a cap from a tube secured to her collar. Inside was a rolled piece of paper he fished out with his little finger. He read the message quickly then flattened the paper against the wall of the nearest building, turning it to its blank side to scroll his reply. When he was done, he rolled in anew and secured it back inside the tube on the dog's collar.

"Go home, Rayn," Aro ordered. At two short blows from the whistle, the dog barked twice and hurried away. Aro watched her go until she was well out of sight before retracing his steps back to The Yard.

Miika heard Aro stir and climb out of bed, but he kept his eyes shut tight until Aro snuck from the room before he jumped up and followed. He could barely hear Aro's soft footfalls in the dark but managed to shadow the man through the halls and down the stairs. Miika's heart raced as he watched a man he called "friend" sneak out into the dark. Perhaps the rat they sought was much closer than they anticipated. Rage bubbled up at the betrayal when Aro hopped the fence and disappeared down the river. He waited several long moments to see if Aro would return right away, and, when he didn't, Miika turned on his heels and rushed back to their shared quarters.

Aro's knapsack sat on the floor next to his bed. Miika knelt beside it, flipped open the top, and started rifling through it. Clothes, playing cards, toiletries, medicine kit — Miika pulled it all from the bag and set it aside as he looked for anything incriminating. There was a book of short stories and witticisms with most of its pages missing, used to construct Aro's tiny, folded creations, a half dozen of which littered the bottom of his pack. A small leather satchel yielded nasty-smelling square bits that looked like dried meat.

Miika's stomach filled with ice when his fingers wrapped around a small glass bottle. Inside were dozens of small white tablets. His first thought was of Shaila and the odd sickness she came down with days ago. Miika uncorked the bottle and shook one of the pills out into his palm. He snapped it in half, smelled it, then tasted it against the tip of his tongue. They were nothing he'd seen before. Was Aro drugging people? Perhaps Amii? Miika had the sudden urge to check on the girl in the adjoining room and began hastily stuffing Aro's things back into the pack.

A squeak of a floorboard alerted him to danger, and he swiveled and knocked the sword away which had been about to skewer him in the back. He was still on his knees and struggled to get to his feet, but his opponent, a masked, unknown Mark, was content to keep him pinned where he was. Strikes were coming hard and fast, and Miika blocked and dodged the best he could from the floor. A punch to the face left him dazed, but he shook it off and landed his own blow to the gut of his attacker.

The unknown Mark doubled over but recovered soon enough to strike again at Miika's face. Miika clasped the man's wrist and squeezed with a twist until the blade clattered to the floor, then he kicked out at his knees. The Mark jumped back to avoid the blow and yanked his wrist from Miika's grasp. From inside his robes, he produced a weighted leather club Miika knew all too well. The club caught Miika in the jaw, and he fell sideways against the bed in a daze. It came down again, this time smashing hard into Miika's kneecap which shattered under the blow. Miika howled in pain then watched in horror as Amii opened her door across the room. Miika's attacker noticed the girl as well and prepared to make a dive for her.

"Run, Amii!" Miika shouted. He pulled the pistol from inside his robes and took aim.

The Mark refocused his attention on Miika and grabbed Miika's arm, forcing it to the side where he smashed Miika's wrist against the wood of the bed frame as hard as he could, over and over again. There was a crack of breaking bone, and the gun fell from Miika's limp fingers. It bounced across the bed and onto the floor.

The man in the mask wasn't going to let Miika have the upper hand again. He straddled Miika and rained blows to his head and chest with the club. Miika grabbed the Mark by the throat, but darkness was starting to creep in, and his fingers refused to tighten. With one final blow from the club to his temple, Miika fell unconscious.

⇜

Amii watched The Mark who had just knocked Miika unconscious retrieve his blade and raise it high over Miika's chest.

"Get away from him!" she screamed in a panic.

He started and hesitated long enough for Amii to dive for the gun on the floor. She gripped the heavy weapon in her left hand and tried to steady it with the right despite her broken arm, shaking violently all the while. The Mark rose and faced her. He took a step forward, obviously convinced she lacked the guts to take a life, but Amii was done letting anyone hurt her or the ones she loved. She raised the gun and yanked back the trigger, but the force of the shot nearly knocked her on her backside. She missed completely and almost dropped the weapon. She readied to shoot again, but the Mark was already running and soon vanished out the door.

Once he was gone, Amii ran across the room and knelt next to Miika. She choked out a sob at the sight of his lifeless, bloody face. She took hold of his shoulder and shook him.

"Miika? Miika!" she called but got no answer.

"Amii!" Aro screamed from the hall, and a second later, he burst into the room. He took in the whole scene, then pushed Amii away as he knelt by Miika instead.

"Is he..." Amii tried to ask.

Aro felt Miika's bloody throat for a moment. "He lives."

"Where were you?"

"I stepped out to relieve myself. I'm sorry."

The room was soon full of men drawn by the noise. Several of them lifted Miika from the floor and carried him away to Boon's clinic. Amii answered as many questions as she could before she asked to see Miika. Aro agreed to escort her.

꿈

Drauses cut down half a dozen men and not a single one would tell him where they were holding Shaila. Rovik didn't deserve this level of loyalty. Or perhaps they feared what Rovik would do to them if they gave him up. Marcel had disappeared, but there were still many guards Drauses could question. One stood in the window of the barn with a rifle, and Drauses knew he'd get no further with the sentry looking out over the lawn. He slipped from shadow to shadow to the barn, examining the walls for a foothold, but they were far too smooth to climb from the outside. Drauses stuck his head in a nearby window and checked that the ground floor was empty before hopping inside.

The lookout was in the hayloft, and he paced back and forth between the northern and eastern windows every few minutes. Drauses knew he dare not try to climb up to the loft—the ladder was ancient and would make far too much noise under his weight—so, instead, he wandered through the hay bales until he stood directly underneath the guard's platform. The wooden planks of the loft's floor were warped, leaving gaps between the boards up to half an inch wide in several places.

Drauses climbed on a nearby hay bale, and as the sentry walked from one side of the loft to the other, he slid the tip of his sword between two boards and waited for the right moment. As the guard stepped overhead, Drauses plunged his sword up to catch the man in the shin. At the same moment the blade made contact, Drauses switched it on to its high setting. The guard convulsed then collapsed to the floor when Drauses switched the sword off again. Through yet another crack in the wood, the Master slit his enemy's throat.

Drauses snuck back out into the dark leaving a stream of red trickling from the loft onto the hay below.

꿈

Amii refused to leave the clinic until Boon told her the truth about Miika's condition. He put the news to her as softly as he could, but it wasn't good. He'd done all he could but wasn't sure when, if ever, Miika would wake. Amii cried, blaming herself for not hearing the commotion and intervening sooner despite Aro's insistence it wasn't her fault. He made her go back to bed, but, before she would, she whispered for him to give her Miika's pistol. He hesitantly took it from his robes and laid it in her waiting palm. While Boon's back was turned, she hid it under Miika's folded robes on a chair near his bed then kissed Miika on his battered cheek before following Aro back to their quarters.

As soon as Amii was tucked away in her room, there was a soft knock on Aro's door. Gragern let himself in without waiting for an invitation, and Aro drew his sword.

"You're supposed to be locked away," Aro said.

"I'm still Liege to this guild. A mere locked door will never hold me." Gragern smiled. "I'm here to sweeten our previous arrangement."

"I thought I made it clear I wasn't interested."

Gragern held out a slip of paper. "You may want to reconsider."

Drauses headed toward the stables, and the smell of horse and hay drifted in the breeze. As he drew up to the doors, a guard stepped out to light a cigarette. Drauses barely had time to grab the man and haul him out of sight. He put his knife to the guard's throat and leaned close.

"Tell me where to find the Lady of the Mark and I'll let you live," Drauses whispered. Finally, he got a nod of cooperation.

"The Cellar," the man said in a rush. "The two metal doors between the mansion and the carriage house."

"Much obliged," Drauses said. Ever a man of his word, he struck the guard across the temple, rendering him unconscious instead of ending his life. The carriage house was just around the corner, so Drauses cut through the stables to save time.

Horses have a sixth sense when it comes to men. They know a man's intentions and sometimes seem able to read his thoughts. The horses in the stables backed away from their stall doors as Drauses marched down the walkway. They knew. This man was a servant of Gindar tonight, sent to deal swift justice to those deserving. They wanted no part of him and made no sound as he passed.

Drauses was growing impatient. He rushed from the stables to the carriage house and around to the side that faced the grand mansion. The metal doors of The Cellar were a hundred yards away, reflective in the moonlight. Two men stood in the doorway of the carriage house, looking out across the yard as they smoked. Drauses slunk back into the dark and headed for the back door.

"How long do you think they'll keep her down there?" one guard asked the other.

"It's not yet been a day. She'd be getting off easy if they let her out now."

"He still plans to take her as his mistress when they're done. Who'd want to lie with one of Straith and Hadra's playthings?"

"Once they're done with her, she'll have forgotten how to suck—" The guard choked on his last word as Drauses' knife flew through the air and plunged into his skull. His partner jumped back a step and whipped around in time to watch Drauses' sword swing up a heartbeat before it cleaved his head off his shoulders.

Drauses retrieved his knife and stowed it in his pocket before stepping over the bodies and heading across the grass toward The Cellar doors. He was relieved to find them unlocked, and he pulled one up enough to slip inside then closed it silently behind him.

The stench hit him first—the metallic, copper tang of blood stuck in his nose as he descended the stone steps. The dim lighting was barely enough to show him the way down, and it cast eerie shadows all around the walls. Once Drauses descended far enough to peer into the room, he froze.

Straith and Hadra, Rovik's notorious executioners, stood wiping down several tools at a counter, their backs to the stairs, not a care in the world. Shaila hung naked in the center of the room by her wrists, her feet dangling limply on the stone floor. He quickly turned away. He couldn't look at her, not yet. There were two more men to deal with first. He moved down the last few steps to the floor and crept closer.

Drauses took his sword in both hands. When he was but an arm's length away, he reared back and plunged it straight through Straith's middle. Hadra's eyes widened at the sight of the blade protruding from his partner's belly, and Straith grasped at the blade with a look of shock, as if he thought it a figment of his imagination.

Hadra picked up a hot stick from his workstation as Drauses yanked his sword free with his boot on Straith's back. The two men faced each other. Hadra's weapon came to life as a rope of glowing blue. Drauses smiled as he switched on his sword, and Hadra's eyes widened at the sight of the electric blade.

The whip drew back and flew at Drauses who let it coil around his blade before he switched it to high. The handle of the whip spit and crackled, and Hadra dropped it with a cry of pain. Drauses switched off his sword then yanked it back to send the handle of the whip flying. He snatched it out of the air and unwound the whip from his blade. Hadra tried to come in swinging, but Drauses was in no mood for a boxing match. With one quick roll and a hard punch between Hadra's legs, Drauses had the executioner doubled over and wheezing.

Drauses wrapped the end of the whip around Hadra's neck from behind, then he threw the handle up over a beam in the ceiling. He yanked down hard, and Hadra lifted off his feet into the air. Drauses coiled the whip again, knotting it up tight around the beam. Hadra's eyes bulged from his face, and his feet kicked madly beneath him. Drauses walked around in front of the executioner, hot hatred boiling his blood, and took hold of Hadra's ankles. He pulled down as hard as he could until, with a final jerk, there was a snap and a gurgle, and Hadra stilled, swinging slowly back and forth at the end of his noose.

Drauses took a deep breath before he turned to confront the pale, lifeless form of the woman he loved. At first glance, he feared she was already dead. She dangled by her arms like a sick, twisted trophy in the middle of the room. Her body was covered in gashes. They'd avoided her breasts, but every other inch of her torso, front and back, was sliced to cause pain. Blood ran down her legs in tiny streams and dripped from her toes to the stone floor below. Two bolts, which he recognized as her own, stuck from her body: one in her shoulder and one in her thigh below an already-oozing wound.

Drauses drew closer, expecting the worst. He touched her throat with a trembling hand, searching desperately for a pulse… and found one, the gods be praised. He had to act fast.

The bolt in her shoulder stuck straight through with the tip protruding out the back, so he broke off the shaft and used the flat side of his knife to shove the bolt through a little further until he could grab it from behind. When he pulled it the rest of the way through, Shaila sucked in a raspy breath, coughed, and cried out in pain.

"Shaila?" he called.

Her eyes fluttered open and focused, like the switch of life being thrown, and she peered at him in disbelief.

"You… you're not real," she muttered.

"I *am* real," he assured her. "I'll take you from this Vedian place, but I must see to this last bolt first."

"No," she whimpered. "Please."

Drauses knelt to examine the bolt in her thigh. It was buried too deeply in the muscle to see the tip. He took out his knife.

"I'm sorry, love," he whispered, and he made an incision below the bolt. Another sharp cry of pain nearly brought him to tears, but he could see the tip. He pressed on. He used his finger and knife to guide the tip out the same direction it went in. Once it was free, he threw the bloodied bolt away, took off his robes, and ripped off a strip of his shirt for a temporary bandage. He tied it tight around her leg over the wound.

Drauses wrapped an arm around her, and, with one quick snick, slit the binding around her wrists, and she fell into his arms. He lowered her to the floor. Her skin was ice cold and ghostly pale. He wrapped her in his robes. Her eyes were closed again as he fed her sticky, blood-encrusted arms into the sleeves. Hadra had keys on his belt, and Drauses retrieved them. It took him four tries to find the right one to unlock the shackles from around her ankles, but once she was free, he sat on the red-slick floor and gathered her into his arms.

"Shaila," he called, but she was lifeless once again. Her honey hair was matted with blood, and her breathing was ragged and shallow.

For a moment, Drauses let his grief consume him. It crushed his soul there on the bloody floor, and he deserved it, he knew. Tears came that he couldn't fight as he touched his forehead to hers.

"Please," he begged, "please forgive me." This beautiful, brave, stubborn woman was his life. If her heart stopped beating, his may as well pump its last right along with hers. If she died, he was the only soul to blame.

Shaking, Drauses forced himself to get to his feet and haul Shaila up into his arms. He turned his back on that place of pain and climbed the stairs. He pushed the metal door open with his shoulder and welcomed the blast of cool, fresh air after the stench of the room below. Just as his feet touched the grass, a cold blade touched the skin of his throat. Drauses froze and clutched Shaila tighter as a black-clad figure circled around to stand in front of him. A gloved hand swept back her hood.

"What, no happy hello?" Rose asked, the tip of her blade still pressed over Drauses' jugular. "It's the least you could give me after I spared you last time."

"You never meant to kill me then," Drauses replied.

"No. The blade I used is a trick designed by a clever, crafty man."

"Roth?"

Rose cocked her head to the side. "You're still full of surprises, Drauses."

"If you don't want me dead, why hinder me now? Remove your blade and let me pass."

Rose shook her head. "You shouldn't have come. I gave you the perfect chance, you fool. Rovik believes you're dead. He no longer worries over you at all. You could've faded away like an old memory, forgotten and untraceable, but now... *now* I have a problem. I'm bound by contract to protect these grounds and see to it any who threatens them meet a swift end. This is twice in as many days one of your guild has swept through this estate causing mayhem. Now here stands both persons responsible. How will it look if I let you pass and disappear into the night?"

"You should concern yourself far more with what'll happen if the body in my arms stops breathing," Drauses said with the hint of a growl.

"If her life ends while you detain me, I promise you, I'll sweep a storm of destruction through this estate the likes of which no one has ever seen."

"So poetic, Drauses," Rose scoffed. "The girl must mean so much to you. A pity her Master is not quicker in the mind, or he could've spared her this fate."

"What do you mean?"

"What was the last thing I said to you in that alleyway, do you remember?" Drauses merely glared on silently, so she continued. "I mentioned *Rubric for My Beloved*, yes? You recited that poem to Amii, you fool, not Shaila. Your ward didn't hear your endearments, and thus couldn't have passed them on to us. I dropped it as a hint to you, and you let it slip right through your fingers. If you'd taken time to think it through instead of letting your emotions cloud you so, you'd have realized your precious Shaila wasn't the one who betrayed you. But you turned on her instead. It's your fault she showed up here alone to take back our daughter."

"Amii is *my* daughter," Drauses sneered. "You've no claim to her since you left her the day she was born."

"I didn't leave her," Rose barked back. "You know the lives of those in the West aren't our own. We're pawns in a greater game. Forces beyond my control took me from her side against my will."

"You should've stood still and let those forces tear you apart rather than abandon your child."

A look of sadness passed across Rose's face, and her anger deflated a bit. "Perhaps," she muttered. She took her blade from Drauses' throat. "I'll let you live again, Drauses, for Amii, but I warn you, this is the last gift of grace you'll get from me. Cross my blade again, and I won't hesitate to cut you down."

"I rather hope I never see you again."

"On that, we can agree. Though we've landed on opposite sides in this war, I wish you no ill will and would rather not soak my blade with your blood."

She sidestepped to let Drauses pass who had no choice but to head across the lawn with his back to her. He could feel her eyes drilling into him as he fled, and he could do nothing but pray she didn't change her mind and run him through with her sword.

❦

Aro came to Amii's bedside in the dark and shook her, calling her name until she sat up, rubbing her bloodshot eyes.

"Wha… Aro? What's wrong?"

"Do you trust me?" he asked.

"You know I do."

"If I asked you to do something utterly mad, would you do it without question?"

She nodded.

He took her hand. "Then get up. Pack your things. We're leaving."

Chapter 22

THE SUN LIT the sky a perfect golden color, the same one Drauses woke to after he and Shaila first made love. She was in his arms now just like that Odavailian morning, but she was pale, bloodied, and broken. Alek's boat pulled up to the Eastern shore, and Drauses rushed across The Yard, thankful Boon's clinic was so close. He kicked the door in without bothering to knock.

"Boon!" Drauses hollered. He laid Shaila across the nearest cot as the doctor stumbled in from his quarters in the back, cleaning his glasses in his nightshirt and nearly tripping over one of his tables.

"Drauses, what…" Boon stuck his glasses on his nose at last and gaped down at Shaila's lifeless body. He pulled the blood-soaked robe from her chest. "Gods…" He snatched up a nearby towel and cleaned away the blood, uncovering the dozens of wounds across her chest and belly.

"Tell me what to do," Drauses pleaded.

"Leave," Boon replied. "I'll work faster and more efficiently without you hovering over my shoulder. I'll call if I need help."

Drauses backed away a few small, uncertain steps toward the door, but then he caught sight of another body lying two cots away and stopped, recognizing the battered face under the cuts and bruises.

"Miika?"

"You need to see Dagon immediately, Drauses," Boon said. "A lot happened while you were away. None of it good."

251

Drauses ran his hands through his hair in dismay as he turned and walked away. Back out in the early morning sunlight, he glanced down at his clothes. He was soaked in blood but had no time to clean up now. He headed for the bunkhouse, but Dagon had already been roused and spilled out of the door before Drauses was yet halfway there. Dagon's eyes widened at the sight of his old friend.

"What happened?" Drauses demanded to know. "Where's Amii?"

"Not here," Dagon replied. Drauses' heart skipped a beat, and he opened his mouth to ask more questions, but Dagon held up his hand. "Amii stopped an unknown Mark from killing Miika in cold blood last night. She tried to blow a hole in the man. 'Tis a pity she missed. If she hadn't been there, Miika would be dead. Not an hour after Miika was brought to the clinic, Aro and Amii disappeared. We think they jumped the fence by the river; there are fresh prints in the mud. We don't know where they've gone or why."

"You've no clue to Aro's intentions? He's your ward."

"None at all. I want to say I know it's not as bad as it looks, that I know Aro would never... but after everything that's happened... I..." Dagon shook his head.

"And the man who attacked Miika?"

"Amii didn't get a look at him. He wore a hood and mask and rushed from the room when Amii took her shot. A moment later, Aro rushed in claiming he was in the toilets. For all we know, he attacked Miika then simply removed his mask and strolled right back into the room. I hate that I suspect him, but Aro seems the most likely culprit now."

Drauses groaned and closed his eyes for a moment then forced them back open again lest he fall asleep on his feet.

"You should retire for a while," Dagon said. "I'll stay near the clinic and get you if there's any news. When was the last time you ate or slept?"

Drauses laughed humorlessly. The last thing he'd consumed was half a glass of whiskey. Before that, his last meal was breakfast with Amii and Shaila at the apartment. As for sleep, the few hours he tossed and turned two nights ago barely counted, but they were all the rest he'd gotten. Drauses rubbed his hands down his sticky, blood-streaked face and didn't answer.

"Go now and clean yourself up at the very least," said Dagon. "You're covered in gore like a creature from nightmares." As if to further drive the point, several wards on their way to breakfast stared at Drauses as they passed.

"I'd rather stay by Shaila until she wakes."

"That wasn't a request," Dagon barked. "Go now, or I'll drag you there myself."

Drauses growled but gave Dagon one stiff nod and stalked away toward his quarters. He still had brothers who cared for his well-being even after all his mistakes of late. He was grateful for the loyalty, though he doubted he deserved it.

Drauses' rooms were a mess of strewn belongings and the shattered glass of whiskey from the night before. He stripped off his ruined clothes and tossed them at the bin, missing it completely as he trudged through the room. The bathroom mirror showed him the beast Dagon claimed he resembled, and he saw now why the wards had stared. His face was splattered with blood from the Odas only knew how many men he'd slain in the night. His chin and cheeks were covered in stubble he had no time nor desire to shave. His eyes were bloodshot.

The shower was hot thanks to Julta's genius, and Drauses closed his eyes under the water as it relaxed his aching muscles. It'd been years since he'd caused chaos the likes of which he wreaked last night. Drauses had thought the ruthless killer he used to be was long gone, buried by the age and wisdom of a Master passed his prime, but the thought of the woman he loved suffering at the hands of Rovik's men had set loose that blood-thirsty demon of old who, as it turned out, was lying in wait this whole time, as deadly and furious as ever. Even now, he fought to push it back, but a burning anger in his chest refused to die. The desire to hunt Aro to the ends of the Earth was overwhelming, and the image of Rovik hanging naked and bloody by his wrists set Drauses' heart thumping wildly. He wanted revenge. He wanted snapping bones and pleas of mercy. He wanted death.

Drauses beat his fists against the wall so hard two tiles cracked under the strain. This was all his fault. He was nothing but a hard-headed, hot-blooded fool. His own pride and arrogance had led them all here:

to Shaila bleeding buckets for his ignorance, to Miika lying lifeless and broken for his blindness, and his daughter missing for placing his trust in the wrong man yet again. And Dagon wanted him to lead? He'd lead them all to ruin as Liege; surely, they must all see that now. Gragern had tried more than once to sully Drauses' name, but Drauses had gone and done that himself well enough.

Once he was as clean as he could manage in his state of mind, Drauses dried and dressed and headed back across The Yard.

Dagon was leaning against the wall by the clinic door. "You look better," he said as Drauses approached.

"How is she?"

Dagon shoved the door open. "See for yourself."

Shaila was sitting up on her cot with Boon hovering nearby when Drauses came inside. She stared absentmindedly into her lap until she heard the door close behind him. Her eyes were hollow as they slid up and locked onto his. It chilled his blood to ice. Boon motioned Drauses away to a far side of the room, and the Master obeyed, though his eyes still lingered on Shaila who went back to regarding her lap with a blank stare.

"How is she?" Drauses asked a second time.

"She'll live."

"None of your vague answers right now, Boon," Drauses said through gritted teeth. "Tell it to me straight, I beg you."

The physician clicked his tongue but must have decided Drauses' wrath was worse than a slip of confidentiality. "Most of her wounds are superficial. They were made to cause pain, not to kill. The worst of them was a gunshot to the thigh. Someone dug the bullet out with a knife and not gently. There's deep tissue damage that'll take years to heal completely, if ever. Her wrists took quite an abuse as well. Those joints aren't meant to carry the weight of the human body. The right looks mild and should recover, but the left suffered more."

"I broke that same wrist years ago," Drauses admitted with a fresh pang of guilt.

Boon raised a brow but asked no questions. "Previous injury would explain that, yes. I'll monitor it closely, but she may lose feeling in those fingers."

"But she'll be alright?"

"Physically? Yes, Drauses, she's fine. But torture damages more than the body. Wounds of the mind, I can't mend. She's spoken not a word since she awoke. Shaila's as brave and stubborn as any of you, but I don't know what to expect."

Drauses looked over his shoulder at Shaila. She was gazing at Miika's bed. Drauses wished Miika would wake. Perhaps he could help nurse Shaila's mind to better health. As anxious as Drauses was to see her, to tell her how sorry he was for all that had happened between them, the thought of approaching her now terrified him. Perhaps it'd be better to leave her alone.

"Go and sit with her," Boon urged, following his thoughts. "That's all you can do right now, and I doubt very much she'll mind."

At Boon's urging, Drauses made his way across the room, and Shaila watched him come with a flicker of interest in her eyes that gave him hope. Perhaps she didn't hate him after all. He'd explain himself, beg her forgiveness, grovel at her feet, whatever it took to put things right. He sat on the cot next to hers and rested his arms on his knees. She eyed him for a moment, then began fiddling with the new braces on her wrists.

"Amii arrived near sunset yesterday," Drauses said softly, launching into speech without knowing exactly what he'd say until he said it and not stopping to give his words much thought otherwise. He simply talked, and she listened. "She wandered the sewers for quite a time, but she's smart and brave and eventually found her way to Alek. I found more of those devices in the pockets of all our allies. Once I leave here, I'll conduct a thorough search of the entire grounds and ensure every one of them is rounded up and destroyed." Drauses glanced over his shoulder at the ward in the next bed. "Amii saved Miika's life," he said proudly. "She took a shot at his attacker with a pistol. Such fire she has. I think she gets it from you."

Shaila sat quiet and detached, avoiding Drauses' eyes.

"Shaila."

She glanced up, but the look in her eyes made his stomach hurt. It was a look of betrayal and heartbreak, of suffering and sacrifice he knew he could never repay.

"Please, speak to me," he begged.

"What would you like me to say?" she asked. Her voice was gruff as if she badly needed a drink, but she was speaking which made his heart swell with joy.

He slid closer. "Just hearing your voice is enough. I was afraid I never would again."

"If I'd managed to steal away with Amii, you never would've. I planned to drop her at your doorstep and disappear."

"Why? This is your home."

"Outsiders aren't welcome at headquarters. You dismissed me."

"I said those words in anger. They carry no weight until council is taken with the Liege. Since he's under question right now, it'll fall to our next Elder to make that call."

"And if I no longer wish to be a Lady of the Mark?" she asked.

Drauses fell pale, and he swallowed hard. "Wards are free to go at any time, as I told you the night we met. But I urge you not to do so. I'll do whatever you ask of me. You can have a new Master, if that's your wish. I'm sure any man here would gladly take you as his ward."

Shaila continued to fiddle with her braces, deep in thought. "I'd like to think on it awhile."

"Take all the time you need." He reached to touch her knee, but she moved it away. His arm fell to his lap instead. "I'm so sorry. Those words are pale compared to this guilt I feel. I'll never forgive myself for... any of this." He was the one to look away this time.

"You came for me. You stopped my pain and stole me away. I harbor no grudges, Drauses." She said it softly but without forgiveness.

"I wish that were true, but I know it's not. If it were, you'd stay here with us... with me."

Shaila gasped. He looked up in hope, but her eyes were drawn to something behind him. Drauses turned in time to watch Miika reach up and touch his battered face with a moan. Shaila flung back her blankets and threw her legs over the side of her cot. When she stood, she stumbled, and Drauses made to catch her, but she pulled free of him and limped away on her own. Drauses stayed where he was, miserably sullen as she rushed to Miika's bedside.

"Miika?" Shaila said.

His eyes opened to slits to gaze at her face, then they widened in recognition. "Are you truly here? Or am I dreaming?"

"No dreams," she said as she took his hand. "I'm here."

Miika slowly raised an arm and pulled her into a painful but no less crushing hug. Drauses watched from a distance, feeling as if someone had plunged a knife in his gut. Perhaps this would be her future. Miika had never doubted her, never let his loyalty waver for a second. He deserved her if any man did. Drauses rose to leave and give them privacy.

"Master Drauses," Miika called as the Master reached the door. "Our rat. I believe it may be Aro, sir."

"What?" Shaila said in alarm.

"I watched him hop the fence in the dark and was attacked as I searched his things. I can't be certain, but it all seems highly suspect."

"I believe we can agree Aro is most certainly our corrupted brother," Drauses concurred. "He took Amii and disappeared last night."

"Amii is gone?" Shaila asked.

Drauses nodded sadly.

"Then it was all for nothing?"

They sat in miserable silence until Drauses couldn't take it anymore. "I'll gather the Masters to council. We'll decide how to handle our unscrupulous Liege and start our process for choosing a new Elder. I plan to petition to name you a Master as well, Miika."

"No," Miika replied.

"No?"

"I'd rather be given a new Master. Let one of our brothers deem me worthy."

"Miika," Shaila chided.

"This is my wish," he insisted.

"If you're certain, then I'll see it done," Drauses said. "I'll be back when this mess is over."

Drauses made rounds through The Yard and asked every Master to join him in council. They trickled into the bunkhouse and assembled in one of the large first-floor meeting rooms around a long wooden table. Drauses and Dagon scoured every pocket for disks and disposed of any that were missed by Dagon's purge earlier that morning, then Drauses started the meeting with the full tale of their corrupted Liege and the ward who brought it all to light.

◆

Shaila sat on the cot next to Miika's with a small smile on her face. She was overjoyed to see her friend awake and well. Though she ached from head to toe, and likely he did as well, she was grateful they were both alive and safe once more.

"Are you alright?" Miika asked.

Shaila nodded, but her smile slipped a little.

"Shaila."

She looked back to his face, swallowed hard, and shook her head.

He took her hand. "Talk to me."

"I don't know who to trust anymore," she said in a whisper. "Aro, the brother we considered a closest friend, has been named a traitor. Someone tried to kill you, possibly that same brother, but possibly yet another black heart among us. We know Gragern is poison, but we don't know how far his influence has spread. And Drauses..." She hesitated. Drauses' crimes weren't of betrayal or corruption. It wasn't fair to throw him in with such unsavory sorts. She sighed, lost for the proper words.

"You should've seen him after you left," Miika said. "Even before I gave him your note, he was a broken man. He marched into that office to see you, but you were gone. I've never seen him so upset. I've no doubt he was on his way to make things right."

"So I should just forgive those things he said in anger?" she asked, swiping a finger under a moist eye. "He aimed a blade at my heart and hit his mark. Broken trust is hard to mend."

"He'll mend it. Give him time."

"How do you know?"

"Because I would."

Shaila laughed one bitter bark of mirth then shook her head. "You men are hopeless. I should carry a journal and jot down all the ridiculous things said in my company. I could publish a whole tome and make a fortune."

"What would you call it?" Miika asked in amusement.

Shaila thought hard for a moment then smiled. *"Renditions of the Witless Male."*

Miika laughed then coughed, winced, and went on laughing anyway. "Oh gods, that hurts."

"Then stop, you fool," Shaila said with a snort.

"Just throw me in with the witless wonders."

They were both lost in painful shakes of laughter.

⤚

A Man of the Mark, concealed under hood and mask, stepped silently down the hall to the Liege's door and knocked three times before letting himself in. The Elder had a knapsack packed in front of his desk, but he stood staring out the window, in no rush to leave.

"The Masters have gathered for council," the Mark said. "It's time."

"I've unfinished business here. I intend to see it through before we go."

"What business?"

"The Lady of the Mark," Gragern said with a sneer. "I want to pull her beating heart from her chest. She's the source of all my trouble. She lifted Drauses' regard amongst the Masters, turned my ward against me, and refuses to die. My last act as Liege here will be to end her life, and you'll help me."

"Will I now? You're not *my* master, Gragern."

"Perhaps, but your place here must remain confidential for you to continue pleasing your brother and sovereign. Help me kill Shaila, and I won't announce you as a traitor."

"I could just kill you. You're expendable."

Gragern fingered the hilt of his sword with a smile. "By all means, step up and try it, whelp. Learn firsthand what made me Elder Master from the start." He waited, but the Mark made no move toward him. "I thought not. Let's kill the miserable whore and slip away while the Masters are in council. Help me subdue her, but *I* wish to be the one to end her life."

With a sigh and a nod, the masked Mark agreed, and only then did Gragern take up his pack and head for the door.

Chapter 23

MIIKA HELD SHAILA'S hand in his while a deck of cards balanced on her palm.

"Now you ask them to draw the top card from the deck to distract your audience," Miika instructed, and he drew the card himself to demonstrate.

"Is it your card?" Shaila asked as a jest, knowing full well it wasn't.

He smiled at her. "Yes."

"Liar. Your card is right… right…" She grasped under his pillow, but the card was nowhere to be found.

"Looking for this?" he asked, and he took the card from under *her* pillow instead.

"You trickster! How did you do that?"

Miika gave her a mischievous grin.

The clinic door burst open, and Gragern strolled in, flanked by a Man of the Mark hidden behind a mask. Shaila jumped from the bed and lunged for a scalpel on a nearby counter. Boon came running from a back room, but the unknown Mark pounced on him and knocked him hard in the temple with the hilt of his blade. Boon crumpled, and the Mark set his sights on Shaila instead.

Miika threw his legs out of bed, but Shaila doubted he would get far in his condition. His sword lay a few steps away, resting atop his folded robes on a chair, but as soon as he placed weight on his ruined knee, the leg gave out. He yelled in pain but started hopping on one foot, clutching cots and tabletops for balance until he wrapped his fingers around the hilt of his weapon.

Shaila overturned a table of supplies to slow the Mark's advance. She had no sword, no crossbow, no gun. She could do plenty with just her hands, as sore as they were, but he had the reach of a sword in his favor. Miika was on his feet, but she knew that wouldn't last. It was a miracle he was even conscious. Her own sudden jump from bed had pulled stitches loose in her thigh, and blood was already soaking through her pants.

The Mark swung his sword at her middle, then at her legs, and Shaila jumped back to avoid the blade as it hissed through the air. She rolled once to the side, trying to get closer without being skewered, but the move caused every wound on her belly and back to burn in protest. She wouldn't be able to do it again. With a swipe of the scalpel, she sliced the man's leg, then struck toward his face. He knocked the blow away. He struck back with the hilt of his sword, but she blocked him, refusing to give him an opening despite her pain.

Gragern drew his sword as Miika drew his from its sheath, and Shaila heard the two blades come together in a clash. She didn't dare even a glance to see how her friend fared. She managed to snag the Mark by the wrist, and with a twist and a press of her thumb to a pressure point, he dropped his sword. They were more evenly matched now. She attacked with the scalpel, aiming for the Mark's throat, but he took the blow to the arm instead. He punched her leg over the blood seeping through her pants, and Shaila screamed. She stumbled back, knocking into a chair and sending it tumbling. The Mark kicked her meager weapon from her hand then knocked her to the floor. He came down on top of her and wrapped his arm around her neck to hold her there. Now Shaila could do nothing *but* watch as Miika struggled with Gragern across the room.

Miika held his sword tight in both hands, but pain was clear on his face, and he stumbled on even the simplest swing. The Elder smiled and kicked him in his bad knee. The ward screamed and fell back against a counter, shoving hard against it to stay on his feet as Gragern moved in. They locked blades again, but then Miika punched the Elder in the face, broken wrist be damned. The Elder took a step back, and Miika spun on his good leg to swing his sword with everything he had, but it wasn't enough. The Elder blocked the blow and kicked Miika in the stomach. Miika doubled over, Gragern pulled back his sword, and the two men locked eyes for a breathless moment before Gragern thrust forward, plunging his blade straight through Miika's middle.

"No! Miika!" Shaila screamed in fury from the floor. She kicked her legs and tore at her captor's arms to no avail.

Gragern yanked his blade away, and Miika fell on his back, clutching his ravaged gut as dark blood gushed between his fingers.

His ward no longer a threat, Gragern rounded on Shaila, his eyes wide with crazed bloodlust and his sword slicked red. He stalked her way. Shaila no longer cared. All she saw was Miika, and she watched him roll and crawl across the floor leaving a trail of blood in his wake.

"This is for all the trouble you've caused me," Gragern spat.

Shaila began to pray.

A gunshot rang out, and Gragern jerked forward a step. He looked down at his chest in wonder as a dark red spot began to grow across his shirt. A second shot brought another patch of red to the right of the first. He stumbled, dropped his sword, then stared at Shaila in awe before he toppled to the floor. Miika was propped up against an overturned chair, his folded robes clutched to the hole in his gut and his pistol raised to the spot Gragern had just been standing. Shaila watched the last of the strength drain from her dear friend's face, and he dropped the gun as he, too, collapsed lifelessly to the floor.

Gragern's sword was inches from Shaila's face. She put her hands together and brought her elbow back as hard as she could into the Mark's gut. His grip at her throat loosened enough for her to turn and punch him in the face. He let her go. Shaila lunged across the floor for the blade, but he dove for it at the same time. Both their hands landed on the hilt, but Shaila lurched forward and sank her teeth into his arm until he let go with a cry of misery. She drew the blade, smashed him in the teeth with the hilt, then kneed him hard in the ribs until he rolled onto his back.

Shaila straddled her enemy and raised the sword, aiming for his heart. The Mark reached up and wrapped both hands around the blade, screaming as it cut his fingers to the bone. Shaila thrust down with all her might and plunged the sword straight into the Mark's chest. His legs kicked as his heart beat its last few pumps, then he stilled as the organ died, speared by steel. Shaila tore away his mask in a rage and paused in shock as she recognized the lifeless face staring back at her.

It was Xeda.

The shock of her discovery barely registered before she dismissed it and crawled away across the floor to Miika's side. A wave of relief brought her to tears when his eyes opened at her touch.

"You won," he said weakly. "I knew you would."

"Don't you even think of dying on me! I'll wake Boon."

"No!" He reached for her, his bloody hand shaking. "Stay with me."

Her lips trembled as she hauled him into her lap and held him close. "I'm so sorry. I failed you."

"No, you didn't."

"You deserve so much more." Her voice broke on a sob. "Happiness, friendship, love—"

"I found all that already... for a short time." He wiped a tear from her face. She took his hand and clutched it to her cheek. "Drauses is a lucky man. More than he knows."

He fell into a coughing fit, and Shaila hugged him closer, praying for more time, just one more minute.

"You... you should forgive him," Miika continued. Blood trickled from the corner of his mouth at the same time a tear fell down the side of his face. Shaila wiped both away with her sleeve. "We're only men, capable... of mistakes. Wit...witless wonders," he said with a shaky laugh.

Shaila forced her voice to remain steady as she asked in a whisper, "Do you want to hear a secret?"

"Tell me." Miika's voice was fading, costing him more and more precious strength with every word.

"I'm with child."

Miika's eyes widened, then he smiled again. "Good. My life for two. It's a fair trade."

There were shouts from nearby, but Shaila paid them no mind, giving all her attention to the man in her arms whose light was slowly dying in his stunning green eyes.

"Will you... will..."

"Anything, Miika."

"K...kiss me."

Shaila caressed his cheek then kissed him softly on his lips, which were tender and warm like the man himself. She broke away when his hand grew limp in hers, clutching him tighter still.

"Miika?"

He was gone.

⸙

The sound of gunshots sent the Masters rushing from the bunkhouse. Drauses got to the clinic first and took in the whole bloody scene. Xeda was lying on his back with a sword stuck in his chest. A few feet away, Gragern lay in a pool of blood, his dead eyes peering toward the door. Shaila sat on the floor clutching Miika in her arms. Even Boon was sprawled in a heap by his office door.

Dagon ran up behind Drauses and froze. "By the gods..."

Drauses ran across the room to Shaila. She was a bloody mess and shook violently as she held Miika tight in her lap. Drauses knelt and found Shaila's cheek resting against Miika's forehead. Her eyes were closed as she prayed quietly. Drauses felt for a pulse at Miika's neck. Finding none, he squeezed his eyes shut for a single, heartbroken moment. He touched Shaila's arm and called to her. She didn't seem to hear him and went on praying.

Others were filling the room now. Several men gathered around Boon and tried to rouse him. Ithail found Xeda amongst the fallen and knelt next to the boy with a cry of misery. Dagon tried to comfort him, but Ithail pushed him away, having none of it. Drauses called Dagon instead, and his friend stepped around the bodies and the gore to join him.

"Take him," Drauses said with a nod toward Miika.

Dagon tried to pull Miika away.

"No!" Shaila snarled, gripping Miika tighter. "Don't touch him!"

Drauses wrapped his arms around Shaila, hauling her to his chest as Dagon inched Miika from her grip. When they were finally separated, Shaila turned on Drauses and struck him in the chest over and over again with a scream of fury for every blow as her misery gave way to pure, hot anger. Her strength ran dry quickly, and she stilled. With a cry of utter pain that broke Drauses' heart, she threw her arms around his neck and started to sob.

"Is she injured?" Dagon asked.

"There's no telling through all the blood, but I don't think so."

"Get her out of here." Dagon helped his friend to his feet with Shaila in his arms.

Boon sat up on the floor, rubbing the knot forming on the side of his head as Drauses headed for the door. The doctor called to him, but Drauses paid him no mind as he carried Shaila out and across The Yard.

He took her to his room. Her eyes were closed when he set her on his bed, but when he tried to pull away to get a clean towel from his bathroom, she grabbed his hand.

"Stay with me," she whispered.

He stripped off his sodden robes and laid next to her, sweeping a few stray strands of hair from her tear-streaked face.

"I'm so sorry, Shaila."

Shaila closed her eyes and rolled closer, burying her face in his chest. Within minutes, she fell asleep.

∽

Rovik was furious once again. Stationery, vases, paintings, and even his desk chair flew across his office. Marcel was on his knees on the floor with his hands bound behind his back. Rose stood a short distance away, leaning against the wall, watching the spectacle with amusement.

"What by Vediida happened?" Rovik screamed. "Gragern is dead; our inside man is dead; Aro has disappeared with Amii; Shaila is back with the guild; and Drauses lives! Have I missed anything?" He overturned his desk with a scream of rage.

"I think that sums it up nicely," Rose said sweetly.

"Don't push me, Rose!" Rovik fumed. He punched Marcel in the face, and the guard fell to his side on the floor. "And you..." Rovik kicked him hard in the stomach. "I'd take you to The Cellar, but Drauses has killed my executioners as well as half my guards! You never felt compelled to warn me the Master still lived? Your brother is dead. You've no more cards to play." Rovik drew a knife from his belt.

"No," Marcel pleaded as he thrashed for freedom. "No, please! No!"

Rovik kicked Marcel onto his back and plunged the knife deep into the guard's belly. Marcel screamed in pain as Rovik twisted the blade then sliced it clear up to his chest. Marcel lay gutted like a fish, screaming as he bled his guts onto the carpet. His cries died away to gasps as he drew his last few breaths before he stilled and went silent.

"Now you have to clean that up," Rose chimed cheerfully.

Rovik stalked across the room toward her, the bloody knife still clutched in his hand. He came nose to nose with her and plunged the blade into the wall not an inch from her cheek. She didn't flinch.

"Aren't you the least bit afraid?" he asked.

"Of you?" she scoffed, then she laughed.

Rovik took hold of her robes and slammed her hard against the wall. "How about now?"

"You won't hurt me, Uncle." She pried his hands from her robes. "You know what would happen if you did."

"I'd never hurt you anyway, girl. The gods help me, I've a soft spot for you." He bucked his hips against hers. "A hard one, too."

"You disgust me," she spat, pushing him away.

"Be careful," Rovik warned. "I may not be able to touch you, but your brother wouldn't be pleased if I told him you were anything less than cordial."

Rose glared but shut her mouth.

"Much better. Now, I want to meet this inventor friend of yours. What's his name?"

"Roth. What do you want with him?"

"He and I are going to think of a way to deal with the guild, even if it means laying waste to the entire East side once and for all. Good riddance, I say."

"You should be cautious where you aim lest you hit our girl."

"I'm starting to care less and less about Amii's safety."

Rose growled. "Repeat that. I dare you."

"If she keeps putting herself in the line of fire, the girl may well find herself hit, Rose."

"I won't let you hurt my child!"

"Your brother and I have reached an agreement. You've no say in the matter."

Rose shoved away from the wall and turned to leave. "We'll see about that."

Rovik called her to a halt. "If you're thinking of betraying me, ask yourself what your brother would do if he learned Drauses lives despite your claims otherwise. I doubt that conversation would go well for you."

Rose spit at Rovik's feet then strolled out, slamming the door so hard in her wake the last painting saved from his tantrum fell from the wall into the growing pool of blood on the floor.

Drauses blinked awake to find the most beautiful woman he'd ever seen lying at his side, and for the briefest moment, he forgot the horrible events of the past few days and smiled at her. When she didn't smile back, he noticed her swollen, reddened eyes and the smear of dried blood on her neck, and he remembered.

Shaila sat up without a word, and Drauses got up from the bed with a heavy heart. He stared down at her, but she avoided him, sniffling as she patted her eyes with a sodden sleeve.

"You should clean up," Drauses said. "The shower is hot; you're welcome to it."

"What happens now, Drauses?" she asked, her voice small and full of pain.

Drauses wished he could summon the words to make things right between them, but he knew none existed, so he stuck to facts. "Now I call the Masters back to council, and we start our process to elect our new Liege. We must decide how Gragern's passing will be recorded in our records and whether he or Xeda will have funeral fires. Miika must be prepared, his pyre built—"

"He should be laid to rest as a Master."

"Yes, he should," Drauses concurred. "I'll bring it up in council. I doubt there will be any objections."

"It's the least we can do for him." A tear slid down the side of her nose, and she wiped it hastily away.

Drauses' guilt rushed in harder than ever, crushing his heart under the weight of his failures—failures he knew were responsible for her pain. That weight dragged him down to his knees, and he sank at her feet.

"Shaila, I'm so sorry. Miika's death lies on my shoulders. I know how much he meant to you, and I failed to protect him as I promised. And after I took a traitor's word over yours and treated you like... I..." He took one of her hands in both of his and bowed his head over it as his shoulders began to shake. "Please, forgive me," he begged with a shaky sob.

✦

Shaila covered her gaping mouth with her hand, at a loss for what to say or do. Drauses was the strongest and most disciplined man she knew, and yet here he was, falling apart on his knees. For her. Such vulnerability brought tears to her eyes, and she stroked his hair, leaned down, and kissed the top of his head.

"Drauses," she murmured, "Miika's death is Gragern's sin, not yours. I loved him," she admitted. There was no point denying it to herself, or to Drauses who no doubt knew the truth already. "But there are others I love just as dearly." She picked her Master's head up from her lap, and the tears in his eyes took her breath away. "As much as I cared for Miika, I always loved you more."

Drauses closed his eyes, in pain or relief, she couldn't tell which.

"When I found you hanging in The Cellar, I wanted to die," he admitted, his voice full of raw emotion. "All I could think was how I was the one who drove you there, how all your pain was my doing."

She hugged him close and went on petting his hair as he let go of all his crushing guilt. He relaxed into her arms with his head to her chest. In that moment, she comforted, eased the pain of grief and the worries of past failures, showed strength in her forgiveness and her wisdom, and he bowed his heart to her in thankful submission. In that moment, she was Master, and he was ward.

"Please, Shaila, don't leave," he said quietly. "Take a new Master if you must, but stay, I beg you, though I know I have no right."

"I need time, Drauses."

"I understand." He touched her cheek. "I only hope…"

She softly removed his hand from her face. "If it's meant to be, it must mend on its own, along with our trust."

Drauses gave a sullen nod. "You're right." He gave her hand a final squeeze before pulling away. "I have to go. Will you be alright?"

"I'll be fine. Go. See to Miika and meet with our brothers."

Drauses took her hand again and kissed her knuckles. "I'll never doubt you again. I know those words are hollow, but I swear to you I'll prove them in time. I love you."

⤚

Dagon updated Drauses on everything they'd learned while he and Shaila were resting. The Masters conducted a thorough search of the grounds, and all listening devices were destroyed along with a receiver they found under Xeda's bed in the bunkhouse. A search of the ward's belongings yielded dozens of communications with Marcel who turned out to be Xeda's older brother, much to everyone's surprise. There were also instructions on how to sabotage Julta's communication boxes with orders to ensure only Shaila and Drauses heard Miika's call for help during the Black Blades' attack as they moved south. Marcel's last few messages mentioned a plan to force Aro to steal Amii away. Such news was equally hard for Drauses to hear as it was for Dagon to deliver.

Once again in council and with Gragern no longer a threat, the rest of the Marks were at last told of Miika's long-time struggles and suffering at the Liege's hand. Drauses petitioned to have Miika marked in their records as a Master. Not a man objected, and Miika was deemed a Master of the Mark on the spot.

Tradition dictated the Masters take three days to decide whom they wished to be their new Liege. Afterward, they would all meet again and cast their votes. Drauses considered mentioning his relationship with

Shaila for sake of honesty with his brothers, but, not knowing if there was anything left between him and Shaila to tell, he decided to wait and bring the issue directly to whomever the group cast as their new Elder Master. It was an odd thing, he mused, praying for a reason to break his codes.

✥

Boon came to see Shaila at Drauses' urging, and though she tried to convince him she was fine, the physician insisted he inspect every wound for torn stitches or unexpected bleeding. The only place she'd been further abused was her thigh which needed several stitches replaced. Boon then wanted to give her a medication to ward off infection since she'd been covered in more than one man's blood, but she was leery of the needle, uncertain if its contents were safe while expecting.

"Boon, I have to tell you something before you stick me with that," Shaila said.

"What is it?" he asked as he tapped the air from the syringe.

"I believe I'm… with child."

Boon paused. "Oh?"

"I don't know if… if the child still lives after…"

"Have you bled?"

She shook her head.

"If you were in danger of losing the babe, you no doubt would've already." It was Boon's turn to look sheepish. "Is Drauses the father?"

Shaila hesitated at first but decided to trust him and nodded. "I beg you to keep such news to yourself for the time being. I haven't yet told Drauses about the babe, and few know of our relationship—"

Boon burst out laughing. "Shaila, dear, everyone knows. No man acts as Drauses has these past few days unless he's in love. It's been the talk of The Yard since we arrived."

Shaila was horrified, but Boon clapped her on the shoulder with a smile.

"Fret not," he said. "From the bits of gossip I've gleaned, it seems the guild holds no grudges, except perhaps that the Lady of the Mark's heart has been claimed already." He took her arm and delivered the shot. "And after so much loss of late, what man wouldn't rejoice at the happy

270

news of a child born out of love?" He looked at her quizzically. "This *is* happy news, yes?"

"I've yet to decide."

"Perhaps it'd help you make up your mind if you told Drauses. He'll need to be notified as soon as possible anyway. Greater care must be taken with you in training from now on."

Shaila nodded, her mind abuzz with all the ways she could tell Drauses he was to be a father again. Her stomach twisted in knots at the thought. Surely Boon was right and Drauses would be happy when she told him… but was that what she wanted? Or would she rather he reject this child and give her the last reason she needed to leave his side and the guild entirely? There was a numbness in her heart she couldn't shake, and there was still the burning pain of Miika's loss she felt in every inch of her soul. At the thought of Miika, his last words came to her in a rush that brought instant tears to her eyes.

"We're only men, capable… of mistakes. Wit…witless wonders."

The pain of losing Miika was agony. The pain of losing Drauses, she knew, would be unbearable. He'd been a hotheaded fool, there was no question, but she did still love him. Whether that was enough to mend what had broken between them, only time would tell.

Chapter 24

THE NEXT DAY, Miika's pyre was finished, and preparations were made. Boon saw to the body while Julta put the final touches on a blade fit for a Master. Gragern and Xeda were gone, taken and buried far from headquarters. They would get no funeral fires to send them on to Odavail. Drauses was helping stack wood around the bottom of the pyre when a yell rose up from the gate as it opened. Marks nearby drew their weapons, and a few went running outside the wall.

Three men dragged Aro into The Yard and tossed him on his knees in the dirt. He raised his hands in the air in surrender without a fight. He no longer wore a sling on his arm and looked in perfect health. Drauses vowed to fix that. The Master drew his blade as he stalked toward the ward. Aro eyed the sword with dread but made no move to defend himself.

"Master Drauses, I can explain."

Drauses stopped, his fingers flexing around the hilt of his sword. He studied Aro, fighting the urge to knock the ward to the ground and draw blood. "What did you do with Amii?" he asked instead.

"She's safe," Aro replied in a rush.

Drauses curled his lip back in a sneer and pointed his sword at Aro's heart. "Answer me, whelp, or I'll bleed you dry right here."

"I came to see if it was safe—"

"Her location, Aro! I won't ask again."

"Stop!" Amii bolted in the gate and across The Yard. She skidded to a stop between Aro and her father who lowered his weapon immediately. She offered Aro her hand as he got to his feet.

"I told you to wait," Aro chastised.

"And let him slit your throat?" She rounded on Drauses. "Stab first, ask questions later, that's Drauses' way."

The accusation stung, but Drauses had to admit she wasn't far off the mark. "Will someone please explain what in Vedia is going on?"

"I will," Aro said as he brushed dirt from his robes. "But first, whose pyre is that?" Drauses' face fell, and Aro went pale. "Shaila?"

"Miika."

Aro winced and gazed across The Yard toward the pyre.

Amii put her hand over her mouth, tears springing to her eyes. "I was too late."

"No," Drauses replied, and he set his hand on the girl's shoulder. "You saved Miika's life, little one. He woke up in the clinic yesterday morning. He no doubt would've made a full recovery, but Gragern came for Shaila, and Miika intervened. If you hadn't saved Miika when you did, he wouldn't have been there to protect Shaila when she needed him."

"You brought Shaila back?"

"I did."

Amii wrapped her arms around her father's middle. Drauses hugged his daughter back, happy to see her safe as well, before he looked again at Aro.

"What happened?" Drauses asked.

"Gragern had information about my family," Aro said. "He tried once before to make me end Miika's life by threatening their safety. What he didn't know was I moved my siblings after the factory was hit by our enemies. He tried again to threaten me, demanding I take Amii to Rovik or he'd go after my loved ones. Once I realized he didn't know their new whereabouts, I decided to take Amii away from here under the ruse I'd take her West. They were determined to snatch Amii away again, and I didn't know who to trust after Miika was attacked, so I took her some-place I knew was safe."

Amii looked up from Drauses' arms and smiled. "I met Aro's broth-ers, all *four* of them! And their dog! It was quite fun."

"I took her to stay with my family," Aro explained. "I watched from a distance for any sign it was safe to return to The Yard. When I saw you were building a pyre, I knew something awful had happened. I came closer to see for myself if we could come back, but the guards at the gate saw me. *Someone* was supposed to stay behind until I gave her leave to join me." Aro looked sternly at Amii who merely shrugged her shoulders. "Which reminds me." Aro faced the gate and gave one long, shrill whistle. In the distance, an answering signal came back a few seconds later.

"What was that?" Drauses asked.

"Aro sent his brothers away," Amii said, and she waved to persons unseen.

"My two eldest siblings came with us today," Aro said. "I just told them to go home."

"You could've invited them in," Drauses offered. "Gragern and the one who acted as spy are gone."

"No, thank you. I'd rather keep my family as safe as possible. It was bad enough that I went to them with Amii."

Drauses shook his head, bemused. "Aro, I must say, what you did was utter madness, foolish, and dangerous."

"Yes, sir."

Drauses held out his hand. "It's exactly what I would've done."

Aro smiled with relief and clasped Drauses' hand in a firm shake.

"You placed your loyalty with Amii and saw to her safety above all else," Drauses continued. "Well done."

"Thank you."

"You should hunt down your Master right away. He was beside himself when suspicions rose against you. If I know my oldest friend, he'll be nursing a bottle alone in his quarters."

Drauses, Aro, Dagon, and Shaila walked across The Yard with Miika between them on a stretcher of red. Donned in his robes, Miika's hood was up, but he wore no mask. Miika had been hiding for far too long. They laid him with care atop his pyre.

Drauses brought the new Master's blade to the table. The sword had never taken a life nor been touched by a single drop of blood, and it never would be. He placed the hilt in Miika's hand over his chest. The blade would rest with its Master, who was never given the chance to wield it.

Shaila came next to say goodbye. She studied Miika's face and marveled at how peaceful he looked. He would know no more pain or misery. They'd granted him what he'd always wanted by making him a Master, but Shaila had failed him. Her promise from the start was to deliver him from his life of injustice, but not like this, not to this end. She'd set events in motion that ended here with her best friend lying ready for his funeral fire.

"You once told me you wished to be someone's hero," she whispered near his ear. "You were *my* hero, brother, a true white knight. You died believing your life for mine was a fair trade, and I'll spend the rest of my days living to make you proud. You'll never come to regret your sacrifice, I promise."

She laid her hand over his where he clutched his sword. From her pocket, she took a single playing card. Only Miika would understand its chosen suit and face. She slipped it inside his robes over his heart, then brushed a kiss across his cheek.

"We live and die by the sword, it's true," she said, "but we also live on in the hearts of those who love us. You'll live on in my heart, Miika. Forever." She squeezed his hand in final farewell then went to stand next to Drauses.

Julta rushed forward and handed Drauses a torch doused in oil, lit the end, and fell back again. Drauses walked slowly alongside Miika's pyre, dragging the torch across the wood until the flames roared, then he tossed in the torch and turned to regard the gathered men.

"Today we lay to rest a Master who never had the chance to show how much he cared for his brothers and his guild," he said. "As Men of the Mark, we've all made sacrifices. Miika gave his life to deliver us from a corrupted Liege and a murderous brother. His death will not have been in vain. From his ashes, our guild will be born anew, free of past poisons. This is Miika's gift to us, and we won't waste it. Not while we still have blood to give." Drauses turned back to the blazing table. "Rest well, brother. Until we meet again."

Shaila wiped the tears from her cheeks then bowed her head to pray.

"We fight beside our brothers with honor and pride. Today one has fallen, and we weep in pain of loss. We pray... his..." Shaila's words trailed off, her grief making it impossible for her to continue. Her brothers spoke up together to finish the prayer for her.

"We pray his soul pass safely through the gates of Odavail. May he guide us forward while we fight in his stead. While we still have blood to give."

With nothing left to do or say, Shaila gave in and let her tears fall unhindered as fire carried away one of the bravest men she'd ever known.

❧

Drauses watched from a distance as the fire burned low. Shaila stood near the blaze for a long time, staring into the flames. Aro brought her a chair, and Amii sat in the dirt at her feet. Most of the men had wandered away, and a sadness lingered throughout the grounds. His brothers were spent from too much pain, too much loss and all work as they went from one catastrophe to another. Drauses remembered the oath he made to see his guild bond like in days of old, so he went searching for Dagon. He found him by the river with Aro.

The duo had several empty bottles balanced atop a piece of driftwood. Aro aimed a pistol at the bottles, and Dagon issued several suggestions before the ward fired and one bottle exploded in a shower of shards.

"A lesson in marksmanship?" Drauses asked as he drew near. Dagon nodded for Aro to continue without him then came to stand beside Drauses.

"That pistol belonged to Miika," Dagon said. "I thought Aro should have it. I hope you don't mind."

"Not at all. Perhaps we should arm our wards with guns more often. Our enemies in the West prefer them, it seems."

"I think it's safe to say we know now what was in the shipment Rovik received. The Black Blades had no firearms when they first attacked us."

Drauses nodded in agreement. "The sovereign must have realized his black-clad cowards can't swing blades with any skill, so he armed them with bullets to do their fighting for them."

"Our brothers of old didn't have the resources for firearms, but times have changed. It might take some time to find enough guns to arm all of us as well, but it can be done."

Aro shot again and another bottle shattered.

"This time, step back a dozen paces, Aro," Dagon called. "Test your skill at greater distances."

Aro did as asked, and the next bottle fell at his shot. He backed away yet further and hit the next bottle with as much ease.

"He's a natural marksman," Drauses remarked.

Aro was well out of earshot now and continued to put more distance between himself and his targets.

"If I'm honest, I'd hoped it'd take longer for him to catch on," Dagon said.

"Why?"

Dagon sighed. "I've nothing left to teach him. As soon as we choose a new Liege, I plan to make Aro a Master."

Drauses clapped his old friend on the shoulder. "A bittersweet thing, to be sure. Will you take a new ward?"

"I don't know. Perhaps it's time to let the next generation train our youth."

"You're younger than I am, Dagon, or have you forgotten all the jests you've made about it over the years?"

Dagon laughed. "I haven't forgotten, brother. And just look at the ward you've trained. Perhaps we become better mentors with age. Or maybe it's because she's a lady. One has to wonder what difference that makes."

"You could train a Lady of the Mark yourself and find out."

Dagon scratched the stubble at his chin thoughtfully as if the idea had never occurred to him before. Aro was an impossible distance away now, and with one last shot, he struck the final bottle off the wood. Several other wards and Masters had gathered to watch, and they all applauded Aro's skill as the last bottle fell.

"How is Ithail?" Drauses asked once the noise had settled.

"Heartbroken over losing Xeda, but hurt worse, I think, by the ward's betrayal. I offer words of comfort where I can, but I know how I felt when we thought Aro a traitor. There's nothing I can say to erase that anger and pain. Our wards, we come to think of them as blood, brothers and sons alike. I understand now how you must've felt when Marcel turned on you, Drauses. How you found the courage to take Shaila as your protégé so soon after such a betrayal, I'll never know."

Drauses was reminded again of the pain so many must be feeling after their losses of late. "I think it's time to throw that carouse we spoke of before."

"I thought you said we'd have to clear it with our new Liege first."

"No Elder to ask for permission means no Elder to care either way," Drauses said with a wicked grin. "It'll encourage discussion about our new leader. This brotherhood was neglected under Gragern, splintered from the inside. Those cracks need mending. Let's bond and repair them, show whichever man we'll soon choose as Elder exactly what we'll expect of him. Our new Liege must understand the ways in which Gragern failed if he's to lead us down the right path."

"Wise words, brother. Let's do it."

"Tomorrow we'll build a bonfire," Drauses declared. "We'll pull tables and chairs into The Yard, gather every deck of cards, every bottle of drink. I know several of the men play instruments. They could take them out, dust them off, and entertain. We'll need more wood, lots of it. We could've roasted a pig or a deer if we had more time."

"I know of a place barely an hour's walk from here where there are fowl aplenty. I could take a few men in the morning and come back with a load of birds to roast. They would cook faster than a whole hog anyway."

"That'd do nicely."

Dagon smiled. "There's also that old case of Sazeen we hid in the—"

Drauses coughed loudly then chuckled. "That's our age-old secret from when we were but wards. Don't spill it now, after all these years."

"Should we crack open a few bottles? For blood and brotherhood?"

"I suppose now is as good a time as any."

"I'll stop and steal a few from our stash on my way back from tomorrow's hunt."

❧

The next morning, before even the slightest hint of dawn, Dagon, Aro, and four men who could best handle bows all set out for Dagon's hunting spot. Drauses saw them off, wishing them good luck and a bountiful hunt. He helped the others gather wood from nearby buildings, and they stacked it for a bonfire in the middle of The Yard. Julta, with his crafty tools, constructed two long spits for roasting fowl. He even designed a complicated device that spun the spikes, keeping them in constant motion for even cooking.

Dawn broke to a clear and sunny morning as the men dragged tables into The Yard and surrounded them with benches and chairs. Drauses asked his brothers to round up any games or bottles of spirits they had squirreled away, and soon the tables were laden with cards and drink. Dagon and his hunting party returned in a few short hours, loaded with fowl, and they got to work preparing the animals to cook. The Yard began to smell of roasting meat as everyone gathered, and lively talk and laughter rose up around the fire.

Shaila sat at a table with Aro, Dagon, and Amii, and they beckoned for Drauses to join them in a game of Suits. Drauses had never been very good at cards. He thought back to that game of naked Spindle he lost so miserably years ago but took a seat and the hand of cards Shaila offered him nonetheless.

After only one game, the birds were finished cooking, and the men all took turns carving the meat off the bones. It was delicious and juicy and washed down nicely with the bottles of Sazeen Dagon produced to the men's delight. More games of cards and dice were starting around the tables, plus a game of skill that required a trusting ward lay his hand flat on a table as his brothers took turns striking the spaces between his fingers with a blade at increasing speed. Drauses eyed that particular game nervously but decided not to interfere quite yet. If the players took too much whiskey to that table, he'd have to break up the game, lest fingers begin to fly.

As the sun began to set and dusk crept across the sky, they threw more wood on the fire and stoked the flames. It lit The Yard and kept them warm as the games and talk continued well into the night. Drauses sat in a chair near the fire after loading on more wood. Through the flames, he could see Shaila sitting across from him. She was smiling at long last, then she laughed at something Dagon said. Amii bounded up to her side, and the two most important people in his life smiled and laughed together. It filled his heart with joy.

Whenever Shaila had spoken to Drauses throughout the day, it had been pleasant enough, but withdrawn as well. They had not had a single moment alone since the morning they reconciled, if that was truly what they'd done at all. He ached to hold her, make love to her, and be assured all was right between them, but she'd asked for time and trust. He was determined to give her both, even if the distance killed him.

One of the wards started playing a pan flute. Soon after a bandura joined in. Two more wind instruments began to play as well, and they were soon surrounded by cheerful music. Amii stood and danced by herself for a moment before Aro grasped her hand and twirled her under his arm. She smiled wide with a giggle of pure delight as he swept her up in a dance. Who knew the ward could dance so gracefully?

A moment later, Dagon held out his hand to Shaila who blinked up at him in surprise. She smiled in amusement and rose from her seat, letting Dagon pull her into a dance as well. Drauses felt a pang of jealousy in his gut, but he stifled it. It was only Dagon after all. He wouldn't begrudge his closest friend one dance with the Lady of the Mark.

Dagon spun Shaila away then back close to his chest. He leaned in and whispered something near her ear that made her laugh again in delight.

Maybe *half* a dance.

Drauses rose and headed around the fire. Dagon saw him coming and smiled knowingly. He relinquished Shaila's hand without a word and excused himself to the sidelines as Drauses pulled her close. He looked at her warily, unsure what she would say at his intrusion, but she merely shook her head and chuckled.

"What's so funny?" he asked.

"Dagon and I were betting how long you'd last before you swept in and took his place."

"Who won the bet?"

"He did. He guessed you couldn't hold out to the end of this song. I argued you had better self-control than that. Seems I was wrong."

Drauses tightened his grip on her and was relieved when she stepped closer as they danced. "If it'd been any other man, I would've intervened sooner."

Shaila laughed, and the sound made Drauses' heart soar. "Perhaps you should see Boon for treatment of acute jealousy."

"There's no cure for it. Especially when it involves a lady finest fair."

Shaila clicked her tongue. "That ridiculous poem. If men only knew how silly they sound when they recite it. I'll have you know, ladies don't fall for such tricks of charm."

"They don't?" he challenged, then he began to recite:

> *"Not flower, sweet, or silvered jewel*
> *would I present to her, this creature*
> *who fell from paradise of sky*
> *to walk amongst those undeserving.*
> *What gift to give this Earthen angel*
> *with soul bright as a star?*
> *That which gives me life*
> *to draw breath, sing songs, make love:*
> *my heart is all I have*
> *and she will own it ever more*
> *straight from my breast still beating*
> *to live on in her good graces*
> *till she returns to Odavail to fly."*

"Ridiculous," Shaila whispered. Her lips twitched.

"And yet you smile." Drauses smiled, too, but his face fell again shortly after.

"What's the matter?" she asked.

"I need to tell you something." She nodded for him to continue, and he dropped his voice to a whisper near her ear. "As soon as we elect a new Liege, I plan to tell him about us. I want to know how you feel about it beforehand."

"We talked about this before. We agreed to do this once Gragern was dealt with."

"I know. But after everything that's happened…" Drauses sighed and shook his head, trying to find the words without demanding she make promises she wasn't ready to make. "We were bathed deep in Pera's light when we made those plans. Things aren't the same now. I wondered if you'd want to make new plans instead."

Shaila clicked her tongue. "Oh, Drauses…" she uttered. "I told you already, foolish man, that I love you as I did before. But my heart has known so much pain. I must give it time to rest and heal before I give it back to you." She touched their joined hands to his chest. "Tell our new Liege whatever you like. I stand ready to do whatever needs to be done to stay at your side."

Drauses peered around to be sure they were still not overheard, then he asked, "And if he insists one of us take our leave of the guild?"

Shaila blinked in surprise. "You think it'll come to that?"

"I don't know. Nothing like this has ever happened before."

Shaila danced in silence as she considered it. "I've had some time to think, Drauses, and… I don't want to be parted from you," she said, and it looked as if the confession lessened some load from her heart. She relaxed a bit in his arms. "No matter what that means."

"You'd leave the guild for me?" His heart soared.

"If it were that or watch you walk away without me, I'd join you in an instant."

"But what of Amii? I could never leave her behind."

"Neither could I. We'll have to take her with us and see her delivered back when the time comes for her to rise as sovereign. Though I fear what Aro will do. He'd never let her go, nor would Amii be parted from him."

"Perhaps he'd come with us," Drauses mused. "Dagon plans to make Aro a Master after our new Liege is appointed. He'd be free to take his leave from headquarters for a time without reprimand. We could give him the choice. He has family, too, after all. He may understand and go along, for Amii."

Shaila nodded. "Our plans are laid then. Now, stop worrying about such things and enjoy the party."

The song came to an end, and she pulled away. He tightened his hand on hers before she could slip it free, and she looked back. He ached to pull her back, to steal a kiss, to dance to one more song, or forever, but as badly as it broke his heart to do so, he let her go instead. Whatever look he had on his face made her pause, and she stared at him until Amii called her away.

The men continued to eat, drink, and dance well into the night, and though Drauses made rounds throughout them all, stopping at every table to make small talk with the Masters, not one of his brothers mentioned their upcoming vote. If Drauses mentioned it himself, he got only vague replies and a prompt change in subject.

Dagon, on the other hand, seemed to have the opposite luck. He laughed his way from group to group with warm handshakes and hugs, and Drauses often found him bent close over the tables, talking in private, hushed whispers to several Masters at once. Drauses came over to join in one such talk only for the whole group, Dagon included, to fall silent as soon as he sat down. He gave up and went to bed, leaving them to their secret whispering around the dying fire.

Chapter 25

SHAILA LAY AWAKE in the bed next to Amii's in the ladies' quarters, the image of Drauses' pain-filled face as she left him after their dance twisting her heart in her chest and refusing to let her sleep. When she could bear it no longer, she slipped from under the covers and snuck across the room. Aro was snoring in the bed closest to Amii's door in the next room. Shaila crept past and out into the hallway, setting the door silently back in its frame behind her so as not to wake him.

She descended the stairs in the dark, trailed her fingers along the wall of the first-floor hallway, and stopped at the fourth door on the right. The knob turned with no resistance, and she let herself in.

Drauses was lying on his back, wide awake, and he jumped up when she entered. He came to her tentatively, as if she might change her mind if he startled her. She didn't and went willingly into his arms with a soft sigh. When he kissed her, she felt no remorse, no anger, and no pain in her heart, only that familiar heat in her blood and stirring desire in her middle. She deepened their kiss, and Drauses moaned in longing.

He stripped off her robes, and she stripped off his shirt, pausing to kiss his chest, neck, and face as the cloth inched up his body. She tore open the front of his pants, shoved them down, and knelt to take him in her mouth.

"No," he said, his voice deep and rumbling. He hauled her back to her feet. "There's only one way I want you on your knees."

He ushered her backward toward the bed until her legs bumped the mattress. He turned her so he was at her back, kissing her neck as he urged her up onto the bed on her knees. Once there was room for him, he joined her there, pulled her back into his chest, touched her throat, her breasts, then lower between her legs. A soft moan escaped her lips, and a moment later, he slid inside her from behind and thrust deep. She gasped at the feel of him buried so deeply in her body then moaned deeper when he did it again.

"Oh Gods…"

She flung her hair over his shoulder as she leaned back against him then turned to meet his mouth with her own. His tongue slipped between her teeth as her legs began to shake. Her hand went up to clutch his hair, and she whimpered against his lips. The pumping of his hips, the delving of his tongue, the feel of his hands sweeping over every inch of her skin sent her body into flight until she cried out as she came apart.

✧

The sound of Shaila losing herself was nearly enough to make Drauses do so himself, but he wasn't ready for this to be over yet. He kept up his kissing, his rhythm, and his touch. She was building again. He could feel her muscles clenching around him where he rocked inside her. Suddenly, her mouth pulled away from his. The look of surrender, tenderness, and love in her eyes made his chest tighten. She trailed her fingers down his temple, his cheek, and his throat.

"I love you," she whispered.

Drauses lost control. He buried his face in her hair and let himself go harder, faster, until she called out his name in a second sweet release. It pushed him over the edge, and he followed her up into the heights of blissful pleasure as his body detonated.

The hours of the night ticked by as they both slept wrapped around each other in a tangle of limbs and sheets. In the dark, she curled close to him, kissed him, made love to him more than once, and without saying so in words, made one thing perfectly clear.

He was forgiven.

✧

The Masters all made their way to the large first-floor meeting room for council at dawn the next morning. As soon as the last Master wandered in, the door was closed, and they all gathered together around the long table in the center of the room.

"We all know why we're here," Drauses said. "So, without further ado, I propose we cast our votes for our new Liege."

"That won't be necessary," Dagon said. "We already know who we wish to lead us. We can take a formal vote if you wish, Drauses, but all but one in this room will vote the same, I assure you."

"This decision was made without me?" Drauses asked. His suspicions from the previous evening were confirmed. His respect with his brothers must've slipped so far they no longer trusted him enough to consult with him. This didn't bode well for him and Shaila.

"Vote for whomever you like," Ithail said, "but we all vote for one man."

"Alright then," Drauses said calmly, though his heart hammered in his chest. "Who is it?"

Dagon smiled. "It's you, of course."

Drauses' mouth fell open.

"It was unanimous," Ithail added. The men around the room nodded in agreement. "We all know who led this guild these past many weeks, and it wasn't Gragern. Where our Liege failed us, you took charge without hesitation. We noticed."

Though ever grateful for his brothers' loyalties, Drauses hung his head at this news. The guild needed a Liege loyal to their cause above all else, and he knew there was someone, more than one someone, he was loyal to above his Brothers of the Mark.

"I decline," Drauses said.

There was a murmur of shock throughout the room.

Dagon cleared his throat. "I know you have concerns. You've voiced them to me at length. You fear you'll go mad stuck at headquarters, dictating and watching from the sidelines while we fight this war without you. But, Drauses, the reason we chose you for this position is because we no longer want a Liege like the ones we've had in the past. Perhaps it is time for someone to redefine what it means to be the Elder Master. If you'd rather swing your sword with us than stay behind, as the Liege, you could certainly choose to do so, and not a man would object."

Drauses had to admit, such an arrangement did sound promising, but it didn't change the situation he was in at present. "That's not why I must turn you down."

Dagon cocked his head. "Why then?"

Drauses heaved a deep sigh. It was time to confess his transgressions. "Gragern thought me unfit to lead. On this point, I'm afraid I must agree. Our Elder Master should be the pillar of the Men of the Mark, the one to look up to above all others. I'm not that man. I've broken our code. I laid with Shaila." He couldn't meet his comrades' eyes. "Masters are not to lie with their wards, our laws say so, and I can't lead the guild if I can't abide by our own codes."

When he looked up from the table, the others all looked amused, several of them smiling and others shaking their heads with rolling eyes. Dagon laughed.

"How blind do you think we are?" Ithail asked.

"Come again?" said Drauses.

"We've known for some time about your relationship with the Lady of the Mark," Dagon said. "It's painfully obvious you're more than mere Master and ward. That doesn't change anything. We still want you as our Liege."

"But the code—"

"Was written years ago when Masters took wards as young as twelve," said Dagon. "That rule was to protect young boys from abuse. Shaila is a grown woman, capable of making her own choices. The code doesn't apply here."

"That is a technicality," Drauses said with a dismissive wave of his hand. "Besides, Shaila and I have decided we won't be parted. In our previous council, we all agreed the Elder Master would no longer be allowed a ward lest we have a repeat of what happened to Miika. How can Shaila stay at my side if I become Liege?"

"That's easy," said Ithail. "Make her a Master."

Dagon nodded in agreement. "As a Master, Shaila would be free to train with whomever she wishes. If that happens to be you and only you for the foreseeable future, that's her choice to make. She's earned it after her actions of late."

There was a murmur of agreement.

Drauses considered this but then shook his head. "I won't keep secrets from her, and, as the Liege, I'd be honor-bound to keep many."

"You'd want to confide in her?" Dagon asked, deep in thought.

"Perhaps she could make some vow of confidence," Ithail offered with a shrug. "Something official to be marked in our records."

Dagon's face lit with sudden inspiration, and he smiled. "A marriage vow."

"What?" Drauses asked in surprise.

"How did that old prayer go?" Dagon asked no one in particular. "The one they used to use in official ceremonies. It mentioned confidences, did it not?"

"I don't—"

"Does anyone have a book of prayer in their quarters?"

Drauses sat in a stunned fog as a book was found. His brothers studied the passage in question, concluded it did in fact mention keeping confidences, and all turned to stare at him with happy smiles.

"Marry Shaila?" Drauses uttered. As he said the words, he considered the notion for the first time: standing together with hands clasped, vowing in front of friends and the gods alike to never be parted, to be forever husband and wife. "My wife." His heart soared.

"Not just your wife," Dagon said, "but our Lady Liege: partner to the Elder Master in ruling the Marks."

Drauses leaned forward in his chair. "You'd accept a woman of just three and twenty as an equal to your Liege?"

"As if Shaila were a mere woman," Ithail said with a bark of laughter. "She can best any of our wards, many of us Masters, and even you, Drauses, when she's angry. We've all seen her bring you to your knees."

"This is your wish then? That I become Liege with Shaila as my partner, my wife and confidant in all things to do with leading the guild?"

"It is," said Ithail.

Dagon nodded as did the other Masters around the room.

Drauses blinked, bemused. "If that's your wish, then I accept."

Dagon rose from his chair and clapped Drauses on the shoulder. "Fantastic! But you know there's one small matter you must address first, don't you?"

"What's that?"

"You have to get Shaila to agree to marry you."

The Masters all roared with laughter at the fresh look of horror on Drauses' face.

∽

Drauses headed across The Yard, pondering how he'd keep the council's decision from Shaila. They'd agreed to give him two days to figure out how to propose marriage. After that, the news would be shared freely. He went straight from council to Julta's workshop.

"Julta, I need your help," Drauses said as he took a seat at the little man's counter.

"You're here, Master Drauses, so I must assume so," Julta replied with a smirk.

"I need you to craft for me."

"Oh? Please tell me my ears don't deceive me! That sword must have impressed you more than I thought."

"You heard me right, Julta, and the sword is a spectacular weapon to be sure, but this isn't for me."

"Don't keep me in such suspense!"

"First, I need a Master's blade. For Shaila."

"That's too easy!" Julta barked with a slap on the counter. "If that's all you're here to ask of me, I'll be deeply disappointed."

"I also need a ring, a proposal ring, in Shaila's size."

Julta stared, mouth agape, at Drauses for a long, silent moment. "Oh..." he uttered in horror. "Oh no, no, no. I'm no jeweler, sir, oh no! How shall I ever craft a piece fitting for such a woman?"

"Relax, Julta. I believe you're more than capable."

"Silver. I need silver. No, I have silver. Plenty for this anyway. I have stones, too. Diamonds? No, no, no. No diamonds. Far too plain, clear like glass. Blech. A color! I need a color, Master Drauses. One that fits the Lady of the Mark."

Drauses stroked his chin, picturing his Shaila always dressed in Mark's robes or the breathtaking dress she wore to the theater what felt like a lifetime ago. He smiled.

"Red, I think."

"Red! Of course. The color of the Marks. Perfect. A ruby. I have several. Give me a day, Master Drauses. A day to create."

"Only one day?"

"I shan't sleep tonight for thought of such an important piece."

"There's one more thing."

"I don't know that I can accomplish any more right now," Julta said with a sigh of exasperation.

"This requires no labor." Drauses dug a paper out of his pocket and handed it to Julta. "I'd like to find these people. I know you have connections. Can you circulate these names among them? Make it known throughout Trista's East side that I wish to see these persons about a matter of great importance. It's time-sensitive."

"Hmm. I've never tried to track down *people* before. I shall do my best, sir. My very best indeed."

⸺

Shaila was beginning to suspect Drauses thought her infected with some horrible contagion. He quickly left rooms when she entered, crossed The Yard in the opposite direction when he spied her, and kept busy with various tasks that put distance between them all day. Though she tried several times to corner and question him about the council's decision that morning, he always managed to slip away.

She questioned Aro who told her his own Master was avoiding questions as well. She cornered Dagon around midday, but he begged his leave of her, claiming he had important business to attend to. Had Drauses asked after his and Shaila's relationship with the new Liege? Had he been told they must cease their tryst? Perhaps he'd changed his mind and no longer wished to leave the guild for her. When he headed for his quarters that evening, she stalked after him, determined to wring the answers from him by any means necessary.

Standing in front of his door, she almost changed her mind. If he wished to stay away from her, she shouldn't force her company. She turned to go, hesitated, raised her hand to knock, then shook her head and walked in without warning. Drauses froze at the sight of her as she strolled in. She shut the door behind her and locked him in a cold stare.

"Can I help you, my lady?" he asked with a smile.

"Help me? Yes. You can help me, Drauses. Please help me understand why the man who claimed such passionate love for me last night has had not a word to say to me all day. In fact, he seems more like a ghost than a man: rarely seen, darting around corners and through doorways the moment I come near. Did you meet with the other Masters this morning?"

"I did."

"Have they chosen a new Liege?"

"They have."

"Are you purposely being vague?"

"I am."

"Do you plan to tell me what happened during council this morning?"

"No, my lady."

Shaila growled in frustration. "Why in Vedia not?"

"The Masters were asked not to discuss it yet."

"Why?"

"If I told you, that would be discussing it, would it not?" He was smirking, and Shaila was growing angry.

"You can discuss such with *me*. I can be trusted to keep a secret."

"Someone once told me *'you need not know every answer lest you take all the mystery out of life.'*"

"I shall drag these answers from you one way or another!"

Drauses pulled his shirt up over his head, flinging it away across the room. He stepped closer. "I promise you, my lady, I will tell you everything in time. But, for tonight, you'll get no answers from me."

He was trying to distract her, but she vowed not to let him. "Surely you don't mean to make me worry," she said, playing for sympathy.

He smiled, wise to her game. He undid his pants and let them slide down over his hips to pool at his feet. He stepped free of them and came closer yet. Shaila backed up, but he rushed in and caught her, snaking his arms around her middle and yanking her close. Pressed against his naked body, she was, admittedly, very distracted. He kissed a spot under her ear that drew a sigh from deep in her chest. His hands untied her robes and pushed them up over her shoulders. She let them fall to the floor.

"I know what you're doing," she muttered.

He reached for her shirt and swept it up off her body. "I'm making love to a beautiful woman," Drauses murmured. His fingers trailed down to her pants where they made short work of the buttons. She kicked them off along with her boots.

Drauses' hands slid down her arms, around her back, and down to her backside where he grabbed her and hauled her up onto his hips. She gasped in surprise and wrapped her legs around his waist to keep from falling. Her arms looped around his neck as he carried her across the room.

There was a desk against the far wall. With a sweep of his arm, Drauses knocked everything off the top of it. He laid her across the wood before sinking to his knees. With a tug, he pulled her to the edge of the desk then set her legs over his shoulders and put his mouth to her. Shaila muttered his name as pleasure washed over her in waves. She pushed up onto her elbows to watch, and the sight of his lips and tongue on her body wound her tighter, faster, until she burst wide open for him with a cry of surrender.

Drauses climbed back to his feet and settled between her thighs. With one swift thrust, he buried himself inside her. The rocking of his hips set the desk bumping against the wall but neither of them noticed. Shaila sat up and threw her arms around his neck while he moved inside her, arching her back to take him deeper still. She nuzzled his throat and kissed him there, right over his racing pulse. A moment later, she buried her face into his neck as she cried out again in rapture. He captured her mouth in a deep kiss as he came apart right after her.

❧

Drauses woke before the sun. He slithered carefully from the bed and managed to dress without a sound as Shaila slept. She roused and reached for him as he snuck out the door. She sat up in a rage just before the door snapped shut behind him. He chuckled from the other side at the sound of her frustrated cry. He'd managed to slip away. Again.

꿏

Far to the north of the city, beyond even the sight of the Men of the Mark and their spies, a large boat sat moored at the Western shore. It was a cargo ship, a relic of times when Trista held trade with Se Trosk A Vol a century ago. Now, Black Blades bustled to and fro carrying equipment and firearms onto the massive vessel. One man knelt by a large cannon on the deck with an odd metal helmet strapped over his face for protection as he welded.

"Roth!"

Roth snuffed out his torch and stood, lifting the helmet to the top of his head as he stepped to the edge of the boat and peered down at Rovik standing on the bank below. He'd heard the sovereign was coming to check on their progress today but had hoped he wouldn't have to interact with the man himself.

"Are we still on schedule?" Rovik asked.

"If all continues to go well, we should be done within the time we discussed," Roth called back, his voice deep and booming. "If you keep interrupting me, however, we'll certainly see delays."

Rovik grumbled and stalked away.

Roth made to lower his helmet again, but a voice from behind stopped him.

"Have you had any flashes of genius on how to sabotage this ridiculous floating arsenal?" Rose asked.

"Not yet," he said with a cautious glance around the deck. "And keep your voice down."

"These men are mine. None of them will take our secrets to Rovik."

"It makes me nervous." Roth picked up a rag and attempted to clean his hands, but the grime wouldn't be wiped away with a dry cloth, so he gave up and tossed it aside. "What you're asking of me, I don't know that it can be done. To make this vessel both perform as it ought and malfunction at the right moment while still keeping us clear of blame—"

"Don't worry about blame," she said. "If anyone so much as threatens you, I'll end them."

Roth shook his head. "We both know there are those, be they few, who can do as they like to me, and you'd be powerless to stop them."

"Are you doubting me?" she asked with a deadly glint in her eye.

As fiery as she was, Roth knew Rose had more sense than that. "If it came to it, you wouldn't stand against them. No sense in both of us dying, now is there?"

"I won't let that happen." Rose strolled close and ripped the helmet off his head. His long black hair tumbled down across his shoulders. A diamond earring dangled from his left lobe and glinted in the sunlight. He smiled as she pulled him close and kissed him passionately. He took her lower lip between his teeth, biting hard enough to make her gasp. She gave his lip the same treatment, sending a shiver of pure desire straight to his groin.

As always, he pulled away first. "I have work to do."

"Are you angry with me?" Rose asked.

Roth sighed. "No. I'm not happy about being dragged into this, but I know that's not your fault. I also know why you've asked this of me, and I agree that it must be done for Amii's sake, but I'm not used to sneaking around in the shadows, Rose. I'm not like you. I design and build. Betrayal and secrets are *your* specialty."

"I know, lover. This is the last time I'll ask something like this of you." She leaned closer and spoke in a whisper for his ears only. "When this is over, and I know Amii is safe once and for all, we're leaving."

Roth resisted the urge to roll his eyes. "Where would we go? How far could we get before your brother caught up to us?"

"I'll run with you for the rest of my life if that's what it takes."

This time he did roll his eyes. "You've said such things before; every time Amii is involved…" He shook his head. "I'm not Drauses. I've no intention of sweeping you up and carrying you away into the sunset. You know that. Spare us both your dramatics and let me get back to work." He took his helmet back from her.

Rose huffed and turned away. As she stalked off, Roth put his helmet back on, lit his torch, and went back to the task at hand.

Chapter 26

JULTA POLISHED THE ring with a rag one final time before holding it out to Drauses on his palm. Though slender along its bottom, the top of the band was a wide, elegant knot of silver strands. In the center, amongst the tangled design, sat a ruby of deepest red. Drauses ached to see it on Shaila's hand.

"Perhaps you missed your calling as a jeweler, Julta," Drauses remarked. "It's beautiful."

"I worry more what the lady will think," Julta said, wringing his hands on the counter.

"I hope she loves it. For both our sakes." Drauses put the jewel in his pocket. "What of the other task I set you to?"

"I've heard nothing yet, apologies."

"Let me know the moment you do."

"Yes, Master Drauses."

As Drauses headed back across The Yard, Shaila came stomping his way. It was time to put his plans into motion. He smiled at her, and when she opened her mouth to again make her demands for answers, he spoke before she had the chance.

"Care to spar with me?" he asked.

She looked flummoxed at first but then shook herself and asked, "You wish to train? Now?"

"I do."

She narrowed her eyes at him and crossed her arms. "I must warn you, I'm quite vexed with you at the moment. The last time we trained when I was in a mood, it didn't turn out so well for either of us."

"I'd argue that session turned out just fine," he said with a wink. "I'll take my chances."

Though still eyeing him suspiciously, Shaila followed him across The Yard toward the westernmost building, the first floor of which had been transformed into a grand training room. Drauses held open the door for her, and as she stepped inside ahead of him, he waved a hand over his shoulder to Dagon who stood watching a short distance away. With Dagon's help, word quickly spread throughout the grounds that the Lady of the Mark was training with her Master again. It was the men's favorite spectacle, so it took little convincing on Dagon's part to spur Masters and wards alike across The Yard to watch the show.

Shaila plucked two training swords from the wall. She threw one to Drauses as men began to file into the room, leaning their backs against the walls in expectation. Drauses' grin grew with the crowd.

"I'd like to make a wager," he said.

"On our match?" Shaila asked. "What are your terms?"

"If I win, I get to ask you one question, and you must answer truthfully."

"And if *I* win?"

"You may ask me *two* questions which *I* must answer truthfully."

Shaila nodded. "Very well." She stepped closer and added in a whisper, "I won't be gentle."

"I'd be disappointed otherwise."

They bowed in unison then rushed forward and came together in a clash of steel.

⁂

The battle waged for over thirty minutes. Shaila's thigh burned from the sudden exercise. Both she and Drauses were exhausted and sweating profusely, but Shaila refused to yield. Drauses' sleeve was smeared with blood from his nose where she'd clocked him with the hilt of her sword. Shaila's eyebrow was split where he'd landed a blow of his own.

296

The room was stifling with so many bodies crammed inside. Even Aro and Amii had wandered in and stood next to Dagon by the wall.

Shaila smiled at Drauses as he put his hands on his knees for a moment, fighting for breath. "Perhaps we should call it a draw," she suggested.

"Only if you fear you'll lose."

She shrugged. "Suit yourself."

Shaila swung up with her sword toward Drauses' chin, and he blocked it before striking back hard and fast. She expected this, for her Master always tried to end the fight fast when he grew tired. She drew back her stance, forcing him to draw closer to keep up his attack. She met his sword and knocked it to the side with her own. A man of perfect footwork, Drauses counter-stepped to center himself, and she slipped in for the kill. Shaila wound her leg around his, knocked him in the chest with her shoulder, and yanked out his leg, dropping him hard on his back. She came down on top of him, pressing her knee to his chest and her blade to his throat.

As the crowd applauded her victory, Shaila stood and took a bow then helped Drauses to his feet.

"I win," she said. "So now, you must make good on our bargain." Those who were about to leave the room paused, their attention drawn anew.

Drauses looked far too smug as he replied, "So I do. What's your first question?"

"Who's our new Liege?"

Silence had fallen in the room as the other wards listened intently.

Drauses smiled. "I am."

Fresh applause and a roar of cheers rose at the news. Without thinking, Shaila threw her arms around Drauses' neck, her deep relief making her forget they were surrounded by watchful eyes.

"Your next question, my lady?" Drauses asked.

With just two words, he'd answered both her questions, for if Drauses was the Liege, then there was no one standing between them anymore. What should she ask him now then? She touched her chin.

"If you'd won this fight, what question would *you* have asked *me*?"

Drauses smiled triumphantly, and she realized this had been his game all along.

"Shaila," he bid, and it sounded more like a plea. He held out his hand to her and uncurled his fingers to reveal a ring in his palm. She gasped and took a step back in surprise. The silver band and deep red stone were beautiful, but Drauses' blue eyes drew hers above all else. "Will you marry me?"

Amii squealed in delight, but Shaila clamped both her hands over her mouth, shocked clear to her toes. Was he jesting? Surely not. But he must be! In her daze, she failed to reply.

"My lady, I need an answer," he prodded with a nervous smile.

Shaila lowered her hands from her mouth. "Marry you?" she asked in awe.

"I've already vowed never to be parted from you. Let us vow it to the gods as well with promise and prayer. Marry me? That is, if you feel I'm worthy."

"Yes," Shaila said in a whisper.

"Louder," Drauses requested.

"Yes, I will," she replied loud and clear, though her voice broke in an effort not to cry.

This time the applause was deafening. Drauses dropped his weapon and slid the ring on her finger, then he kissed her in front of the entire guild.

Shaila's heartbeat was deafening in her ears, and her face felt like it was on fire. All the worry of what would come should their secret be found out was gone. There was nothing left to stop them from loving each other openly now... except... Shaila still had one secret left to tell. But with Drauses' proposal came a fresh wave of relief. If he wanted her as his bride, surely he would rejoice at the news of a child.

Shaila was still in a daze when Drauses pulled away and turned to address the gathered men she'd nearly forgotten about.

"In council, we took our brother Miika's unfortunate situation to heart and decided together that our Liege would no longer be allowed a ward," he said.

Shaila looked up from her ring in concern, but Drauses gave her a reassuring smile.

"To honor our newest law," he continued, "and as my first act as

Liege, I'll be giving Shaila leave of me. She has proven herself far more than I could ever ask of her, as much as any Master could hope his ward would. I name her a Master this day. I've also asked her, in audience of you all, to be my wife. The day we are wed, she will become your Lady Liege and my equal in this guild.

"Shaila and I will be two halves of the same position of power. I'll consult with her and she with me on all matters to do with leading you." He held his hand out to Shaila who took it with a squeeze. "Please don't hesitate to come to either of us with concerns or suggestions within the guild. We'll listen, and, unlike our late Liege, we vow to act within the best interests of this guild always. Whether Liege, Master, or ward, we are all brothers and sisters, comrades in arms who stand together while we still have blood to give!"

"While we still have blood to give!" the men chanted back.

Dagon waved from the back of the room, and Drauses nodded. "I've stolen the light long enough. I believe Dagon has an announcement as well."

"Indeed, I do," Dagon said as he picked his way through the crowd. "Aro, join me."

Aro's eyes widened, but he left Amii's side for the first time in days to stand beside his Master.

Dagon regarded the gathering with a sad smile. "Over the past few seasons, my ward has shown the kind of bravery, initiative, and loyalty we come to expect from every Brother of the Mark. There's little left for me to teach him, so today, in front of all his brothers-in-arms and our new Liege, I name him a Master as well."

Aro smiled in happy surprise as his brothers applauded. The two Masters, old and new, shook hands, then Aro pulled Dagon into a one-armed hug and spoke private words only for Dagon's ears. Shaila watched as Dagon closed his eyes, warmed nearly to tears by whatever Aro said.

"Thank you all for the audience," Drauses said. "You're dismissed."

As the Marks filed out of the room again, Amii tore across the mat and leapt at Drauses with a squeezing hug. "I'm so proud to call you father," she said.

"Not nearly as proud as I am to call you daughter," he said with a smile, then he kissed her on the cheek. When he set Amii down, he took Shaila's hand again and examined the jewel on her finger. He kissed her knuckles lovingly.

When Aro and Dagon came to offer congratulations, Aro shared a sad look with Shaila, and the guild's newest Masters drew away for a private word.

"I wish Miika were here to see such a joyous day for us both," Aro said.

Shaila smiled sadly. "He did see it, Aro. He no doubt cheered for us from Odavail."

"I blame myself," he admitted. "I know taking Amii to safety was more important, but the doubt still weighs heavy in my heart. Maybe if I'd been here…"

Shaila touched his arm. "I blame myself too. I set Miika on this path, but Miika's problems started long before we were part of them. We'll drive ourselves mad with ifs and maybes. All we can do now is ask our fallen brother and dear friend to guide us forward for the rest of our days. I choose to believe he does this happily already."

Aro nodded then grinned. "Wise words, *Lady Liege*."

"Oh gods!" Shaila exclaimed. "I may never get used to hearing that."

"You'd better. No man here will call you anything else from now on. Except Master Drauses, of course."

"And what of *your* new title, *Master Aro?*"

It was Aro's turn to be taken aback. He cocked his head to the side then laughed. Shaila joined him, and they snickered together in wonder until Amii came bounding up to hug Shaila in congratulations.

"Can I see the ring?" the girl asked, and she sighed at the sight of the jewel. "Someday, I hope a man will give me something as beautiful."

"It will be as beautiful as you, little one," Shaila cooed, then for reasons unknown, she glanced at Aro. Amii soon drew the towering Master deep in conversation, and the two of them wandered away together. Shaila watched them go and smiled to herself. "Beautiful, indeed."

❧

Rose stood just inside the door in Rovik's office when Roth walked in to announce the sovereign's new ship was ready and awaiting her maiden voyage. The calculating smile on her uncle's face at the news made her uncomfortable, and she wished Roth hadn't walked so close to the sovereign's desk. He was too far away for her to protect him.

Rovik smiled and stood from his chair, walking around the desk to Roth who eyed the sovereign warily.

"And it will function as it ought, yes?" Rovik asked.

"Of course, my sovereign," Roth replied with conviction.

Rovik leaned a little nearer, and Rose tensed. "And my niece didn't ask you to sabotage my vessel in any way?"

Rose watched with pride as Roth kept eye contact, never flinching. "No, sir. She didn't."

"Well done," Rovik said with a fresh smile. "If I didn't know my Rose as well as I do, that lie may have convinced me."

"It's not—"

Rovik punched Roth in the stomach, and Rose took a menacing step closer, but Roth held up a hand to stop her.

"Admit what you had him do, and I won't touch him again," Rovik said.

"We did nothing to your precious vessel," Rose spat.

Rovik shrugged and struck Roth again, this time with a knee between the legs. Roth went down on both knees, gasping. Rovik looked again to Rose, but she said not a word. A knee to the face sent Roth sprawling across the carpet with a bloodied nose.

"Enough!" Rose yelled. "We didn't sabotage the boat, Uncle. You have my word."

Rovik regarded her for a long moment then dragged Roth up onto his feet. He called for the guards standing duty outside his office and shoved Roth at them.

"Take him to The Cellar."

"No!" Rose drew her blade and stood between Roth and the guards who both drew their guns on her.

"Stop!" Roth yelled. He stepped around Rose, between her and the guns. "I'll go."

Rose rounded on Rovik. "What is the meaning of this betrayal? We've done all you asked!"

"This is insurance," Rovik said. "If my ship does its job tomorrow, Roth will be returned to you, unharmed. But if the boat sinks or something equally suspicious happens, I'll grant my new executioner leave to do as he pleases. Perhaps you've heard of him. His name is Vynus."

Rose paled at the name.

"He came highly recommended by your brother," Rovik continued. "I bet he'll be more than generous with his work to impress his new employer."

Rose shared a look of agony with Roth. As he'd predicted, there was nothing she could do as the guards seized him by the arms and hauled him away.

⁓

"Julta," Shaila called from the workshop counter.

The man peeked out from his back room for little more than a second, then disappeared again.

Shaila heard him swear from behind the wall, and she chuckled. "Well, come here."

Begrudgingly, he came to the counter but refused to meet her eyes.

"Is there nothing you wish to ask me, Julta?"

"No, ma'am... Lady Liege, no."

She seized Julta by the chin and forced him to look at her. "It's the most beautiful thing you've ever crafted, Julta. Nothing could've made me happier."

Julta burst into a hysterical fit of laughter. He danced about for a moment then groaned and sank into a nearby chair. "Please, never let Master Drauses request such a thing from me again," he begged. "I fear my heart won't take it."

"You always ask for a challenge."

"Not that challenging! I prefer weaponry. Oh, yes! That reminds me!"

Julta sprang back to his feet and dashed across the room. He came back to the counter with a long sword tucked in a beautifully carved sheath. A nervous, excited giggle escaped him as he held it out to her. The mad glint in his eyes made her almost afraid to take it from him.

"Your new Master's blade," Julta said.

He laid the weapon on the counter, and she wrapped her fingers around the hilt. Shaila squinted at the blade as it slid from its sheath. It wasn't whole. It gave the impression from a distance that it was one solid piece of steel, but upon closer inspection, she could see the lines that cut the blade into several dozen individual pieces.

"Stand up and step back," Julta commanded. He pointed at the hilt. "Spin the end one hundred and eighty degrees clockwise."

"Half a turn clockwise," Shaila muttered as she spun the end of the hilt.

With a slight rumble under her palm, the sword fell apart. No. It was still together but no longer a blade. The pieces of steel had separated but were still strung together by a complex system of steel cables that ran down their centers. Though still technically connected, each arrow-head-shaped piece of steel pivoted independently and was sharpened on all sides. She flicked her wrist and the weapon slithered back and forth like a snake.

"Blade whip," Julta said proudly. "I've been working on this design for years but never had an appropriate wielder. I've finally found one. Turn the end back to its original position."

Shaila did so, and the hilt vibrated again. One second the weapon was a whip, the next it snapped back and was once again a solid blade. She swung it in a graceful arc, then spun with an upward swipe. It was much heavier than her old sword, but Master blades were often heftier and much more ornate. This one had a cluster of small rubies set in the end of the hilt as well as bands of braided gold and red metal woven around the base in a complex knot with more rubies nestled between the strands. It matched her ring perfectly and was easily the most gorgeous weapon she'd ever seen.

"I must issue fair warning, Lady Liege," Julta said, growing quite serious. "This weapon will take years to master. Use the whip with caution until you know how to wield it. It could injure you or nearby comrades if used improperly. The blade I'm confident you can handle; its brother will be a much harder beast to tame."

"If it's so hard a weapon to use, why give it to *me*?"

"The ward who was named Master within a season, who the Marks accept as Lady Liege, dedicates herself to this guild, its cause, its Elder Master: she can wield this weapon, I've no doubts."

"I'm honored, Julta."

"Oh, I have more," Julta announced, and he darted across the room again. He came back with a familiar-looking silver rectangle attached to two leather straps.

"My crossbow!" Shaila exclaimed. "How did you get it back from Rovik's estate?"

"It's your crossbow's twin," he corrected her. "I always make more than one of my weapons." Julta winked and pushed it across the counter to her.

Shaila strapped on her new weapons. The blade was heavy on her hip, but she liked the feel of it. She wondered what Drauses would say about it, then she smiled; perhaps she could make him jealous.

In the night, a vessel filled to the brim with firepower and black-clad men sailed down the river toward the south of the city. Not a soul was awake to witness its passing. It was just before dawn when the river bend came into sight, and the engines died away so as not to wake the Men of the Mark downstream. As the sun began to rise, they made their final preparations and sailed around the bend.

Shaila and Drauses spent the night on the third floor of the bunkhouse, which was remodeled for the Liege and included its own quarters, bathroom, and spacious office. Though at first the thought of staying in rooms where Gragern once lingered made Shaila pull a face, Drauses reminded her the late Elder was an incurable insomniac and spent most of his time in his office rather than his quarters. The bed, therefore, had stood empty for those few days Gragern was in residence. Shaila's unrest faded as Drauses spent all hours of the night showing her how happy and grateful he was that she would soon be his bride. With no threat of discovery, no worry that they may one day be separated, they found new heights of passion and pleasure that deepened their devotion to each other.

The next morning, in the moments of dawn as the sun lit their new rooms, Shaila stood in the spacious bathroom and studied herself in the mirror. Her stomach swam and cramped as it did almost every morning now. She struggled not to give in to the nausea since Drauses was in the next room. It was getting harder to hide it from him. Soon, her body would begin to change, and he would notice. Already she could see the signs herself, though they were still too subtle for eyes other than her own to see. She smiled to herself. It was time.

She went back to the bedroom where Drauses sat on the bed, lacing his boots. He was not yet fully dressed as he still lacked a shirt and robes. Her eyes lingered, enjoying the view. He looked up to catch her staring.

"You look as if you're bursting to tell me something," he remarked.

"I am."

He stood and crossed the room to her. She stayed in the bathroom doorway, hesitant and anxious.

"Say whatever it is you wish, my lady. If it comes from your lips, it'll no doubt bring me nothing but joy."

Shaila stared into his eyes and opened her mouth to spill her secret. From the near distance came a deafening boom, and a second later, the whole building shook as if struck by a quake from the depths of the Earth. Screams erupted in the halls below as another boom and quake hit, closer this time. Shaila rushed for her clothes as Drauses finished dressing as well. Just as Shaila tightened the belt of her sword around her waist, the wall behind her exploded in a shower of wood as a ball of iron hurled through the room. She rolled away, and Drauses took her arm and hauled her out into the hall.

"What in Vedia was that?" Shaila yelled as they stood staring back through the door at the ravaged bedroom.

"A cannonball!"

"Cannons?" Shaila shared a look of utter horror with Drauses, clutching his arm in fear. "Amii!"

They whirled in unison and rushed away down the hall.

Chapter 27

AS DRAUSES AND Shaila drew close to the stairwell, a group of Black Blades spilled out of the door at the end of the hall. Shaila drew her crossbow and struck the first one dead from a distance. The next Blade fell a second later, split from navel to chin by Drauses' sword. The third pulled a gun, but Shaila kicked it away, took hold of the man's robes in both hands, and spun him toward Drauses who plunged his blade in the man's back. Shaila drew her own sword and, with a mighty swing, cleaved the head off a fourth Blade as he came through the door. Their fifth and last enemy raised his gun.

"Down!" Drauses called as he drew his knife from his robes. Shaila dropped to a knee as Drauses threw the knife over her head, and it stuck into the Black Blade's neck. Shaila rose, took hold of Drauses' knife, and tore out the man's throat. As the Blade fell, she tossed the knife back to Drauses. They moved together into the stairwell.

The second-floor hall was already full of their enemies, both living and dead. Shaila ran ahead and kicked a Black Blade hard in the chest. She followed with a kick to his knee, a palm to his nose, then an elbow to his kidney before she wrapped her arm around his throat and snapped his neck in time to ready her crossbow and fire a bolt up through the chin of a Blade who tried to rush in for a quick kill. The last few Black Blades in the hall eyed her with dread then turned and ran like cowards. Shaila snatched the sword from a dead man at her feet and threw it like a spear. It skewered one Blade in the back as his comrades rounded the corner. The hall was full only of bodies now, and Shaila stood shaking in fury and covered in blood amidst the carnage. She caught Drauses staring in awe.

"A mighty Lady Liege indeed," he uttered with a grin.

"Aro," Shaila called. "It's us. Hold your fire." She and Drauses rounded the doorway to Amii's quarters.

Aro stood in the middle of the room, gun raised and ready with a terrified Amii hiding behind him. The floor was littered with half a dozen Black Blades who'd managed to enter the room with three more in the hallway full of bullet holes. Aro was out of breath and covered in blood with a look of pure rage on his face as he slammed bullets into his pistol.

"Has Rovik lost all sense?" he thundered. "He'll get Amii killed!"

"It seems he's reached a new height of desperation," Drauses said. He beckoned to Amii who left Aro's side to hug her father in relief that he was unharmed. "We must go. Now!"

Aro nodded and readied his pistol, loaded once more, but as they all turned for the door, another cannon boomed, and the ball crashed through the wall to Aro's left. Aro dove away from the blast as Drauses yanked Amii against his chest to shield her from hurling wood and brick. In the commotion, no one heard the Blade running down the hall, but Shaila saw him come in the door.

"Behind you!" Shaila yelled. Drauses heard her warning, but he still held his daughter in his arms. He released the girl, shoving her away before a hot stick wrapped around his torso. The bright blue whip sent painful shocks through Drauses' chest, and he screamed.

Aro fired from the floor and hit the Blade in the temple. As he fell, the hot stick fell with him, but the damage was already done. Drauses' eyes met Shaila's for a breathless second, then he collapsed along with the Blade to the floor.

"Drauses!" Shaila hit her knees and shook him, called his name, but he stayed still and silent.

Aro knelt and put a finger to Drauses' neck. He looked at Shaila in shock and shook his head.

Amii burst into hysterical tears and threw herself across her father's chest. "No! No, no, no!"

Aro stared at Shaila, and she stared right back, lost for words and drowning in painful realization. Drauses was gone. That truth sank its teeth in her heart, and a lancing pain cut through her chest. She took Drauses' robes in both her hands and shook him.

"You can't leave us!" she screamed. "Drauses!" Though her lungs worked to bring her air, she was suffocating. He couldn't be gone. This was Drauses, thought invincible by his comrades and enemies alike, but, within seconds, with one strike, he was swept away to join his gods. This can't be the end. Though sense said she couldn't fall apart right now, Shaila began to weep right along with Amii, clutching as much of him as her arms could reach as if holding him tighter might bring him back.

Aro was speaking, his mouth forming words but making no sound, and even Amii's sobs were silent. All Shaila heard was the drumming of her own heart in her ears. Drauses had warned her this day would come, the day he fell and left her behind to fight alone, but she couldn't do it. She'd stay here beside him until death claimed her too.

A nearby rumble and another quake toppled yet more of the gaping wall nearby, and Aro threw himself over both girls to protect them from raining rubble. When the dust cleared, he touched Shaila's cheek, and she looked at him in wonder.

"Help me, please," he begged, and this time, she heard him. "Amii needs you!"

Drauses' last act had been to push his daughter to safety. His death would be in vain if the girl fell here as well. With one last choking sob, Shaila released Drauses' robes and latched onto Amii's instead. She hauled the girl away and up into her arms.

"No!" Amii screamed as Aro ushered them into the hall. "We can't leave him! Go back, go back! He's not dead! He can't be dead!"

With Amii sobbing in her ear and the image of Drauses' lifeless face burned in her mind, Shaila knew her own heart would likely stop beating out of grief at any moment.

Her Man of the Mark was no more.

✤

From across the street, on an upper floor of yet another of the East side's abandoned ruins, Rose watched as Rovik's boat opened fire on The Yard. Though the Marks positioned at the gate got it open when the trouble started, precious few of them managed to slip out to safety. Most now huddled in doorways and windows or hid between buildings as they fought their black-clad enemies, not daring to cross The Yard lest they be struck down by the cannons. Rose knew they need only hold out a moment longer.

Right on cue, the guns one by one ceased to fire until, with one last blast, all fell quiet. Roth's sabotage had worked, just as he'd assured her it would. Rose sobbed one deep cry of misery. He'd done exactly as she'd asked him. The boat sat useless in the water for the moment, allowing the guild precious time to flee. Rose watched as Men of the Mark poured out of the gate. Somewhere in that tide of red robes was her daughter; she was sure of it.

Rose had organized Amii's escape, but, in doing so, she'd traded the life of one person she loved for another. She lost either way. Her stomach twisted in guilt at the thought of what Vynus would soon be doing to her lover. Roth never asked to be a part of this; she was always the one to run to him with her problems, and he always fixed them, was always faithful to her above all others. In return, he'd pay the price for his loyalty and for her failure to keep him safe.

Rose turned away from the window and wiped away her pitiful tears. Soon the sovereign's men would discover Roth's sabotage and fix it. It would be too late by then; the guild would be gone. She would be too.

A bomb went off in his chest. That was the only explanation he had for the sudden flash of pain over his heart. It was a short pain though, less than a second, and he was soon slipping back into black nothingness despite how hard he fought to open his eyes.

The bomb went off again, and this time Drauses' eyes popped open as his body arched off the floor. He screamed as pain lashed through his entire body for a few agonizing seconds, then it stopped as suddenly as it started. He lay panting on his back as his heart raced in his chest.

Drauses rolled to his stomach with a groan of pure misery. It took three tries, then as soon as he managed to stand, his stomach rolled, and he held himself up against the wall as he vomited all over the dead Black Blades, clutching his throbbing chest. Every muscle in his body ached, and a spot over his heart burned like Vedian fire.

What happened? His last memory was of Shaila's face as he fell. How long had he been lying here? No more than a moment or two, if he had to guess. There were shouts from outside, but the cannons were no longer booming.

Drauses staggered across the room to the hole in the wall and peered out. The ship was no longer firing. His Brothers of the Mark rushed across The Yard toward the gate, fighting Black Blades as they went. In the morning light, he made out Shaila running across The Yard with Amii. Aro followed on their heels, firing his pistol back at their pursuers. Drauses' family was headed for safety. He needed to join them.

He knelt and picked up his sword, sheathing it back onto his hip. He would never make it to the gate alone in his condition. Unless… he threw off his red robes and snatched the cleanest black ones he could find from a dead man on the floor. Drauses pulled them on and flipped up the hood.

He kept his head down as he made his way through the hall and down the stairs. Several Blades rushed by but barely gave him a passing glance. Out in The Yard, he was more surrounded, and he lowered his face even more. He headed straight for the gate, but his plan was thwarted when the Black Blades shoved it closed. He changed course, heading instead for the nearby storage rooms.

Drauses' head ached, and he was suddenly exhausted. Whatever had happened to bring him back from the dead had been far too rough; his body wasn't taking it well. He shuffled into the storage building and headed for the basement. With luck, this would be the last place his enemies would look for stragglers.

Drauses collapsed on the floor between the shelves and put his back to the wall. He had to rest. He'd sit here for a moment and gather his strength.

꒰

Dagon directed everyone down the street and inside a nearby building, an old carriage house. One of its double doors was long gone, the wood likely scavenged for building materials or firewood, but it was well out of firing range from the boat. Shaila and Aro followed the crowd as they rushed inside.

Shaila finally let go of Amii. "Watch her," she ordered Aro, then she went back outside to Dagon. "Is this everyone? How many have we lost?"

"At least three," said Dagon. "I watched that many fall myself. I kept them away from the walls as best I could until we got outside, then we avoided open spaces until the boat stopped firing."

"Where's Boon?"

"Already tending to the wounded."

"And Julta?"

"With Boon. Where's Drauses?"

Faced with the question, Shaila couldn't answer. She shook her head and disappeared back inside with the last of the men. Dagon followed her to the back of the carriage house where Boon was passing around supplies from a knapsack he'd managed to bring with him. Amii and Aro sat together nearby. Julta stitched a gash in Aro's arm while Amii wept into his other shoulder. Aro held the girl close and gave Shaila a reassuring nod when she came to check on them both. Dagon shadowed her as she wandered amongst the men, checking for any serious injuries. Boon assured her they'd see no more casualties.

"I want a head count immediately, Boon," she ordered.

"Right away."

The men all stared at her, and Shaila realized what she had to do in Drauses' stead.

"The Blades have shut the gates on any who may still be in The Yard," she announced. "If you know for certain of a fallen brother, report his name to Boon. Otherwise, any of you free of serious injury, gather and prepare. We must launch a counterattack as soon as possible, both to aid any brothers captured by our enemies and to roust those bastards from our headquarters. Those who lack weapons, borrow from your wounded brothers and fight with me. By the gods, I won't let them take another home from us! Not while I still have blood to give. What say you?"

The men roared with approval and rushed to do as she asked, shouting to their comrades and passing weapons about in eager preparation.

"My Lady Liege," Dagon called.

Shaila closed her eyes. She knew what he wanted but didn't know if she could say it aloud. She had to keep herself together, her Brothers of the Mark now looked to her for leadership, but recounting Drauses' death would be her undoing. Dagon wasn't going to let her evade him, however. He grabbed her by the arm, their codes be damned, and forced her to face him. In her eyes, he read the words she couldn't bring herself to say, and his face twisted with pain.

"How did he fall?"

"A hot stick," Shaila said, her chest contracting at the words. A tear tumbled down her cheek. She swiped it away and tore her arm from Dagon's grasp.

Boon came rushing up to Shaila's side. "How exactly did Drauses fall?" he asked with interest.

"Not now, Boon," she muttered.

"Now, Shaila, it's important," he insisted. Julta lingered behind him, clinging to every word. "How was Drauses struck down?"

"A hot stick struck him in the chest, and he just—"

Boon exchanged an odd look with Julta.

"How long did you wait before you left him?" Julta asked in a rush.

"But a moment," Aro said as he walked up. "I urged us away as soon as I could."

Boon and Julta regarded each other again.

"Did it fail?" Boon asked.

"I'm confident it functioned exactly as I designed it to," Julta replied. "It wasn't enough time. I warned you too great a shock would—"

"What are the two of you muttering about?" Shaila asked. "Speak straight with me, now!"

"We placed a device—" Boon said.

"I built it; Boon installed it," Julta interrupted.

"It's meant to ensure if Drauses was ever shocked in the chest by a hot stick, it would immediately shock him again."

Julta nodded vigorously. "The device is charged by the initial shock from the hot stick and uses the energy to deliver a shock of its own."

"Why on Earth would you shock him twice?" Shaila asked.

"Electric shock knocks the heart out of rhythm," Boon explained. "A second shock can put it back."

"You mean restart the heart?" Aro asked.

"You can't *restart* a non-beating heart," Julta said in disgust. "Even *I* know that."

"Then how is it Drauses survived before?" Shaila asked. "He said his heart was stopped by that hot stick years ago."

"The Odas help me," Boon muttered, rubbing his temples. "I've explained this to him before. His heart didn't *stop*. It was in distress but never ceased beating."

"What brought him back?"

"I shocked him with the hot stick again," Dagon replied. "I was with him that day. We were both just wards. I watched the weapon take him down and couldn't rouse him, so I coiled it over his chest and shocked him again, only for a second."

"It was quite a revelation," said Boon. "I was fascinated that Dagon was able to bring Drauses' heart back to proper rhythm this way. I've put many years of study into the phenomenon since."

"I checked the Liege for a pulse before we left him," Aro said.

"You wouldn't find one," Boon replied. "Blood wasn't pumping, but that doesn't mean the heart was dead."

"You mean Drauses still lived when we left him behind?" Shaila asked. Her hopes were rising but so was her panic.

"It's possible."

"Where is this device?" Shaila asked. "I saw no gadgets on Drauses' person."

Julta smiled while Boon looked sheepish and guilty.

"What did the two of you do?" Dagon asked.

"It's in his chest," Boon admitted.

"Close to his heart," Julta added proudly.

Shaila gaped at them. "You put something *inside* him? When? How?"

"I installed it the day you brought him, shot and bleeding, back to the factory near a season ago," said Boon.

"Drauses will beat you both bloody for taking such liberties without his knowledge or consent!"

Dagon laughed. "He'll be absolutely furious."

"Hot sticks have claimed the lives of many Marks in the past," said Boon. "Julta's devices would help—"

"Devices?" Aro asked in alarm. "Are there others walking around with these machines in their chests?"

"There are four."

"Do they know?" Shaila asked.

Boon shook his head.

"I'm shocked, Boon," said Shaila. "You take the confidence of your charges so seriously. It's not like you to break trust."

"I take their safety far more seriously, Shaila. You know as well as I Drauses would've never allowed me to do this." He looked her in the eyes. "Don't ask me which among these men are more stubborn."

"It's a toss," she said with a hint of a smile twitching at the corners of her mouth.

"I did it to keep them alive, which is my highest priority."

Julta giggled. "I just wanted to put my toys to use."

Shaila ran her hands down her face. "The two of you…" She shook her head and sighed once deeply. "Later. What about Drauses? Would we have known if his device worked?"

"You would know when it fired," said Julta. "It would send the body into spasms."

"That never happened," Aro replied. "Your device must've failed."

"No," Julta protested. "It worked. The shock was too great and delayed the device's response. I designed it this way intentionally, for if it fired with too much force it would burn the heart instead of aiding it. The device needed time to adjust its output. It would've fired when it was ready."

"If that's true, Julta, we left Drauses behind, alone, and surrounded by our enemies," Shaila announced. "I need to know you're certain beyond any doubt."

Julta stood up tall. "I'm certain my device functioned exactly as I meant it to."

"Then I must go back for him."

"Shaila," Dagon bid, "you can't. You're our Elder in Drauses' stead. You can't place yourself in such danger."

"Drauses and I aren't yet wed. I'm not your Lady Liege."

"That's a technicality we would overlook if—"

"Drauses is your Elder Master," Shaila said, and her voice took on an edge of authority, the tone of the leader she needed to be in this moment. "He needs us. Furthermore, I'm fairly certain the Masters decided the Liege of the Marks would no longer remain behind while his comrades do the fighting for him. Was that all smoke to appease Drauses so he would agree to be your Elder, or did you mean it?"

Dagon was taken aback. "We... we meant it, of course, but—"

"Then I'll hear no more of this 'you can't place yourself in such danger' nonsense. Am I understood?"

"Yes, my Lady Liege," Dagon said with a small smile and a nod.

"Good. I'll allow a man or two to accompany me, but I'm going back for Drauses."

"I'll go with you," Aro said.

"I will as well," said Dagon.

"We need a plan to get rid of that blasted boat," Shaila said. "Any ideas? Why did it stop firing?"

"Blasted boat," Julta mumbled, seemingly deep in thought.

"Ran out of ammunition?" Aro offered. A second later there was a boom of a cannon.

"Well, that answers that," Dagon said as another cannon fired. "It seems they've fixed things. We lack the firepower to—"

"*Blasted* boat!" Julta exclaimed, making his comrades all jump in surprise. "Yes! Explosives!"

"You mean my bolts?" Shaila asked, touching her crossbow.

"Bigger!" Julta began to pace, muttering to himself as he walked to and fro. He drew imaginary figures in his palm then shook out his hand as if to knock the numbers away and started over. "In my workshop, there's a box of gel. It looks like a brick, but it's soft to the touch. It's a new explosive material I recently acquired. With that and a few other things, I'm sure I can sink that vessel."

"You aim to come with us?" Aro asked in surprise.

"I must. I'll have to construct the explosives."

"Your workshop is on the far side of The Yard, Julta," Shaila said. "We'd have to cross all the way to the river within sight of the boat."

"Get me there, and I'll get you what you need."

"We could swim in from the river," Aro suggested.

"That won't work," Dagon said with a look of shame. "I can't swim."

"You should stay here then, Dagon," Shaila said. "You can watch over Amii and organize the men to attack once the boat goes down. And if the worst should come to pass, you can carry on in our stead."

"That kind of remark doesn't make me want to stay behind, Lady Liege," Dagon grumbled.

"I'm sorry, but it's the truth of it. This must be done. Aro and I are confident swimmers."

"As am I," said Julta.

"Someone needs to go on if all else fails," Shaila said. "There's no one else I trust more than you to do that. I'm sure Drauses would feel the same if he were here to cast a vote."

"I agree," Aro said.

Dagon looked from Shaila to Aro then to Julta. "It seems I'm outnumbered."

"I'll go explain this to Amii," Aro said with a grimace before heading off to do just that.

"Be ready to storm the gate once the boat is down, Dagon," Shaila ordered. "I want every one of those black-clad bastards out of our home!"

"Yes, ma'am."

"No, you're not!" Amii yelled from across the room. "I forbid you!"

"I think Aro needs a hand," said Shaila. "Our future sovereign's temper matches her father's."

Dagon laughed as Shaila went to rescue Aro from Amii's fury.

Drauses woke when the cannons began firing again. There were voices nearby. His respite was over for now. Drauses climbed to his feet and did his best to walk off his aches and pains. He felt better. Barely. He drew his sword and stepped behind a set of shelves by the stairs as two Blades came down into the cellar.

"More dry goods," one man grumbled.

"Where in Vedia are their weapons?" asked the other.

Drauses reached around from behind the shelf and snagged the nearest man by the neck. He yanked the Black Blade backward onto his sword until the tip stuck several inches out of his chest. His partner jumped and drew his gun. Drauses switched on his sword, grabbed the hilt with both hands, and shoved hard until the two men smashed together. Though Drauses' sword slid but an inch or two into the second Blade, its electric charge shot through both bodies, incapacitating the one who still lived. Drauses yanked his sword free, and both men fell to the ground. He stood over the still-breathing Blade and set the tip of his sword to the man's chest.

"You'll all become well acquainted with our weapons soon enough," Drauses muttered, then he drove his sword through the man's heart.

Chapter 28

THE JESPA'S WATERS were chilly this time of year. Aro swam about twenty or so yards in front of Julta and Shaila, sticking close to the Western shore. When he drew close to the boat, he went under the water to stay undetected. He surfaced next to the boat's hull and waited for Julta and Shaila to catch up before moving on. They swam together along the boat to the side closest to land.

With a nod, Aro struck out toward the shore first. The fence had been smashed flat by cannons and dozens of trampling feet. Once they reached solid ground, the three of them dashed through the shallow water to the side of Boon's clinic. As the building closest to the water, the clinic was a wreck. The workshop behind it, however, looked barely disturbed. When they reached the front of the shop, Julta called them to a halt.

"Wait here," he whispered before darting around the corner up to the door. He stood to the side and turned the handle then flung the door inward and jumped back. Several bolts shot from inside the workshop and out through the doorway. They each stuck in the dirt, and Julta gathered them up before motioning to his comrades to join him.

"What was that, Julta?" Aro asked as they entered the empty workshop.

"You booby trap your door to shoot people?" Shaila asked.

"Not all the time! Just at night... and when I'm not there... and when I'm sleeping... and..." he shrugged and dashed away, gathering the things he needed from shelves and boxes and drawers. He produced a brick of a putty-like substance, slapped it on the counter, and split it in half. He fiddled with an odd string and some tubing for several minutes while mumbling to himself and ignoring Aro and Shaila's questions. He glared at the string, down at the putty, studied his notes, the string again, then swore.

"What's the problem?" Shaila asked.

"N... nothing. Who'll be placing the explosives?"

Aro raised his hand. "I will. I'm a faster swimmer." He gave Shaila a wink. "That's how I won that wager and caught Master Dagon's attention."

Julta handed Aro both pieces of putty. "Place these on the sides of the boat just above the water line," he instructed. "Stick these tubes deep into the gel. I attached fuses. We want both charges to blow near the same time. Two charges, bigger hole, faster sinking. Twist the ends together, light them both, and the charges should blow simultaneously."

Aro eyed the short fuses. "How long will these take to burn?"

"That length should burn for about seven seconds."

"Seven seconds? How am I supposed to get back to shore before—" Aro realized then why Julta looked so nervous. "Oh."

Julta grimaced. "It's... unlikely you'll have time to reach a safe distance."

"Absolutely not," Shaila fumed. "Make the fuses longer."

"I can't. The fuses must burn while wet. These are my own design, and this is all I have. I'm sorry." Julta was wringing his hands with a look of deep pain on his face.

"It's alright, Julta," Aro said calmly. He took the pieces of tubing and fuses and put them in his pants pocket.

"I can't let you do this," Shaila said. "Give those to me. We'll find another way."

"I'm a strong swimmer. I may be able to—"

"I suggest you dive," said Julta. "Don't swim for the shore but dive straight down. The water might help protect you." Julta held out the little silver box he used to light the funeral torches. "This is simple flint and steel. It'll take extra strikes to light when wet."

Aro reached to take it, but Shaila grabbed his arm. "Aro, no. Give me the fuses. Now." She held out her hand. He reached in his pocket, but as soon as her hand fell from his arm, he snatched the box from Julta and bolted out the door.

"Aro!" Shaila screamed after him, but he ignored her and sprinted for the water.

Aro kicked off his boots and tore off his robes before he dove back into the icy river and swam as fast as he could for the boat. He was shivering when he reached the hull. The two lumps of explosives slapped easily to the metal, and he slid the tubing into the gel as Julta told him. The flint and steel shook in his hand as he struggled to light it with cold fingers. It took a dozen tries before a spark caught and lit a flame. He said a silent prayer as sparkling fire began to burn up the length of the fuses.

Aro breathed deep and dove straight down into the water. The river here was very deep; he couldn't see through the darkness and the temperature dropped the further down he swam. An undercurrent hit him hard and swept him to the side. Instead of fighting it, Aro turned and swam with the current the best he could as it pushed him downstream. He heard the explosion and felt a blast of painful pressure squeeze the air from his chest.

He was out of breath and stuck in the current. The same force that had saved him from the blast now threatened to drown him. His arms and legs pumped as hard as they could to escape the current's pull as his lungs burned for oxygen. When at last he felt calm water around him again, he struck out for the surface, but his thoughts were clouding and his sight fading as his body began shutting down. His arms and legs were heavy, but there was daylight above him. If he could keep going a few more feet...

The burning in his chest was too much to ignore, and his body sucked in water, making him panic.

Just a few more feet. Please.

A blackness, heavy and cold, swallowed him.

Amii...

᪐

Drauses walked The Yard, watching from under his black hood as his enemies searched buildings for survivors and weapons. Though they'd closed and locked the gate, none of them stood guard over it. Through the holes the cannons had blown in the wall, Drauses caught flashes of red as several Marks hurried down the sidewalk and took position by the gate. They were preparing to launch a counterattack. Though how they planned to do it with the boat still firing balls of iron, he knew not. There was a sudden, deafening explosion from behind him, and he whipped around to see the boat engulfed in smoke and flames.

In the resulting commotion, Drauses ran for the gate. He threw the lock and yanked the gate open to let in his brothers then made himself scarce lest they mistake him for one of their enemies. With a clear path, the Marks, led by Dagon, rushed in and began cutting down men in black. Drauses followed a group of three Black Blades as they tried to slip away into the bunkhouse and dealt with all three before they realized an enemy hid among them. He moved further into the building, looking for more lost sheep to slaughter.

Aro should have surfaced by now. The boat was destroyed, and the few men inside had abandoned the guns and were fleeing on foot. The front gate was open, and Black Blades rushed to fight the wave of red robes that now flooded into The Yard. Shaila watched the water for Aro's head to break the surface, but he was nowhere to be seen. Something was wrong. She ran along the shore, following the river as she searched for a sign. The Odas only knew how far the currents would take him.

She stripped off her robes, her blade, and her boots as she ran, leaving them strewn up the shoreline. She caught a hint of red in the water downstream and ran faster to catch up. She drew up next to Aro in the water in time to watch him sink back out of sight. Shaila swore and sprinted down the riverbank before diving in.

Shaila could see Aro's shirt in the water, slowly sinking out of sight. She struggled to get to him before the currents carried him away. Her fingers felt fabric in the water, and she snatched a handful before heading back for the surface. Her head broke free, and she gasped for air as she wrapped an arm around Aro's chest and struggled to pull him along with her. Twice, she was yanked back under the surface and almost lost her hold on him, swallowing mouthful after mouthful of river water before the ground came up to meet her feet. She looped both her arms under Aro's and dragged him up onto dry land. She laid him on his back in the stones.

Aro wasn't breathing. Shaila's knowledge of resuscitation was basic at best since she'd never needed to do it before, but she had to try. She pinched his nose, put her mouth to his, and breathed air into his lungs. She did this twice before pressing down on his chest several times. It had no effect.

"Aro, please," she begged. "Don't you leave me too! Miika can't have you yet."

Shaila tried again, breathing more air into his mouth, pressing his chest harder and longer. She repeated the pattern three more times, but still, Aro didn't stir. In one last desperate act, she struck him hard in the chest with a closed fist.

Aro's eyes snapped open, and he rolled to the side, spitting, coughing, and clutching his chest as he choked for air.

Shaila sent up a prayer of thanks before she yanked the Master onto his back once more, fisted her hands in his shirt, and gave him several hard shakes.

"I ought to strangle you, you deranged fool!" she screamed, then she sobbed with relief and yanked him into a fierce hug. "I thought I'd lost another friend."

Aro hugged her back. "Ap-p-pologies, Lady L-L-Liege." His mouth chattered from the cold. "N-n-next time I'll tr-try not to d-drown."

"There better never be a next time. Amii would never forgive me if anything happened to you. Neither would I." Shaila got to her feet and gave him a hand up onto his. "Come. Let's go help our brothers reclaim our home and find out once and for all if Drauses is alive or dead."

Dagon was barking orders left and right when Shaila and Aro joined him, still dripping wet from the river.

"Any word of Drauses?" Shaila asked.

"Not yet," Dagon replied.

"I'll check where we last saw him."

The stairs and halls of the bunkhouse were littered with the bodies of the men she and Drauses had cut down only hours ago. Shaila maneuvered through the limbs and pools of blood toward the ladies' quarters. She paused near the door to prepare herself before rounding the corner. She spotted the red robes on the floor. At first, she thought it was her beloved's body right where they'd left it, but then she realized they were empty. She walked over and picked them up. They were definitely Drauses'; his favorite knife was still concealed in the inside pocket.

There was a footstep behind her, and she drew her sword and whipped around. Steel clashed against steel as her blade met another. The Black Blade made no move to strike back, so she swept his weapon away and brought the end of her sword back to plunge it through his middle.

"Shaila!"

She froze and focused on the face within the black hood, on the scar down his left cheek, his deep blue eyes, that familiar bump on his nose. She knew that face. Dare she believe? While Boon and Julta had prattled on about devices and electric shocks, she'd been hesitant to hope, wishing not to have her heart broken twice. He swept his hood back, and his long brown waves fell across his shoulders. She dropped her sword, instant tears welling in her eyes.

"Drauses."

He pulled her into his arms and held her close. She unfastened the black robes and threw them away in disgust then trailed her hands over every inch of his chest and back, up his neck, then down his arms.

"I'm alright," he said.

She shook her head. "No. You're alive by mere dumb luck and our friends' crazy schemes. I nearly lost you. I watched you fall—" She was losing the control she'd struggled to keep the last few frightening hours. Miika's funeral fire came to mind, and she choked on a sob that Drauses had come so close to being next.

Drauses pulled her into his arms. "Please, don't cry for what might've been. I'm here. You ought to know by now it'd take much more to rip me away from you."

"Let's not test your grip, my Liege," she said, wiping her eyes with her sleeve. "I don't know how much more my heart can bear."

"Shaila?" Aro called.

"Here! We're both here."

Aro swept into the room. "Master Drauses," he said with a sigh of relief. "Julta's device worked after all."

"Device?" Drauses asked.

Shaila winced. "Yes. The one that brought you back after you fell."

"Julta gave me no such gadget."

"He did," Aro said. "You just never knew."

"What in Vedia are you talking about?"

"The day you were shot, Boon and Julta planted a device for this purpose," Aro explained. "It was to save your life if you were ever struck down by a hot stick like you were before."

Drauses made a face. "What do you mean '*planted?*'"

Aro bit his lip and looked at Shaila who placed her hand over Drauses' heart. He gazed down at his chest then shook his head. His face burned red as he turned and swept from the room. Shaila followed.

⌘

The last of the Black Blades had been slain. The Yard was theirs once again, though it needed countless new repairs. The Marks were rounding up bodies, cleaning up debris, and receiving treatments for various injuries in front of Boon's clinic. The building was a ruined mess, and Boon had to dart in and out of the rubble for supplies to treat the wounded. Six lifeless bodies lay on the ground nearby, covered by their robes in respect.

Drauses stalked across The Yard and made straight for the doctor. Boon saw him coming and froze in wide-eyed wonder as the Master approached.

"Drauses," Shaila called from behind him, her tone one of cautious warning.

Boon took several steps back. "Let me explain."

"Explain? *Explain?*" Drauses raged. "You cut open my chest and stuck in one of Julta's contraptions without my knowledge while I lay unconscious and unable to object!"

"And it saved your life."

"You didn't think I deserved to know you'd taken such a liberty?"

"We were afraid you'd demand it be removed."

"I'm demanding that now. *Take it out!*"

"No."

Drauses tilted his head, stunned at Boon's daring. "What do you mean, '*no*'?"

"Your continued health and safety were why we did what we did, Julta and I. Now that you're the new Liege, it's even more important you be looked after to the best of our ability. The device worked, and your continued success with it could save countless other lives, Drauses."

Drauses snorted. "So, I'm to leave this bit of metal and wires inside my chest for your amusement?"

"Our amusement?" said Shaila. She took Drauses by the elbow and yanked him around to face her. "You think I found it *amusing* to watch you be struck down? You think Aro was *amused* to feel your throat and find no pulse? And Amii. Do you think she found *amusement* in watching her father fall protecting her? I don't ever wish to tear her away from your lifeless body again. I'm asking you to at least consider this, for the guild, for your daughter, and for me."

As if on cue, Amii came rushing across The Yard. "Father!" she cried as she plowed into his middle, wrapping her arms around him and bursting into tears. He hugged her close and studied Shaila, then Dagon, then Boon. He looked down at his six dead brothers, imagining his family's grief if he were lying beside them.

"Alright," he said, but with a caustic glance at Boon he added, "But if you ever take such a liberty again with any man in this guild without their knowledge, we'll revisit this conversation, and you won't like the outcome."

"I understand," Boon said.

"If there are any others you've defiled in this way, tell them immediately. They deserve to know."

Drauses walked away with his daughter tucked under one arm. He beckoned to Shaila and pulled her in close to his other side. With his family safe once again, his anger faded and was replaced with relief and gratitude to the Odas for watching over them, and yes, maybe to Boon and Julta, too, for their mad schemes, though it'd be some time before he thanked them, if he ever did. He kissed Shaila on the temple, breathing deep of her sweet scent.

'*By the Gods,*' he vowed to himself, '*Rovik will never come after them again.*' They had to stop running. It was time to bring this fight to Rovik and end it, once and for all.

⤚⤙

Rovik came down the stone stairs into The Cellar, breathing deep with a smile. If fear had a scent, it would be the copper aroma of ichor mixed with sweat and piss.

Roth sat naked in a chair in the middle of the room with his wrists bound behind him and each ankle strapped to a chair leg. Unconscious for the moment, his head lolled down, chin to chest.

Rovik walked up and grabbed Roth by the hair, yanking his head back to study his face. Roth's left eye was a swollen, bloody mess; his nose was broken and crooked; one ear was bleeding where his piercing had been torn out; his bare chest was covered in burns; and the missing earring had been shoved through his right nipple.

"Wake him up," Rovik ordered.

Vynus waved a small glass vial under Roth's nose until he gasped and coughed, turning his head away from the sickening smell of ammonia.

"Good morning," Rovik greeted with a smile. Roth glared at him through his good eye. "You'll be happy to know your sabotage worked exactly as you and your lady planned. Because of your insubordination, the Men of the Mark suffered minimal losses. Well done indeed." He leaned closer and lost his smile. "Now you'll rot down here until you beg me for death."

"We both know this was my fate either way," Roth muttered through split lips. "Your man touched me long before your boat ever set sail. You're jealous, Rovik. You're jealous I have Rose and you don't."

"So sorry for the miscommunication." Rovik smiled anew. "Though you're right about your fate. Rose can't have distractions. Her brother and I agreed that you were becoming too much of an attachment for her. I may have been persuaded to give you a quick death with very little pain had you been truthful with me before. Since you chose to lie to my face, you'll instead suffer for your betrayal to your country."

Roth chuckled with a wince. "I did Jesparia a service by helping the Men of the Mark. Someday, and I believe it'll be soon, they'll end you and restore balance."

"Jesparia was a twisted mess of self-loathing long before I came along. My people don't wish to be united, East and West. Try to force the two together, and they'll tear each other apart far worse than before."

"You're a fool, Rovik."

Rovik flicked the fresh piercing in Roth's breast. Roth slammed his teeth together, refusing to scream.

"That's good," said Rovik. "It'll make the sound all the sweeter in the end." He nodded to Vynus. "Remember: minimal blood loss and no infections." He smiled back down at Roth. "Your lady isn't coming for you. Rose has disappeared and abandoned you, and the men you risked so much to save don't even know you exist."

As Vynus drew close with his scalpel and a sickening smile, Roth began to mutter in prayer, but when steel met flesh, he could no longer contain his screams. Rovik watched from across the room, chuckling at the sight and smell of fresh blood.

Chapter 29

MORE FUNERAL FIRES.

Drauses was tired of laying his brothers to rest. Once the flames carried away their fallen, he called the Masters to council. This time, Shaila stood at his side as he regarded them all.

"Three times this past season we've laid beloved brothers atop pyres," Drauses began. "The loss we've known of late has been catastrophic. If this last attack has taught me anything, it's that Rovik no longer concerns himself with Amii's safety. If he no longer cares if the girl lives or dies, he must be close to naming a new successor. We can't let that happen. If we allow Rovik to choose a new heir, all our efforts will have been in vain, our brothers' lives lost pointlessly."

Drauses stood and leaned on the table, glancing to each Master in turn around the room as he continued. "I'll run and hide from our enemies no longer. I won't watch my guild die a slow, bleeding death as Rovik picks us off one by one. We should rally our strength and aim a strike of our own."

"Many of us echo your thoughts, brother," Ithail said. "We've laid waste to so many Black Blades during their two strikes against us. There can't be many of them left."

"That's my hope," said Drauses.

Shaila stood and spoke in council for the first time. "Amii will be thirteen in a few short weeks and can take her place as sovereign. She'll have the love of the West to calm the anger of Rovik's downfall, and she'll have the East's support with the Men of the Mark at her side."

"We never planned for Amii to take her place as sovereign so soon," Dagon said. "She's still so young."

"She can handle it," Drauses said with pride. "And she'll have us behind her. Always."

Though this was Aro's first council, too, he threw himself into the discussion as Shaila did. "Regardless of her age, we chose Amii to rule us long ago," he said. "This guild has made sacrifices, grieved losses, and felt the pain of betrayal, but we've also done what many thought impossible and secured a new ruler for Jesparia. We've cut away our own corruption and placed two powerful Masters as our leaders. We're as strong as we've ever been, and Amii is stronger than you know. I agree with my Liege. Now is our time. Now is *her* time."

"Thank you, Aro," Drauses said with a nod of gratitude.

There were many nods and words of agreement around the table.

"Let's take a vote," Dagon called. "All in favor of a strike on the sovereign's estate and setting Amii as our sovereign now."

Dagon took a count for their records, but Drauses didn't need to hear the number. Most raised their hands.

"Then we've work to do," Shaila said, her tone one of such conviction it sent a shiver up Drauses' spine. "As soon as preparations can be made, Rovik's estate will run red with blood."

᷍

As the men all bustled about The Yard preparing for battle, Shaila stood by the river, staring out into the water, deep in thought. After a while, Drauses came to stand beside her.

"What's troubling you?" he asked.

"The pyres, they made me think of Miika," she admitted, willing herself not to cry.

"You miss your friend."

"I do. Terribly so."

Drauses wrapped his arms around her and pulled her close. "I admit I felt such jealousy watching how close you and Miika grew, but I'd gladly go back to living with that envy to have him alive and well at your side again."

"I know you would." She turned in his arms and looked deep into his eyes. "Do something for me?"

"Anything."

"Stay close to me tomorrow. I won't ask you to stay behind while you send your brothers off to battle, but if you receive so much as a scratch, I'll kill you myself."

Drauses laughed. "A mere scratch will earn me death?"

"Hmm, perhaps not." She traced the scar on his cheek. "How about this then: for every new mark I find on your body tomorrow eve, I'll not warm your bed for a night."

Drauses winced. "You wound me, Lady Liege. You'd deny me your sweet lovemaking?"

"To encourage you to be safe? I would."

"I think you overestimate your self-control. I can be very persuasive."

Shaila smiled. "Challenge accepted, Master Drauses."

There were yells for Drauses from across The Yard.

"My Liege!" Dagon called. "A man at the gate claims you sent for him."

Drauses grinned like a youth neck-deep in mischief. "Let him in."

"What are you up to?" Shaila asked as they started toward the gate together, but he went on grinning, refusing to answer.

As they drew nearer, Shaila squinted at the man who came in the gate, recognizing him, though at first, she didn't know from where. Her heart fluttered when his short, bronze hair came into view, now streaked with grey. His slim physique hadn't changed one bit, neither had his raggedy brown robes, though they had more holes than she remembered. By the time she was close enough to know for sure, she was sobbing. She ran the last few yards and wrapped her arms around the man's neck, squeezing him tight.

"Shaila?" he uttered in disbelief, hugging her back.

"I can't believe you're here," she said tearfully. "I went to see you shortly after I came back East, but the house was empty."

"I moved south a few years ago. I live not far from here, in fact."

"You know this man, Lady Liege?" Dagon asked.

"I daresay I do," Shaila replied, taking both the man's hands in her own. "This is my father, Kiidon."

"Gods, you're so beautiful," Kiidon said, touching his daughter's cheek with tears running down his own. "You always were. My little Eastern jewel."

"Oh, papa." She put her hand over his, closing her eyes and soaking in its warmth on her face. Her father. She had her father back. But how? She looked at Drauses. "Did you do this?"

Drauses nodded. "I sent word through the city that I wished to see him as soon as possible." He smiled. "Shaila, will you marry me today? Right now? With your father here to take part?"

Shaila beamed. "Yes, my Liege. I will."

"Marriage?" Kiidon asked in surprise.

Drauses stood up straighter and offered his hand. "Allow me to introduce myself, sir. I'm Master Drauses, Liege to the Men of the Mark. I've asked Shaila to be my wife and Lady Liege at my side. With your blessing, of course."

"As if she needs my permission," Kiidon replied with a laugh. He shook Drauses' hand anyway. "Shaila never does anything against her will and lets no one, man or woman, stand in her way."

Drauses laughed.

"What of Mother?" Shaila asked. "Why didn't she come with you?"

Kiidon lost his smile, and a sudden pain filled his eyes. "Your mother passed four years ago, darling. Forgive me, but I had no way of contacting you."

Shaila gasped a little at the news

Drauses put an arm around her. "I'm sorry."

"Four years ago," she said sadly. "She passed before I came back East."

"How *did* you end up back on this side of the river?" Kiidon asked. "And how on Earth did you end up with the Men of the Mark? I remember your fascination with the stories as a girl but never dreamed you'd one day join them."

"Why don't the two of you talk in private while I see to our wedding arrangements?" Drauses offered. "You've no doubt much to catch up on."

❦

It was just moments before sundown when Drauses summoned one and all to the riverbank. He handed Kiidon a book of prayers so worn it looked ready to spew its pages.

"I'd like very much if you'd lead this ceremony as the bride's father," Drauses requested.

"I'd be honored, sir," Kiidon said, and he opened the book and found the proper page.

Drauses looked at his bride. "Dagon will stand with me as a union brother," he said. "Who would you like to stand at your side?"

Shaila smiled and held her hand out to Amii. The girl skipped up and took Shaila's hand with a giggle of glee.

Kiidon stood with his back to the water, the setting sun sinking low in the sky behind him. Drauses and Shaila stood facing each other as prayers were read. The Men of the Mark all repeated the prayers when asked, as did Drauses and Shaila. Marriage bands were called for and Julta bounded forward, producing two slim silver rings.

Kiidon asked for any words of promise from the couple. Having no pre-written words to read, Drauses was about to shake his head, but peering into Shaila's beautiful face, he changed his mind and said what was in his heart as it came to him.

"From the moment I laid eyes on you, I was captivated by your beauty and your spirit. Our lives have been so intertwined since that fateful night that I no longer know where I end and you begin, and I find I don't mind a bit. The only thing I regret is taking so long to tell you how much you mean to me. My lady finest fair, I take you as my wife and pray to the Odas to never be parted from you from this day forward."

Shaila had to take a moment to compose herself after his speech, but then she found her own way to tell him how much he meant to her in return.

"The moment you swept in that window years ago, you swept right into my heart as well. Though I had no way of knowing we'd end up here someday, something inside me said if I let you slip away, I'd regret it for the rest of my life. It took me two years to understand everything Lady

Fate gave me that night. My Liege, I take you as my husband and pray to the Odas to help me bring you as much love and joy as you bring me from this day forward."

With a shaking hand, Drauses slid the silver band on her finger next to her ruby ring. Shaila did the same for him, and, with a kiss, their marriage was sealed. Their gathered brothers applauded with rowdy cheers, but Drauses and Shaila didn't hear the noise as they came together for another long kiss, lost in their own sweet world of two.

✦

The men lit a fire in The Yard, and though it wasn't the carouse they'd thrown before, they sat, talked, and rejoiced in each other's company as the day wound to a close. As soon as he found a free moment, Drauses drew Dagon aside for a private word.

"I have an assignment for you, brother," Drauses said.

"What might that be?" Dagon asked.

"I know you're eager to join the fight tomorrow, but I'd like you to take Amii and go far away from here. Come sunrise, The Yard will be all but abandoned. She can't stay here so unprotected."

Dagon chewed his cheek and glared. "Do you think I'm weak, my Liege?"

"Of course not. Why would you ask such a thing?"

"Because this is the second time I've been asked to stay behind. I'm beginning to think myself incompetent."

"You're the first I'd trust with this assignment, and Shaila trusted you to lead the guild in our stead should the worst come to pass. That shows the faith we have in you, no incompetence on your part."

Dagon snorted, but then, after a moment's consideration, he said, "Very well. I'll slip away with the girl when you and the rest head upriver."

"You need to leave tonight. Immediately, in fact."

"Why?"

"Walk with me to gather Amii and her things, and I'll explain what I need you to do for us."

✦

Rose should have fled the city by now. It was unwise to linger with a target on her back, but, no matter how hard she tried, she couldn't leave, not without knowing if Roth was alive or dead. She knew better than to hope. It was likely his life ended the moment Rovik's ship ceased firing. As much as she tried to convince herself, Rose could stand it no longer. As the night dragged on, Rose made her way to the Eastern shore of the Jespa.

When she drew close to where Alek usually moored at night, she saw in the moonlight that the boatman was already talking to someone, someone dressed in red robes and hood with a smaller figure, a girl, at his side.

"Amii?" Rose whispered, and, though she knew she shouldn't, she walked down the alley toward the trio, making no attempt to silence her footsteps as she did. When she drew close, the Mark whirled, blade drawn. Her heart sank a bit when she realized it wasn't Drauses.

"I mean you no harm," Rose announced with her hands up and open to show she held no weapon.

"Perhaps not," the Mark replied, "but I'm sure there are no less than a dozen others nearby with such intentions. Amii, get in the boat."

"That won't be necessary. I'm alone. I thought you were Drauses."

"I recognize your voice," said Amii. "You helped Marcel kidnap me and tried to kill my father!"

The Mark at the girl's side drew closer to her.

"I made it look as if I meant to end his life, child, but it was never my intent to see it through."

"Who are you?" the Mark asked.

"My name is Rose."

Amii's eyes widened with recognition.

"Yes, little one," Rose said. "I'm your mother."

Amii glanced from Rose to her companion and back again. "My mother is dead. Rovik told me so."

"Rovik speaks no truths, child. Surely you know that by now."

Amii took a step forward, but the Man of the Mark swept her back with his arm.

"I want to see for myself, Dagon," the girl said.

"I can't allow that, Amii," Dagon replied. "She's a Black Blade. We can't trust her."

"Dagon? Drauses' friend of old?" Rose asked. "He spoke highly of you once upon a time."

"I could say the same of you, but times change."

"Lower your hood," Amii requested.

Rose did as she asked, letting her hair fall around her shoulders.

Amii gaped. "You look just like me."

"I rather think it's the other way around," Rose said.

"What do you want from us?" Dagon asked.

"I want nothing from you at all. I came to ask Alek for passage across the river."

"Alek's services are needed elsewhere tonight."

"I understand. No problem. There's more than one way across the Jespa. Where are you taking the girl?"

Dagon smiled. "You're the last person I'd share that information with."

"Drauses is planning something foolish, isn't he? Why else would he send you away with his flesh and blood?"

"Father always looks out for my well-being above all else," Amii said, accusation heavy in her tone.

"I know. That's why I chose not to end his life. He is good for you. Far better than I would've been. I'll never ask your forgiveness for leaving you, Amii. It's likely the best kindness I could've shown you. I wasn't meant to be a mother."

"I could never forgive you anyway," Amii said, though her tone was free of resentment. "I have a new mother now, in case you've not heard. Father and Shaila were married today."

Rose felt an instant pang of regret. It could've been her at Drauses' side. It would've been if she'd been worthier, a little smarter years ago, a bit braver. Alas, it wasn't her fate to stand with the fabled Man of the Mark. Rose smiled through her pain.

"My congratulations to them both," she said. "Marriage is a long-ago abandoned ceremony in the East. I hope they start a revival of the tradition."

Dagon cleared his throat. "We must be on our way, Amii."

"As must I," Rose agreed. "Until we meet again."

"I won't hold my breath," Amii muttered.

Dagon ushered the girl into the boat.

Rose lifted her hood, turned, and marched away down the darkened street, willing herself not to glance back at the young and beautiful girl who had her eyes, her hair, her fiery temper... Rose glanced over her shoulder as Alek's boat pushed away from the shore and started up the river.

Amii never looked back.

⤝

The sun was still hours away from rising. The Men of the Mark rested as well as their anxious minds would let them, except for one. Shaila flung her hair back over her shoulders as she arched over Drauses, riding him slowly, driving him wild. He had his instructions. He wasn't allowed to touch, nor move his hips. He had to lie there and accept her teasing pace, as she posed over top of him for his viewing. He ached to touch her, to roll her over and bury himself inside her, but she was his Master tonight.

Just as she did the night before their move to The Yard, Shaila was doing all she knew to erase his qualms. Only this time, she did it as his bride. The thought sent a delicious shiver through his body, and he could bear it no longer. His hands came up to touch her, his palms sliding over the soft skin of her hips, up her belly and chest to caress her breasts. She leaned over him, her hair pooling on his shoulder as she kissed him. Her scent, her warmth, her tongue all drove him mad, and he bucked his hips beneath her. Instead of chastising him, she began to move with him.

"My lady finest fair," Drauses muttered, "I take you as my wife and pray to the Odas to never be parted from you from this day forward."

"My Liege," Shaila replied, "I take you as my husband and pray to the Odas to help me bring you as much love and joy as you bring me from this day forward."

Drauses rolled and thrust deeply inside her, and she cried out his name with unbridled passion, no longer the least bit afraid of who might hear her. As the rest of the night slipped by, they didn't concern themselves with what the day might bring; instead, their minds thought of nothing but their victory as two halves of the same whole who were lucky enough to find and complete each other.

9th and 50 of Autumn, Jesparia's 9th and 20 year of Rovik

Before the sun rose on the morning of battle, the Men of the Mark gathered in The Yard near the river as Alek came speeding up the water, leading half a dozen more boats behind him. Alek hopped onto the shore and shook Drauses' hand.

"I've brought friends as you requested," said Alek.

"Very good," Drauses said. "We couldn't do this without you. Did you see Amii and Dagon off safely?"

"I did."

Drauses broke the men into groups and ushered them into the boats before he and Shaila boarded Alek's vessel. As soon as Shaila was seated, Alek held out a familiar leather quiver full of bolts with a smile.

"Dagon asked me to give you this."

"I asked Dagon to retrieve them for you before he and Amii set off," Drauses explained.

"Thank you both," Shaila said. She strapped them on, happy to be fully armed once again as they set sail in the dark toward Polco Street.

Chapter 30

ALL WENT SMOOTHLY during the sail from The Yard to the Western bank. From there, Julta produced a heavy set of clippers the men used to cut away a section of the fencing large enough to walk through two abreast. They headed, quick and silent, down Polco Street, sticking to the shadows cast by the early morning light. Not a block away from the estate, Drauses gave the signal, and the men parted, splitting into two even groups. The first group, led by Drauses and Shaila, turned the corner and moved down the alley next to the estate's towering walls. The other group, headed by Aro, continued down Polco Street and lined up with their backs against the wall, a skip or two from the front gate.

Drauses let himself in the side entrance the same as he did the night he came for Shaila, shaking his head at the absolute ignorance that they hadn't changed their security since then. The lock gave way to his pick with ease, and he and Shaila swept into the grounds followed closely by their men. With no cover of darkness to shield them anymore, it was no time at all before the first guard spotted them and the alarm was raised. The Men of the Mark drew their blades and clashed against the blades and whips of Rovik's guards.

∽

Rose watched from across the street as the Marks marched on the estate. She saw Drauses lead half of them down the side alley to the servant's entrance, but she didn't recognize the towering man who led the second group toward the front gate. They huddled against the wall there until the screaming began. Signaled by the sounds of chaos, the Mark leading the second group burst into the guards' shack by the front gate. Several gunshots blasted, then a moment later the gate creaked open. The long and lean Man of the Mark rejoined his men and led them forward onto the grounds.

Rose threw off her black robes and tossed them away. Dressed in civilian attire as she was now, no one would turn their blades on her unless she struck first. The sword and knife on her hips might still raise suspicions, but she'd take that risk over leaving the weapons behind. She crossed the street and slipped in the gate behind the last of the Marks. Though she wasn't their ally, she wouldn't cross blades with Drauses' men if she could help it.

The Marks here split into two groups at their leader's urging. One team stormed the mansion through the front door while the other headed around the side of the house toward the stables and barn. Rose followed the men into the house from a distance. While they swept down hallways and up the main staircase, Rose let them go on ahead and instead headed for a side door to a small hallway. To the right of this hall was a staff dining room with a window that looked out toward the carriage house. The Cellar was twenty yards from that window. The riflemen in the barn would be able to see her, but if she went out through the window and ran fast across the lawn, she might get down The Cellar's stairs before being spotted since they would be busy firing on Men of the Mark.

As Rose turned to enter the dining room, Vynus burst through the door at the end of the hall, no doubt attempting to escape the carnage throughout the house. He spotted Rose, smiled, then began to laugh.

"You must be here for your toy," he said.

"Where is he?" she screamed.

"Wherever they take the carcasses once I'm done with them. The river would be my guess."

Rose's heart tore in two. She began to shake, biting back a sob as his words confirmed what she'd already known in her heart. Roth was dead. Her eyes bore into Vynus where he stood, and she drew her blade. He turned on his heels for the door, willing to take his chances with the Men of the Mark rather than face the Lady Blade.

Rose ran down the hall at a full sprint, her sword clutched in both hands, and as Vynus turned the handle and the door cracked open, her blade plunged into his lower back. There were no tricks to her weapon this time, and the blade speared clear through him. The tip stuck hard into the wood of the door, and Vynus stood nailed to it, writhing on her blade like a worm on a hook. She pulled a knife from her belt and plunged it up between his legs. His screams echoed up the hallway as she twisted the blade from side to side. When she withdrew it, all manner of fluids fell to the carpet.

She withdrew her sword and left the blubbering, pathetic man to bleed to death on the floor. Somewhere in this house, her uncle cowered like a scared rat. She would find him and make him pay for her pain in blood.

Aro saw a woman he didn't recognize head into the house behind Ithail's team. He wanted to investigate, but he had a job to do and couldn't afford the loss in time. He and his team headed around the west side of the house as Drauses had instructed, and Aro spotted the barn the Liege had warned them about in the distance. No sooner did he find the window of the hayloft than a rifle shot rang out with a crack, and the bullet passed by Aro's left, not an inch from his shoulder. He rolled and darted inside the carriage house.

Aro rushed through the carriage house and jumped outside through a back window then dashed to the back of the stables. He moved inside through the large sliding door and ran down the aisle past the horses who whinnied as he flew by. With his back to the wall, Aro took a quick peek around the corner at the barn. He looked for but a heartbeat to spot his target in the window before hiding again behind the wall to ready himself. The horse in the stall he was leaning against poked her head over the door just over his shoulder. She snorted at him then nibbled on the collar of his robes. He absentmindedly scratched the end of her nose as he said a prayer to calm his nerves, then he leaned out of the doorway again, took a knee for stability, and took aim.

Down the sight of the pistol, he could see the man in the loft staring straight back with his rifle. Aro fired first, and the rifleman jerked then fell out the window to the ground below. Aro ran across the yard and hopped in the window of the barn. There was a second man in the loft taking shots out of an eastern window at Drauses and Shaila's men.

Aro started up the ladder, and the guard heard him coming. As Aro's head came up into the loft, Rovik's man took aim with the rifle. Aro ducked as his enemy took his shot, and the wood above the ladder exploded in a shower of splinters. As the rifleman racked another bullet into the chamber, Aro popped back up and fired once with his pistol, striking the guard in the neck. As the rifleman clutched his gushing throat, Aro climbed up into the loft. With a hard kick, he sent the guard flying backward out the window.

The rifleman had dropped his gun, and Aro picked it up out of curiosity. He looked through the sight mounted on top and was surprised at the sudden magnification of his aim. He walked to the window and peered through the scope down to the yard below. Drauses, Shaila, and their team waited behind cover as guards poured into the yard through the back door of the house. Aro took aim at one and fired. The unexpected kick of the rifle jolted him back, but he hit his target, and one of the guards fell, a hole punched clear through his chest.

Aro smiled, racked the rifle, and aimed again.

❧

Drauses heard the rifle still firing but quickly realized Rovik's men were falling to its bullets now. He looked around the shed he and Shaila used as cover and watched the gunman fire again, taking down a guard in the grass halfway between them and the house. Drauses waved at the window, and Aro took down the rifle and waved back briefly before lifting the scope back to his eye and firing on. Drauses smiled and darted out from behind the shed.

"Move up, brothers," Drauses called. "Aro will cover us from above."

Aro's men rushed around the western corner of the house as Drauses' men swept from the opposite direction, and the two waves of men in red came together in the grass. Shaila ran across the yard toward the house, and Drauses followed. A man darted out the back door, pistol drawn, and Shaila drew her crossbow, but before she could fire, there was a blast from Aro's rifle, and the guard's head exploded in a shower of blood and bone. Shaila peered up at the window of the barn and blew a kiss at their expert marksman before she and Drauses entered the house.

Aro's second team had not yet reached the back of the mansion. Guards moved about the hall on this floor, firing at the Marks in the backyard through the windows. At the sight of Drauses and Shaila, they turned their attention to them instead. Shaila rolled, shot a man in the forehead with her crossbow, then ran down the hall to meet the blade of the next guard. Drauses swept on ahead, taking down the next guard in line before ducking at Shaila's command as she fired her crossbow over his head. The two of them had the hall emptied in no time.

Men of the Mark began trickling into the house, having run out of Rovik's men to slaughter outside. Drauses sent them in teams of four to check the upper floors. He organized the rest to strike the second floor where they'd face the most resistance.

"Has anyone heard where Rovik is hiding?" Drauses asked.

"He hides not, my Liege," Ithail answered as he burst into the hall from a nearby corridor. "It's my understanding he sits in his quarters on the third floor, awaiting his fate."

"Let's not keep our sovereign in suspense," Shaila quipped.

She and Drauses headed for the third floor, cutting a bloody path up the staircase as Rovik's men tried and failed to seek shelter on lower floors. On the third-floor landing, Drauses held the door open and ushered her through with a playful bow.

"After you," he said with a smirk.

Shaila laughed. "My hero."

In the third-floor hallway, three guards rushed around a corner and skidded to a halt at the sight of Drauses and Shaila. Drauses drew his small knife from his robes and whipped it down the hall where it buried into the chest of the first guard. Shaila rolled ahead and came up with a swing of her sword that split the second guard's belly open. The final guard pulled a hot stick, and it lit bright blue. Drauses switched on his sword to deal with him, but Shaila stepped between them with a growl of fury.

"Not this time," she muttered, and she spun the end of the hilt on her blade. "It's my turn."

Drauses watched in disbelief as her sword fell away and became a long whip of steel. She took two large steps forward and drew the weapon back to strike as Rovik's guard mustered the last of his bravery and rushed at her, hot stick drawn. Shaila rolled under his blow and came up with a swing of her own. Her whip slashed across the guard's back, and he screamed in agony. Shaila spun and her whip sliced higher this time, right across the back of the guard's neck with enough force it beheaded him on the spot.

Drauses walked up and gripped her arm, raising it to inspect her weapon closely.

"Julta?" he asked.

"Who else?"

Drauses fingered the whip, inspecting the backs of the pieces to see how they fit together to make a solid blade, but he wasn't expecting them to be sharpened on all sides and hissed as one slit his thumb open.

Shaila clucked her tongue. "That's mark number one, my Liege."

"It was self-inflicted!" Drauses defended.

Shaila laughed and shook the blood and bone from her whip before spinning the hilt of her weapon again. Each sliver of steel stacked against its brothers until they formed a single solid blade once more.

Drauses shook his head. "I keep waiting for the day you no longer surprise me. You must be nearly out of ways by now."

Shaila wiped her blade clean on her pant leg. "I wouldn't bet on that, my Liege." She wrapped her arm around Drauses' neck. "I can shock you to your toes anytime I wish."

"Oh? Then do it now. Show me this power you think you wield so effortlessly."

Shaila kissed him then brought her mouth close to his ear. "I'm with child, Drauses," she whispered.

Drauses' lips parted on a startled breath. He stared into her eyes, searching for any signs of jest.

"A babe?" he uttered.

Shaila nodded with a smile and pulled away, scampering off down the hall. Drauses stood in shock a moment before following after his Lady Liege who laughed with glee at the look on his face.

Once Rovik's men had all been dealt with in the yard, Aro climbed down out of the hay loft and joined his brothers in the grass. He sent a ward to escort Boon and Julta onto the grounds from their safe haven across the street. Boon started treating the few Marks who were wounded in the fight, but Aro noted the guild had seen no casualties. The newest Master smiled with pride at how much he and his brothers could accomplish with one well-organized strike under the orders of a competent Liege.

As he moved about the yard to aid his brothers, Aro noticed two metal doors in the grass between the mansion and the carriage house. Out of curiosity, he crossed the lawn and pulled them open. An awful smell poured out that sent Aro staggering back with a groan. Though weary of what he'd find, he crept down the stone steps, pistol drawn. Below was a large stone room the walls of which were lined with all manner of tools and weapons. The floor was splattered with various bodily fluids, and Aro could no longer stomach breathing through his nose. Near the far wall, a body laid across a table, bound wrist and ankle, across its surface.

Aro came closer, expecting to find a corpse. A man laid naked across the tabletop on his back, his body a battered mess of blood and bruises as well as incisions all fresh and still oozing around their stitches. Though obviously a man, the genitals had been removed. Aro had to turn away from the gore, looking instead to the man's chest, which, he was surprised to note, still rose and fell with ragged breath.

Aro called up for Boon. The physician's face paled and his step faltered when he came down the stairs, but when Aro pointed him to the motionless man on the table, the doctor came closer to investigate without delay. He did a quick inspection of the incisions then peered about the room.

There was a bloody bucket in a nearby corner, and Boon looked inside, moving its contents around with a random tool he plucked from the wall.

"The gallbladder, spleen, appendix, and genitals," Boon announced. "All organs that can be harvested without the death of their victim."

Aro did his best not to be sick. "My gods," he muttered in horror. "Will he live?"

"Perhaps, but he may not wish to."

Aro touched the bound man on his shoulder, and he immediately thrashed away from the Master's touch.

"No! No! Please, no more!"

"We mean you no harm," Aro assured him. "You're safe now."

"Kill me," the bound man begged as tears and blood dripped down his face. "Just kill me. Let me die. Please, let me die. Please. Please."

Boon walked away toward the various shelves and came back with an old glass bottle.

"What is that?" Aro asked.

Boon pulled his sleeve down over his hand and doused the fabric with liquid from the bottle. "It's Ether. It's an archaic medicine, but it'll do for now." Boon came to the side of the table and held his sleeve over the bound man's mouth and nose. After a moment, the man quit struggling and stared up at Boon with wide, frightened eyes.

"This will bring you peace for now," Boon said. "We'll take you away from here to safety."

When the man's eyes finally closed, Boon removed his sleeve, and he and Aro worked to free his arms and legs. Boon checked all wounds were clean and stitched before declaring him safe to move. Aro stripped off his robes to wrap them around the broken and abused body, then he and Boon gently lifted the stranger from the table and carried him toward the house.

⁐

On the third floor, Drauses and Shaila stood outside Rovik's bedroom door with the last of his guards lying dead on the floor at their feet. Shaila regarded her husband with a nod before turning the handle and shoving the door open which banged against the wall. Rovik stood by the window, watching the Marks move about in the backyard below. He sipped a glass of whiskey as if he had not a care in the world. When Shaila and Drauses walked in, he peered over his shoulder at them.

"The two of you are quite a sight," Rovik mused. "Splattered in blood and gore like creatures of nightmares."

"Just yours," said Shaila.

"Congratulations on your victory," Rovik said as he turned from the window, swirling his whiskey before taking a deep drink. It was an image Shaila knew so well it sent her stomach rolling. "It seems your men made short work of mine. But what, now, will you do with me?"

"You'll be tried and publicly executed for your crimes against your country," said Drauses.

"Crimes against my country?" Rovik scoffed. "My country thrived while I sat as sovereign. My people adore me."

"Half of them," Shaila corrected. "Like many sovereigns before you, you basked in the approval of the West while condemning the East to death and suffering. I think once all Jesparia's people speak as one, you'll find their loyalties don't lie with you as much as you think they do."

"Do your precious supporters know how you like to cause others pain?" Drauses asked. "That Vedian cellar in your backyard, how many beyond the walls of this estate know about that? Or about the countless women who warmed your bed for years only never to be seen again? The West will know soon enough how sick you are. They'll accept Amii as their sovereign with open arms."

"Little Amii," Rovik said with a sigh. "I was wrong about her. More than once. The little one who threw herself over my chest to protect me not so long ago is gone. Despite what she may tell you or what you may think, I loved her as my own."

"If that were true, you never would've sent that floating arsenal down the river to rain death on us all while she was among us," Drauses replied. "That choice was your undoing, Rovik. The day you disregarded Amii's safety was the day you sealed your fate."

"I rather think it was the day I took Shaila as my mistress," Rovik said thoughtfully. "I was undone by a beautiful woman. She'll be *your* undoing someday as well," he said with a nod at Drauses.

"I doubt that."

"I don't," Rovik sneered, and he drew a pistol from inside his jacket. He aimed it at Drauses' heart. Shaila knocked Drauses to the floor, and the shot flew over them both. Rovik took aim again as Drauses threw his knife from the floor. It stuck into Rovik's hand, and the sovereign shouted in pain and dropped the pistol. Shaila fired her crossbow and an electric bolt buried itself into Rovik's chest. He crumpled as it incapacitated him. When the bolt's charge was used up, Shaila came down on top of him, sword drawn and ready to slice open his throat.

"Shaila!" Drauses called.

She didn't look away from Rovik's face, but she tilted her head slightly to show she was listening.

"He's not worth it," said Drauses as he got to his feet. "Don't repeat my mistakes."

She stared down at Rovik, the desire to bleed the man dry making her hands shake with anticipation. For the second time, she felt the vengeance she sought right at her fingertips. With one motion, she could make him pay for every ounce of pain and humiliation he'd caused her and so many others. What person had he wronged more than all of that?

Amii.

Shaila was poised to swipe her blade under Rovik's chin, but the thought of Amii living the first twelve years of her life in his shadow, not knowing the father who yearned to love her was just across the river, taken from her mother the moment she first drew breath, made her pause. Rovik's downfall ought to be a public trial and execution to usher in Amii's reign properly. It was the least Rovik could do for the girl with the last of his wretched existence.

Shaila took the blade from Rovik's neck, but he wasn't saved from her fury entirely. Instead of slitting his throat, she punched him in the face so many times her hand went numb before she finally climbed back to her feet. Drauses came and dragged the bloody sovereign to his knees. Drauses bound Rovik's hands behind his back, then pulled him up and marched him from the room.

As Rovik went through the doorway ahead of Drauses, Rose spun across in front of him, blade in hand. Rovik hit his knees, and Shaila pushed her way past Drauses to watch as the Archdynast stared up at Rose with the last few seconds of his life, blood pouring down his chest from his slit throat. Rose glared down at Rovik in hatred, then shoved him in the chest with her boot. He fell to his back on the floor, choking on his own blood. Only when he stilled did Rose look up.

"Apologies," she said.

"His life wasn't yours to take," Shaila snapped.

"Perhaps not, but it's done. Make it known the decision was beyond your control. No blame will fall to Amii."

The two women regarded each other, each remembering the last time they saw one another. They locked eyes, and, though they both knew there would never be a spark of friendship between them, mutual respect won over old grudges. They nodded once to each other in understanding. Drauses' gaze flicked from one woman to the other then back again.

"What agreement did the two of you just make?" he asked.

"Not to kill each other," said Shaila.

"For the moment," Rose said sweetly. "I won't be lingering here. Once I leave, this truce ends."

Shaila gave another nod. "Agreed."

The three of them turned and walked away down the hall, leaving Rovik's body lying on the floor, his stony eyes staring after them as they went.

Chapter 31

AS DRAUSES, SHAILA, and Rose entered the first-floor hall, Aro and Boon came in the back door carrying an unconscious man between them wrapped in Aro's robes.

"Who's this?" Shaila asked.

"We found him bound in a cellar in the yard," Aro explained.

Rose sprang forward. "Let me see!" She took the man's chin and tilted his head up then covered her mouth with her hand.

"Do you know him?" Drauses asked.

"Yes," Rose uttered. "His name is Roth."

"Julta's brother Roth?" Drauses asked.

"Roth has a brother?" Rose asked.

"*Julta* has a brother?" Shaila asked.

"Vynus, Rovik's executioner, told me Roth was dead," Rose said.

"He may be unless we act swiftly," said Boon.

Shaila ushered them toward the staff quarters, and Aro and Boon hauled Roth into the nearest bedroom. The doctor ushered everyone from the room as he always did.

"Are you alright?" Shaila asked Aro. "You look pale."

"That place," Aro said. "The things they did to that man..." He shuddered.

Shaila knew what he meant, having been subjected to the horrors of The Cellar herself.

"Come with me," she bid, and Aro followed her back through the halls and out to the backyard.

"Julta!" Shaila called. "We need you a moment." The little man bounded to their side as Shaila marched across the lawn to a shed near the back wall. It was locked. Aro raised his pistol to shoot the lock off, but Shaila set her hand on the gun.

"I wouldn't do that," Shaila warned. Drauses was standing near the house, having shadowed them out of curiosity, watching from a distance. "Don't stand and gape, Drauses," she called to him. "Come use your handy tool and let us in this building."

Drauses came to do her bidding. As he worked the lock, Julta peered down at the rifle in Aro's hand and snatched up the weapon.

"Hey!" Aro cried, but Julta ignored him as he yanked open the bolt to stare into the chamber, inspected the barrel, and peered down the sight.

Julta huffed in disgust. "I can make you something much better than this.

Aro snatched the rifle back. "Until you do, I'll keep this one, thank you kindly."

The shed doors swung open to reveal walls and shelves lined with equipment and weapons. Julta's eyes lit up at the sight of it all.

"We need an explosive," said Shaila. "Something strong enough to cave in stone and steel."

Julta bounced up and down for a moment before rushing headlong into the shed. He darted from one shelf to another, snatching things down at random. He stood at a short workbench tinkering with his findings, and it was no time at all before he came back to them holding a jumble of putty, tubes, and fuses.

"I'll take it," Aro offered. He winked at Shaila. "I promise not to drown this time."

Shaila *tsked* and made a face at him that made Julta giggle, then she touched Julta's shoulder. "This shed is now the property of the Men of the Mark. Its contents are all yours."

Julta peered back into the shed with a look of wondrous excitement. "All mine?" he muttered.

Shaila and Aro headed back across the grass toward The Cellar, and

Julta hesitated a moment before following too. Aro insisted the inventor wait above as he and Shaila went down one final time. As Aro set the explosive and prepared the fuse, Shaila looked around, battling the memories of hopelessness and pain the room brought. This destruction would help lay all that to rest for her and for every soul who'd suffered within these walls.

"It's set," Aro said. "Are you ready?"

Shaila nodded, and, using Julta's little silver box, Aro lit the fuse. They ran up the steps and across the yard to where Julta stood at a safe distance. A moment later, the ground exploded in a shower of dirt, grass, and stone. The Cellar caved in on itself, and Shaila, Aro, and Julta cheered and clapped. Drauses laughed, and even Rose smiled at the sight of the smoke. Rovik's playhouse was no more.

᠍

Roth woke in a bed with no memory of how he got there. He ached from head to toe, particularly around his middle where he knew he'd been gutted like a freshly hunted deer. He moved to touch his face and was surprised to find his hands unbound. His left eye felt odd, as if it no longer fit in its socket. He touched it gently and found it covered in a bandage. Just this simple movement of his arm sent ripples of sharp pain throughout his body. He hissed and groaned in agony.

"Hello," said a voice to his right, and Roth turned his good eye to watch an older, balding man approach the bed. Roth prepared to roll away and flee if needed, but the man raised his unarmed hands to show he meant no harm.

"My name is Dr. Rikar. I'm with the Men of the Mark. We found you in an underground cellar and brought you to safety. Our enemies here have been dealt with and will threaten you no longer."

"The Men of the Mark?" Roth replied, his voice weak and rough. "Is Julta with you?"

"Yes, but he hasn't yet been told you're here. Master Drauses wishes to speak to you first."

"Then bring him."

"We need to discuss your condition first."

"I know what's been done," Roth said bitterly. "I need no recounting."

"You know what's been taken?"

Roth nodded. "I was awake as they did their deeds."

The doctor paled and closed his eyes for a moment in horror. "I suspected as much. If Drauses gives his consent, I'll gladly aid you in any way I can to ensure you live a normal life. Steps can be taken to encourage your body to perform as it ought despite what's been done."

"Nothing about my life will be normal from this day forward. I'm no longer a man."

"That's not the truth of it. The only thing we know for certain is you'll not father children. Beyond that, nothing is impossible. You are most assuredly still a man."

"And my eye?" Roth asked.

Dr. Rikar frowned. "I won't know the extent of the damage until swelling subsides, but I doubt very much you'll ever see out of it again. May I ask what they did?"

Roth swallowed hard and turned his gaze to the ceiling. "Vynus stuck me with a screwdriver." At a particularly vicious wave of agony, he shook with a breathless moan.

The doctor came a step closer. "I can give you something for the pain. It'll help you rest."

"I want to see my brother first."

"As you wish. I'll fetch Drauses and be back to check on you."

The doctor took his leave, and it was not more than a minute or two when the door opened again. This time, a tall Man of the Mark with a scar on his face walked in, followed closely by a woman with golden-brown hair that fell clear to her backside. She also wore robes of red, announcing her as the fabled Lady of the Mark that Roth had heard so much about. Her beauty was comparable to Rose's, he noted. They approached his bedside together.

"I'm Master Drauses," the man said. "I'm Liege to the Men of the Mark. This is my wife, Shaila, our Lady Liege."

Shaila smiled. "You are Roth?"

"I am."

"I told your brother you're here," she said. "He waits just down the hall. We'll send him in once we've had a chance to talk."

"What do you want to know?"

"Why were you being held by Rovik's executioner?" Drauses asked.

"I engineered his ship full of guns and rigged them all to fail. Rose knew Amii would be in danger. She asked me to ensure your men could get her to safety."

"How did you make the guns fail?" Shaila asked.

"I compromised the touch holes on the cannons. They melted closed as the guns heated. It only took a shot or two to render each gun useless until the vents could be reopened."

"And you did this at Rose's request?" Drauses asked.

"I did. Though I'd have gladly done it anyway. I want nothing more than to bring an end to Rovik's reign."

"Rovik is dead," Drauses announced. "I need to know where your loyalties lie now. Rose was with the Black Blades who were working for Rovik, except now she seems to have turned on her comrades and Rovik both. Who do *you* stand with?"

"I stood with the Blades many years beside Rose, but we always opposed Rovik, each for our own reasons. Rose moved as her own piece in this game of war, but I remained on the sidelines, aiding her when she asked me. If she's left the Black Blades as you say, I'll have to decide if I should do the same. Hestus will show little mercy either way."

"Hestus?" Drauses said in surprise. "Rose's brother?"

"He leads the Black Blades. Didn't you know?"

"We had little knowledge of the Blades at all until a season ago," said Shaila. "Their leader was never mentioned by name, though we never had the chance to ask after him before."

"Hestus at the head of the Black Blades explains a lot," Drauses said. "I found it hard to understand why Rose would vow herself to such a cause, blades swung merely for coin. She had higher standards once upon a time, but she always harbored a deep respect and loyalty for her brother."

"Indeed," Roth agreed. "He was why she left Amii with Rovik under the ruse of her death. That is the way of the Blades, you see. Unlike the

Marks who keep their lovers and families once they join your brotherhood, the Blades are told they must sever all ties. We let our loved ones think us dead and gone. No one left to mourn us at our true passing that way. No questions asked, no fuss. When Hestus called on her to join his newly banded mercenaries after Amii was born, her father forced her to choose him over the babe. She trained his men, but, as you no doubt know by now, not many ever came close to her in skill."

"What services did *you* provide the Black Blades?" Drauses asked.

"Weaponry, reconnaissance—both audio and visual—and the types of sabotage you've already witnessed. The listening devices planted amongst your men were my design."

"The blade Rose used to stab me?"

Roth nodded. "I made her that weapon, yes. She needed your death to look convincing."

"Do you pose any threat to my family?" Drauses asked. "I'm more than willing to extend our hospitality and allow Boon to care for you, but I'll leave no man unattended who may risk the lives of my brothers and loved ones."

"I've no grudges against you and yours. I assume you plan to place Amii as our sovereign, and I support that notion. I hope she unites our people once more."

"That is our hope as well," Shaila said. Roth coughed once and groaned with a grimace. Shaila touched Drauses' arm. "We'll leave you for now. Julta will be around directly."

Shaila took Drauses by the elbow. Though the Elder was clearly not done speaking, he let his wife lead him from the room. Roth smiled in amusement at how such a mighty man could fall to the whims of a beautiful woman as easily as any other.

✦

Rose watched from a distance as Drauses and Shaila left Roth's room and Julta entered it, leaving the door open behind him when he did. She crept down the hall and stood with her back to the wall just outside it, closing her eyes with relief at the sound of Roth's voice as he greeted his younger brother.

"Hello, Springs." She could tell by his tone that he was smiling.

"You died," Julta said so quietly Rose barely heard him. "I burned you to Odavail."

"I let you believe that for a long time. I'm sorry, brother. Though I don't deserve it, I pray you can forgive me for it someday."

"Someday?" Julta asked. "Am I not allowed to forgive you now?"

"If you wish."

"I have you back. I won't waste a single moment on any kind of quarrel with you, unless... unless you plan to disappear again once you recover."

"I don't know where I'll go once I'm able."

'With me, love, like we planned,' Rose thought to herself.

"Please stay where I can see you."

Rose's heart skipped a frantic beat. If anything could come between them, it would be this: a love far stronger than the one he'd found with her. A brother's love. There was a long silence during which she closed her eyes and chanted the words she wished he'd say over and over in her head, but when Roth spoke, the words he chose instead brought instant tears to her eyes.

"I've caused you enough grief over these past years," Roth said. "I'll bring you no more. If you wish me tethered to your side for the rest of my days, that's where I'll stay, Julta. I owe you this much."

Julta giggled with glee. "Now that Amii is soon to be our sovereign, she'll unite East and West. There will be a high demand for services we can easily provide. Let's open a workshop together. We can combine our expertise to help Trista heal and grow anew. What say you?"

"I'm not a Man of the Mark. You'd have to leave the guild. I can't ask that of you."

"I'd leave them for you. For this."

"I'd be honored to work beside you. If that's truly what you want."

Boon came down the hall with a vial and syringe in his hand. He stopped at the sight of Rose near the door. She raised a finger to her lips, pushed off the wall, and turned to walk away. But then she hesitated and looked back at Boon.

"Take care of him," she whispered, her voice cracking in heartbreak.

Boon nodded, and Rose took her leave, first of the hall, then of the house, then the estate entirely. She crossed the street and only then looked back. Drauses stood watching her from the mansion's grand entrance, his face unreadable and handsome as ever. They stared at each other for a long moment before Rose turned on her heels and disappeared into the city streets.

᪥

The grounds were abuzz for the next few days as bodies were disposed of, repairs were made, and all of Rovik's possessions were swept from the mansion. Drauses wanted everything to be perfect before he signaled Dagon to bring Amii to her new home, but there was a single detail he'd been fretting over since Rovik's demise. As he sat motionless on the bed in his temporary quarters, frozen in thought right in the middle of dressing one morning, Shaila confronted him.

"Alright, out with it," she demanded.

"Out with what?" Drauses asked, bewildered.

"Whatever it is that's occupied your mind these past few days. Whenever I look at you, you're in another place or time. What's distracting you?"

Drauses sighed. "It's Amii, or rather who'll protect her once she's placed as sovereign. This will be her home now, and, as much as I'd like to look after her myself, I am the Liege. We have to be with the guild, return to The Yard. The next best thing to me guarding her myself would be to place a fellow Man of the Mark at her side, but I don't know who it should be or how to choose the man."

"Why not let Amii choose?"

Drauses rolled his eyes. "It's no mystery at all who the girl would pick. Not that I think lowly of him, but Aro is only newly a Master. He lacks expertise gained through years of experience."

"Skill isn't the only importance in this decision, Drauses. Far from it. Amii is still a child, one who is bound to make mistakes as she ages, like any other. She needs someone she can confide in, someone she trusts. Aro is her closest companion. She'd share all with him and keep no secrets, and the closer her protector is, the better he can shield her."

"I'm uncomfortable placing one so young at her side."

Shaila studied her husband with a raised brow. "Oh, now I see," she said with a slight smile. "You fear something might develop between them as Amii ages. Is that it?"

"She dotes on him so. It's clear she already holds him in too high regard."

Shaila crossed her arms. "And you'll be sparing her what, exactly, by taking away the man who means so much to her?"

Drauses winced. "Don't say it like that, please. I don't wish to cause her pain—"

"Do you think it'd be wrong if Amii and Aro fell in love someday?"

"I can't think about that. She's too young."

"We both know Aro better than that. He would never take advantage of Amii's youth."

Drauses sighed. "No, he wouldn't."

Shaila came to sit beside him. "Tell me, my Liege, would you protect me from danger?"

Drauses sputtered, thrown by her sudden change of subject. "I have in the past. I try every day. And I would in future, of course."

"Would you take a bullet for me? A blade for me? Lay down your life for mine?"

"Yes."

"Why?"

Drauses chuckled, wise to her game. "Because I love you," he admitted.

"And I you," Shaila replied as she touched his cheek. "You think the strength and success of our brotherhood lies in skill alone, Drauses, but that's not the truth of it. It lies in each man's willingness to make sacrifices for his brothers, to lay down his life for them without a second thought. It's love that makes a person, man or woman, go to incredible lengths, just as I did when I went back to the mansion for Amii. I did it because I love her, and you. Aro would lay down his life for Amii in an instant. You know he would."

Drauses sighed in defeat. "Yes, alright, I see the truth in your words, Lady Liege, but what about Aro's desires? Will he want to leave the brotherhood to act as a personal bodyguard for the rest of his life? Never be allowed to take a ward? Perhaps he'd prefer not to take on such a responsibility. But if we allow Amii to choose…"

"Hmm, yes," Shaila mused. "We'll have to think on that one, won't we?"

"I'm sure my Lady Liege will help me find a solution," Drauses said with a smile.

Shaila looked down at her hands clasped over her belly, and Drauses touched her chin to raise her eyes back to his own.

"What is it?" he asked.

"I was worried your silence was due to the news I shared with you."

"You thought I was unhappy about the babe?"

"For a moment."

"Nothing could be further from the truth," he said as he touched her belly. "I'm both excited and grateful beyond words! Not only do I get to be a father twice, but this time I get to be here from beginning to end. I get to watch you both grow."

Shaila huffed. "Please, don't mention growing. I'd rather not think about that part."

"You can grow as big as you like, my love, you'll still be my lady finest fair."

"Oh, to Vedia with you and that blasted poem, Drauses!" she fumed, though she couldn't help but smile.

Drauses swept her up into a kiss which quickly grew into more. The house bustled about as the morning passed without a single sign of the Lieges as they stole time for themselves, bathed in Pera's light.

Chapter 32

3rd and 60 of Autumn, Jesparia's 1st year of Amii

DRAUSES CALLED EVERY Man of the Mark to the foyer, and he and Shaila stood at the bottom of the grand staircase as everyone gathered. Amii was in attendance, as was Boon and Julta, who were taking a rare break from sitting at Roth's bedside. They all whispered together, speculating at what their Liege was about to announce.

"I've called you all together today because an important decision must be made," Drauses began. "We've announced Amii as sovereign of our country, with an official ceremony to take place on her thirteenth birthday in a few weeks' time. As her father, as well as the Liege to the guild who worked so hard to install her here, I'm responsible for placing someone at Amii's side to act as head of security for this estate, as well as Amii's most trusted guard and adviser as she moves forward as sovereign. It should come as no surprise that I feel it best if one of our own takes this position.

"I've struggled these past few days with which man I should choose for this assignment or even how to choose just one from amongst my many capable brothers. After much discussion, our Lady Liege and I have decided to ask for volunteers. It's important to note that this assignment will be lifelong. Whichever man goes, though still a Man of the Mark, will no longer receive any other assignments, will reside full time here at this estate, and will be unable to take a ward from this day forward. Consider it carefully before you offer your blade. My fellow Marks, who here is willing to stand at Amii's shoulder and wield his blade for her for the rest of his days?"

Many men stepped forward, over half, which pleased Drauses. He noted without surprise that Aro was among them.

"I'm happy to see so many are willing to take this as seriously as I do. However, I won't be making the final decision." Drauses beckoned to Amii who hurried across the room to stand next to her father. "Amii, I want you to choose from this group of men who you'd like to stand at your side. Choose wisely, for the man you pick will be your guard for as long as you stand as leader of Jesparia."

"This is no decision at all," said Amii, then she crossed her arms. "In fact, I'll be quite cross if the man himself doesn't already know I chose him."

Drauses looked at the group of men and found Aro already shaking his head in amusement, stifling a laugh. "Aro," he called, but the Master in question was already making his way through the crowd. He came to stand in front of his Liege, head bowed. "Starting today, this very moment, you'll be taking leave of us. Shaila and I present you with the lifelong assignment of guard and adviser to our beloved sovereign. Do you accept?"

"Yes, my liege," Aro said.

"Then take your place at Amii's side. Know that if you ever require aid, the guild stands ready to assist as you remain a Man of the Mark and forever our brother."

Aro bowed to his Liege, and then he turned to Amii. He drew his sword and set the tip of the blade to the floor at his sovereign's feet, taking a knee in front of her.

"My blade is yours, my lady," he vowed with a smile. "I promise to wield it in your name until the Odas take me and to never shed a drop of blood to soil your honor. Any who wish to harm you will have to cut through me first, for I offer my life as a shield for yours this day, and every day, till the end of days. My blade is yours forever, on my honor as a Man of the Mark, while I still have blood to give."

"Oh, Aro," Amii gushed with a sob, and she threw her arms around his neck in a crushing hug. "I'll make you proud, I promise."

"You already have, little one," Aro replied as he hugged her back.

Drauses shared a look with his wife who tried and failed to hide a smile as the Men of the Mark all broke into applause.

✍

Aro had just finished a celebratory hug with Shaila when Drauses motioned him aside.

"I need a private word," said Drauses.

"Of course, my Liege," Aro replied, and he followed Drauses a short distance away.

"I hope you realize the importance of the position Amii has trusted you with," Drauses said.

"I do, sir."

"We allowed her to choose because she trusts you. You'll be her protector and counselor, sure, but also much more than that. You're her closest friend. She'll confide her secrets to you, good and bad, and you'll share in both her triumphs and her failures. Don't ever abuse such power or allow anyone to exploit your knowledge of her."

Aro bristled. "Those things I said weren't for show," he said, his voice sharp with indignation. "I'd never betray Amii, sir. Never."

Drauses studied Aro anew, and Aro expected a stern word or two for his tone. To his surprise, the Liege didn't chastise him but bowed his head instead. "I meant no offense, Aro. I know you're a better man than that."

Aro was taken aback. "Thank you, sir."

"What would you say to training with me a couple of times a week? Not that I doubt your abilities or those of your former Master who trained you. I merely wish to pass on any knowledge or skill I can, for Amii's sake."

"I... I'd be honored. It's well known your skills know no equal, except perhaps for our Lady Liege."

"She brings such pride to the guild," Drauses said with a smile. "I'm fortunate to have found a woman as wise as she who's also a master of battle and deadly beautiful. I suspect Amii will be just as handsome someday. Let me give you some words of wisdom." Drauses clapped Aro hard on the shoulder making him jump. "Deadly beautiful women often have even deadlier fathers who won't take kindly to a man taking liberties where he ought not. Do you understand?"

Aro locked eyes with his Liege. "Perfectly, sir."

"Good," Drauses replied cheerfully, releasing Aro's shoulder. "Tomorrow, we'll start recruiting guards for this estate. You and I will go through the applicants together and choose the best the city has to offer to guard Amii's new home."

"Till tomorrow then."

Drauses nodded and walked away. Before Aro had quite recovered himself from the exchange, Shaila stepped up to take Drauses' place.

"I have something for you," she said, checking over her shoulder to be sure they weren't overheard. She passed over a small leather pouch held shut with a leather cord hooked around a button. Aro opened it to find several small tools one would find in a medicine kit.

"Boon, Julta, and I put our minds together and fashioned this for you," Shaila explained. "It contains several useful tools to stop bleeding including a packet of powder of Boon's design meant to clot blood on contact. Julta made the case small enough to fit in the pocket of your robes. Considering your condition, you're to keep this with you at all times from this day forward. As your Lady Liege, I'm insisting on it. As your friend, I'm asking you to take care of yourself to the best of your abilities. This will help."

Aro fingered the tools, recognizing a few as ones he carried in his much bigger, far less portable kit. No one had ever done anything like this for him before.

"You had this made before Amii made her choice," he said.

Shaila winked at him. "We knew the outcome of this meeting before it was ever called. We have faith in you, Aro. You're the one for this assignment. There was no question, only formalities. You and Amii chose each other." She drew closer and lowered her voice. "Whatever Drauses muttered to you just now, with that look on his face he thinks is so intimidating, don't take it to heart. He's merely being a father with a beautiful young daughter to look after. Do good by Amii in all things, wherever life takes the both of you, and Drauses will be ever grateful and supportive. As will I."

"I will, Lady Liege. I promise."

Shaila leaned up on her toes and dusted a quick kiss on his cheek before strolling away.

✍

Nearly the moment Shaila rejoined her husband, who was discussing supply runs with Dagon on the other side of the room, she spotted Julta making his way through what was left of the gathered crowd in the foyer toward them.

"Master Drauses, Master Shaila," he said. "I must speak to you both in private."

Drauses and Shaila exchanged a look.

Dagon cleared his throat. "I'll take my leave and begin our preparations."

"Thank you, Dagon," Drauses said with a nod. Once Dagon was out of earshot, Drauses turned to Julta. "Yes?"

Julta cleared his throat and wrung his hands. "Now that my brother is on the mend," he said, his eyes locked on Drauses' boots, "I need to know what I'm allowed to take with me from my shop once he's well enough to travel."

"*Take*, Julta? Are you leaving us?" Shaila asked.

"I am. My brother and I wish to open a shop together. Since he's not part of the guild, we'll find a place in the city to create for all of Trista."

Drauses and Shaila regarded each other.

"What could be better than one genius inventor?" Shaila asked.

"Two," Drauses said with a small smile. He turned back to Julta. "That won't be necessary. You *and* your brother are welcome to stay at The Yard and make use of your workshop there, as well as all the supplies retrieved from this estate."

"Roth may join the guild?" Julta exclaimed.

"If that is his wish," Shaila said. "If he brings us even half the service you have over the years, he'll be a welcome addition to the guild indeed."

"But... but what about a shop?" Julta asked. "We want to create for more than just the guild."

"I think something could be arranged," Shaila said. She looked at Drauses who nodded.

"I'll ask the men to scout for a suitable location," Drauses said. "Someplace close to headquarters where you and your brother can bring your genius to all of Trista. Perhaps Boon would be interested in such an arrangement as well since you're all so fond of... gadgets," he said with a small huff.

Julta stared at them, wide-eyed and speechless until, in a display of affection most unusual for him, he leapt forward and wrapped first Drauses then Shaila in quick, fierce hugs. "Thank you, thank you," he said, tripping over his own feet as he backed away, turned, and rushed off.

Drauses shook his head in bemusement. Shaila touched his arm.

"That was a good choice," she said.

"So much is changing," said Drauses, touching his temple. "It makes my head spin."

"One thing never will."

Drauses pulled her close. "Tell me."

"I love you, husband."

"The best decision I ever made was taking you away with me that night so long ago. I shudder to think where we would be without our Lady of the Mark."

Shaila placed her hands on the sides of his face, her thumb tracing the scar down his left cheek. The room, the Marks, Trista, and all of Jesparia fell away as they stole one selfish moment for themselves with a passionate kiss.

Epilogue

ON AMII'S THIRTEENTH birthday, she took her place as sovereign of Jesparia. With the Men of the Mark behind her, she not only had the courage to lead but endless guidance at her request. As she once dreamt she would, she led her country with her own strengths and not as a puppet for the likes of men. Wherever she went, Aro shadowed her, always stationed at her shoulder.

Under Amii's rule, the walls between the East and West were torn away and bridges long ago destroyed were rebuilt as first Trista, then all of Jesparia, once again became one. Buildings were repaired, businesses reopened, and the old Sazeen brewery was restored to give many in the East side employment, a luxury few had ever known.

Farmers along the outskirts of the city now had new reasons to sow acres of crops to fuel the stills with needed grain. With the capital city reopened to trade once more, Jesparia's neighbors took notice, and trade requests began to flow into Trista in increasing numbers. Jesparian Whiskey and lumber soon began to travel all across Oda Karrith both by river and in wagons. This brought the coin the city desperately needed to repair and heal after nearly a hundred years of hardship and ruination.

The Men of the Mark were hailed as heroes, but Drauses knew their victories were the result of one choice, one moment, one woman: the Lady of the Mark.

8th and 20 of Autumn, Jesparia's 2nd year of Amii

Rose sank to her knees on the floor with her hands bound behind her back. She spit a gob of blood onto the carpet with a sneer as a man in black robes and mask stood over her, staring at her in deep thought.

"Did you honestly think I'd never catch you?" he asked. "It took me nearly a year, but I caught up with you just as you knew I would."

"It was worth a try," Rose replied.

"You've stopped nothing. I will still become sovereign just as Rovik and I planned. You've merely delayed the process."

"What choice did I have? Either way, I kill a loved one, my kin, with my own hands."

"Amii will only die if she refuses to cooperate."

"She won't surrender to you, Hestus. She has too much of her father in her."

"Then she'll go down with the rest of them. Amii will learn those who stand on the backs of men have the furthest to fall." Hestus reached down and took Rose's chin in his hand, tilting her face up to look deep into her eyes. "The question remains whether *you* will surrender, Rose. Or would you rather join your child as I rip the hearts from every Man of the Mark and all who stand beside them? Oh my, will the blood flow… until they have no more to give."

The End

If you liked this story, please consider leaving a review!

Join other readers to discuss this book and get updates about the series in our private Facebook group:
https://www.facebook.com/groups/readersofthemark

Follow the author:

- Twitter: @Alex44Fantasy
- Instagram: mxalex44
- TikTok: MxAlex44
- Facebook: https://www.facebook.com/alex.mx.1671/

Or visit their website at mxalexwrites.com.

Glossary

Numbers, dates, and time:

Numbers in Jesparia are spoken and recorded by ones, then tens, then hundreds, for all numbers greater than 20 and less than 1,000. Once a number becomes larger than 1,000, it is spoken as a string of numbers with no places. For long numbers ending in many zeros, the speaker adds "with _" for how many zeros are to be added to the end of the string. The commas dividing the number every three places are then added after the number is written in full.

For example, the number 29 is spoken and recorded as "nine and twenty" or "9 and 20." A larger number, such as 129, would still be recorded the same way: "nine, twenty, and one hundred." One step further and the number switches to the alternate format. 1,290 is then spoken as simply "one, two, nine, zero" with the comma being added after the number is written down. If the number is *far* larger, say 1,290,000,000, then this would still be spoken as "one, two, nine," but then the speaker would add "with seven," meaning 7 zeros are to be added after the 9. For very large, complex numbers with no zeros, it is simply easier to write them down rather than recite them orally for both speaker and listener alike.

Years are broken into four seasons: Spring, Summer, Autumn, and Winter. These seasons mark their corresponding seasonal weather as one would normally expect, but the word "season" is also used as a measurement of time that could span multiple "weather seasons." For example, the time between the 50th of Summer and the 50th of Autumn would be measured and referred to as a season, though it technically spans two partial *weather* seasons.

Years are recorded individually in each country, corresponding to that region's current reigning sovereign, and roll over to the next year on the first day of Spring. Those who communicate outside their country must be knowledgeable of their neighbor's current sovereign year to keep the dates straight. Where in Jesparia the year is the "*7th and 20 year of Rovik*", that same year in Fraidan, their closest neighbor to the west, is actually the "*19th year of Lystia.*"

It is also important to note that when a new sovereign takes over in any country, the first year of their reign is marked on the day they took over, no matter what season in that year they became sovereign. For example, the day Rovik became sovereign of Jesparia, it officially became the "*1st year of Rovik,*" regardless if that day happened to be the first day of Spring, the last day of Winter, or any day in between. The days leading up to Rovik's appointment are still considered the year of the previous sovereign's reign, however, as the year did not officially become Rovik's until the exact day he overthrew his predecessor. Also, when the new year began the following Spring, it became the "*2nd year of Rovik,*" whether Rovik sat as sovereign a full four seasons or not.

The Gods of Jesparia:

The religion in Jesparia is polytheistic. Though the sciences are often quite advanced for the times, Jesparians still hold tightly to their deeply spiritual beliefs and customs of old. In the Jesparian faith, there are two realms of gods and spirits: Vedia and Odavail, The Realm of the Sinful and The Realm of the Pure, respectively. Below is a list of all the gods, also referred to collectively as "the Odas," and a brief description of each one's specific place in Jesparian worship.

Heniira – The moon goddess.

Those who seek safety or protection pray to Heniira, for she is a symbol of sanctuary. She was the first of the gods to realize Earth's potential for intelligent life. She fell in love with the first primitive humans to walk the planet and vowed to watch over them as they continued to evolve. After a flying ball of rock nearly destroyed Earth, Heniira decided to ensure her beloved beings would be forever protected by plucking out one of her own eyes and setting it in motion around the planet as a guardian, thus creating the moon.

In early times before science was better able to explain such things, the moon's phases were thought to be Heniira's eye slowly blinking over the course of a lunar cycle. On the days the moon went black, the "closed" moon, the goddess was believed to be resting. A full moon is referred to as an "open" moon and is celebrated as a day when Heniira's protection is the strongest since nothing can hide from her full gaze. Though the cycles of the moon are obviously better understood now, the "open" and "closed" lunar days are still recognized as important times of worship to those who often pray to Heniira, and Jesparian art, both past and present, often depicts the moon as a giant eye in the sky instead of a white orb.

The closed and open moons are particularly associated with the birth of children. A babe born during a closed moon must be blessed at a harana dedicated solely to Heniira at the very next open moon. Otherwise, the child has not been "seen" by the guardian goddess and cannot receive her blessings nor her protection. On the other hand, a child born during an *open* moon is said to be favored by the moon goddess. The umbilical cords of these children are coveted by devoted worshippers who use them as relics, but mothers of open moon babes prefer to throw the cords into rivers, lakes, or the sea. It is believed that Remlar, the god of water and Heniira's twin brother, then takes the cords to his sister as an offering for the child's good fortune. Originally a ritual only for babes born during an open moon, the practice of throwing the umbilical cords into open water has spread to include nearly all children born under the Jesparian faith.

Remlar – The god of water.

Remlar protects all bodies of water and the aquatic life within them. He sinks ships if he believes the crew harbors ill will of any kind. Though all captains pray to him for safe passage, captains and crews of fishing vessels are particularly devoted to Remlar, for he's the one who decides which ships receive a bountiful catch and which ones return home empty-handed. Those deemed unworthy may be dragged down in merciless storms which are considered manifestations of his notoriously foul temper.

Remlar is Heniira's twin brother, which was thought to explain why the tides and the moon are so closely related. Though a sibling to the kind and merciful moon goddess, Remlar is considered one of the most ill-tempered gods. He is often depicted as a sea monster with many heads that watch over the seas in all directions. Though his rage is renowned, so is his unconditional love for his sister, who is said to be the only one able to handle the hot-blooded sea god. Remlar sometimes appears alone in art, either as a monster or a fierce warrior who wields the sea as a weapon, while other times he's drawn as a plume of water woven around the moon, his beloved twin sister's image.

The legend of Vediida and Masiila, the rulers of the underworld:

When Heniira first fell in love with the beings of Earth, Remlar was the first god she convinced of mankind's potential. Out of love for his sister, Remlar also devoted himself to Earth and its mortal beings as the god of water. Heniira believed humans were divine, and, after a time, she convinced her brother to take a female human lover, for she swore that any children born by man and god combined would surely be creatures of ultimate power and divinity. So it was that Remlar took a human lover who birthed him twin babes: one boy and one girl.

Vediida – The god of the underworld (Vedia).

Vediida is Remlar's son born of a mortal woman. The child was born second of the twins, and a complication during his birth resulted in the young mother's death. Heniira wept at the news, for she knew this omen meant the child would be cursed.

Vediida grew to be a strong but greedy man who hungered for the power he felt he was owed as half a god. He is the youngest of the male gods and is often depicted as a handsome youth dressed all in black with a calculating grin, or sometimes as black bones bathed in flame. He spent his years on Earth bringing terror and destruction to anyone unfortunate enough to encounter him. He started the first wars and brought famine and plague to Earth out of spite toward his godly father who gave him life only to leave him stranded in the world of mortals. Thankfully, Vediida's time on Earth was short, for the first time he took sail across the seas, Remlar sank the vessel and drowned Vediida in the most violent storm known to man. It is said the waves crashed, lightning cracked, and no ships dared sail the seas for a full season as Remlar both raged at Vediida's foolishness and grieved the necessary death of his only son.

As punishment for his crimes, Vediida was not allowed to join the pure souls in Odavail after death and was banished to the underworld instead. His power as half a god would not let him be just another wandering, burning soul, however, and he soon became the lord of the sinful and master of the underworld, which he renamed after himself. Vedia is a place of suffering for evil souls that burns constantly with fires hotter than any found in the mortal world. Only the wicked dwell there, with one exception.

Masiila - The goddess of healing and the underworld.

Remlar's other child, Vediida's sister Masiila, chose a much different life than her brother. She became a healer, dedicating her life to helping humans in any way she could. During her long life on Earth, she saved countless lives, cured three of her brother's plagues, and once brought a stillborn babe back to life in her arms. She was loved by any and all who met her and was every bit the angelic being Heniira had imagined, so much so that when she died, the gods offered her a place in Odavail at their side without hesitation.

Though she wept with happiness at the gods' offer, Masiila refused to join them in Odavail. Much like the love Remlar has for Heniira, Masiila loves her brother dearly, despite his foolish and wicked ways, and declared she could never live where Vediida was not allowed to dwell. She chose instead to go to the underworld to be with her brother and keep him honest, ensuring he only ever took the souls he was owed and never a pure one. Her sacrifice only made the gods respect her more, and so they agreed to let Remlar give his daughter three gifts to take with her to Vedia.

Remlar's first gift was a bell made of diamonds, Earth's most precious stone. If Masiila should need her father, the ringing of the bell would summon him to her side. The second gift was a robe woven from renistrila, Earth's most beautiful blossom. The flowers never wilted and forever bathed her in their perfume, even in the fires of Vedia. The third and most powerful gift was a basin carved from a branch of The Tree of Prayer, Earth's most sacred treasure. When filled with seawater, the basin showed Masiila those among mankind who worshipped her and prayed for her help in healing. And so it was that the goddess of medicine used this window to Earth to continue helping mankind even from the depths of the underworld.

Masiila and Vediida, children of gods and man alike, are two sides of the same coin, the good and the evil that can come when gods meddle in the lives of men. Though their story was not at all the one Heniira had in mind for them, Masiila and Vediida did both bring about the highest blessing of Odavail, one which Heniira felt made her and Remlar's mistake worth the trouble in the end. After both Remlar's children passed on from the mortal world, the rest of the gods decided to devote themselves to mankind, having witnessed firsthand the power and the ruin that could come from their continued absence on Earth. And so, the rest of the Odas slowly grew to love man as passionately as Heniira, though she remains mankind's most devoted guardian.

Gindar – The god of death, war, and domestication.

Riding upon a great black steed, Gindar decides who dies, when, and by what means. He earned his post by conquering his brother Purgadon, who served as the previous god of death. Soldiers pray to this god to favor them in battle, to spare their lives, and bring them victory but—if the worst should come to pass—that he grant them swift and honorable deaths instead. He and his horse gather the souls of the departed and deliver them to either Vedia or Odavail, wherever they are fated to spend eternity.

The name of Gindar's horse has been lost throughout the ages, but it is still widely known that the animal lacks eyes. As a blind steed, he relies solely on Gindar for direction, and Gindar cannot do his job of rounding up the souls of the dead without his mount. This is thought to symbolize the balance of man and domesticated animals and how one requires a trust and understanding of the other to coexist efficiently. Man needs animals in life but with them comes a responsibility of man to care for his charges and see to it they are not led astray.

Purgadon – The first god of death.

As Gindar's older brother, Purgadon was the original god of death and war. It was he who first broke the great black stallion and began rounding up the souls of the departed. Gindar accused Purgadon of plotting to bring about an apocalypse that would end all life on Earth. Heniira begged Gindar to intervene, so he fought and slew Purgadon then banished his soul to Vedia where he is held as prisoner.

Some believe Purgadon was wrongfully accused by Gindar who merely yearned for the power his elder brother wielded. They wait for the day Purgadon escapes his prison, returns to seek vengeance on his brother, and takes back his rightful place amongst the gods in Odavail. Of those who follow this path of worship, there are some who believe Gindar himself plots to one day end all life on Earth, and they pray when that day comes, Purgadon can break his bonds in time to save the world from ruin.

Pera – The goddess of love and fertility.

Pera is the shepherd of all creatures in love, be them human or animal. The lonely pray to her to find their life-long partners. Couples pray to her to grant them children. She draws lovers together by altering their sight. This phenomenon, called "Pera's light," allows soul mates to see one another perfectly through the eyes of true love.

This goddess' story is somewhat controversial, as love is such a passionate emotion, for better or for worse. Some choose to believe Pera and the god Wote are lovers, and that he shares his never-ending knowledge with her to help her pair together the correct couples in love. Others, particularly the ones who've suffered heartbreak or unrequited love, believe Pera gains her inspiration for choosing lovers from her lifelong pining for Wote who does not return her regard. This would explain why some love is doomed and painful from the start.

Pera is often drawn as a startlingly beautiful maiden in a long flowing dress with a strip of cloth tied over her eyes, for it is said that she gouged out her own eyes to blind herself shortly after becoming the goddess of love for mankind. This is thought to embody true love as being deeper than physical attraction because if Pera cannot see the one she chooses to love, then their beauty, or lack thereof, plays no part in her devotion. The fact that Wote, her suspected lover, is often drawn as an aged cripple likely helped fuel this belief. This feature has sometimes resulted in the goddess of love being confused with Heniira in some art since the moon goddess is also drawn missing an eye. Drawing Pera with eyes is considered taboo and often symbolizes an artist's nihilism.

Wote – The god of knowledge.

This god is believed to know every shred of wisdom in the world and the universe beyond. He can see all events of the past, present, and future in perfect clarity. Those who seek to learn pray to him for perseverance. Many pray to him for answers to their troubles, but this is usually considered a foolish waste of prayer, for though he can see the future, Wote is selective when sharing such knowledge with man or even with his fellow gods. He believes they should intervene in human fates as little as possible, though he may make exceptions for Pera, depending on one's beliefs concerning their relationship.

Wote is the oldest of the gods and is depicted in texts as an old man with a long, grey beard who leans heavily on a walking stick and wears an ancient key around his neck. What the key is meant to open is the subject of much speculation. Wote is Heniira and Remlar's father, though their mother is unknown. This fact only fuels the belief that Wote and Pera are lovers, for that would make the love goddess the twins' mother, but this is purely speculation as none of the old teachings or texts ever name her as such. Pera and Heniira's similar features in art dating back hundreds of years is also further evidence the two could be related, and many choose to believe this is the case despite the lack of tangible proof.

The Tree of Prayer:

The Tree of Prayer is considered the most sacred place on Earth. No mortal man can prove to have seen it with his own eyes, and yet its existence is rarely questioned. Planted high on top of a hill on an island in the middle of Remlar's deepest sea, the tree is so tall its highest branches are thought to stretch clear to Odavail, thus, in a sense, the tree is directly connected to the Odas themselves.

In art, the Tree of Prayer is drawn towering over the very island it inhabits with long, often intricately intertwined branches and deep red leaves that never fall, while the ground around its base blooms with countless renistrila blossoms every Spring, Summer, and Autumn. Any prayers uttered at its base are guaranteed to be heard by the gods, but it is not guaranteed they will be answered. Remlar trimmed the tree's thickest branch to make the basin he gave to his daughter Masiila to take with her to the underworld.

Other Terms:

Greeg – A deep green fish most commonly found in the Jespa River.

Harana – A building of worship. Haranas can either dedicate their worship to one specific god or all the Odas collectively.

Renistrila (aka reni) – Renistrila is a bright flower that blooms in many different colors, though most often a deep blue. It is the first flower to bloom in Spring and the last to die in Autumn, thus its birth and death often mark the beginning and the end of those two seasons. It is often found along riverbanks where currents are weakest, as well as along the shores of ponds and lakes. A single blossom can grow as large as ten inches in diameter. It is considered by many as the most beautiful blossom in the world and is often included in many religious ceremonies due to its affiliation with the Tree of Prayer and the healing goddess, Masiila. Coincidentally, its leaves have natural healing benefits and were used in ancient times as an antibiotic.

Sazeen Whiskey – The treasured brew of Jesparia. Sazeen was Jesparia's main export for over fifty years, and its recipe was a deeply guarded secret known only to those who worked in advanced positions in the Trista brewery. Worker strikes eventually brought brewing to a halt. The honey-sweetened spirit was in high demand even before the brewery's demise, so the few bottles that survived thereafter were bought and sold at prices so high that only the richest families could afford even a taste of it, though a few bottles were hidden away throughout Trista's East side.

Lightning Source UK Ltd.
Milton Keynes UK
UKHW050221150223
416791UK00017BA/315/J